FERAL SINS

FERAL SINS

SUZANNE WRIGHT

Text copyright © 2012 Suzanne Wright

Published by Montlake Romance
P.O. Box 400818
Las Vegas, NV 89140

ISBN-13: 9781611097184
ISBN-10: 1611097185

To my amazing husband and gorgeous children—the three

most fabulous people in the world

CHAPTER ONE

W hat in God's name was that smell?

It wasn't a bad smell, mused a slowly waking Taryn, whose eyelids were too heavy to lift. It sure didn't belong in her bed, though. Her sleep-fogged brain was able to tell her three things. One, the smell was actually a person's scent—a most delicious scent: fresh pine, spring rain, and cedar wood. Two, the alluring scent belonged to a male. And three, that male was a wolf shifter, just like her. Taryn Warner did not smuggle strange guys into the pack house, even if they did smell delicious.

Forcing a droopy eye open, she peeked at the space beside her and was able to confirm her suspicion that the mystery male was long gone. Swiveling her head—which felt unnaturally heavy— she peered at her alarm clock. Or, at least, she would have if it hadn't done a disappearing act. Along with her bedside table. And these silky sheets beneath her, she suddenly realized, were not her sheets.

With a start, she sat up. And cursed. Nope, she wasn't in her room. In fact, she wasn't even in her home. Scanning her surroundings warily, her eyes widened in response to not only the luxury around her, but also the realization that she was inside what looked to be a freaking cave. *A cave?*

It was no Stone Age cave, though. Hell, no. The light-cream sandstone walls were all perfectly smooth apart from the occasional niche that was being used as a mini shelf. The floors were covered with a plush beige carpet that looked invitingly soft. There was a very masculine-style triple wardrobe and large set of drawers, both a dark oak that matched the headboard of the platform bed. The bed itself was under a smooth arch that had been hewn into the cave, making it cozy despite the enormity of the bed. But not cozy enough that she was enjoying this freaky little scenario.

Although her inner wolf was on the alert, she wasn't nervous or anxious. Taryn snickered. Her dumb wolf didn't even have the sense to worry that she was in a strange place—a cave, no less—that she had no memory of arriving in. It was probably a good thing that she was latent.

So...had she gone out with Shaya and somehow ended up going home with a guy? That didn't ring true. For one thing, she couldn't recall arranging a night out, let alone actually venturing out. Moreover, her position as pack healer meant she was constantly on call and so getting ridiculously drunk was something she never did. Also, she was fully clothed—casual clothing that she would never wear on a night out—and there was no smell of sex on her or the bed.

What was the last thing she remembered doing? Despite the fogginess in her brain, she could recall heading to the Internet café at around noon. She sure didn't remember getting there. Of course, it was worth noting that she suffered from NRS syndrome (Never Remembers Shit), but this was different. It was like there was a gap in her memory.

Taryn drew the air around her into her system, filtering through the various scents. She could smell only two individuals besides herself and the yummy-smelling wolf. Another male and a female, both of whom were also unfamiliar wolf shifters. At least she could be sure that she wasn't in the grasp of Roscoe, that dick Alpha, who didn't give a crap that she didn't want to be claimed by him. For that matter, her father didn't give a crap either; he was too busy trying to build an alliance with the other pack, and if that meant using his daughter to get it, he happily would.

She wished she could say that it was just because he was so desperate for an alliance. But no, her dad already had plenty of alliances with other packs. He simply didn't have time for his only child because, as a latent, she was a blow to his pride, an aberration in his bloodline. In his mind, being responsible for her conception meant that she was his weakness. She put his greatness into question for the rest of the pack. Or so he thought. He certainly wouldn't bother putting her photo on a milk carton if she never returned home from wherever the hell she was.

Spotting a set of beige curtains, she flicked the bedcover aside and rose from the bed. Dizziness momentarily rushed over her and she swayed. Jesus, what was with her? Staggering to the curtains with sluggish, ungraceful movements, she parted them to reveal a bay window—a window that was unfortunately locked. Rather than morning, it was more like late afternoon. Did that mean she hadn't spent the night here and had been here only a few hours? Or did it mean she had just had one hell of a sleep?

Her eyebrows almost hit her hairline as she took in the view. Most packs had a massive luxury lodge surrounded by a number of cabins. Some even had lodges situated on cliffs. But this place wasn't on a cliff—it *was* the cliff. With arched, lighted balconies and smooth stairways leading to different levels, it was like one of those ancient cave dwellings meets the town of Bedrock.

What. The. Fuck?

Below was grass. Grass. More grass. A huge forest. So, from what she could tell, she was in some kind of huge cave system in the middle of no-man's-land. She had heard of caves being hollowed out and turned into homes or even hotels, but never had she expected they could be made to have such a warm, contemporary look. Something told her she was still in California somewhere, but she had a feeling the cab ride home was going to be expensive. Good thing her kidnapper was wealthy. Especially since there didn't seem to be any sign of her purse anywhere. If this was all a joke, she *so* didn't get it.

Smoothing out the bane of her existence that couldn't seem to decide what shade of blonde it wanted to be, she headed for the door on shaky legs. She might have been cautious if she wasn't so annoyed, woozy, and confused. Besides, she figured that if these wolves intended to hurt her they would have done so already, and they definitely wouldn't have left her to sleep on such a comfy bed in an extravagant room.

She tugged on the door handle, but to her horror and frustration, the door was locked. *Locked?* "Hey!" she called out as she knocked loudly. No response. "Helloooooooooo!" Still nothing.

So, to sum up, she was in a strange place around strange shifters and she was being *confined*? Well, *now* her wolf was pissed. Being cooped up was enough to infuriate and agitate any shifter. "Hello! This is your captive speaking! Open the freaking door!"

A chuckle preceded the turning of a key and then the door slowly swung open. Taryn found herself face-to-face—well, face-to-chest—with what could only be described as a living, breathing mountain. Another wolf. She arched a brow at his cocky, devilish smirk, wondering what could possibly be so amusing.

"You're awake. Good."

"And just which dwarf might you be?" No, it wasn't a good time to make jokes, but she was a sarcastic bitch and when she was pissed off the sarcasm took on a life of its own.

His smirk widened. "The Alpha wants to speak to you."

"And your Alpha is…?"

He winked. "Follow me."

Rolling her eyes at his cocky swagger, Taryn followed him through a tunnel that took them deeper into the mountain. Seeing the occasional turnoff, she realized that it was actually a network of tunnels, like some kind of giant ant colony. Just like in the bedroom, the light-cream walls were so smooth they actually looked soft. Her wolf was going crazy at the strange, unfamiliar scents, wanting Taryn to explore the place. "Mind telling me where I am?"

"All will be revealed shortly," he drawled.

"How about how I got here?" she asked irritably.

"The Alpha will explain everything to you."

She couldn't contain a growl, but it seemed to amuse him.

Soon they came to a large black door, which Mountain Man held open while she passed through. They were now in a huge open-plan kitchen that was surprisingly modern and stylish with its oak cabinets, black marble countertop, and platinum appliances. In the center of the large space was a long oak dining table around which a small number of male wolf shifters hovered. All heads turned as she entered and the crowd split, giving her a view of who sat at the table. Her jaw almost hit the floor.

Motherfucker. Trey Coleman.

Now she knew that she hadn't come here willingly. Even if she had been on a night out and gotten hammered, no amount of alcohol would have distracted her from the fact that this guy was a psycho. He was kind of like the black mamba snake: fiercely aggressive, had a bad reputation, and was respected, admired, and feared all at the same time. That had a lot to do with the rumor that at the delicate age of fourteen he had challenged and almost killed a mature Alpha male. A mature Alpha male who had also been his father.

If what Taryn had heard was correct, Trey had been banished rather than earning the position of Alpha male. The act had caused a divide in the pack, and those who hadn't agreed with the decision had left with him. Together they had formed their own pack, with Trey as Alpha male, and earned their own territory through battles with other packs. So far this particular Alpha was undefeated…which was probably because his wolf tended to turn feral during battles. And here she was with him. She couldn't help but get the feeling that the universe was laughing behind her back.

Given that she was in the company of—or, more accurately, being confined by—a person who wasn't at all mentally stable, you would think her wolf would be at least a little nervous. Taryn certainly was beneath her anger. Oh, not at all! Her wolf wanted to rub against him enticingly, recognizing his scent as the one from the bedroom. Tramp.

Okay, Taryn could concede that the homicidal nutcase was seriously hot. His harsh scowl and the sharpness in his arctic-blue eyes seemed only to add to it. His T-shirt didn't hide his broad shoulders, defined upper body, or washboard abs. Ripped, that was what he was. Ordinarily, Taryn didn't much like the highlander look, but she found that she couldn't help but admire that physique. In addition, both her body and her wolf reacted helplessly to the power that was practically buzzing around him; he wore authority like a second skin. Perversely, his hard, penetrating stare was heating her blood rather than affronting her. His eyes had taken on a glazed, hungry look that both thrilled and startled her. It made her wolf growl in excitement. The primal lust that gripped her was so intense it almost hurt.

Well, that was just great. Maybe she was developing Stockholm syndrome or something.

In any case, no way would her inconvenient attraction to him inspire her to react to him as her body and her wolf wanted—and as many other females often did, if his reputation as a rake had any substance. Her father was also the dark, rugged, brooding, dangerous type, and he was a pain in the padded ass. Betraying nothing about her appreciation of him as a male specimen, Taryn simply returned his full-on alpha stare with one of her own. Oh, her wolf may be latent, but she was still an alpha wolf.

Trey regarded the female before him curiously. He had been told that she was latent. Add in that she was a tiny little thing, away from her pack, and in *his* company, and surely you would have yourself a flighty deer. But there was no fear in her expression, nor was it wafting from her like fumes as he would have expected. Instead, she was royally pissed. Apparently, he had become so used to the scent of fear that he now found himself a little thrown.

He also found that he was becoming painfully hard as a raw basic hunger surged through him, beating at his self-control. She wasn't beautiful in that oh-so-obvious, in-your-face way, but in a natural, understated way. Although she was slender, she had mouthwatering curves that had all sorts of fantasies playing around in his head. It was her mouth that had most of his attention, though; it was plush, carnal, and made a guy think impure thoughts. A mouth that was currently set into a hard line, communicating how livid she was. Still, the stench of fear hadn't permeated the air. Maybe she just didn't recognize him. "Do you know who I am?"

Taryn rolled her eyes. "Why don't we just skip to the part where you tell me how the hell I got here and why exactly I'm here at all, Coleman?"

Everyone around her stiffened and an uncomfortable hush fell upon the room. Obviously they were all waiting for the guy to explode. Yeah? Well, she had had enough of intimidating, dominating males. Had had enough of boyfriends who seemed to think that her being latent meant she had to be submissive and meek. Had had enough of her father trying to force her to mate with a sleazy Alpha for his own sly reasons. Had had enough of said sleazy Alpha who was so determined to mate with her that he had cornered and bitten her without her permission, believing he had marked her as his. And now psycho boy here had obviously kidnapped her. Forgive her if she had reached her limit!

Trey smiled inwardly at her feistiness. He had been told enough times that he had an intimidating presence. All his life, even before he'd earned his reputation, people had been wary of him, and it had kind of irritated him. His grandmother blamed his seemingly permanent scowl as well as the dominant vibes that surrounded him.

This female, however, wasn't shrinking away from him or the intensity of his gaze. And he knew it was intense. He knew that his eyes were so completely focused on her and every single line and curve of her hot little body that it should have been enough to make her look away, squirm, or scowl. She didn't even flinch under his scrutiny. Instead, she met his hard stare boldly, and it occurred to him that it was very possible that he had found someone who could outstare him. This was obviously a female who was used to taking shit from people—probably as a result of being latent. Her fiery nature pleased his wolf, who didn't respect tremblers. He would bet she had a wicked temper.

Instinctively, Trey inhaled deeply to investigate the scent of the female, just as he did with anyone he met for the first time. *Fuck.* The exotic fusion of coconut, lime, and pineapple seemed to slam into his system and shoot straight to his hard cock, making it jerk. His wolf growled his arousal, wanting to further investigate this female with the mouthwatering scent. "Why don't you sit," he invited, gesturing to the seat opposite him. His strong attraction to her would be a good thing if she agreed to his deal.

Taryn would have refused his invitation, but to do that would give the impression that she was feeling too intimidated. She couldn't afford to show weakness. After taking the seat, she said, "So you were going to explain what this is all about?" If she hadn't been so in need of answers, she would have avoided talking to him at all. That rough, gravelly voice caressed her senses and almost succeeded in making her shudder.

"My Beta and my Head Enforcer brought you here a few hours ago."

"What? Why? And how did they even get me to go with them?"

"They drugged you."

Taryn gaped. He was too flippant and unremorseful for her liking. "They did *what*?"

"At the café. After you left and the drowsiness kicked in as you were walking home, Dante and Tao took you and brought you to me."

"If it makes you feel any better," began Mountain Man, "you still fought me and Tao like a wildcat before you went away with the fairies to dreamland." He lifted his T-shirt to show her a set of claw marks that spanned his chest. *Her* marks, she realized. Although she was latent, she could partially shift. She also realized that Mountain Man was amused rather than angry.

"*Wildcat* is an understatement. No one ever marks our Beta," a tall, olive-skinned wolf who she presumed was Tao—her other kidnapper—told her. With his athletic build and chocolate-brown hair, he was more her type. Unfortunately, her wolf was growling her disagreement; she rather liked psycho boy.

"And the purpose of Operation Drug and Kidnap the Female Wolf is what, exactly?" Her tone made it clear that no answer could possibly placate her.

Trey's inward smile surfaced. She would be perfect for what he had in mind. In order to know for sure, he needed to tell some sweet little lies first and feel her out, find out if his suspicions about her supposed mating were true. "Roscoe Weston."

Her wolf growled inside her head at the name. "What about him?"

"He has something I want. Something that he owes me."

"Ah, and now you believe you have something he wants and that there's going to be some sort of trade going on." It was just her luck that she would get stuck in the middle of Alpha games.

"You're not so much insurance as you are a little reminder that he owes me and I'm not a patient man."

And she wasn't a patient woman. Nor was she partial to being drugged and kidnapped. But did anyone give a shit? No. It could be that she was latent or just that she was small, but people tended to judge her as being delicate, skittish, and submissive. "Look, maybe in your culture it's perfectly fine to drug and abduct a person, but it sure as shit isn't acceptable in mine."

"As soon as Roscoe arrives, you can leave."

That wasn't exactly fan-freaking-tastic news. A part of her wanted to rant and rave, but what good would it do? She would only end up being confined in that damn bedroom again and that would drive her and her wolf crazy. Also, she was a believer that it was best to have your enemy in sight. "Have you called him yet?"

"He'll be here soon," he lied. In truth, he hadn't contacted Roscoe and he had no intention of doing so.

"Well, then, can the captive get a coffee or what?" she asked no one in particular.

Aside from psycho boy, Dante, and Tao, there were four other males in the room: a broad frowner with a military haircut, a gorgeous blond with caramel skin, a tall wolf with tousled dark curls and a clown-wide smile, and a burly, rugged guy with claw-mark scars across one cheek. It occurred to her that she could just label them Grumpy, Blondie, Smiley, and Burly.

Other than Dante—who seemed strangely fascinated with her for having managed to claw him—none of the wolves looked at all pleased about her presence. She guessed that they weren't fans of her dad. Not many were. Even the wolf who was wearing a huge grin looked intrigued as opposed to friendly, and she had the feeling that his smile was permanently there. Or maybe he was imagining what it would feel like to rip out her throat and hand it bow-tied to her asshole of a father. With his arrogance, deviousness, and "I own the world and can do whatever the hell

I want" attitude, her dad was as good at collecting enemies as he was at gathering alliances. Even those who allied themselves with him only did so because of how influential he was—it was all just politics.

In response to her question, Trey nodded to a grinning Marcus, who switched on the coffee machine and retrieved a mug from the cupboard. Trey tilted his head as he considered her. "You know, you're not what I'd expected."

"Is that right?" she said flatly.

"Roscoe usually likes airheads and submissives." Blonde as she was, she didn't have that bimbo look about her. There was no missing the sharp, keen mind behind those charcoal-gray eyes. "Funny how a person's true mate can be the opposite of what they go for."

"He's not my true mate." It came out snappier than she had intended.

"If you haven't found your true mate yet, why would you mate with someone else? It's not like you haven't got plenty of time to find him. You can't be much older than twenty-four, twenty-five."

"My mate's dead. He died when we were kids."

"Well, then, that's something you and I have in common. I also lost my mate a long time ago, before I was able to claim her."

Taryn took in his solemn expression and felt a pang of sympathy for him. The loss of a mate wasn't something others could understand unless they had experienced that kind of pain themselves. "Sorry."

He simply shrugged a little. "Hmm, now you and Roscoe as a couple make even less sense. If you're not true mates, then that means he's *chosen* a spitfire. It really must be love."

"Huh." Taryn had to bite back a snort. Love? Yeah, right. The reason Roscoe was so determined to fuck her was simply because she hadn't responded to his charm and apparently his ego couldn't handle the blow. As for why he wanted to take her as his mate…The only thing she could figure was that he wanted an alliance with her dad.

"When's the mating ceremony scheduled for?" asked Trey.

Oh, there would be *no* mating ceremony. Roscoe was keen to get it over with because her dad had insisted on there being one before he would hand her over completely—only so he had an excuse to have a get-together with all his allies and look like the big man. No way would she bind herself to someone she didn't care for or even like. Then there was the matter of Roscoe being a control freak; she had picked that up from his interactions with his enforcers, all of whom he intimidated. She didn't believe they were scared of him in a physical sense. It was as though he had some sort of hold over them, like he held their secrets in the palm of his hand or something like that.

Also, if the rumors were right, Roscoe got his kicks from inflicting pain on women. Considering he had forced his mark on her in the middle of a nightclub, she had no problem believing that. She had expected him to strike her after she practically crushed his balls with her hand in retaliation, but when he could finally stand and had finished panting, he'd merely smiled. It was a creepy smile that swore revenge, but he hadn't stopped her from walking away. Apparently, he was biding his time.

To escape the mating, her first stop had been her dad. As he wanted the alliance, she wasn't getting any help from that corner. Her next stop should be her Alpha, but as her dad *was* the Alpha, that avenue was closed to her. She could try leaving the pack, but that wouldn't improve her situation. As a lone wolf, without any protection, pack, or territory, she would be easy pickings, and Roscoe would undoubtedly be the picker.

The only other person she had was her uncle—her deceased mother's youngest brother—whom she hadn't seen since he mated into another pack ten years ago. Her plan was to ask him to approach his Alpha with the idea of accepting her into his pack, but she wasn't optimistic. Although she was a healer, she was also latent and she couldn't envision any Alpha being particularly interested in taking in a latent wolf. The question was, even if the Alpha did take her in, would he be prepared to challenge Roscoe if he—angry at being thwarted as only a control freak could be—came to bring her back?

She thought about telling Trey that she liked Roscoe even less than he did, but sometimes it was a case of "better the devil you know"—and this particular devil was possibly worse than Roscoe. Instead of answering his question, she got herself comfy on the seat, crossing her legs yoga-like, and sipped the coffee that Smiley had placed in front of her.

"Does your silence mean you haven't set a date yet?"

"Oh, didn't I answer? That's probably because it's none of your business."

He felt his mouth twitch into a smile. "You must be looking forward to soon becoming an Alpha female of a pack."

Something about his tone had her frowning. "Are power-hungry females the only type you've known?"

He shrugged. "Isn't it what every female wolf dreams of?"

"Oh, yes, and I'm bowled over with excitement at my upcoming position."

Strangely, he found that he liked her sarcastic streak. "I thought you were a healer."

"I am."

"Typically they have gentle natures."

"I fall flat there."

"I heard you're quite a powerful healer."

She was. There were three different types of healers. Some worked on an emotional level, neutralizing or healing emotional wounds. Others drew the aches and pains into themselves, acting more as a sedative and ensuring a speedy recovery. Then there were those like Taryn, who could heal the actual wounds within minutes, guaranteeing a recovery.

"Do you always sit in odd positions?"

"Just be thankful I'm not sitting on your countertop. That's where I usually sit when I'm in the kitchen." Maybe because it reminded her of all the times her mom had sat her there while they baked together, maybe not.

"What about in the bedroom?" he asked with what he knew was a wicked, suggestive grin. "Do you get in odd positions in there too?"

"Depends if the male can succeed in pinning me down."

"Ah, of course. You're an alpha." And alphas, whether they were leaders of their own pack or just alpha by nature, didn't surrender without males proving their dominance. Just the idea of fighting to have Taryn submit to him had his cock throbbing and his balls aching. He knew she'd fight him like a wildcat.

He liked his women strong and feisty, but they were often too intimidated by him to challenge him. If they weren't intimidated by his unapproachable air, it was the heavy dominant vibe he gave off. If it wasn't either of those that intimidated them, it was how close his wolf was to the surface. That was if they weren't scared enough initially by his reputation. The only female who had ever stood up to him—and still did so on a regular basis—was his grandmother.

"Do you have any cookies or something to go with this coffee?"

Marcus placed a pack of Trey's grandmother's cookies beside her mug and she immediately delved into them. Trey's gaze was helplessly drawn to her carnal mouth as she chewed. Images of those lips around his cock flashed through his mind, making his wolf growl inside his head. Then his entire body clenched as she sucked the dribbles of coffee from the tips of her fingers. *Well, fuck.* What made the whole thing even more of a turn-on was that she clearly had no idea she was being watched by every male in the room. She was innocently and unknowingly provocative. Of course Roscoe would want her, but it was still difficult to understand him taking a spitfire for a mate. He was too controlling to mate with a strong-willed woman.

What Trey found even more difficult to understand was why Taryn would want Roscoe as a mate. Yeah, he knew females tended to like Roscoe and his charming ways that hid his coldness, but Taryn seemed like someone who would snort at flowery words and oppose being with someone who wanted to control her. It didn't make sense. *They* didn't make sense. That was why he was thinking that maybe his suspicions about their supposed mating had truth in them.

One of his enforcers, Dominic, had come to Trey with the story of how he had stumbled upon Roscoe and a female wolf having some sort of struggle. Dominic had been ready to interfere when he saw the fresh bite on her skin—a claiming. He had walked away then; no shifter with any sense would try to interfere in a row between mates. Still, the whole scene had bugged Dominic, because she hadn't looked willing. What Trey hadn't been able to figure out was why she would allow anyone to get away with forcing his mark on her. Her father was Alpha of the pack, for Christ's sake. Surely he wouldn't allow that.

Trey knew the kind of things Roscoe Weston was capable of. Claiming an unwilling female would be nothing to him. Maybe if that female was submissive it would be nothing much to her, but Trey had known Taryn Warner for only five minutes and already he could tell that she was far from submissive or complacent. It didn't make any sense. There was another thing supporting his suspicion that there was something very wrong about this mating..."You don't smell of him."

Thank God, Taryn refrained from saying aloud. Although Roscoe had left his mark on her, he hadn't been able to imprint on her. Two wolves who weren't true mates could still come together as mates and have a tight bond through the process of imprinting. That process couldn't be sparked unless there were strong emotions involved, and it required a lot of physical contact. When two wolves were imprinted, their scents mixed and they developed a sort of metaphysical link. Even if Taryn ended up mated to Roscoe, they would never have that link, because there was no way they would ever imprint. Unless the emotion of hate was able to spark it, of course. "Hmm" was her only response.

At that second, she dropped a cookie in her coffee; taking advantage of her distraction, Trey reached across the table and tugged her T-shirt aside to bare her shoulder. What he saw there made him growl.

Taryn jerked back, gaping and scowling. "What the hell are you doing?"

"Why would you cover it with makeup?"

"What?"

"Your mark. A female wears her male's mark with pride; you're covering yours. Did he force his mark on you?"

Totally thrown by the sudden turnabout in the conversation, Taryn was pretty much speechless.

"Taryn," he drawled menacingly before demanding, "answer my question."

His bullying tone had her straightening in her seat. "Look, psycho boy, I don't know what your problem is—though I'd imagine it's difficult to spell out even for your psychiatrist—but no matter what's going on between you and Roscoe, it doesn't give you the right to know anything about what's going on between *me* and Roscoe."

"Maybe not, but I still want an answer," he said in a gentler voice. "Did he claim you against your will?"

Although there wasn't really a reason to hide it, pride and distrust still had her denying it. "Do I seem like the kind of person who would allow something like that?"

"I have no doubt that you're trying to find a way out of mating with him if it's not what you want, but I don't think you've found one. Now, did he claim you against your will?"

"What does it matter to you?"

Trey took that as a yes. "Does your father know?"

She spoke quickly, hoping that if she just satisfied his curiosity he'd back off. "My dad's a proud man whose only child is a latent daughter. He sees an alliance with a wolf as powerful as Roscoe to be the best thing that's ever come out of my existence."

"Your mother?"

"Died when I was nine."

"You don't have other relatives who'll help?"

Taryn was about ready to scream at this guy. Not only was he poking at a very raw wound, but her body was reacting to him in a way that unsettled her. Her fingers itched to touch him and to comb through his short, dark hair to find out if it was as silky as it looked. The primitive hunger crushing her had her insides churning, and there was some throbbing going on in some very interesting places. There had to be something wrong with her if she was attracted to a psycho. But, strangely, she didn't feel in danger with him. *Definitely Stockholm syndrome.* "This is not your problem and it has nothing to do with whatever's going on between you and Roscoe."

He twisted his mouth and cocked his head. "What if I said I could help you?"

Her heart almost stopped. "Why would you do that? How could you even do that?"

"You could join my pack."

Okay, well, that was unexpected. "What could you possibly gain from that?" she asked, immediately suspicious.

"A healer."

Yeah, sure. "There's more."

"Yes, there's more. I have a proposition for you. I believe that we can help each other out."

He rooted in his jeans pocket and pulled out a small sachet. "Inside this is a pill like the one you were drugged with earlier, but a little stronger. If after our conversation you decide to decline my offer, I'll ask you to take it. When you wake up, your memory will again be fuzzy and you will have lost the past ten hours."

"You want to drug me again? It wasn't bad enough that you drugged me the first time?"

"Let me ask you this. If any of my enforcers had approached you and asked you to meet me here at my pack house, would you have gone along peacefully?"

Of course not. "Point taken." Begrudgingly. "What's this proposition of yours?"

"I'm sure you've heard all about how I supposedly beat the hell out of my own father when I was fourteen. Well, it's true. I did. And for very good reasons, none of which are important right now. I won the right to be Alpha, but my dad, my uncle, and many other males banded together to banish me. I was just a juvenile; I couldn't take them all on. So I left, along with some from the pack who disagreed with what had happened. We formed our own pack, which we called the Phoenix Pack—"

"That was my idea," interjected Dante. "You know…because we rose from nothing."

Clearing his throat, Trey continued, "Anyway, we then got ourselves some territory and we've been content enough here. I was never interested in getting involved with any political bullshit or making alliances, so we always kept pretty much to ourselves. Unfortunately, that's come back to bite me right on the ass."

He settled back in his seat, crossing his legs beneath the table. "A few weeks ago, my dad passed away. Since my uncle was Beta, he has now taken over as Alpha, but apparently, that's not enough for him. He has applied to the council for his pack and mine to be united as one again with him as Alpha. Personally, I think it's because he wants our territory, but it's probably to piss me off too. The council arranged a date for us both to meet in the presence of a mediator to see if the issue can be resolved without violence."

Shifter councils formed only to appease anxious humans who didn't like the shifter way of solving disputes—namely, violence. Taryn didn't much like it either, but it had always been part of shifter culture. The agreement made with the humans was that the shifter council would insist that packs would have to appeal to the council before starting any disputes with other packs. If the matter couldn't be solved through mediation, the protocol was that exactly three months had to pass before either pack could act on the challenge—the council's way of giving tempers a chance to calm, hoping an amicable agreement could be reached within that period.

It was clear to Trey by the expression on Taryn's face that although she was listening intently, she didn't have a clue where he was going with this. "Of course I'm going to oppose his request, which means he'll then have to back down or officially challenge me. I know him well enough to know he will not back down. An agreement won't be reached within the three-month period that the council will impose, not in this case. There'll be an out-and-out battle between the packs—one that I have absolutely no problem with. But I know my father had plenty of alliances and all of those will now be my uncle's. Naturally, he's going to ask for aid from those alliances and we'll easily be outnumbered."

Taryn gave him a helpless shrug. "I'm sorry to hear things are pretty shitty, but I really don't see what I can do—unless you're interested in a sarcastic comment—and I don't see what any of this has to do with Roscoe."

"This has to do with me needing a mate…and you needing a way of being out of Roscoe's reach."

Taryn's entire body stiffened. Surely, he wasn't suggesting what she thought he was.

"I need alliances, Taryn. Your dad collects them like they're coupons. If I had an alliance with him, I would have a link to *his* alliances and then I'd have plenty of wolves to call on for this battle. Maybe it will make my uncle hesitate, maybe it won't. In any case, the situation will be evened out."

Alliances, alliances, alliances. "So you're asking me to reject a guy who wants nothing more than an alliance with my dad, all in favor of a guy with exactly the same motive?" She snickered. "You could probably arrange an alliance without using me, so why not just contact him?"

But she already knew the answer to that. Lance Warner was cunning and ruthless, known for sniffing out a person's weakness and leaping on it. He would see how much Trey needed him and would exploit it. Probably by demanding some of his territory or by insisting he owed him a "favor." Being indebted to an Alpha like him was never a good thing. Alliances formed through a mating, on the other hand, were more balanced.

"There's a very big difference between what it would mean to mate with me and what it would mean to mate with Roscoe."

"What's that?"

"With me, it doesn't have to be permanent." And he'd never hurt her, unlike Roscoe.

Confused, Taryn shook her head. "Wolves mate for life."

"Yes, but I don't want cosmic, soul-moving, imprinting shit in my life." In fact, he was pretty sure he wouldn't be capable of feeling the kind of emotions that kept a mating alive. "Of course we'd have to make everyone believe this is the real deal and that we've mated for life, but all I need is for you to remain with me as my mate until the battle is over."

"Well, then, you don't necessarily need me to mate with you. You just need me to act as though I'm mated to you."

He shook his head. "That wouldn't work, because I'd need to mark you. The second I do, you'll be classed as my mate. It will be a real mating, just not a forever-after one."

A big issue, though, was that Taryn was sure her wolf would be accepting of his mark and wouldn't understand that this was to be a short-term thing. It still wouldn't be difficult to break the mating link, because she and Trey wouldn't imprint on each other, but it would be very uncomfortable for her wolf. And that was just one of many problems. "Look, even if I wanted to take you up on your offer, I couldn't. My dad and Roscoe have signed contracts, and my dad's elated at the idea of having an alliance with Roscoe. He won't stop it."

He had thought as much. "Unless you make him believe that we're true mates."

Her tone was flat as she spoke. "I told you, my mate is dead. Everyone in the pack knows I lost him."

"Many times, shifters have mistaken a close childhood friend as their future mate. You'll just need people to believe that was the case with you."

She shook her head. "I couldn't do that to Joey. I couldn't shit on his memory like that. I *won't* shit on his memory like that."

Knowing he needed to tread carefully, he kept his tone gentle. "You think he'd prefer for you to be stuck in a mating with a wolf you don't want? Do you think he'd want that for you? Would you have wanted it for him?"

"It still doesn't seem right," she mumbled.

He was impressed by her loyalty. "It's not like we can make it look as though we met, fell head over heels, and then decided to mate. We don't have the time, and given my reputation, it wouldn't look realistic. It would also give your dad room to argue your choice of mate. If it's believed that we're true mates, he can't oppose that—it's beyond his control."

"What about your pack? Won't they know it's bullshit?"

Not wanting to go into the specifics, he kept his reply vague. "It's a shitty story, but let's just keep it at I hadn't acknowledged to others that she was my mate." That had made her death all the worse, and then he hadn't felt like he had the right to speak of her. Not many knew the complete truth, and that was how he liked it. "When I informed my pack a few weeks ago of my plan to mate, I also informed them that my true mate died a long time ago. That's all they need to know."

And that's all you *need to know*, he didn't say, but Taryn heard. She might have bristled at that, but it would have been hypocritical; losing Joey wasn't a matter she spoke of unless she had to.

"They will play along that we're true mates if it helps us keep our territory and stops my uncle from taking over the pack." Unfortunately, not all of them were supportive of a Warner being in their pack, but telling her that wouldn't be a wise move.

A part of Taryn wondered why she was hesitating. She wanted to get away from Roscoe, didn't she? Well, here was her chance. But it wasn't as simple as that, was it? No, because her chance came in the form of another big, bad Alpha who had a price for his help. Hell, two wolves—two *Alpha* wolves— suddenly wanted to mate her, yet neither actually cared even a tiny bit about her. She was a means to an end. Not exactly flat- tering, and it certainly stung.

Taryn was surprised by just how much it stung, considering that she hadn't envisioned ever wanting to take a mate; it would have felt like she was betraying Joey. That might not make a lot of sense, given that they were kids when he died, but Joey had been the one person in the world created for her, just for her. Created to care for her, to accept her, to love her.

And because of that, just as Trey had pointed out, Joey wouldn't have wanted her to be trapped in a mating she didn't want. Joey would have wanted, no, *expected*, her to do whatever it took to escape that fate. This particular avenue, however, might be a bit too complicated.

"Even if I did agree to this deal, I don't see how we could fake a mating bond. It's an extremely intimate thing. Mates are all touchy-feely, they don't spend a minute apart, they smell of each other, they wear each other's mark, and they have some kind of link that helps them sense each other's mood. How in the hell could we ever fake a metaphysical connection like that?"

"We'll only need to fake it when anyone outside my pack is around, and that won't be often. Knowing that your freedom from Roscoe depends on this should help you dramatically with your acting skills."

The man has an answer for everything, grumbled Taryn inwardly. Could she do this? Could she pull this off? It wasn't in her nature to cower from anything challenging, no matter how much danger or risk it involved. Maybe it had a lot to do with her latency; continually proving herself had always been a way of gaining some measure of respect. But this wasn't just some kind of dare. This was her life and all about what direction she wanted it to take.

She sighed and ran a hand through her hair. "My dad's not stupid, unfortunately. He knows I don't want to be mated to Roscoe. If I walk up to him and say 'Hey, Dad, guess what, it turns out my true mate's not dead and I found him,' he's going to accuse me of trying to play him."

"And that's why we'll need to be publicly seen to 'discover' each other. Maybe at one of the shifter clubs. No one other than my wolves will know we've met before that claiming."

Okay, that was a good idea. But would it work?

Taryn stifled the urge to groan as indecision racked her mind and body. Her wolf wasn't undecided. Oh no. With her elemental nature, her wolf wasn't interested in details or problems; she was only interested in whether Trey was a potential mate. She liked his confidence, his determination, his heavy air of dominance, and she absolutely loved his scent. Her wolf was totally fine with letting Trey mark her. In fact, she was craving it. Not good.

"Have you thought about what it'll mean to claim me, even temporarily?" she asked. "Your wolf will know I'm not your true mate, and he may even understand that you don't consider this a permanent mating, but those will be itty-bitty details to him. If you bite and mark me, your wolf is going to see me as all *his* in every way. That means he'll be—"

"Crazily possessive, crazily jealous, and crazily protective," finished Trey. "That will help us with faking a mating bond. Though I'm sure that his understanding that you're not my true mate will be enough to keep him under control." His wolf was currently quiet inside his head, completely focused on Taryn as he waited for her response. His wolf approved of Trey's choice. He had identified her wolf as dominant and assertive, and he very much liked Taryn the woman too. Liked her innate sensuality, liked her loyal streak, and he especially liked her spunk. Just as Trey did. And her scent...God, her scent.

He could sense that she was close, so close, to accepting his proposition. He didn't blame her for being wary or hesitant, but she had to know he was the lesser of two evils. "Taryn, I'm offering you a way out. If I were you, I'd take it. Unless you want to end up bound to Roscoe for the rest of your life."

"That would never happen, no matter what."

"Maybe not. It seems to me, though, that there aren't any other avenues open to you right now."

"I was planning to go to my uncle's pack."

Oh, he hadn't doubted that she had some plan up her sleeve. "You trust his Alpha to take you in, to protect you against Roscoe when he comes for you? And he *will* come for you."

She swallowed hard. "I don't know if I can trust his Alpha, because I've never met him, but I don't know if I can trust you to protect me either. I know Roscoe won't just bow down and accept it; he has too much pride for that. He'll most likely turn up and challenge you. Are you saying you would honestly accept that challenge, that you would fight to keep me in your pack?" She didn't hide the skepticism from her voice.

"Yes, I would," he stated firmly. "I need this mating as much as you. You can still contact your uncle after joining me and then see about switching packs afterward. Three months, at the most, is the length of time I'll need you to stay. Mediators don't usually ask packs to take longer than that to civilly sort out the matter.

You could then say you've realized you were wrong about me being your true mate, whatever."

A few months in a mating with psycho boy versus a lifetime with Roscoe…In theory it should be easy for Taryn to take Trey up on his offer, but not when she considered that she would be handing herself over to someone who literally was the big bad wolf. Her instincts told her he wouldn't harm her, and although they had never let her down before, that wasn't to say that they weren't letting her down now.

He raised his brows questioningly. "Well, Taryn, do we have a deal?" He shook the pill packet. "Or would you like another long nap?"

"There's one thing I really don't get. Why me? From what I've heard, you've never had any problems reeling in females. Surely, it would have been a lot easier for you to approach an unmated female and ask her to play mates. I'm sure plenty of those females have Alphas that have the same kind of alliances my dad has."

"As much as it's going to be a pain in the ass having to convince everyone that your mate was never your mate, it would be even more complicated to convince an unmated female to pretend I'm her mate. To let another male mark her, even if it were temporary, would be like betraying her true mate, even if she hadn't found him yet. Sure, I know females who are power hungry enough that they would find the prospect of becoming Alpha female of my pack more important than waiting for their true mate. But then I'd be stuck with them. When I heard of your situation, I figured we could help each other."

Taryn made a noise that was something between a sigh and a groan. There were so many issues, so many unanswered questions. She supposed that when it came down to it, however, the question of most importance was: Was she truly prepared to do what it took to remove herself from Roscoe's reach? Returning her gaze to Trey, she sighed again, and then nodded.

He gave her a crooked smile. "Right decision."

"So when do we do this?"

"This weekend. I have my meeting with my uncle and the mediator on Saturday afternoon, so the matter can't wait. I take it you usually go to a shifter club on weekends?"

She nodded. "I go to The Pulse every Friday night. It's the nearest club to my pack house. I have to stay local in case I'm needed to do some healing."

"It's best not to do anything out of the norm for you. Friday night I want you to go to the club as usual. If you can, stay near the bar. At some point I'll find you and we'll 'stumble upon' each other. I think you'll find that everything will move very fast from there. Then afterward you'll come home with me. In the meantime, go about your business the way you usually do. I'll give you my number in case there's some reason you need to get in touch. Try not to use it unless you have to." He didn't like that this gave her four days to change her mind, but this was the plan with the most potential.

Again she nodded.

"You can't tell anyone about this, Taryn. Not even your best friend. Especially when there's a risk that someone will consider you safer with Roscoe."

Unfortunately, he was right. Her two best friends, Shaya and Caleb, were pretty protective of her, and they seemed to find Roscoe completely charming. They didn't see the coldness behind his smile. They would do everything they could to discourage her from mating with psycho boy here, and if that didn't work they would most definitely go tattle. Even if she had been utterly convinced that they would be supportive, she wouldn't have told them. It wouldn't be fair to place them in the position of keeping secrets from their Alphas.

Not liking her silence, he said, "I mean it, Taryn. You have to keep your mouth shut about this. You don't tell a soul."

She bristled at the ring of command in his voice. "We should probably clear this up right now, psycho boy. I don't have a submissive bone in my body, so don't bark at me unless you're happy to be ignored."

The word *submissive* had his mind conjuring images of her tied up, bent over, and begging him to take her. He couldn't hold back a devilish smile, and he was sure by the way her charcoal-gray eyes narrowed that she knew just what was going through his head. "We'll see. So, can we shake on it?"

Taryn clasped his offered hand. "Note this: if you try to hand me over to Roscoe when he comes, I'll claw your balls off."

CHAPTER TWO ⊙

No sooner had Taryn closed the front door behind her than a voice was booming, "Where the hell have you been?"

It was always a surprise when her dad sought her out. Usually Lance Warner was indifferent to Taryn and could even go a whole day without talking to her. What was more surprising was that he seemed to believe she should be hanging around, just in case he wanted to see her or to bestow some attention on her. She was pretty sure it confused him that she didn't respond to his indifference by constantly striving to gain his attention and approval. But Taryn wasn't going to beg for the scraps from anyone's table.

"What is it?" She knew no one needed healing. She would have received a text message if that were the problem.

"It's almost time for the evening meal."

Since when did he care if she missed a meal?

"Roscoe's going to be here soon. You have about two minutes to change."

Ah. "Why would I change? And why wasn't I told he was coming?"

Lance snickered. "Because you would have done a disappearing act, just to be awkward. You know, I still don't know why you're so set against him. I never would have thought you'd attract an Alpha in a million years. Hell, a wolf shouldn't want to be bound to a latent unless he has no choice. You should be grateful."

"Grateful to be mated to someone I don't like, let alone care for?"

"You'll just have to grow to care about him, won't you," he snapped. "I want this alliance and you are *not* going to mess this up for me. Now get upstairs and change into something…I don't know…"

"Slutty," she offered. "You want me to look slutty." It would have been a shock if he hadn't been doing this every time an unmated male came here since she was fifteen. It still managed to hurt each time. "He already bit me and you've already exchanged contracts, so it looks like we can skip the seduction stage."

"While you're denying him, there's still a chance he'll back out."

She searched his expression. "Doesn't it matter to you at all that this will make me miserable? I know you must have heard the rumors about him and how he treats women. Does none of that matter to you?"

"It'll be good for you to mate with someone who has a firm hand. You could use the discipline. Maybe he can be the one who manages to teach you the meaning of respect."

Taryn couldn't help that her mouth fell open. She had thought that her dad was just ignoring the rumors, blinding himself to them to escape the guilt. In fact, he felt none. He was perfectly content with the idea of handing her over to someone who would beat her, and he wouldn't even be angry with Roscoe for doing it.

She took a step forward until she was invading his personal space, something that no wolf should do to her Alpha, but in that moment he wasn't her Alpha or her father. He was just an asshole. "You know, for the first time in my life I'm actually glad

Mom's not around. If she'd been here to hear this, it would have broken her heart."

He actually laughed. "You forget, Taryn, she died before it became clear you're latent. She wouldn't have wanted anything more to do with you than I do."

Taryn smiled. She knew he didn't really believe that, just as she knew that Cecilia Warner wouldn't have cared about the latency. "You know, jamming your fingers into your ears might just prevent all that hot air from gushing out of your mouth."

"You disrespectful little bitch," he gritted out as he raised his hand to slap her.

She didn't cower. "Go on, do it."

"I'd really rather you didn't, Lance," said a voice from the doorway. They both turned to see Roscoe removing his leather jacket, flanked by two of his enforcers. As usual, he looked like he'd just walked out of a photo shoot. A blond god, some of the females called him. Taryn thought of him more as the Antichrist. "When you signed that contract, you signed her over to me."

In other words, the only person who had the right to slap her was him.

"Until the mating ceremony, I'm still her Alpha, Roscoe. Remember that."

"And as her mate, I'd feel obliged to protect her if you were to lay a hand on her." He turned to Taryn and smiled. "Nice to see you again, beautiful."

Taryn almost shuddered. He had that same look in his eyes that he'd had when he'd bitten her. As that was something that was a kind of rape to her wolf, she was going crazy now inside Taryn—growling, pacing, flexing her claws.

This was one of the things that most annoyed Taryn about being latent. When her wolf was frenzied, her anger and frustration had nowhere to go and it was like a pressure gradually expanding inside Taryn's chest. People tended to think that because her wolf didn't physically show herself, she must therefore be subdued and weak in spirit. Taryn wasn't sure how it was for other latent wolves, but that certainly was not the case for her.

Her wolf was a big presence within her. She didn't understand that she couldn't surface. She didn't understand that it was pointless to tug at the reins, pointless to try to fight Taryn's will. So, in general, her wolf was bold, difficult, and pushed her instincts and desires on Taryn. Right now, her wolf's desire was to take a swipe at the smarmy bastard in front of her. When he leaned down to kiss her, she turned her head away, but his mouth still managed to catch her ear.

Lance released a tired sigh. "Let's go. Everybody will be waiting for us."

As they made their way to the dining room, Roscoe attempted to hold her hand. She shot him a look that swore violence and curled her upper lip. His response was a smile. She kind of got the feeling that he liked seeing her riled. Damned if she could figure out why. He should find her rebellious behavior insulting and exasperating. She'd rather hoped he would anyway.

"You'll be sitting at the head table tonight, Taryn," Lance announced as they entered the room. She had to resist the urge to growl. Although she was the Alpha's daughter and the pack healer, ordinarily she would sit at another table, with Shaya and Caleb.

Of course Lance placed her beside Roscoe. She wasn't thrilled to find her dad's bodyguard seated at her other side. Like most of the others in the pack, he had been nice to her when she was a kid, before puberty hit and her wolf didn't surface. Maybe if Lance had still been accepting of her then things would have been different, but by dismissing her as unimportant and weak, he had pinned a big, fat target on her back.

What had saved her from a dozen beatings was that in spite of her latency she still had shifter speed and strength. Of course it hadn't saved her from all of them. She had worked to become the best hand-to-hand combatant, and to be fitter and more agile than anyone within the pack. The bodyguard's ego was still sore after the time he had sneaked into her room in the middle of the night, only to end up with a broken nose and a dislocated jaw.

Quickly the food was brought out and everyone was eating greedily while listening to Roscoe answer all of Lance's questions about his pack and the times he had been challenged in the past. Taryn rolled her eyes as she saw how many of the females were staring in utter admiration at Roscoe, clinging to his every word. Even Shaya, for Christ's sake! The males were also staring at him, all pretty pissed with him for his effect on the females.

She simply didn't understand how everyone could be so taken in by him. Yes, he was charming, had a warm smile, and was very nice to look at, but there was something very wrong with his eyes. There was so much ice there. No matter how wide his smile was, it never reached his eyes. From the second she had met him, he had rubbed her and her wolf the wrong way, yet no one else seemed to have sensed that... wrongness about him.

"You haven't eaten much," he whispered in her ear.

She didn't bother responding. How he could expect her to have an appetite right now she couldn't imagine.

"If you're done we could go for a walk. Alone."

Slowly she turned her head and gave him an expression that said "You've got to be kidding me." Ignoring his chuckle, she resumed poking at her food with her fork.

"You could at least make a little effort to talk to me. I came all this way just to see you."

Well, then, wasn't he a fool?

"You know, if things are really bad with you and your dad, we could both talk to him and try negotiating you coming to stay with me for a few days."

At one point, had she given him the impression that she was gullible?

He sighed. "Come on, Taryn, you can't tell me you wouldn't like getting away from here for a while. You could see where you're going to be living, meet some of the wolves from my pack. You'll soon be their Alpha female. Don't you want to get to know them?"

No, not even a little bit. And she would never be their Alpha female.

"They're eager to meet you. In a few days, I'll be going to Australia. You could come."

"Is there no way you could just go sit on a cactus or something?" He actually smiled at that. What was wrong with this guy? Surprising her, his hand slid around her neck—a gesture of ownership. Enraged, she jumped to her feet and kicked his chair out from under him. She snarled down at him, where he was splayed out on the floor, "Don't you *ever* touch me like that! I don't belong to you. I'll never belong to you!"

What made the whole thing even worse was that he was smiling. He had wanted her to lose control. He was enjoying being able to get her so incensed. Cursing, she stormed out of the room, ignoring the gasps, the horrified mumblings, and her dad's bellows. She didn't stop marching until she was outside.

The cool evening air was like a soothing caress—one she so desperately needed. She took several calming breaths, trying to ease not only her own anger, but that of her wolf. Her wolf was raging over how that male had held her with proprietorship.

It was only minutes later when she heard footsteps approaching and his scent drifted toward her. He sighed as he halted a few feet behind her. "Taryn, it really is time you stopped fighting me. I think we've proven who the more dominant one is."

She turned slowly, clenching her fists. "All you proved when you bit me is that you can physically overpower me and you have sharp teeth, just like I proved that I can deliver some serious pain to your groin whenever you use them on me. None of that has anything to do with dominance."

"You might want to know that your father and I have arranged the mating ceremony to take place on the next full moon, which is a week from now."

She couldn't help but gape. "You know, I can't work out whether you have selective hearing or just don't give a shit about a single word you hear. *I do not want to mate with you.* In fact, I would rather have a porcupine brutally shoved up into my rectum than mate with you."

He shrugged. "I've already claimed you."

"I don't accept that claim."

"Your father does."

She shook her head incredulously. It occurred to her that getting angry with this wolf never helped her cause. Maybe if she tried being diplomatic? "What is all this really about? You don't even like me. Why would you want me as your mate?"

"Of course I like you."

"If it's an alliance with Lance you want, I'm pretty sure you could get it without mating me."

He looked at her curiously. "You truly don't see your own worth, do you? I wasn't sure if it was an act at first."

"You don't need a pack healer. You already have one."

He folded his arms across his chest. "I'm not talking about your worth as a pack member. I'm talking about your worth as a person, as a female. You're a very beautiful, sensual, refreshing female. Totally without artifice. You have just as many alpha vibes emitting from you as any other female alpha, latent or not. And as for your iron will…I never thought I would meet a person more stubborn than me."

So he recognized that she was more stubborn than he and yet they were still having this discussion? She failed to see the logic in that. "Look, you and me…We don't sing from the same hymn sheets; we're not even the slightest bit compatible. You need a nice, submissive female who'll say and do what you tell her to and make all the right noises at the appropriate times. Me, I'm just going to piss you off."

"You're right, Taryn, I do like my females submissive. And that is exactly what you will be when we mate."

And he really believed that, she could tell. "You must seriously be smoking crack."

He laughed. "The delusional one in this situation is you, Taryn."

"I'll never mate with you. Never."

His look was sympathetic. "It's sad that you actually think you'll win this battle."

"It's sad that you even started this battle. Why would you want me when you know I don't want you? Why would you want me when you know I'd fight you every step of the way?" The chilling smile he gave her made everything suddenly click into place. "You don't want me in spite of those things. You want me *because* of those things. You get your kicks out of forcing yourself on women."

"No, not forcing myself on them. I'm not a rapist. But I love a challenge, and I love to be in control. Power is a heady thing for me. What greater power is there than to be able to own someone who doesn't want you, someone whose will you can break, bit by bit, until she has gone from a spirited, dominant, independent individual to a person who is totally submissive to you?"

It took a few seconds for Taryn to be able to speak. "You're sick."

He jiggled his head. "Maybe I seem that way to you now, but just think, Taryn. A year from now you will want nothing more than to please me in every way I want to be pleased."

"Never," she bit out.

"I won't need to force you. You will crave my dominance and my direction. I'm looking forward to you moving into my home. Then we can begin your training."

"Sick, delusional, and suicidal. That's what you are."

"Suicidal?" He sounded amused.

"I'd kill you before I let you touch me."

"You really would try to, wouldn't you? Even if it meant risking your own life."

"If I mated with you, I'd be practically dead anyway," she spat. "Being some little slave for you wouldn't be a life."

"I don't think I've ever met a female who has more resistance to the idea of submission than you."

"My resistance is to the idea of submitting to *you*."

His creepy smile widened. "And that just makes the whole thing so much sweeter."

Oh, he was so very, very, very sick. "It will never happen."

"I'll remind you of this conversation in a year's time. It will be interesting to know what you make of it then." With that, he strolled back toward the house, leaving her standing there, gaping.

It was honestly like talking to someone who didn't understand your language, someone who also had a hard-on for the "lord and master" lifestyle and intended to take it to the extreme. Suddenly the idea of taking her chances by just packing a bag right now and leaving the pack to do the lone wolf thing seemed worth the risk. *Four more days until I meet up with Trey*, she reminded herself. In four days she could be free of her father. Moreover, there would be no way that sicko could get near her.

Almost as if her father or Roscoe, or maybe even both, had suspected she was a flight risk, it was decided that evening that her whereabouts for the entire twenty-four hours of each day up until the mating ceremony would be monitored. If she was at home, one of her dad's enforcers was to accompany her around the property. If she left pack territory for any reason, she was to be tailed by two more of his enforcers. Protection, they called it. Yeah, right.

After only one day of being spied on and followed wherever she went, Taryn was more than pissed. She was a bomb waiting to go off. She couldn't even relax in the knowledge that she had her arrangement with Trey. There was still a chance that it could fall through. She needed a backup plan.

The constant surveillance had made it hard for her to get into her dad's office to hunt down her uncle's address and contact number—even if she didn't end up seeking refuge with her uncle, she still hoped to contact him at some point. Eventually she found the details, but the cell phone had been disconnected. Fuck it all!

If Trey's plan fell through, she was prepared to drive all the way to that address and beg her uncle's Alpha to give her sanctuary. *Maybe* if he liked her uncle *a lot*, he would take pity on her. It would be convincing him not to hand her over to Roscoe or Lance that would be the problem after that. Really, though, what else could she do?

Knowing that she would never be able to come back here, no matter what happened, Taryn packed a large duffel bag complete with clothes, passport, and a few sentimental objects, with the plan that she could stash it in her car, ready for Friday night. Unlike the other wolves, she always drove to the club, as she was constantly on call in case someone from her pack needed healing.

She didn't have a lot of stuff, so it wasn't hard to sift through it and take only the things she really liked or wanted. Her dad had forbidden her from getting an actual job that paid wages, wanting her here at all times due to being the pack healer. The only times she ever had money to buy herself things were when he gave her some, which wasn't often. One thing she had learned from her mom was the importance of saving money, so at least she had some to take with her.

The problem was getting the duffel bag to the car without her constant companion seeing. She figured that her best chance of making Perry a little distracted was if she seemed the most boring person imaginable. Of course that wouldn't be enough, because she was considered a flight risk. Her best hope was to appear to be angry, but drained of the will to fight, hoping to pass as someone resigned to her fate. So that was what she did.

After another two days, Perry became less vigilant, and she found a moment to stash the duffel bag in the trunk. Then she busied herself concentrating on what she would do if Trey didn't appear at the club. She knew she was going to her uncle, but what she *hadn't* mastered was just how she would do that while being watched so closely.

She figured that her best option would be to disappear in a crowd of people. If she could slip away from the club while her dad's enforcers were still inside, she might have a chance at getting away. She *had* to have a chance. She couldn't mate with that sicko.

Finally, Friday morning came. It had felt more like two weeks than four days. She had remembered what Trey had said about not doing anything out of the norm, but there was one thing she had to do before she left. Her usual visit to Joey's and her mom's graves was every other Sunday, but Perry didn't seem suspicious. Surprised, but not suspicious. Although there was a chance this might seem suspicious to him later, it wasn't something she could leave without doing.

She went to her mom's grave first and, as usual, spent a few minutes tidying it up by replacing the decaying flowers with a fresh bunch. Silently she apologized to Cecilia Warner for this being the last time she would ever be able to visit, and for not being able to have the kind of loving relationship with Lance that Cecilia would have wanted.

Her eyes filled as she gave Joey's grave the same treatment as her mom's. She then sat in front of it as she silently spoke to him.

Hey, Joe. I don't know how much you guys up there know about what goes on down here, but there's been some really weird crap going on. Remember I told you last time about that weird-ass Alpha my dad is trying to force me to mate with? Well, it turns out he's also a very sick son of a bitch, and my dad doesn't even give a shit.

There's this other Alpha who's offered me a deal that would get me out of this, but it means I'd have to mate with him. It wouldn't be a real mating, because all he wants is an alliance with my dad and it will only be temporary. The thing is…I need to make everyone believe that he's my true mate, which means I'm going to be telling them that you never were. And I'm so sorry for this, so fucking sorry, but I can't see any other way out.

People say I must wish I'd never found you if it meant you were going to die before we even had a chance to have the mating bond, but I don't wish that, you know. Never have. We might not have mated, but we did *have a bond.*

I'm so sorry, but this is the last time I'll be here. My dad's not going to let me come back after this, but you can bet your ass that I'll still be talking to you sometimes. I'll find a river just like we used to and I'll go sit there and talk to you. And you better listen too, Joseph Winters, because you always had a habit of switching off when you thought I'd been talking for too long.

You've probably switched off now. Okay, it's fair to say that I've been jabbering on. She stood, wiping the tears from her cheeks, as she said the words she always said just before leaving. *Miss you, love you.*

Then, with a heavy heart, she turned away and began walking back toward the pack house. And it hurt so, so much knowing she'd never be back. It was like there was a huge constriction around her chest that tightened with each step.

"He was a good kid," Perry stated.

"Yeah."

"He won't hate you for mating with Roscoe, you know. He wouldn't want you living your life alone. And Roscoe's not a bad guy."

Deciding that arguing would only make Perry more likely to watch her more closely, she continued with her "I'm pissed but resigned" act.

Knowing that she would never again see the graves of the two most important people to her, Taryn would have spent the next few hours in a gloomy mood if it hadn't been for her dad's fantastic news. Roscoe was due to arrive Sunday for another visit. That put her thoughts back in order like nothing else could have. Not only did it remind her exactly why she was doing this, but it helped her shove aside the guilt—guilt that had been heightened by how her body and her wolf reacted to Trey.

It wasn't that she had never desired a guy before, but the desire had never been this intense before. If Taryn had met him under different circumstances, she would most likely have run far and fast from that desire. As much as she had always told herself that one day she would mate, whenever she had gotten involved with a guy she had found herself involuntarily holding back. Although she craved safety, protection, and the type of connection that only mates had, the craving made her hate herself, because she felt as though she was betraying Joey. A part of her knew that wasn't the case, but it didn't change how she felt. If she ever particularly liked a guy, her instinct was to stay the hell away from him.

Therein lay the problem with Trey...She wouldn't be able to stay clear of him. Not only because they needed to spend time together to pull off the true mate stuff, but because they would be mated. It wouldn't matter that what brought them together wasn't love or even a desire to be mated. The second he marked her and she accepted him, they would be classed as mates and their wolves would make it damn difficult for them to keep a physical distance.

She was pretty sure she wouldn't need to work hard to keep an emotional gulf between them, because neither she nor Trey wanted to imprint on each other. Still, the idea of being around someone who could so easily prime her body with just a look was, to say the least, disconcerting. It didn't help that her wolf had such a big thing for him.

Figuring it was important that Trey knew, she sent him a text message around midday to warn him about her dad having her followed. The whole claiming might work out better if his enforcers were aware that they might have to either distract or fight off two of Lance's enforcers.

It was eight thirty when Shaya and Caleb finally came knocking on her bedroom door. They had all been best friends since they were kids. Joey had been the leader of their little group, and it had hit every one of them hard when he died. These two people had seen how badly Taryn had dealt with Joey's death. They would remember how Joey had been so protective and possessive of her. As such, they would be the most difficult to convince that Trey was her true mate. Hell, she might not be able to convince them at all. She would feel a little guilty lying to them like that, betraying their friendship.

It's act well or mate with Roscoe.

"You ready to go?" Caleb asked as he fiddled with the collar of his shirt.

"Yep," she replied.

"Hey, you look great," Shaya remarked in her usual giddy voice as she took in Taryn's sapphire-blue silk dress and matching heels.

Caleb nodded his agreement. "I'm not sure Roscoe will like that you're going out looking like that, without him around to keep other wolves away." As they began walking down the stairs, he added, "I still can't believe you put him on his ass at dinner the other night."

Shaya shrugged. "Looked to me like he kind of liked it. It's only what he should expect if he picks a dominant female."

"Taryn, I wanted to ask," began Caleb. "Do you seriously not want him, or is this some big thing that dominant females do? Do they make the males really work for it?"

Deciding it was best not to launch into how much she detested Roscoe *right* before apparently stumbling upon her true mate, she bit her lip. "It's our way of testing if the male's a worthy mate." That wasn't a lie. Alpha females didn't submit without the male proving his dominance. It was just that in this case that didn't apply, because Roscoe had never been a consideration.

"Oh, I think he's definitely worthy," said Shaya with a smirk. "I'd do him."

Taryn rolled her eyes, smiling. "There aren't many people you wouldn't do."

Shaya jiggled her head as she conceded that, making her short auburn tresses dance around. She talked a lot about other people she would do as Taryn drove them to the shifter club in her Hyundai Tucson. Caleb then criticized each one of her choices, purely to annoy her. Taryn laughed when she was supposed to and spoke wherever necessary, but mainly she was concentrating on keeping herself and her wolf calm. How could she, though, when her nerves were shot?

When Taryn finally pulled up outside The Pulse, her dad's enforcers parked their own car two spaces behind. She prayed—literally—that they would follow her inside. If it came to her needing to resort to plan B, she couldn't exactly sneak off in her car if they were outside watching over it. Relief swept over her when they began following at a discreet distance.

A nervous sigh escaped Taryn as she entered The Pulse. Although some clubs allowed both humans and shifters to enter, this club was open only to shifters. Her wolf picked up on her anxiety, but didn't understand what was really happening. Confused and frustrated, her wolf was pacing within her, clawing at her. In addition to that, as a creature with the most basic instincts, her wolf wanted to investigate some of the male scents and hiss at some of the female scents. Yeah, her wolf could be a right bitch when she was all worked up.

"You okay?" Caleb asked as he halted behind her. Great, he'd sensed something was off.

"My wolf's not having a good day. She's practically clawing at my insides in an effort to get out. Sometimes I think my being latent is harder for her than it is for me."

Shaya shot her a sympathetic smile. "The feeling of being trapped must drive her wild."

Taryn nodded. "Come on, let's go get a drink." And try to stay near the bar so Trey could easily find her. She sidled through the incredibly tight crowd on her way to the bar. The incidental social touches soothed her wolf a little.

The owner of the club and head bartender, Roger, looked up as they reached the bar. In greeting, he nodded at her, Caleb, and Shaya. "What can I get you all?"

A Valium, maybe? "The usual for me please, Roger." Being constantly on call, she mostly stuck to Coca-Cola when she went on a night out. Depressing, but a drunken healer wasn't a good one.

As Caleb ordered a beer and Shaya ordered some weird cocktail, Taryn discreetly searched for her dad's enforcers, Oscar and Perry. They stood at the other end of the bar, chatting while still alert. At least there was a decent distance between them all. She had to resist the urge to scan for any sign of Trey.

She, Caleb, and Shaya found some vacant stools by the bar and got comfortable as they drank and chatted. Although she was fully part of their conversation, it was always at the forefront of her mind that her life was about to change. She was about to enter a temporary mating with the wolf shifter equivalent of the black mamba snake, who had a worryingly overwhelming effect on her body. To add to that, she would never be returning to her dad's pack, and this could even be the very last time she saw her two best friends.

"Thank God you're here! I need your help badly."

A curse flew out of Taryn's mouth as she looked up to see Nicole, one of her packmates. She had run over everything in her head before coming, but she hadn't once accounted for someone needing her for her healing skills right in the middle of her fake claiming. Crap. As the pack healer, it wasn't like she could refuse to help, and she didn't want to.

"It's Ashley," explained Nicole as she took Taryn's hand, pulled her from the stool, and began to lead her through the tight throngs of people. Shaya and Caleb followed closely behind them. The combination of the brushing of bodies against her and strange hands occasionally fondling her as she went by further soothed Taryn's wolf, while simultaneously rousing her.

"What's wrong with her?" asked Taryn.

"She's barely conscious. I guess she must have taken something, but Taryn, you know Ashley doesn't do drugs."

Nicole abruptly stopped. Not because they had reached Ashley, but because there was such a large crowd of shifters huddled together that it was like coming up against a wall. Clearly, there was a very powerful Alpha male somewhere within that crowd who was being both protected and harassed. She wondered if it was Trey. A shudder rippled down her spine as she thought of what was to come—if he found her, that was.

Advancing farther involved a lot of foot squashing and elbow clashing, but eventually they stopped before a chair where Nicole's boyfriend, Richie, stood as though on guard. He gave them all a nod in greeting. In the chair was Ashley, slouched, pale, and limp.

Nicole crouched before her and rubbed her forearm. "Ashley?"

The small redhead opened her eyes slightly, but her expression was pretty vacant. Yep, she'd been drugged, all right.

Nicole, worrying her lower lip, rose and turned to Taryn. "Can you help?" She knew that Taryn didn't have to help anyone who had been dumb enough to drug herself into a practically catatonic state, but Taryn had to agree with Nicole—Ashley wasn't the type of person who would do drugs.

"You think Roger will let us use his office? I can't heal her here."

"I'll go ask him," said Caleb. Before she could say a word, his tall form had disappeared in the crowd.

"Do you think someone spiked her drink?" asked Shaya.

"She was fine up until those hyenas were sniffing around her," said Nicole in a panicky voice, twirling a blonde curl around her finger.

Richie nodded. "They looked like a bad bunch, so I chased them off."

Taryn puffed. "Roger's going to be so pissed off. Not only is someone using drugs in his establishment, but they're using them to spike people's drinks."

"You not with Roscoe tonight?" asked Richie.

"It's only a few days until the mating ceremony," said Nicole. "You must be pretty excited."

"Hey, it was really cool when you knocked him out of his chair," Richie said with a grin. Clearly, Nicole had been one of the females staring at Roscoe, pissing Richie off.

"What had he done?"

Taryn ran a hand through her hair, hoping she didn't look as stressed out as she was feeling. "You know how it is with Alpha females and making sure their mates are worthy." Feeling a tap on her shoulder, Taryn swerved to find Caleb. "Roger said it was okay?"

Caleb nodded. "He's waiting by the door with the key. He likes to keep it locked."

"Come on, then, people, let's get Ashley moved."

Taryn grabbed Ashley's purse as Richie and Caleb each draped one of Ashley's arms over their shoulders and lifted her from the chair. She didn't react, other than to let out a low, whiny moan. With Nicole and Shaya on either side of her, Taryn led the way to the office, making room through the crowds for the guys to carry Ashley without dropping her on her ass.

Five footsteps later Taryn accidentally bumped into a curvy brunette. A familiar curvy brunette. Everything about her was false: her breasts, her plush upper lip, her eyelashes, her nails. God, even the length of her hair wasn't natural—she clearly wore hair extensions. Hell, she was so fake she probably had *Made in China* stamped somewhere on her body. Taryn would happily have ignored her if she hadn't turned and sneered, speaking in that acidic tone of hers.

"Well, if it isn't the latent."

After listening to Brodie's crap for years, Taryn could only roll her eyes and sigh. "*Must* we go through this every time? Yeah, I'm latent, get over it."

"Should you even be in here? This is a shifter club and, when you think about it, you don't really count as one, do you?"

Noting how loud and obvious Brodie was being and just how close she was to the notorious Alpha of the local Falcon Pack, realization dawned. "Oh, you're putting on a show for the big, bad Alpha here. I'm sure he's very impressed hearing you mouth off to someone who you clearly believe is weaker than you."

Shaya snorted. "You'd think she would have learned her lesson years ago when you kicked her ass at the school prom."

Brodie's face scrunched up in mortification. "I had a migraine that day."

"Sure you did," Caleb said dryly.

Turning her attention back to Taryn, Brodie shot her a wicked smirk. "How's your dad? Is he doing as good as when I left him last night?"

Her wolf growled inside her head. "You know, one day you're going to get seriously banged up and need healing, and I'm not going to do a damn thing about it."

"Ooh, did I touch a nerve?"

"You get *on* my nerves, does that count? Now as much as this might surprise you, Brodie, the world doesn't revolve around you. I have shit to do, including helping out Ashley here, so run along."

She stepped a little closer, pouting. "But I'm having fun. Aren't you, little freak?"

With a speed that Brodie obviously hadn't been expecting, Taryn grabbed her mop of hair and yanked down her head to connect with Taryn's sharply rising knee. There was a crunch—her nose, probably. Then she flung a squealing yet dazed Brodie aside and watched as she landed awkwardly on her ass. "I am now."

Ignoring the claps and cheers—did all guys love watching females fight?—Taryn continued making her way to the office. Roger unlocked and held open the door, allowing them all to enter before clearing off the surface of his bureau. The guys carefully laid Ashley on top of it.

Knowing the drill, Nicole opened the window and then stood against the far wall with Caleb, Shaya, Roger, and Richie to give Taryn some space. Taryn placed her palm over Ashley's forehead and, as quick as that, there were patches of luminous lights shining through Ashley's skin, indicating where the drug had done the most damage. The first light was coming from her stomach, making her baby-pink dress give off a neon glow. The other was beneath her scalp, gleaming behind her red hair.

Taryn bent over and opened Ashley's mouth, as if she would give her mouth-to-mouth, which wasn't far from the truth. She put her mouth to Ashley's and then inhaled deeply until she tasted the foulness she had been expecting. When she could breathe in no more, she lifted her head and turned it toward the window before blowing all the foulness out of her lungs. It escaped her mouth in a whoosh of what looked like black particles and zoomed out of the window.

She repeated the process over and over until Ashley's stomach and scalp no longer glowed, indicating that all of what had been polluting her insides was gone. Taryn then stumbled backward, breathless and a little weak. "She should wake up soon."

Caleb urged her into Roger's leather office chair and placed a bottle of water in her hand.

Shaya shook her head. "No matter how many times I see you do that, it always amazes me."

"So...you extracted the drug from her system?" asked Roger.

"No," said Taryn. "I can't explain it well, but it's like I extract the *badness*."

"Like...the bad effects of the drug or illness or injury?"

Nodding, she replied, "Kind of, yeah."

"That was so cool," gasped Nicole. "Even cooler than when you broke Brodie's nose. You going to heal her?"

Taryn tilted her head as she considered it. "Nah."

CHAPTER THREE

Three times Trey had strolled the length of the bar, searching for Taryn. Where the hell was she? For a second, he wondered if she had backed out, but the thought had left his head as quickly as it came. Taryn Warner wasn't the type to wriggle out of a deal.

He knew she had been in this exact spot not so long ago. Her scent still lingered and it was reasonably fresh. His wolf growled at the exotic smell, wanting to hunt her down. To hunt her down and mark her, claiming her as his.

"Her scent disappeared not far from here," said Dante as he reappeared at Trey's side. "Looks like she went into the private office and she hasn't come back out yet."

"What would she be doing in the boss's private office?" If anything sexual was going on, Trey would kill him. Surprised by the vehemence behind that thought, he double-blinked. The sight of his Beta and three enforcers grinning told him that they knew what he'd been thinking. They had all warned him that because his wolf was so near to the surface, his possessive streak would be hard to control. Know-it-all bastards.

What they couldn't know was that his body reacted to Taryn in a way that it never had to another female. He tried to think of it as a good thing; it meant the sex would be amazing. But he didn't like that she seemed to have some sort of power over his body, not to mention his wolf. Already he was feeling possessive of her, for God's sake.

Intending to answer his own question of where she was, Trey began edging through the throngs of people toward the office. He was barely three feet away when the door opened and Taryn walked out, looking pale and shaky. He knew that look. It was the same look his old pack healer had worn whenever she had used her gift. Concern—relatively unfamiliar and unwelcome—traveled through him, but then a smile split her lips at something her friend had said and a shaft of lust shot through his system.

Seeing that she hadn't noticed him, he stayed where he was and waited for her to near him. Once she was close, he deliberately bumped into her and watched in satisfaction as surprise and then lust flashed in her eyes.

Oh God, thought Taryn as she saw the heated, determined expression on Trey's face. His enticing male scent surrounded her, blocking all else. Her wolf shot to alertness and growled her arousal. Taryn held still as he buried his nose in the crook of her neck and inhaled deeply. When his face returned to hers, his eyes had turned wolf and he was so unbelievably focused on her that they might as well have been the only two people in the club. She knew it was an act, but her body still reacted and her clit began to throb in time with her overactive pulse.

Knowing what she was supposed to do, Taryn placed her nose at the junction of his neck and shoulder and, just like he had done to her, took in his delicious scent on a long inhale. She didn't have to fake being drunk on it. As Taryn returned her gaze to his, Trey's hands landed on her hips and he tugged her to him. Then he pretty much took her over. His mouth crushed hers as his tongue thrust forcefully into her mouth, sweeping against her own. The kiss was dominant and possessive as he took the response he wanted, demanding her submission.

One hand collared her throat possessively as his other clutched her ass, branding it as his. She didn't realize she was grinding against him until he hoisted her up and curved her legs around his hips to better the friction. Helplessly she moaned her pleasure into his mouth, digging her nails into his back. If the growl that rumbled up his chest was anything to go by, he liked to be scratched.

Trey couldn't believe how responsive Taryn was. The whole claiming might be an act, but he knew that her body's reaction wasn't forced or exaggerated. She was like fire and he couldn't help but revel in it, in her taste, in her scent, in the feel of her skin, and in how her body seemed to conform perfectly to his. It shouldn't have been possible that a slender person could fit snugly against someone as broad and burly as he was, and yet she did. Those little moans she was making were driving him insane, and he wanted nothing more than to flip up her dress and fuck her right there. Only his awareness that there was a nearby threat to their claiming kept him from thrusting into her.

Pulling his mouth from hers, Trey moved his hand from her throat to tangle in her hair as he kissed and nibbled his way down her throat, before settling in the juncture of her neck and shoulder. He scraped his teeth over the spot, letting her know what was to come. When he was sure her climax was near, he bit down hard, breaking the skin and tasting blood. Instantly she shattered, groaning and shuddering. He sucked strongly on the patch of skin he had bitten, being sure to leave a distinct mark that couldn't be considered anything other than what it was. A claiming.

As quick as that, a rush swept through Trey and he felt a sort of snap in his head, similar to what he'd felt with each of his pack members when they blooded. Then he sensed her through the pack link—not her thoughts, but her fiery, spicy, sensual presence. It was done; she was his to protect as his mate and part of his pack. His wolf growled his approval, urging Trey to sweep her away to their territory, away from the threat that her dad's enforcers presented. He pulled back to admire his work and swiped his tongue over the mark, liking the look of it on Taryn's skin and how she trembled in response.

Taryn knew her face was a mask of surprise, and she knew everyone would mistake it for her shock at supposedly finding her mate. Her surprise, however, was genuine. She hadn't expected Trey to be able to pull that kind of response from her body, even with the effect he seemed to have on her. She had practically melted for him and he hadn't even really touched her. And when his teeth had sunk into her skin…it was as though an electric current had traveled through her, sparking her release. Not like when Roscoe had bitten her against her will; that had left her feeling violated and enraged.

Her ever-present connection with her dad as Alpha had now disappeared and was replaced with this new connection. Lance's presence in her mind had always felt invasive because of his aversion to her; he was all ice and arrogance and deviousness. But Trey was so different; he was strength and danger and raw sexuality. His presence inside her was like an anchor to her wolf, who was a little smug right now, since she was a big fan of psycho boy.

"Trey," he said gruffly as he slid her down his body, as if introducing himself. It was pretty common that two wolves could mark each other before exchanging names, swept away by the urge to claim.

She smiled. "Taryn."

Trey almost rolled his eyes when Dante said, "Hey, congratulations, Alpha."

"Oh. My. God," said Shaya, gazing wide-eyed at them.

And so it begins, Taryn grumbled inwardly, turning to see that many of her pack had observed the claiming and were staring. Every face was the picture of shock. Even Oscar and Perry, who looked as though they had been trying to get past Tao and Dante, were stock-still and gaping.

"Hand Taryn over," demanded Perry. The unsteadiness of his voice suggested he was aware of who Trey was. "As her father's enforcers, we are responsible for her."

Trey gripped her hip possessively and growled at him. "Not anymore you're not."

Their eyes were dancing continually from him to Taryn. They didn't look so determined to try to get to her now, she noticed. That could have had a lot to do with the scowl on Trey's face and the death threat in his eyes. Unless he was dumb, a shifter didn't dare attempt to separate mates, and as unbelievable as it might have seemed, that was indeed what she and Trey looked to be. Still, Perry's and Oscar's dedication to her dad meant that they couldn't just let her go on her merry way, especially since they all believed she would be mating Roscoe.

Oscar straightened to his full height. "Release Taryn or we will be forced to contact her Alpha."

"He's no longer her Alpha. You know that."

"There doesn't have to be any trouble. Just let her go."

Instead, Trey locked his arm around her waist and released a deep, rumbly, "fuck off" growl that had everyone around them tensing. "She's mine."

"Taryn," said Shaya in a pleasant voice, "why don't you come over here and—" Trey's growl cut her off.

"She's not yours," Caleb stated through gritted teeth before fixing his gaze on Taryn. "You know he's not your mate, Taryn. You're confused or something, but you—"

Abruptly Perry reached out to grab her arm, and she gasped. Before she knew what was happening, she was behind Trey, whose hand was wrapped tightly around Perry's throat. Tao was restraining Oscar to prevent him from interfering, while Trey's enforcers Smiley (he wasn't smiling now) and Burly were on either side of her in protective stances.

"Don't. Touch. My. Mate." Trey bit out each word.

"She's already mated," Perry somehow managed to wheeze out. "She's mated to Roscoe Weston."

"If she'd been mated, I couldn't have claimed her—you know that. And you just watched me claim her."

"Her dad won't allow it."

Trey smiled. "It's already done. Now, here's what you're going to do. You're going to start by getting the fuck away from me and *my mate*. Then you're going to call your Alpha and tell him to inform Roscoe Weston that he won't be touching her ever again. If your Alpha has a problem with any of that, I'll be right here. But he should know in advance that she won't be leaving here with anyone but me."

The steel in his voice had Taryn's wolf growling her approval. The dumb animal was impressed by his dominant display, liked that he was shielding and protecting her. She wasn't even averse to the idea of him squeezing Perry's throat a little tighter, despite that the guy had lowered his eyes in a sign of submission. She could understand why—Trey had a certain intensity about him that always made him seem intimidating, but this was different. He was menacing, fierce, unyielding. Every word had been a command and rang with power and authority. It had Taryn feeling a little flushed, if she was honest.

"Roscoe gets here on Sunday," warned Perry. "He'll come for you."

Trey laughed. "Oh, I certainly hope he does." With that, he flung Perry away from him and signaled for Tao to release Oscar. He then turned his back on them, communicating his lack of fear, and snaked his arm around Taryn's waist to pull her tight against him. "Time to look mesmerized by each other while we have a little chat," he whispered in her ear.

Wrapping her arms around his neck, she locked her gaze with his and fixed a smile on her face. His answering smile was devilish. "My dad's going to shit a brick. He'll have felt my disconnection from the pack by now."

"I think he's already on his way here. When the enforcers first tried interfering, one of the males from your pack announced to a female that he was going to call him. Are you going to be okay watching what happens next? I don't want to battle with your father and risk the chance of an alliance, but there's a possibility that the confrontation will lead to a battle." He wasn't expecting to be granted an alliance straight away, not when Warner was going to be pissed about having his daughter taken from him.

"He won't want the fight any more than you do. He'll know you're a more dominant wolf and that you'll most likely defeat him—he won't want to chance looking weak in front of his pack, in case it inspired one of them to challenge his position."

"You're going to have to openly claim I'm your true mate, Taryn," he reminded her gently as he breezed his thumb over his mark. "Are you going to be able to do that?"

It took a good deal of effort not to let the smile drop from her face. "Yes. I know what has to be done."

He brushed his lips against hers. "Good girl. How's your wolf doing? Did she want you to fight me off when I marked you?"

She shook her head. "She likes you."

Trey smiled crookedly. "You say that like it makes her stupid."

"She's impressed by your level of dominance."

That surprised him. "Not intimidated?"

"No. She thinks you're strong enough to take her on; she doesn't like weaklings. It's your scent she likes most."

His wolf really liked hers. Trey inhaled deeply, taking that exotic scent into his lungs. "My wolf's riding me hard. He wants to complete the claiming." Grinding against her, he spoke into her ear, "And I need to be inside your hot little body."

It was true that the mating technically wouldn't be complete without them consummating it, but as it wasn't a mating in the truest sense, Taryn had figured that the drive to have sex wouldn't be as strong. Instead, her wolf and her body were craving that completeness.

Trey slipped his hand under her dress and boldly cupped her. "This is where I'll be very, very soon, Taryn," he promised—more like threatened. "Inside you, filling you with my come, and making you scream."

"I've met guys like you before. They talk the talk but, well… talking doesn't exactly get people to orgasm, does it?"

Trey smiled wickedly. "When I fuck you, Taryn—and make no mistake about it, baby, I *will* fuck you—the only talking you'll be doing is begging me to let you come. And don't doubt that I'll make you come. Not just the once. You'll come over and over again, until *I* decide you've had enough. Until I decide that *I've* had enough."

"Hmm. That's all very fascinating, but you're forgetting one very important thing."

"And what's that?"

"My guess, Tarzan, is that you're very used to Janes; you don't just want total obedience, you *expect* it. I'm not sure you'd know what to do with a woman who would bite you, scratch you, and curse you to hell and back if she wasn't getting her own way. You want my submission, you're going to have to battle for it."

He hadn't thought he could get any harder. She was right in her assumption that he was only used to submissive women; females were too cautious around him to fight him for dominance. He didn't crave submission, but he liked it. And he sure as shit liked the thought of Taryn, his mate, submitting to him. The idea of having to fight for and earn the right to her submission… Fuck. "I'll look forward to the upcoming battle."

"And just so you know in advance, big boy, I never beg." All alphas had a big thing for begging, especially when it came to their mates, and Taryn needed him to know that it wouldn't be happening. "Don't take that as a challenge, because it's genuinely not meant as one. It's just something I never do."

Trey didn't have to ask to understand why. It was because that would mean she had completely surrendered, given her complete submission, and Taryn wasn't prepared to do that for anyone. He understood that need to not be totally vulnerable to another person.

"Now that we've cleared that up"—he curled both arms around her, resting his hands on her ass—"I'll ask…do you think we're fooling anybody?"

"I think most of them are having a little trouble accepting that I'd been wrong about Joey, but they can't deny to themselves what they've just seen." Or what they thought they'd seen. She realized now that if they hadn't done things this way, no one would have bought it. "I don't think any of them believe this is some kind of prearranged thing. More like they're wondering if it's out-of-control lust or something."

He nodded. "They might be able to think of a reason why you would lie about being mated, but they won't be able to come up with a reason why I would."

As his head tipped to the side and his eyes turned wolf, Taryn gasped. His gaze was glued to her shoulder and she knew exactly what it was that had his wolf fighting to surface. She had to refrain from flinching as he released a menacing growl. If she, the female his wolf saw as his, showed any fear of him, it would offend and aggravate him. He was already very much on edge right now.

Knowing what the animal wanted and needed, she said, "Go on." He didn't hesitate. Just bent his head and bit down hard over Roscoe's mark, sucking and licking the skin to replace it with his own mark. When he lifted his head again, it was Trey looking back at her. Apparently, his wolf was satisfied enough that he was willing to retreat.

Trey wasn't surprised by his wolf's jealous reaction to the sight of the fading bite from the other wolf's teeth on Taryn's flesh, but he was surprised that she had accommodated his wolf's basic need to replace the mark with his own. By abruptly more or less chomping on her shoulder, he had done what Roscoe had.

"You didn't struggle," he said, knowing he sounded a little mystified. He wouldn't have expected Taryn, a latent wolf, to understand how difficult it could be to rein in the animal's instinct when the beast lived as close to the surface as Trey's did.

She sighed. "You and I aren't really all that different when it comes to our wolves. My wolf constantly reaches for the surface, because she has no understanding of why she's trapped. Being trapped frustrates her and all that frustration fuels her spirit, making her brash and testing. And that brash, testy spirit then constantly rides me, trying to force her urges or needs on me—it's really her only way of surfacing. So I understand more than you might think about how it is for you to have your wolf so close. Not that I'll always placate him—it's probably best you understand that now. But both she and I know when to push and when to yield."

That was something that only a true alpha could do. Trey found that he respected Taryn Warner, and that wasn't something he could say for a lot of people. "It wouldn't be much fun if you placated me or my wolf all the time." His head whipped around when one of the females spoke.

"Taryn, do you think we could just talk alone for a second?"

Taryn guessed that Shaya thought she might think more clearly if she was away from Trey. She had been about to respond when Richie tapped Shaya on the shoulder.

"Getting in between mates isn't a good idea," he told Shaya. "Especially when they've only just claimed each other."

"But they can't be—" She stopped midsentence and Taryn knew why. Her dad had arrived.

As soon as Lance Warner spotted her, he strolled toward her, clenching his fists. His eyes darted from her to Trey. "What the hell is this?" Then he saw the mark on her neck and his eyes bulged.

"I've found my mate," she declared in a steady voice.

"Your mate?" he repeated tonelessly. "What the hell are you talking about, girl?"

"You're not happy for me, Daddy Dearest? Why am I not surprised?"

Lance fixed his glare on Trey. "Let go of my daughter." There was a slight tremor to his voice that betrayed his nervousness.

"That's not going to happen."

"What's your game here? We all know she isn't your mate. What would you want with her, with a *latent*?"

"Careful," said Trey in a deceptively patient voice, not liking the derogatory way Lance spoke of Taryn.

"You want to trade her for some of my land, is that it?"

Trey laughed, and it wasn't a nice sound. "If I wanted some of your territory, I'd have challenged you, Alpha to Alpha. And believe me, I'd have won."

"Well, if this isn't about territory, then what the hell is it all about?"

"Um, Alpha," Richie began, "we all just saw what happened. It looked like true mates finding each other."

Relief washed over Taryn as she saw many of the wolves around them nodding their agreement with Richie.

"No!" insisted Lance. He pointed hard at her. "You're doing this just to spite me, you little bitch!"

"Hey," snapped Trey as he advanced a step toward Lance. "Be very, very careful. Paper-thin fucking ice."

Taryn almost shivered. The words had been delivered in such a lethal, authoritative tone that her dad had actually resisted the urge to snap back at Trey. "The decision was taken out of anyone's hands by nature itself, Dad."

"Nature? If you're talking about your rebellious nature, then yeah, nature is what caused this. You're doing it to get out of mating with Roscoe. We both know that Joey was your true mate."

"I thought so too, but as unbelievable as it might seem, I was wrong." God, it hurt to say that.

"No. I remember the way you were when he died. You wouldn't talk, barely ate, never left the house. You were like that for over six months."

"That probably had a lot to do with me having lost my mom in the very same accident."

He went to take a step toward her, but Trey's growl halted his advance. He snarled at Trey. "Even if the kid wasn't her true mate, it makes no difference, she's already mated! She's mated to Roscoe Weston."

"As I said to your enforcer, if that had been true, I wouldn't have been able to claim her."

"Well, I think you'll find Roscoe will disagree with you on that. And so do I. She's coming home with me." He signaled to Perry and Oscar to grab her.

"Try it," Trey bit out, his face like thunder and his eyes flashing with anger. "I can guarantee you won't like what happens." Wisely, the enforcers didn't try it.

"What are you waiting for?" Lance growled at Perry and Oscar.

Oscar shrugged. "It's like Richie said. We saw what happened. It sure looked like true mates—"

Lance shook his head. "There's something I'm missing here."

Taryn used his own words against him. "With your view of the world, I would have thought you'd find this easy enough to accept. According to you, a wolf wouldn't want a latent for a mate unless he had no choice in the matter."

"That's true," Lance said with a snicker. "I don't even know why Roscoe wants you, why anyone *would*."

A second later, he was pressed against the wall with Trey's hand around his neck. "It's almost as though you want me to rip your throat out," he growled, fighting his wolf from surfacing and doing just that. He hadn't wanted there to be any violence, but Taryn had been right. Although they weren't true mates and this whole thing was to be temporary, his wolf wasn't hung up on those details, wasn't held back by them. His wolf was an elemental being who acted mostly on instinct, and since he'd marked Taryn Warner, his wolf regarded her as his. His to protect, to comfort, to shelter, to possess. And Trey agreed.

This whole thing hit too close to home, making Trey think of his own father. His dad had been pretty attentive and protective… right up until the seer within the pack, when Trey was just five, had told Rick Coleman that Trey would one day usurp his position as Alpha. After that, his father had pretty much disowned him and left his care to his maternal grandmother—when he wasn't busy taunting him or using him as a punching bag. His mom had tried to fix the divide between them, but she was too much of a submissive wolf to have had any influence on his father.

"Get the hell off me!"

"But I'm comfortable here." Watching Lance try to glance around, Trey smiled. "No one's going to help you. Unlike you, they know better than to try to get between mates. Says a lot about you as an Alpha if no one is willing to offer their life for yours."

"She's my daughter—"

"And she's my mate. She's mine. *No one* keeps her from me. *No one* insults her. And *no one*—and I mean no one—talks to her the way you just did, understand me?"

"Just tell me what it is you really want," snarled Lance. "You just that desperate for a pack healer that you'd tie yourself to a latent?"

Tightening his hold on Lance's throat, Trey smacked his opponent's head against the wall. "Didn't I just tell you no one insults my mate? Not very bright, are you?" He gave Taryn a baffled look. "You sure you two are related?"

She shrugged one shoulder delicately. "I do look a lot like the maintenance guy." Going to stand beside Trey, she cocked her head at Lance. "I don't know what your problem is, Daddy Dearest. You can't stand the sight of me. You should be pleased that I'm leaving the pack. Oh, and you should also stop insulting me if you expect Trey to release you any time soon."

Lance stared at her with a disbelieving look on his red-purple face. "You honestly believe he isn't playing some kind of game? He's using you, Taryn. When you realize that for yourself, don't think you'll be welcome back in my pack."

She gave him a sad smile. "I stopped being welcome the day you realized I was latent. But then, you always were an ass, weren't you."

"Is that what this is? Revenge? You know how bad I want that alliance."

Trey snickered. "What, an alliance with me wouldn't mean anything to you?"

Lance's gaze shot to Trey. It was obvious he hadn't thought of it that way, and she could almost see the wheels turning in his head.

She released a bored sigh. "Trey, just leave him." But Trey didn't. He seemed to be having too much fun watching her dad struggle to breathe. "Come on, he's a waste of skin and fur."

After a deep, calming breath, Trey ever so slowly released Lance and stepped back. "This is what the situation is, Warner. Taryn is my mate, she is now part of my pack, and Roscoe Weston will not touch her ever again. If he has any kind of issue with that, he is free to come to my territory. I'll be waiting." He held his hand out to Taryn. "Come on, baby."

Shooting her dad a withering look, Taryn took Trey's hand and he pulled her against him. His warmth seeped into her body and calmed her wolf even despite the tension. As she looked at Shaya and Caleb and saw the concern and horror on their faces, she felt a stab of guilt.

It's this or being Roscoe's little sex slave! a voice in her head reminded her.

Mouthing "bye" at Shaya and Caleb, she allowed Trey to lead her out of the club.

CHAPTER FOUR

A fter a twenty-five-minute journey, Dante turned the hulking seven-seater Toyota Highlander into a wooded area. Lance Warner's pack territory was a ranch that spanned six acres of land, on which sat a main house where he, his Beta, his bodyguard, and his enforcers lived. Surrounding the main house were several converted barns for the other packmates.

Phoenix Pack territory was nothing like that.

For a start, it had a perimeter fence with an access gate.

"We didn't bother having security on the gate until those human groups that call us abominations formed. They like to stand outside pack houses with their 'Die Demons' banners," Trey explained. "Only pack is granted admittance—or guests, by invitation. It's guarded twenty-four hours." He waved to the shifter on duty, who strolled out of a little security shack and approached the Toyota. "You remember this wolf, right?" Trey asked her. "Ryan's one of the pack's enforcers."

Taryn smiled at the apparently not very talkative Ryan—or Grumpy, as she had branded him a few days ago—who was eyeing her curiously. He made her think of one of those bionic soldiers in sci-fi movies. His movements were a little robotic and he had a real Terminator snarl going on. A guy who wouldn't hesitate to kill if the need arose, she deduced. Still, she didn't feel intimidated. In fact, she was determined to see that impassive expression falter.

"Are you miserable by choice?" As she'd hoped, he was so taken aback that his guard dropped for a split second; his dark eyes widened and his lips twitched. "It's fine and everything. I was just curious about whether you were born looking like you were sucking on a lemon or if the whole gloomy attitude is a life-style choice."

When Ryan's lips curved the *tiniest* bit at one corner, Trey gaped inwardly. For the mostly mute and antisocial Ryan, that was a gushing reception. "Everything went as planned with the claiming," he said to Ryan. "I'll tell you more in the morning at breakfast." Ryan nodded, then patted the vehicle before returning to the shack.

After a short drive over a rocky trail, they finally arrived at Bedrock—there was really no other word for it, was there? She found it amazing that even with light coming from some of the windows, it didn't stand out at all. Unless you were looking for it, you'd probably miss it. "Who did all this?"

"Apparently, the ancestors of the last pack started it a long time ago. It's been added to and modernized over the years. We did a lot of improvements to it ourselves."

"There are actually hotels in places like Turkey that are luxurious cave dwellings just like this," Dante told her as he drove through an opening in the bottom of the mountain, which Taryn soon realized was actually a concealed parking lot.

As she hopped out of the Toyota, she noticed Tao parking her Hyundai Tucson a few spaces away. His sulky expression as he got out of the car was the same one he had worn when Trey ordered him to drive it here for her. "I need to get my bag out of the trunk," she told Trey as she took a step toward her car.

"Tao will get it."

The Head Enforcer froze and a muscle ticked in his jaw. Begrudgingly he retrieved her bag, and Taryn couldn't help smirking at his petulant behavior. The ass shook his head when she went to take the bag from him and stormed past her, following behind Trey and Dante as they strolled out of the opening they had just driven through. Smiley gestured for her to go before him and Burly. Sighing, she removed her high heels and headed for Bedrock.

The night was dark, cool, and silent. The earthy smell, the little sounds of small animals, the wonderful night breeze, the rustling of the tree branches...all of it called to her wolf. She wanted to explore this new woodland, wanted to find out what those unfamiliar scents and sounds were around her. Instead, Taryn was hiking up several narrow flights of steps that had been carved into the mountain wall.

They came to a large door that appeared to be at the center of the other entrances. Then they were going through an indoor maze of tunnels that took them deep into the mountain. Taryn was pretty sure she would get lost if left to wander anywhere alone. Eventually they came to a black door that led to the same kitchen she had sat in only a few days ago.

Realizing that she had pretty much been dismissed as unimportant right now, Taryn hopped onto the black marble counter and grabbed herself a peach from the fruit bowl. Munching happily on it, she listened as all five male wolves sat around the table discussing strategies for when Trey's uncle made his challenge. They were so cool about it that anyone would think they were referring to an Xbox game or something, as opposed to an actual life-and-death situation. There was even a kind of childlike excitement there.

Rolling her eyes, she dug out her cell phone from her purse and read the dozens of text messages she had received from members of the pack. All were asking if the rumor that she had mated Trey Coleman was true. Shaya and Caleb had sent several, both expressing concern about his reputation and trying to convince her that she was wrong about him being her true mate. She knew she would have to respond to them soon, but right now she was feeling too raw.

Aware that all had suddenly gone quiet, she looked up from her cell to find several pairs of eyes focused on her. Surprised, she pulled her finger from her mouth, having sucked off the peach juice. "What?"

Trey cleared his throat. "Nothing." Not liking even the thought of the other males ogling her, he shot them all a cautioning look. Of course, he couldn't blame them. She was so damn sensual and so damn unaware of it.

"By the way," said Dante, grinning from ear to ear, "welcome to the pack, Taryn."

She snorted. "You might not be saying that when Roscoe appears on your territory."

"Are you kidding? We're looking forward to it."

"Yeah, we have to thank you for bringing a bit of life to things around here," agreed Smiley—or Marcus, as he had introduced himself as on the drive here—as he leaned back in his chair. Although he didn't seem any more accepting of her than the others did, he wasn't as antisocial toward her as they were.

"You have to understand, Taryn," said Dante, "we don't get a lot of challenges. This is the most excitement our pack has had in a while."

"Why were your dad's enforcers following you around?" asked Trey.

"When Roscoe came to visit, I wasn't very nice and they considered me a flight risk. The mating ceremony was supposed to take place in a few days."

"Do you think Lance will keep fighting this?" asked Burly. Taryn remembered from their introduction on the journey that his name was Patrick—or Trick, for short.

Trey shook his head. "He might be pissed off and wish things had happened differently, but it's like Taryn said. He'll be worried

I'll defeat him and make him look weak to the rest of his pack. He recognized that my wolf was more dominant than his."

"And the alliance? Do you think we have any chance of getting it?"

Trey looked at her. "What do you think?"

"I'd say yes," she said. "I saw the look on his face when you asked if an alliance with you wouldn't have meant anything to him. It gave him something to think about."

Dante tilted his head at her. "He'll switch loyalties that easily from Roscoe to Trey?"

"As long as he gets an alliance with a powerful Alpha out of this, he'll be content. Give it a few weeks for him to finish sulking and he'll make contact, wanting us to meet up. I'll put money on it."

"You're *that* confident?"

"He's *that* fickle."

"Well, we'll know for sure on Sunday," said Trey. "If he comes along with Roscoe, he's stating that he allies himself with him, no matter the outcome."

"Do you think Roscoe will come as soon as he realizes you've mated Taryn?" asked Dante.

"Yep. What time's he due to arrive on Sunday?" Trey asked her.

"Early in the morning."

"Greta's not due back till after lunch. She'll be disappointed she missed the confrontation."

"Actually, she called earlier to say she'd be arriving in the morning," Trick informed him.

"Greta?" Taryn was glad that none of the possessiveness and jealousy leaked into her voice. Her wolf snapped to alertness, wondering at the mystery female.

"Grandmother," explained Trey.

Taryn didn't like the way he was grinning. It said he was aware of her wolf's immediate response to him saying another female's name with such familiarity. She shot him what she knew was a petulant scowl. He laughed silently.

"She doesn't go out much," said Dante, "but occasionally she goes to stay with her sister, who mated into another pack. I think she might be hoping to try to secure an alliance between that pack and ours. It could have been done a long time ago, but Trey was never interested in making them until now."

"Does the Alpha of that pack have many alliances?"

"Not really, but it would be more than what we have now."

"Then I guess it's a good thing my dad's so fickle." Sighing, she slid smoothly off the countertop. "Where's my bag?"

"Trey's room," Tao told her, his tone unwelcoming. "It's the same room you woke up in last time you were here."

Dante gestured with his hands as he spoke. "Just take a left at the end of this tunnel. You then need to take your second left after that. Then go straight until you come to a junction and take a right."

When her eyes flicked to his, Trey thought he might have seen hesitation there. "Go anywhere else and I'll just hunt you down and drag you to bed."

She rolled her eyes. "Easy there, Flintstone."

"Flintstone?"

"If you're Alpha of a place like this, you're Fred Flintstone. I have no intention of hiding from you. You're mistaking me for one of your submissive Janes. That's not to say there won't be some struggling involved if you expect to get in that bed with me."

"I'll be following you there in about twenty minutes. We'll let the struggling commence then. But what with your wolf riding you so hard to complete the mating, I can't see you struggling that much."

"Ah, so you're a resident of La La Land. I bet you're sultan there too." The sound of Dante's throaty laugh followed her out of the kitchen.

Damn if psycho boy hadn't been right about her wolf's eagerness though. It wasn't just that her wolf craved the feeling of his body possessing hers. The drive to consummate the claiming also had a lot to do with her wolf being anxious that the mating was incomplete. Being back inside Trey's bedroom, where his scent was overbearing, made her wolf a little less restless, but she still didn't like being separated from her male. Not while the mating was half-finished.

Opening the door at the opposite side of the room, she found herself in the most amazing en-suite bathroom. She very much liked the look of the all-glass corner shower, but the masterpiece was the square, spacious bath. It was so humongous you needed to climb a few steps before you could get into it. Unfortunately, she didn't have time for a leisurely soak, so corner shower it was.

A thought struck Taryn as she entered the shower. It was well known that mates found it uncomfortable to be apart for the first few months. Would that apply to her and Trey, or would they be spared because they weren't true mates? She suspected that, in any case, things would always be more trying for her and Trey, due to both their wolves constantly reaching for the surface.

If it *was* going to be really uncomfortable, that could prove a problem. Although she hadn't known Trey for very long, she had picked up that he wasn't a touchy-feely person. For shifters, touch was a *need*. It was as basic as eating and breathing. But Trey didn't seem to experience that craving, or had conditioned himself to ignore it. Yes, he had slid his hands all over her at the club, but that had been for the purpose of their "true mates" act. The second they were in the Toyota, he had released her, and he hadn't touched her since. He always seemed to sit apart or stand apart from the others. If this continued while they were mated, it would be damn hard for their wolves.

As she stepped out of the corner shower, she wrapped a thick white towel around herself and went back into the bedroom, all the while ignoring the way her stomach was clenching at the mere thought of having Trey inside her—not Trey as her mate, but Trey as the man who, merely by looking at her, had an overwhelming effect on her body.

It was no wonder that he had always reeled in females with little effort. *Not that there would be any more reeling.* A split second later, she realized just how much possessiveness had been in that one thought, and she had to roll her eyes.

Hearing a low growl, Taryn slowly turned her head. Trey was closing the bedroom door, and staring at her with such heat in his eyes that she sucked in a breath.

"You have tattoos," he all but growled. Trey had never really thought of tattoos as sexual, but the sight of them on Taryn's body had his cock throbbing. He couldn't decide which he liked best, the anklet or the howling wolf on her shoulder.

She grinned wickedly. "So I do."

All Trey wanted right then was to trace both with his tongue, but he doubted he'd have the self-restraint to take things nice and slow when his lust for her was like a fever in his blood. His wolf was eager to come inside her—another way to mark his mate. But both he and his wolf knew that this was about more than just consummating the claiming. Taryn needed to acknowledge, accept, and admit that she was his mate.

They weren't mates of the soul or even the heart—both of which made it possible for the mating to be temporary—but she had to understand that this didn't make it any less real. They were still mates in the physical sense, which meant that she belonged to him. If he didn't make her understand and admit it, this would never work. He wouldn't have her always throwing in his face that he wasn't her true mate, implying that he didn't have any rights to her. She was his now. Or at least for a short while anyway.

"Lose the towel," he ordered. Not many people would dare to ignore an order from him, but of course, Taryn did. "Lose the towel," he repeated. But she only smiled.

"Honestly, does that usually work?" She could understand if it did. Hell, that implacable, uncompromising tone had very nearly worked on her. She was just so damned horny and her wolf craved his possession, but even her wolf knew he had to prove he was worthy of her surrender.

"I know you're an Alpha, Taryn, but I think you might be forgetting that so am I. Believe me when I say that I *will* have your submission."

"Unleash the beast if you want. I'll try not to laugh, I promise."

His wolf stretched within him, ready and content to catch and subdue his little mate. "Don't make me chase you, baby. Don't make me have to spank that ass." Not that that would be such a bad thing. "Come. Here."

"Yeah, well, ordinarily I would but it's been such a long day and—" Abruptly he dived at her, but she swiftly and skillfully dodged him and managed to place a good distance between them.

"You want this, Taryn." He grinned as her gaze zoomed in on his hands as he unsnapped the buttons of his fly. His painfully hard cock sprang out and she licked her bottom lip. He groaned, then shoved down his jeans and stepped out of them. "I can smell your arousal," he added as he unbuttoned his shirt and had her backing up toward the bed.

"If you say so." Her aloofness might have been more convincing if her voice hadn't been so hoarse with lust. In her defense, his body was unbelievable. All muscle and sinew and power, but not in that over-the-top way with veins popping out or anything. No, it was all sleek, smoothly shaped muscle, made all the better by that golden tan. Her wolf was growling her approval, wanting Taryn to lick a path along that golden skin from the column of his throat to the base of that thick, long cock. It wasn't such a bad idea.

"I can sense how hard your wolf's riding you."

"Jealous that she is and you're not?" Again he rushed at her, but again she dodged him, jumping onto the large bed and then running across it to land nimbly on the other side.

His expression was castigating as he stood on the opposite side of the bed. "You're denying me what's mine. That hot little body is mine now."

"You really believe that? Ah, bless your little heart." His long arm shot out and his hand snagged the end of the towel, whipping it away. Bastard.

As his gaze caressed her naked body and took in all that flawless, creamy skin, Trey actually felt like he'd been poleaxed. Although she was slender, she wasn't skinny or fragile-looking. She was lithe and sinuous with gently and perfectly curved hips, shapely, toned legs, and a gorgeous set of breasts. He'd always gone for voluptuous women, but it became clear to him now that he had seriously underestimated the appeal of small breasts. Taryn's were high, plump, and perfectly rounded, calling his name. His mouth watered as he caught sight of her completely bald pussy. "Mine."

"I'm afraid not, big boy."

He leaped across the bed and grabbed her arm, but she expertly twisted out of his hold and backed away. "You can keep running from me, but it won't change anything."

"I belong to no one but myself."

"That mark right there—*my* mark—says different."

"I'm your mate," she allowed, "but I don't belong to you or anyone else. Well, actually, if you want to get technical about it, I'm not actually your mate yet," she added with a smile.

"Oh, you will be very soon, baby, once I shove my cock inside you." He charged at her with renewed vigor, catching her just as she turned, and crammed her against the wall, her back to his chest.

Taryn struggled and twisted, but his body was like a cage around her. "Move, you son of a—" Then abruptly he plunged a long finger inside her, addressing that aching emptiness, and she practically liquefied against the wall, moaning.

"That's it, baby, be still for me." He kept his thrusts shallow and leisurely, licking his claiming mark and liking her answering tremor. "Feel good?"

"It's all right, I guess."

He had to smile. "It's all right, huh?" She cried out as he plunged another finger inside her. "You're so tight," he groaned. "Tight. Hot. Wet. Mine."

"Wrong."

"Well, baby, while I'm finger-fucking you against this wall and you're moaning like crazy, it sure feels like I own you."

"Never in a million years, asshole," she growled.

"Asshole…Now you're just giving me ideas." He withdrew his fingers and moved one to the puckered hole at the back, circling it teasingly. "One day, I'm going to fuck this gorgeous ass."

"I'm curious, do you retreat into your fantasy world often?" Catching him off guard, she sharply jammed her elbow into his ribs, making him jerk back just enough for her to duck out from under his arm. Sometimes it was good to be small and slim.

To her frustration, she had only gotten a few steps when a strong arm looped around her and he tackled her to the ground. Then she was flipped onto her back and Trey's mouth closed over her nipple and sucked hard. "Oh God," she breathed. Moaning, she cradled his head and scrunched his hair in her hands. Each tug on her nipple sent sparks of pleasure shooting to her clit, making her writhe and squirm beneath him.

It was official—Trey had been mistaken to overlook small breasts. Or maybe it was just because this was his mate that he was unable to release the taut nipple. As he molded and squeezed her other breast, he groaned at how perfectly it fit in his hand. His wolf was growling, urging Trey to take her, to make sure she knew who she belonged to.

Abruptly he meshed his lips with hers, forcing his tongue inside to glide against her own. "I'm going to fuck you now," he rumbled. "I'm going to fuck this body that now belongs to me. Mine," he growled, punctuating it with a bite to her lower lip.

As Taryn met his gaze she saw hunger, anticipation, and determination, and there was something else—possessiveness. "No." She dealt him a harsh blow to the chest, which had him jerking into an upright position. Quickly she flipped to her stomach and was almost fully on her feet when he gripped her by the hips and yanked her down onto his lap. He growled something that sounded like "Got you" and then impaled her on his cock. The pleasure-pain of it had her back arching as she cried out.

Trey groaned as her inner muscles clamped down on him. "Take all of it, Taryn," he demanded through his teeth. He slowly lifted her until only the head of his cock was inside her and then slammed her down onto him. "All of it." He raised her again, enjoying the feel of her juices coating his cock, and then he impaled her to the core, seating himself to the balls. "Oh, fuck yeah." His wolf howled inside his head, loving that he was finally inside Taryn, filling her, stretching her. She was so tight and hot around him that he was close to coming already. As he gave her a moment to adjust to his invasion, he nibbled at her spine and then pulled her back against his chest so he could graze his teeth over his claiming mark. "You okay?"

Okay? She was absolutely freaking amazing. The pressure of his size stretching her stung and burned, but it was a delicious pain and she was reveling in it. She gasped as he suddenly lifted her again. The movement was slow, forcing her to feel every inch of him dragging against her sensitive inner walls. Something between a moan and a whimper escaped her throat.

"Shh," he soothed. "Such a good girl taking all of my cock," he praised as he once again slowly impaled her on himself. Twice more he did it, loving her drawn-out moans and the way she squirmed restlessly. "Are you going to tell me no again?" She shook her head, moaning. This time he lifted her fully off him, then rose to his feet and propped her up on her hands and knees on the bed. "I need it hard and fast, Taryn. Can you take it?"

"Do it."

"Good girl." Gripping her hips, he rammed into her so hard she fell forward, so that she was resting on her elbows. That was even better.

Taryn cried out as he began mercilessly pounding into her with deep, dazing strokes that were zapping her with bliss. Nothing should feel this good, she was sure of it. It had definitely never felt this good before, but she'd known it would be this way—and it had scared her. Now, though, as he tunneled in and out of her, reaching depths that had until now been untouched, there was no fear, only sheer and utter carnal bliss.

As Trey gazed down at all that creamy skin of her back, that *unmarked* creamy skin, he had the urge to bend down and sink his teeth into wherever he could reach. He closed his eyes against the impulse. He wouldn't mark her again, he told himself. He'd fuck her and ensure she knew that she was his, but he wouldn't mark her again. Twice already he had marked her, when the one claiming bite was all they needed. He didn't need to possessively mark her up with claws and teeth to leave his brand all over her, the way his wolf wanted him to. The way Trey the man wanted to.

"Do you like that? Does it feel good having my cock inside you?" Her response was a feverish moan that was a clear yes. "That's a very good thing, because I'm going to be in here often. Taking what's mine."

"Not yours," she growled.

His next thrust was extra hard—a warning, a punishment. "Keep growling at me, keep telling me you're not mine, I dare you."

"I'm not yours." She reached back with one arm and grazed his chest with her claws. Not enough to leave a permanent mark, just enough to caution him. She growled when she felt the slash of claws along the flesh of her lower back—these were deeper, *would* mark. "Don't you dare brand me, you son of a bitch." She gasped as a hand came down sharply on her ass, and then his hand knotted in her hair and he dragged her up so her back was arched against his chest.

"I'll mark you wherever I want," he growled into her ear, still ruthlessly hammering into her. Abruptly he sank his teeth into her nape and his wolf growled his approval. "You're my mate, Taryn. Say it."

She snapped her teeth at him, missing his jaw by mere inches. "Fuck you!"

Again Trey spanked her ass hard. "Let's try that again, shall we. Whose mate are you, Taryn? Who do you belong to?"

"I'm your mate, but I don't belong to you!"

"The two can't be separated; it doesn't work that way."

Pissed off that he was right, Taryn growled her annoyance and struggled against him, but he only tightened his hold on her hair.

"You're not going to get away. Not until I've pumped every ounce of my come inside you. Now, *who do you fucking belong to?*"

After a slight hesitation she conceded with a snarl, "You."

"That's right, baby, and just in case you're ever tempted to forget..." He yanked her head back and bit down hard into the soft flesh of her neck, where it would be visible for all to see.

Just like that, even though she hated what he'd done, a wickedly powerful orgasm crashed into Taryn and she screamed her release.

As her muscles closed bitingly around him, Trey exploded inside her with a loud, guttural growl-groan, marking her with his come just as surely as he'd marked her with his teeth. Shit, he had never fucked like that, never come so damn hard. He couldn't decide if it was a good thing or a bad thing that this female could make him mindless.

As she collapsed forward onto the bed and Trey got a look at her body, he had the urge to slap himself. In addition to his claiming bite and the one he'd given her to cover Roscoe's, there was a bite on her nape, there were claw marks on her back, his handprints on her ass, another bite on the very visible part of her neck, and claw marks on her hips where he'd held her. The worst of it was that every single one of those brands gave him and his wolf a kind of masculine satisfaction.

Goddammit.

CHAPTER FİVE

A n overwhelming need to pee woke Taryn. The rays of moonlight peeking through the curtains had been replaced by sunlight, telling her it was early morning. Her intention to stretch was inhibited by the tanned, muscly arm and leg belonging to the wolf behind her, both of which were draped over her as if to trap her there. She smiled at that. Then her smile widened as she recalled being woken a few times in the night. Yeah, it could be said that they had engaged in a sexual marathon. Trey was insatiable and had impressive stamina, even for a shifter.

Wriggling out from under his hold, she went to answer the call of nature. She found herself staring longingly at the luxurious tub—a hot bath sounded fabulous—but her rumbling stomach had other ideas.

A few minutes later she was dressed and heading through the damn network of tunnels. The familiar black door that led to the kitchen wouldn't be too hard to find; she could just follow the scents of meat and eggs and hot, toasted bread. The chattering stopped as she entered and five strange faces looked at her curiously, though they didn't seem surprised to see her. Obviously, word had gotten out about Trey finally bringing her here.

As simple as this moment was, it was also pivotal. Her stay here wasn't going to be a pleasant one. Being Lance Warner's daughter would be enough to make some wolves give her a hard time. It wouldn't matter that her mating with Trey might ultimately aid their cause. She was still a Warner and there was no way any of them would want to answer to her. Also, the fact that she was latent meant that some people would regard her the same way that Brodie did—as a freak of nature, an easy target, someone who didn't even count as a shifter. They would test her patience and strength, and make her stay here difficult.

As such, there were a few ways she could handle her first few moments in their pack. One, she could present them with a dazzling smile and introduce herself needlessly, hoping to win them over with a friendly attitude. Two, she could act aloof, distant, and ignore any attempts to goad her. Or three, she could just be her usual ray of sarcastic fucking sunshine and tell anyone who pushed her to go eat shit.

A bigger person would have gone with option two, but, well, she was a bitch. So she decided to go with number three. "Look, I'm not much of a morning person, because I tend to sleep through it, so if you're hoping to piss me off, then proceed with extreme caution. We'll get along just fine if you don't treat me any differently than you would a princess." With that, she nodded at the stunned faces and hopped up onto the countertop.

The plump brunette who had been pouring coffee for the others approached her. "You must be Taryn," she said, smiling. "I'm Grace. I cook, clean, and say *shit* a lot."

"Ah, someone who speaks my language."

Grace gestured at the dining table, where croissants, toasted bread, bacon, scrambled eggs, baked beans, sausages, platters of cold meat, various fruits, and cereals were all laid out. "The wolf over there with the glasses and the goatee who's the epitome of geeky, that's my mate, Rhett. The Bill Clinton lookalike is Brock, a cousin of Trey's dad. The guy next to him with the spiky blond hair and the baby face is Cam. And the unfairly gorgeous female opposite him with the unfairly great legs is Cam's mate, Lydia."

"Stop mooning over my mate's legs, Grace," Cam groused playfully before shoveling half a croissant in his mouth.

"You're like a little doll," said Lydia, smiling at Taryn. She was the only one other than Grace who had a smile for her. "No one would ever think you had such a smart, awesome mouth."

"Coffee, tea, or orange juice?" Grace asked while Taryn took one of the empty plates and piled bacon, scrambled eggs, and toasted bread on it.

"Coffee." Plate in hand, she parked her ass back on the counter. At Grace's amused but questioning look, she shrugged. "I always sit on the counter. A little quirk of mine."

Grace's gaze skimmed over her, taking in the various marks of possession that decorated her flesh. "Well, short of having *Property of Trey Coleman* tattooed on your forehead, he couldn't have made it any clearer that he considers you his, could he?"

Very true. In addition to those marks that Trey had left while they consummated the claiming, there were those that he had made during the second, third, and fourth rounds that followed through the night. There was a bite at the hollow of her throat, another on her inner wrist, a third one on the swell of her breast, and also claw marks on both upper arms—and those were only the ones that weren't hidden beneath her black T-shirt, navy jeans, and black leather knee-high boots.

And what had Trey's response been when she told him that he might have overdone it a little with the marking? A shrug followed by a very smug grin.

Maybe it would be fair to say that if she hadn't fought him so hard on the issue of belonging to him, then she wouldn't be in this state. Yeah, but that only applied to the first time. After that, she had conceded belonging to him as his mate, although she had snarled at him with every concession. He hadn't had any need to keep it up.

She wondered if maybe the drive behind it had been that he had sensed that her admission was only halfhearted. Once she had belonged to someone, and when he had been taken from her, it nearly killed her, even though they had never mated. As it was, Joey had taken a chunk of her with him when he died. And that was okay, because that was his chunk to take. But she wouldn't give that much of herself to another person again. Her soul wouldn't survive the loss a second time, as there wouldn't be enough of her left to allow her to live. She would simply exist, breathing in and out and in and out, but nothing more. And this was a male she *would* lose—that was a sure thing. So, yeah, she would belong to Trey on a physical level, but no more than that.

It was actually best that way, as it meant there was no chance whatsoever that the process of imprinting would spark. Despite Trey's mark-happy behavior, he didn't want that any more than she did. It was simply in the nature of the male to want to possess his mate completely, inside and out. This male would just have to make do.

"And I thought *I* looked badly marked up on my claiming night," said Lydia.

"Can I, um, ask," began Rhett. "Is it true that you're, um, latent?" At her nod he added, "Do you still feel your wolf or is she buried deep?"

Grace quickly interrupted. "You should know that Rhett is one of the most curious people to have ever walked the face of the Earth. He's great with computers and anything technical, but he's not an expert with human emotion. It wouldn't occur to him that he might offend you by bringing it up." She shot him a reprimanding glare.

Taryn shrugged. "It's fine. No, my wolf's not buried, she's very much aware and very much a pain in the ass." Rhett seemed about to ask her something else, but a sharp look from Grace had him returning his attention to his meal.

"It's going to be nice having some more female company," said Lydia. "We're way too outnumbered by the males."

Taryn arched a brow. "There aren't many women?"

"Well, there are three others, but they don't really count. Selma and Hope are your typical walking tributes to Barbie, and are both vain and bitchy. And Greta's…well, she's horrid."

"Lydia," censured Brock. "Have a little respect." The look he gave Taryn was withering.

Lydia ignored him. "She thinks she rules the place because she's the Alpha's grandmother, likes to boss us females around. The males can't do any wrong in her eyes. She mothers Trey, Dante, and the enforcers something awful, calls them *her boys*. And, well, she doesn't like females sniffing around her boys."

"She's even worse when it comes to Trey." Grace's smile was sympathetic. "Scares off every female who goes near him."

"Surely she's not going to want to scare me off when Trey needs to claim I'm his mate for his super plan." Their winces said that wouldn't be the case.

"*Need* a Warner? Now that's a joke." The deep voice belonged to a male who, though nowhere near as good-looking or muscular as Trey, bore a few similarities to him. He had the same strong nose and chin, the same arctic-blue eyes, the same height. Whereas Trey's dark scowl somehow looked good on him, it made this guy look creepy. She only had to look at his posture and the flash of bitterness in his eyes to know the guy had a chip on his shoulder. She had to wonder just what that chip was all about. He took a seat beside Lydia and then glared at Taryn. "We don't *need* a Warner, and we don't *need* a latent."

"I don't *need* your approval," retorted Taryn. "So fuck off." That seemed to surprise him, but she wasn't under the illusion that it would shut him up.

Grace sighed. She didn't appear any happier about his presence than Taryn was. "That's Kirk, Brock's son, so he's sort of Trey's cousin." She mouthed, *And an asshole.*

His nostrils flared as he looked at Taryn. "If you think we're all going to bow down to a Warner, think again."

Taryn smiled at Grace. "Isn't it great when just your very existence infuriates someone? You've got to love that kind of power."

The sound of very merry whistling was soon followed by Marcus and Trick's entrance. One look at the marks on her body and that clown grin took over Marcus's face. Trick simply snickered.

"Hey, little sister." Trick ruffled Grace's hair, earning himself a scowl and a smack on the shoulder.

"Go, sit, eat, don't bother me," she grumbled. Chuckling, he took a seat at the table and practically attacked the plate piled with slices of cold meat. "Here," said Grace as she handed Marcus a doggie bag. "See you later."

Marcus opened it and sighed happily. "Is it wrong that I'd sell my soul for your cooking? If you weren't already mated, I'd snap you up."

Grace rolled her eyes but a blush stained her cheeks. Taryn couldn't blame her—the guy was seriously hot. Hell, all the enforcers were. "He's guarding the gate today, so he only has time to pop in and out," she explained to Taryn after he had left the room.

Taryn looked up as Dante entered and went straight to the jug of coffee. He poured some into a Bart Simpson mug, inhaled the aroma deeply, and then took a sip. It was only then that he turned to everyone, apparently equipped to interact with others now that he had caffeine in his system. The instant he saw her he almost choked on his drink. She would have said she didn't look *that* bad, but she did.

"Now I know why you kept yelling at him for biting you." At her raised brow, he explained while grinning wickedly, "As Beta, my room's next to the Alpha's. How does *he* look?"

"You'll see for yourself, won't you." In truth, she hadn't marked Trey. Her wolf had wanted her to, had desperately tried to surface in response to Taryn's resistance. But there was no chance Taryn was going to encourage his wolf's sense of possessiveness by marking him back, not when this was temporary. Also, it would be easier on her wolf when they separated if she hadn't branded him. It would be easier on Taryn too. Trey hadn't questioned her about it or urged her to mark him, so she could conclude that he was on the same wavelength.

Dante took another swig of his coffee. "I said that Trey—although he's not usually possessive—would mark you up proper. The others, including Trey, thought he would be able to rein it in because you aren't true mates. I have to say that I'm kind of enjoying that I was right."

"Your life is that sad?"

"You don't get it. Trey never marks his women. He's always teased us whenever we've gotten even the slightest bit possessive with our partners. I'm just enjoying how the tables have turned."

"To be fair," said Trick, pausing in the demolishing of his cereal, "it's a little different since he mated her."

Dante looked about to say something, but he was distracted by the entrance of Ryan, Dominic, Tao, and Trey. Ryan acknowledged her with a grunt, Dominic with a teeny nod, and Tao with a fierce scowl.

"Yes, it is a fabulous morning and yes, I did have an amazing sleep, thank you," she said to them sweetly.

Just for the hell of it, Trey delivered a sharp nip to her bottom lip before taking a seat at the table with the others. Inwardly he frowned at this strange primal urge to be close to her and touch her. Naturally he ignored it, but his irritation remained. Trey hadn't hungered for touch for a long time, and he didn't like the idea that that might be changing.

He hadn't been too pleased when he woke up to find himself alone. He'd originally hoped to taste her this morning, since oral sex had been out of the question last night, when she was battling his dominance so hard. He hadn't been able to pin her down to taste her and he certainly hadn't been interested in risking sliding his dick between those snapping teeth. Damn if their battles for dominance hadn't been the hottest thing ever though.

Dante leaned back in his seat, smiling at Trey. "So…how come you didn't mark her?"

Low laughs filled the room, but Trey just ignored them. Okay, he'd probably gone a little too far, but he simply liked the look of his mark on Taryn's flesh. Once he'd gotten past his annoyance with himself for his urge to do it, he hadn't held back.

"Poor girl looks like she had a fight with a vampire. Oh, and *you*, Taryn. Damn, you can curse. What did she call you at one point, Trey? Oh, that was it. A motherfucking, ass-licking son of a cocksucking goddamn bitch." Grace and Lydia laughed.

"I'm an expressive person," she said with an innocent shrug.

"I especially liked the part when she threatened to slice your cock off in your sleep if you didn't stop spanking her. So where did she mark you?"

Trey knew the question was rhetorical. Females tended to mark their males around the groin, and obviously Dante figured that was the case with Taryn. Rather than correct him, he allowed him to think that. He wasn't sure why she hadn't marked him. Oh, she'd nipped him and scratched him a few times through the night, but it had only ever been in retaliation and it was never deep enough even to draw blood, let alone mark.

His wolf didn't like it, and Trey was pretty sure that her wolf wouldn't be too pleased about it either. Maybe she would mark him when the battles for dominance had eased, he mused. He didn't bother asking himself why he even gave a shit. This mating stuff fucked with the brain.

"How does it feel to have a female who won't bow down to you?" Dante's grin was roguish.

Trey returned the grin. "It makes life interesting." *Very interesting.*

"I don't know how you can fuck a Warner," snarled Kirk.

An unnerving growl filled the sudden silence and Taryn's wolf began pacing and releasing a growl of her own as if to back up her mate.

Trey's entire focus was on a fidgety Kirk. "Don't. Insult. Taryn. Again." Just like last night, the very idea of anyone insulting her made his blood boil.

Keeping his head bowed, Kirk rose from his seat and stalked out of the kitchen. Brock gave Trey an apologetic smile, and then followed after his son.

"You're right," Taryn said to Grace, who was taking Kirk's now vacant seat. "He is an asshole."

"We'll be leaving here in a couple of hours to head to the meeting with the mediator," Trey told her. "In the meantime, I'll be in my office, but there'll be plenty of people around if you need anything."

Yeah, all of whom are hoping I die a painful death very soon. "I wouldn't have pictured you as the type to have an office."

"I have investments in a number of different businesses, and I like to keep an eye on them. Feel free to wander around or whatever."

"I will once I've been for a run."

The eagerness in her voice surprised him. "You still have that need even though you're latent?"

"My wolf gets restless and uncomfortable if I don't. She still craves that feeling of being free, the kind that comes from running with other wolves." Although these wolves were only temporarily her pack, that didn't affect her wolf.

Trey couldn't imagine how difficult it would be to be latent. He wasn't sure who would have gone crazy first, he or his wolf. The fact that Taryn was not only sane but also free of bitterness and hate demonstrated just how strong a person she was.

As he sat sipping the remainder of his coffee, he watched her chewing on a piece of bacon. Such a simple sight, and yet he couldn't move his eyes from her. There was such an effortless sensuality to her movements. Each one was graceful, almost fluid. The way she chewed her food and licked that carnal mouth had his cock so hard he could probably hammer nails with it.

Dante's eyes were helplessly glued to her—something that Trey wasn't pleased about, but couldn't blame him for. Even his enforcers seemed to begrudgingly admire her innate grace. She really was the most sensual creature he had ever seen. The fact that she was totally without vanity and completely oblivious to how provocative she was only increased the attraction. She was truly nothing like any of the women he had been with in the past.

"Trey?"

Definitely nothing like the female who was currently heading toward the kitchen. *Once*, he had fucked the woman *once*, and yet ever since that night four years ago Selma had acted as though she had rights to him. He'd kind of hoped that she would have moved on by now, but apparently the universe thought it would be more fun this way.

"An ex?" Taryn was surprised at just how much the idea irked her.

"For her to be an ex, there would've had to be some kind of relationship to begin with."

"In other words she's someone you used to fuck?"

"I like to think of her as more of a mistake."

"Trey, is it true?" demanded Selma as she stomped into the kitchen with Hope at her side. Instantly Selma's nostrils flared as she took in the other scents in the room. Her head whipped around to face Taryn. Trey watched as Taryn smiled warmly at her, but there was something dark in that smile, something that warned Selma to be very careful.

Taryn cocked her head at the females. Oh, Lydia hadn't been kidding when she said they were living tributes to Barbie, complete with peroxide-blonde hair, fake tans, and an overabundance of makeup. The taller of the two lowered her eyes at the sight of Taryn, but Trey's "mistake" was mightily pissed. Good.

Selma's focus quickly returned to him. "You mated her? You actually mated her?"

"Why are you so surprised? I told each of you about my plan at our last pack meeting."

"Yeah, but I never thought you'd really do it! She's a *Warner.* And I just—I thought that you and I would mate."

Several snorts snatched Trey's attention. He watched as Dante, his enforcers, Grace, and Lydia all exchanged glances that said Selma was obviously delusional.

Selma planted her hands on her hips. "Aren't you going to introduce me?"

Trey held his hand out invitingly to Taryn. Smiling, she crossed the room and let him pull her onto his lap. "Taryn, Selma. Selma, Taryn."

"Oh, I'm just Selma to you now?"

She had only ever been *just Selma* to him. Of course, he had known that she was hoping he'd mate her and she would have the position of Alpha female. He hadn't known that she thought she had a chance.

Taryn rolled her eyes. "I suppose this is the part where you enlighten me about how you're his ex—perhaps even the love of his life—and then I'm supposed to feel insanely jealous. Sorry, but it's just too early in the morning for me to muster that kind of response. Maybe you should try again later." Though that wasn't to say that Taryn wasn't tempted to slap her purely for having touched Trey—as idiotic as that was.

"Seriously, Trey, you can't honestly have mated *her.* She's not even your type. I mean, she's thin. And mouthy. And small. Even her boobs are on the small side."

"I have nice feet."

"You're not his type!"

"You mean because I can read and write?"

Selma flushed and stamped her foot. "Trey? *Trey?*"

Finally he spared the whining woman a glance. He'd only been half listening to the conversation, as he'd been too busy nuzzling Taryn's neck, breathing in her exotic scent. As he licked over his claiming mark, a tremor ran through her.

Taryn gave him a sideways glance. "Trey, you really shouldn't do that unless you want me to jump you while we have an audience." The ass licked it again.

"Hello!" barked Selma, waving. She was a picture of jealousy.

"Oh, sorry, did you say something?" Taryn asked innocently.

The ringing of Trey's cell phone cut off whatever Selma had been about to say. Seeing that the caller was Ryan, he brought himself and Taryn to their feet. "I'll be back in a minute." With one last lick to his mark, he released her, relishing the flush on her cheeks, and left the room to take the call in private.

As if Selma wasn't staring at her with utter hatred in her eyes and obviously planning her murder, Taryn leaned against the counter as she tackled her last slice of bacon.

"I feel sorry for Trey being stuck with you, even if it's only for a few months. Seriously, Dante, what was he thinking, mating a Warner?"

"You wouldn't have liked her no matter who she was, and we all know why."

"Oh, come on, Dante, if what I've heard is right, she's latent, for God's sake." God, the woman sounded like Brodie.

Taryn sighed. "You know, I really wish people would stop talking about my latency like it's the second coming of Christ. I'm not the only latent shifter."

Selma gave her a pitying look. "You have to admit that a latent couldn't manage being an Alpha female."

"I suppose you would do a much better job."

"Yes, I would. Even if this mating was real, it wouldn't have lasted long. Once Trey and his wolf began to realize just how weak their mate is, their interest in you would have swiftly dwindled. They'd have gone looking for a female wolf who can complement them and their strength. And when that happened, I'd have been waiting."

Trey was just ending the call when the sound of a loud crash hit his ears and had him cursing in surprise. He raced into the kitchen and stared, confounded, at the vision before him. Selma was very ungracefully splayed out on the floor, obviously having smacked her head against the wall, if the trail of blood was anything to go by. Everyone at the table had risen from their seats and stared down at her, wide-eyed. And Taryn...well, she was leaning against the counter, calmly biting into a slice of bacon as if there wasn't a woman moaning and bleeding all over the floor.

"What the hell happened?" he demanded. Taryn's expression was perfectly serene when she peered up at him.

"She fell."

The sound of muffled laughter had his attention returning to the table. Dante, Grace, Lydia, Cam, and Rhett were chuckling so hard they were shaking. Although the others were silent, none of them—not even Hope—had been able to hold back an amused grin.

Taryn sighed. "I think I'll go on that run now. Grace, that breakfast was excellent." She then made her way around a moaning Selma, pointedly ignoring her. "Close your mouth, Trey, or you'll catch flies."

Still totally bemused and also a little horny as a result of her Alpha vibes pulsating around her, Trey stared after Taryn as she pranced out of the room humming a tune he didn't recognize.

"Taryn's one mean bitch," Dante said approvingly.

"Trey, look what she did to me!" whined Selma.

He didn't want to. "Dante, Tao, you coming?" Both rose from the table and thanked Grace before following him out of the room. "What was all that about, anyway?"

"Just Selma being her usual irritating self," replied Dante. "You should've seen the way Taryn picked her up and slung her at the wall. It was awesome."

Tao nodded his agreement, albeit reluctantly. "That female's freakishly strong for her size."

Oh, Trey already knew that from their battles last night. His lips curved into a smile as he imagined battling with her all over again tonight.

Taryn was in a better mood after her short run. The cold breeze on her face, combined with the familiar scents of the forest, had left her feeling refreshed and settled her wolf. Only then had she begun to wander through the maze of tunnels to familiarize herself with what would be her home for the next few months. Three hours later Taryn was in the doorway of the living area, gaping.

A wander around had confirmed that not one inch of the place was anything but spectacular. There were four floors and each one of them featured dozens of en-suite bedrooms, a small kitchenette, and a laundry room. On the fourth floor, where Trey, Dante, and the enforcers slept, there was—in addition to a laundry room—a pool room, a game room, an office, the huge, amazing kitchen, and a large living area. The blend of modern and antique furnishings was a feature throughout the entire place, never once clashing.

She was nothing short of awed and had found something to gasp at in each and every room. But this room…whoa. The audio-visual system was state of the art, the decorative, swirly carvings on the main wall were amazing, and the many armchairs all looked comfy enough to sleep on, but it was the item in the center of the living area that had her attention. *Is it a bed? Is it a sofa?* The freaking thing looked more like a giant cushion.

There had been a sectional sofa in her pack house too, but it wasn't anything like this. The black leather was clearly top quality and it could comfortably seat at least eighteen people. One end was a gorgeous chaise lounge while the other end had a recliner. It was so big and bulky that not only did her ass sink into it, but her feet didn't even touch the floor. It totally dwarfed her. Suddenly she felt like one of the Borrowers.

Oh, she could get used to this luxury. She wasn't a materialistic person, never had been, and she totally agreed that money didn't bring you happiness. Still, she'd rather be depressed wearing Prada than dirty rags.

"Comfy?"

Taryn looked at the doorway to see Tao there, scowling. "If I didn't know any better, I'd think you resented me being comfortable."

He shrugged. "I'm not convinced your dad will give us an alliance, which means we'll have brought all this trouble on ourselves and not even get what the pack needs out of this mating."

"Maybe you should've thought of that before you kidnapped me, huh?"

"Believe me, if I could have talked Trey out of this, I would've, but I respect Trey and I follow his orders."

"That's nice. You can leave now. I promise your idiotic opinion will be noted."

A muscle ticked in his jaw—something that seemed to be a habit with him whenever she was around. "There's nothing idiotic about not wanting Lance Warner's daughter in my house or around my pack. They say the apple doesn't fall far from the tree, don't they."

"Hey, I have a suggestion, why not put a condom over your head—if you're going to act like a complete dick then it makes sense to dress like one." His mouth actually twitched at that, but Taryn just sighed and retrieved the remote control from the round pine coffee table. Switching on the TV, she sought out the sports channels.

Tao came to stand beside the sofa. "You watch boxing?"

"I missed the fight between Jacobs and Leighton last night. I just want to watch the repeat, then you can watch whatever you like."

Frowning, Tao gingerly sat beside her. "Fifty says Leighton won."

Taryn stared at him curiously, then nodded. "Seventy says Jacobs won by knockout."

Well, this was a surprise.

On leaving his office, Trey had followed the trail of Taryn's delicious scent to track her down. Considering how Tao had been treating her up until this point, the last thing Trey would have expected was to find the pair of them laughing and joking while watching boxing on TV. Her response to Selma would have shown the pack that she wasn't an easy target or someone who took any shit, but he hadn't thought it would be enough to win anyone's respect just yet. Clearly, he had been wrong. He should have been glad about that. It was a good thing for her to have Tao as an ally. Strangely, though, Trey found himself wanting to punch his Head Enforcer for putting that smile on her face. His wolf...well, he wanted to gut Tao.

"Ready to go?"

She looked up at him, frowning at the strain in his voice. "Sure." Her frown deepened when, instead of walking on ahead of her with Dominic and Ryan, he waited for her to reach his side. She noticed that Dante was smiling—the kind of smile that said he knew something she didn't. Well, whatever. Trey remained at her side all the way to the car and even sat with her in the backseat, which, for some reason, had Dante's smile widening.

Her wolf enjoyed having her mate so close, enjoyed having his scent cocooning her. Unfortunately, just as Taryn had feared, it was proving to be uncomfortable for her wolf when they parted for too long. She wouldn't have thought that five hours counted as "long," but her wolf had been restless and on edge until the moment he entered the living area. His presence automatically made her feel safe, reassured, and relaxed.

"Has your father been in touch with you yet?" Trey asked her.

"No. He'll be too busy sulking."

"You know there's a chance he'll turn up tomorrow with Roscoe, don't you."

She sighed. "Yeah, I know." She doubted he would, but there was still a chance.

"And you know what will happen if he tries to take you, don't you."

She wondered if he even realized that the hand of the arm he'd hooked around her headrest was now playing with her hair. "Even if he comes, it'll only be Roscoe who'll challenge you."

"I hope you're right. I want that alliance with your father, but there's no chance I'll be able to hold back my wolf if he tries to take you."

The heavy dose of possessiveness in his voice had her lips twitching. What made it more amusing was that she could see how much the unfamiliar sense of possessiveness irritated him. "I did try to warn you that it wouldn't matter to your wolf that we aren't true mates."

He shot her a glare. "Smart-ass."

"Aw, I love you too."

He snorted and faced forward again, resisting the urge to nibble on her bottom lip. And the urge to kiss her. And the urge to lick over his mark. His wolf, on the other hand, liked all three of those ideas and was growling his encouragement at Trey. His wolf had...missed her. He brooded and fretted when he wasn't around her, pushing at Trey to go hunt her down. Whenever he *was* around her, his wolf wanted to lick every inch of her and roll around in her scent. It was dumb and it was pathetic and it made Trey want to kick his wolf's ass.

Eventually they arrived at a restaurant in the next territory that Taryn knew belonged to the mediator's wolf pack. She also knew they wouldn't be having the meeting inside the restaurant, but within the wooded area behind it—a place where many shifters had come to blows in the past when mediation meetings hadn't gone so well. Hopefully, this wouldn't be one of those times.

Seeing the tension in Trey's shoulders as he opened her car door and the way he *very* reluctantly stepped aside, she smiled. "Your wolf doesn't want me to go, does he? He doesn't want me being around the naughty wolf." The poor guy was in totally unfamiliar territory with all this protectiveness and possessiveness.

He narrowed his eyes at her. "I'm glad you find this amusing."

Knowing what would ease his wolf, she did what she hadn't yet seen anyone do. She invaded Trey's personal space, sliding her arms around his waist. She had been up in his personal space plenty of times while he fucked her senseless, but sexual touching and social touching were two very different things, two very different needs. And it seemed like Trey had conditioned himself to ignore the latter need. He stiffened for a few seconds and then his arms went around her, surprising her. Little by little, the tension in him eased as he allowed his wolf to take solace in her closeness and her scent. "Ready?"

"Let's get this over with," he grumbled. In keeping with their true mate act, he took her small hand in his and kept her close as they followed the narrow, pebbly path that ran through the wooded area. Although he had been assured that there would be enough security to guarantee that his uncle couldn't make an abrupt attack, Trey still listened intently as they walked. His hearing picked up nothing other than the scurrying of small forest animals, the even breathing of each member of his pack, and the crunch of fallen dead leaves and sticks beneath their feet.

The path stopped at a clearing and there, at a long wooden table, sat his uncle, three males from Darryl's pack, and a tall, dark guy who he guessed was the mediator. Standing on either side of the table were six tall, bulky males who were clearly members of the security team.

His wolf tensed and growled at Darryl's scent, offended by it. The memories of the day Trey attacked his father slapped him hard. He could remember Rick's sneers, snarls, and the harsh words that had inevitably robbed Trey of all control. Even now, he couldn't regret what he'd done, and he doubted that he ever would.

Forcing away the dark feelings attempting to swamp him, he tightened his hold on Taryn's hand as they strolled over to the table. Everyone stood as they reached it, and Trey watched as Darryl's eyes zoomed in on Taryn and the marks covering her.

"Let's all sit, shall we," suggested the mediator as he took the head seat. Trey sat with Taryn and Dante on either side of him while Tao, Ryan, and Dominic stood behind them.

The evil uncle was not at all what Taryn had been expecting. It was hard to believe he was actually related to Trey. There was no resemblance there at all, except for the strong nose. Darryl's squinty eyes, lazy posture, perfectly parted dark hair, and sly smile all gave off the impression of a smarmy, cunning bastard. She couldn't help feeling satisfied that her presence had thrown him.

"Afternoon, everyone," said the mediator, rubbing his prominent jaw. "My name is Dean Milton and I've been appointed by the council to act as mediator in this dispute. My role is to guide this discussion and aid you in exploring your issues in the hope that an agreement can be reached. Note that both parties are free to leave at any point and that a decision will not be made in your absence. Before we go any further, could each party please introduce themselves, starting with the applicant?"

"Darryl Coleman, Alpha of the Bjorn Pack," the smarmy ass drawled with a self-satisfied smirk. "On my right is my Beta and on my left is my Head Enforcer. At my back are some of my enforcers."

Dean nodded, then looked at Trey. "Now if the respondent could also introduce himself and the wolves with him."

"Trey Coleman, Alpha of the Phoenix Pack. Behind me, you'll see my Head Enforcer and two of my enforcers. On my left is my Beta and on my right"—he stroked a hand through her hair—"is my mate, Taryn." He knew the smile he shot his uncle wasn't a pleasant one.

"Thank you," said Dean. "Now I'll ask you both, beginning with the applicant, to outline the issue as you see it. I ask you not to interrupt each other."

Darryl straightened in his seat. "It's been a long time, Trey. You look well. Can I ask how the rest of the pack are doing?"

"You can, but I won't answer."

"I see you've mated. A beautiful female."

"We're not here to exchange pleasantries, so cut the shit."

After a sigh, Darryl fixed a concerned look on his face. "It is regrettable that our pack divided the way it did. It never sat well with any of us. I, in particular, worried for your safety and that of those who left with you."

Trey heard a snort behind him and thought it might have been Dominic. He was tempted to snort himself.

"A great many of us have carried that guilt. But you know your father. I do not wish to speak ill of the dead, but it is a fact that my brother was too damn stubborn for his own good. He refused to lift the banishment, no matter how hard we appealed to him. As unfortunate as his passing is, it has also given us an opportunity to introduce changes and progressions. And we wish to welcome you back into the pack. With me as Alpha, of course."

Dean arched a brow at Trey. "As the respondent, what is your stance?"

He began massaging Taryn's nape, drawing strength from her closeness to keep his wolf calm. "You always did talk shit, Darryl. I prefer bare facts. Shall I share some with you? A bare fact is that you were right at my father's side when he banished me, encouraging his decision. Another is that if you had really wanted to overrule the banishment you could have, as Beta, applied to the council. A third is that you couldn't care if I live or die; your motivation to unite the pack is not regret or concern. So what the fuck is it?"

Taryn noted that the mediator didn't look in the least bit surprised that Trey wasn't interested in a civil discussion. He could probably see through Darryl's act just as easily as they could.

"I don't blame you for this anger, Trey," said Darryl. "But why not let it go and unite the packs once again?"

"Why not just tell me what this is really all about? Is it my territory that you want? Is it to enlarge the pack? Is it just to be a pain in my ass?"

Where the idea came from she wasn't sure, but an idea suddenly occurred to Taryn. "Maybe he has a perverse wish to see you bow down to him." All eyes darted to her, and then to Darryl.

Dante pursed his lips. "Maybe it's all four."

"You can't tell me that neither you nor your wolf has missed your homeland," said Darryl. "Surely you've dreamed of coming home many times."

Trey blew out a breath and shook his head. "Did I ever wish to return to a place where people who were supposed to care for me had been so eager to sling me out? No, no, I didn't at all. The whole prodigal son thing isn't for me."

"So you have no inclination to unite your pack with Darryl's?" asked Dean.

"None whatsoever," replied Trey.

Darryl's expression turned dark and bitter. "Don't make this become a battle. It's not one you can win."

"Did I introduce my mate properly? I don't think I did, did I? Taryn, meet Darryl Coleman. *Uncle*, meet Taryn Warner." He grinned inwardly at the flicker of unease that crossed Darryl's face.

"Taryn Warner," repeated Dean, smiling at her. "You once healed a friend of mine, Lennox Gellar; his nose had been broken. You were also the person who broke it."

She shrugged. "He deserved it." Oh, and he really had.

"If your reputation's anything to go by, that wasn't your first broken nose." At her unrepentant shrug, he asked, amused, "You don't think that perhaps you have anger management issues?"

"Punching people *is* managing my anger."

Strangely not liking the playful banter going on between his mate and the mediator, Trey tangled a hand in her hair—a shifter gesture of ownership. "Are you going to do the wise thing and drop this?" he asked Darryl.

"The wise thing would be for you to sign an agreement that says our packs are now one and I rule as Alpha."

Taryn couldn't stop the snort from popping out. "And who in La La Land told you that would ever happen? Probably the same person who told you that you're a good liar."

He spluttered. "Excuse me?"

"Oh, come on, you talk so much shit I can smell it on your breath."

"I take it this means no agreement can be reached," Dean said quickly, obviously wanting to stop the conversation from becoming any more argumentative than it already was. "Darryl, do you wish to pursue this further, or are you willing to withdraw your application?"

"I'm not backing down."

Trey leaned forward in his seat. "Then I accept your challenge."

Dean sighed. "You know the drill. Twelve weeks. Twelve weeks must pass before either of you can act on that challenge. Hopefully, you can both come to an amicable agreement within that time."

"How many times does that actually happen?" Taryn asked Dean, curious.

"More often than you might think. About forty-five percent of the time, disputes are nothing but impulsive challenges that neither side particularly cares to follow through with once their tempers have eased. Without that twelve-week cooling-off period, there would be many pointless battles and many pointless deaths. So maybe it wasn't such a bad idea to placate the humans by forming a council."

Darryl snarled, "Unless within that time my nephew agrees to unite the pack, my challenge will be followed through. Those wolves are mine. And I'll very much enjoy taking those caves of yours. Maybe I'll even take your mate as mine."

Trey's menacing growl had everyone jerking. Feeling him tense as if to spring, she squeezed his hand hard enough to cause pain—a sharp pain that would cut through the anger fogging his thoughts. She curled her upper lip at Darryl. "Call me shallow, but I do prefer good-looking guys. And you...well, it seems like the best part of you dried up on your mom's thigh." She probably shouldn't have found it so amusing that he didn't seem to be breathing, but, well, it was a bitch thing.

Dean quickly said, "Meeting over. Trey, I'm going to ask you and your wolves to leave first."

"What do you mean *first*?" griped Darryl.

"In the interest of preventing confrontations from occurring, the protocol is to keep ten minutes between the time that each party leaves."

Eager to be away from Darryl before his wolf surfaced, Trey stood upright, pulling Taryn to her feet. "Let's go, baby."

Surprising him, she leaned against his arm, offering him support that he hadn't known he needed. "I'll be seeing you soon, Darryl," he growled, his eyes flashing wolf. The temptation to tear off his limbs and rip out his throat for trying to lay claim to what was his was riding Trey hard. Satisfied by Darryl's nervous expression, he nodded and stalked back to the Toyota.

Once back in pack territory, Trey closed himself in his office, needing that privacy to fight off the memories haunting him and the gray cloud that seemed to be hanging over him. Yeah, he was a brooder. It wasn't the memory of his dad, severely wounded, that haunted him. Nor was it the memory of how many had suddenly turned against him, just like that. It was a memory of something far worse, something that he shouldn't be able to shove to the back of his mind so it would only haunt him from time to time. But he wasn't a person who *felt* the way everybody else did. He knew instincts, he knew urges, he knew logic, but feelings…not so much.

It wasn't that he was cold, just that he'd closed himself off a long time ago in what he now knew was a defense mechanism. It was most likely a bad thing and strongly linked to his underdeveloped conscience, but it was also one of the things that had made it possible for him to take on the responsibilities of Alpha at fourteen and get his pack through that difficult time of the banishment.

As usual, Dante never left him to brood in peace for long. A knock on the office door half an hour later was followed immediately by Dante's entrance. He was the only wolf who didn't wait for permission to enter, and he was the only one who could get away with it. "Are you done?"

"Is Greta back yet?"

"Got back about ten minutes ago. She's in the kitchen packing away boxes of some weird herbal tea. Um, I think you might want to know that on my way here I saw Taryn going to refill her coffee mug."

Trey groaned. "Shit. Tell me they're not alone."

"Who do you think will start cursing first?"

Sighing, Trey strolled out of his office, en route to the kitchen to rescue his mate from his rather antisocial, borderline psychotic grandmother.

"I don't like you."

Taryn almost laughed at the growling old woman sitting at the table. The second Taryn had entered the kitchen, Greta had begun hovering around as Taryn refilled her mug and then perched herself on the counter, dipping mini cookies in her coffee. Going by how nosy Greta appeared to be, Taryn had been expecting her to ply her with dozens of personal questions. Instead, she had sat in total silence as she watched Taryn's every move, scowling the entire time.

Rather than being irritated, Taryn found herself amused. Greta reminded her of her own bitter grandmother. She also reminded her of Norman Bates's mother in *Psycho*. "Now that's not a very nice welcome for your grandson's mate."

"You might have gotten one if you'd been his true mate," she snapped, flicking her short, fuzzy, graying hair away from her face. "But you're not."

"No, I'm not."

"And I don't like or trust you one little bit."

Taryn gave a slight shrug. "I guess it's a good thing that I don't give a shit."

A dramatic gasp of outrage escaped from Greta. "How dare you speak to me like that! You will watch your language in my presence."

"Yes, ma'am."

"This mating-for-a-deal wouldn't have happened in my day. I told him he didn't need a mate to build alliances—Darryl won't go through with his challenge. But did Trey listen to me? *Noooo.*

And now look what we've ended up with. A tiny little fart with a tarty tongue. All his life I warned him about power-hungry females, but has he listened to me? *Noooo.* He's not only gone and brought one home, but he's mated with her. Well, you just remember that you won't be here for long. And don't expect me to treat you as Alpha female. You're nothing as far as I'm concerned. Just some cling-on slut who wants a position she never would have had if she hadn't made a deal with my grandson."

Taryn cocked her head at the old woman. "So...the dead *do* contact us."

Greta growled and pointed at her. "I've seen your sort before."

"Really?"

"Common. Disrespectful. A hussy—"

"How did you know I was a hussy?" It was a strain not to laugh as the woman became more and more irritated by Taryn's lack of reaction to her taunts. Greta had nothing on her own grandmother.

"—and as if that's not bad enough, you're blonde. That's all we need, isn't it. A bimbo."

"Hmm. I really hope I don't sound condescending—that means talking down to someone—but, you know, you really shouldn't believe everything you think."

Another growl. "My grandson doesn't need a hussy."

"Well, he must want one."

"He'll want you out of here as soon as he sees what you're really like. He'll sling you out. Yeah, and he won't be gentle about it."

"Oh, I do love a rough touch," said Taryn dreamily.

"Think you're funny, do you? Think you're smart?"

"You want to know what I think? Okay. I think you've been behaving as mistress of the place because you're Trey's grand-mother. You look at me and you see a threat to your lovely little world and you don't like it. Well, I'll tell you something, Greta.

If you think I'll be scared away by a sour crone who's so old she dreams in black and white, then you're in for a massive disappointment. I made a deal with Trey, and I'll be here until I've lived up to my half of it. In the meantime, feel free to keep up the insults and the intimidation techniques—all I ask is that if at any point it seems like I care, please tell me, because I really don't want you getting the wrong impression."

Greta, her face purple, slapped her hand down hard on the table. "That's it. Out. I want you out. Now." When Taryn just stared at her, Greta growled, "I. Want. You. Out."

Taryn held up her index finger. "Just give me a second. Attempting to give a fuck...Attempting harder to give a fuck... Sorry, there was an error. Fuck not given."

Both women looked up as Trey and Dante walked in and skidded to a halt. Taryn found her mouth curving at their nervous looks. Obviously they had guessed Greta would be like this. Taryn's wolf settled a little as she picked up her mate's scent. "Aww, Trey, you didn't tell me your grandmother was such a kind, delightful soul."

Trey was surprised by Taryn's smile. Clearly, she was holding up just fine against Greta.

"You really want this trollop as a mate?"

"Watch it, Greta," Trey cautioned in a low voice.

"I don't have to be polite to her. She's nothing but a hussy!"

"You sure like to repeat yourself, don't you, woman," Taryn said with an air of boredom.

"I want her gone!"

He folded his arms across his chest, trying hard to prevent a grin from surfacing. If Greta was looking so flustered and annoyed, then she was obviously losing at the confrontation she had undoubtedly begun for no other reason than she didn't like females around him. "That won't be happening."

"I refuse to accept her as part of my pack!"

"Why is that, exactly?"

"You should hear the way she's been talking to me. Disrespectful is an understatement! Worse, she's a hussy! She won't be faithful to you. She'll be all over your enforcers, spreading herself around them like butter on toast."

"It really is disconcerting just how well you've read me, Greta," said Taryn.

With a growl that had all eyes widening, Greta stood. "I said I want her gone!" She focused on Taryn then. "I want you gone!"

Taryn gave her a mock frown. "Now really, Greta, anger is such an ugly thing."

"It's Ms. Tyler to you, hussy."

"Sure thing, Greta."

Turning to Trey, she ranted, "Have you heard the way she talks to me? She has no respect! She's rude! She's—"

"Staying exactly where she is," finished Trey firmly, hearing his wolf growl his agreement. Trey wasn't a grandson talking to his grandmother now. He was the Alpha talking to a pack member.

"But she's not your true mate and she's not good enough for you!"

"I'm aware that she's not my true mate. It has nothing to do with why she's here."

"She's not good enough for you!"

He had a moment when he considered pulling his hair out. "You don't even know her, so how could you know anything about her or whether or not she's good enough for me?"

"Is it true that she's latent? You picked a latent for an Alpha female?"

Trey was ready to snap at Greta for making such a comment when Alpha waves suddenly reached out and hit them all with the force of a sledgehammer. The vibes clotted the air, smothering him while at the same time invigorating him. He turned to

Taryn to see her glaring at Greta, and realized she was letting his grandmother see exactly how powerful an Alpha her wolf was. Obviously, she'd had enough of being insulted. He couldn't blame her. Unfortunately for him—and probably for Dante too—her dominant display went straight to his cock, hardening it painfully.

"Taryn?" he said softly. She looked at him, smiling, and suddenly the waves eased. "You okay?"

Nodding, Taryn slid from the counter and did a very feline stretch. "I think I should leave the room though. I can feel those hussy urges coming on me already. Probably best if I go before I leap on you or Dante."

Trey looked at his gaping grandmother, who obviously had not expected such a demonstration of power from little Taryn. "I don't want to have to go through this again," he said in a grave tone, knowing how tenacious Greta could be. "She's my mate. Accept it. And if you want her to treat you with respect, then remember it works both ways."

Taryn sighed. "No, she's right. My behavior has been truly unacceptable. Accept my apologies, Ms. Tyler. I know I really should have more respect for the dead." With a grin and a wink, she strutted out of the kitchen, followed closely by Trey and Dante. Her grin widened as she heard an outraged gasp burst out of the old woman.

"Hey, you did good," praised Dante, chuckling. "Didn't cry or anything."

"Something tells me I'll have to put up with that every— Hey!" She gaped at Trey as he snatched the mug from her hand and gave it to Dante. "What the hell are you doing?"

"Baby, you got me hard as a rock after that display of dominance in there. If I'm not inside you in the next five minutes, I'll lose it."

"Oh, hell no!"

Locking his arms around her, Trey carried her through the tunnels, ignoring her kicks and the string of profanities she hurled at him. Once in the bedroom, he dumped her on the bed. "Now I'm going to fuck you and make you come so hard you can't breathe. Deal with it."

CHAPTER SIX

D reams didn't get much better than this.

On one level, Taryn couldn't help finding it a little depressing that her best sexual encounters tended to happen during her sleep, but the pleasure spiking through her body left no room for such thoughts.

A thick, talented finger was stroking in and out of her while sharp teeth nibbled on the back of her shoulder. The thrusts were shallow, leisurely, teasing. She squirmed and tried impaling herself farther, but the finger withdrew—a warning. She moaned her frustration. A low, wicked chuckle was her response and then two fingers plunged inside her and her next moan was of sheer bliss.

Ordinarily Taryn wasn't a huge fan of finger-fucking, but these fingers were extremely clever, hitting all the right nerves with unerring accuracy, as if they knew just how to play her body. If they would only pick up speed...

Oh, and then they did. The teeth stopped grazing her shoulder as that hot mouth drifted to her ear and a tongue swirled inside the shell.

"Come for me, Taryn." The whisper was hoarse and filled with authority. "I want to feel you come all over my fingers."

That was when she woke up and became very aware that she hadn't been dreaming at all. Instantly she stiffened, but obviously knowing she'd fight him, Trey slipped an arm beneath her and locked it tight around her, pinning her arms against her body. "You tricky fucking bastard," she rasped, struggling against his grip and the sensations. But his grip only tightened as he kept her right where he wanted her and pumped his fingers hard and deep, *demanding* her orgasm.

"Come. Now." He bit down hard on the back of her shoulder.

Her traitorous body gave him what he wanted. An orgasm washed over her and her muscles clutched his fingers as she came with a loud cry. Then in one decisive movement he raised her leg, tucked it into the crook of his elbow and drove into her. Oh, she hated him.

Trey groaned as her muscles contracted around his cock. "Fuck, Taryn." She melted against him for a second and then went back to struggling. Well, of course she did. In this particular battle for dominance, he had basically cheated by seducing her in her sleep, but she just felt so damn good around him that he couldn't bring himself to care.

He thought it odd that his appetite for her body hadn't begun to dull yet. He only had to smell her scent or hear her voice to become immediately hard. Unlike Trick and Dominic, Trey wasn't the type to have so little control over his libido or his body. But where Taryn was concerned, it was a whole different matter. He couldn't even blame it on the mating. This primitive hunger had hit him the second he saw her and didn't seem to be going anywhere.

"That's it, baby, fight it," he urged. The little wildcat did. Even though his cock was pistoning away in her pussy, even though her groans told him that she loved it, she still thrashed and fought to be free. Fought his dominance. If he hadn't been as strong as he was, she'd have twisted out of his hold by now—and most likely have snapped his neck. Those flailing hands were clawing at whatever skin they could reach. It was a real good thing her arms were trapped.

"Cocksucking son of a goddamn dick-faced bitch!"

"You're the bitch, baby. *My* little bitch. And I'll fuck my little bitch whenever I want." He knew she was fighting her orgasm, but he also knew by the way her inner muscles were fluttering around his cock that she wouldn't last much longer. Surprising him, she turned her head and snapped her teeth, grazing his face ever so slightly. Growling, he locked his teeth onto her nape and pounded harder. Seconds later she screamed and her pussy spasmed around him, triggering his own orgasm. "Fuck!"

When she finally stopped panting, Taryn gave him a sideways glance as she muttered, "Bastard."

He laughed before bringing the fingers he had fucked her with to his mouth. He hummed appreciatively as he sucked them clean. "I could become addicted to your taste." He wasn't lying. Her taste was just like her: spicy and seductive.

"Let me guess," drawled Taryn with a snort. "You think it's best if you get a regular dose so the addiction stays under control."

Again he was laughing. This female had a wit and an attitude that he could appreciate. He reluctantly withdrew from her body and then, unable to resist, he lightly slapped that pretty little ass before jumping out of bed.

It wasn't until he was in the bathroom that Taryn finally forced herself into an upright position. She shook her head in sheer disbelief at how someone could be so energetic first thing in the morning. Eventually she not so gracefully rose from the bed and stretched her arms above her head. She would bet she looked very much like a contented cat. Well, an orgasm was always a good way to start the day. At that very moment the sound of a cell phone ringing met her ears.

"Trey, phone!"

In seconds he was out of the shower and answering the call. As she saw his eyes flash wolf and his body stiffen, she cursed. She knew exactly what that meant. There went her hope of Roscoe just letting the issue go or, in the event that that failed, him simply leaping to his death.

Instantly questions began swirling around her mind. What if he'd brought hordes of wolves with him? What if Trey got hurt? What if the others got hurt? She couldn't exactly heal any of them if Roscoe spirited her away—and wouldn't that be a fate worse than death.

"That was Ryan. Roscoe's here. He's not going to take you," he assured her, sensing her anxiety through the pack link, as they both frantically began to dress. Within thirty seconds they were at the main entrance to the caves, where many of the pack were already waiting.

"Did Ryan tell you he's brought quite a few wolves with him?" asked Dante in the same tone that someone might ask what time it was. *Men.*

Trey turned to her. "I want you to wait here and—"

"Oh, hell no! This mess is mine and you expect me to sit here twiddling my thumbs, relishing the feeling of my own safety?"

"You're staying."

She smiled. "I believe you were warned before you even mated me not to bark at me unless you're happy to be ignored."

"Taryn," he drawled in an impatient tone, "I am your mate—"

"And I'm stubborn. If you want absolute obedience, get a Labrador. I'm not quite the delicate flower people tend to take me for. Now let's go."

Right then, Trey wanted nothing more than to spank her ass. He didn't want her anywhere near that male who coveted her. Both he and his wolf wanted to know that she was safe, but Trey knew by the look on her face that she would simply ignore him and follow him outside, no matter what he said.

"You don't get to interfere, understand? There will probably be a wolf-against-wolf battle. You stay out of it." He knew that once he was in wolf form and engaged in a battle, there was a good chance that he would go feral.

Taryn was honestly starting to feel sorry for him. He obviously thought he had some sort of authority over her and she believed it would be awhile before it became apparent to him that the female he had taken as his mate did her own thing. "Again I feel I must remind you that I don't do well with orders, but I have no wish to interfere, so the point is moot."

Resisting the urge to shake her, he huffed and turned away, only to find that some of the others were watching the exchange with amusement. He didn't blame them. Here was this dainty little female giving him shit and even managing to get her own way.

Greta growled. "You just had to bring her here, didn't you. Trey, you don't need her. There's no way Darryl will go through with this challenge. Just hand her over and be done with it."

"Can't we hand *her* over instead?" asked Taryn. Was it wrong that she was seriously considering it?

"The hussy's not worth fighting over. If he wants her, let him have her."

"She's mine. No one takes her." Trey nodded at the males around him. "Let's go. Taryn, stay at the rear."

"No."

"What was that?"

"To the outside world I'm Alpha female here, Trey," she reminded him as she slipped on a light denim jacket that matched her jeans. "The Alpha pair always presents a united front when there's a confrontation. I'm not saying that if he challenges you I won't step back, but I won't be shoved to the rear."

The steel in her voice aroused his wolf just as much as it pissed him off. Trey was feeling pretty much the same. "Taryn, you can't expect me or my wolf to be okay with you being in such easy reach of Roscoe, of being in that kind of danger."

Smiling sweetly, she cupped his chin. "I won't be in danger. You'll protect me."

Despite everything that was going on right now, he actually wanted to smile at her impishness. The other males were ducking their heads to hide their grins. "Fine, we present a united front, but only because the mating wouldn't look real if we didn't." He thought that was a pretty good way to save face, but one or two of the males snorted. "Now, let's go."

As one—with Trey and Taryn side by side—they all made their way out of the caves and headed toward the gate.

Taryn marveled at how all the males could walk at such a leisurely pace, yet look extremely menacing at the same time. Each of them suddenly seemed two inches taller than he truly was and had the most sinister look. Even Marcus's usual grin had been replaced by a hostile scowl. Trey...well, that was another matter altogether. Scrap hostile and sinister—the guy looked like he needed a rabies shot. He was a walking promise of death. And her wolf totally approved—yet another indication that she was dumb.

Nearing the gate, they caught sight of several vehicles parked by the security shack. A large number of shifters stood tall beside them. A normally composed Roscoe was scowling with rage, flexing his fists at his sides.

"Oh, good Lord," she said, snorting at the sheer ridiculousness of the number of wolves he had brought with him. Forty against seven? Yeah, very brave. It was a clear attempt at intimidation, but Taryn knew it hadn't had the desired effect. Why Roscoe had thought that Trey—someone who was practically the personification of intimidation—would be rattled was anyone's guess.

When Trey came to a halt twelve feet away from the intruders, Ryan came to join the wall that the Phoenix wolves had made. Roscoe's gaze settled on her and anger flashed across his face, most likely in response to Trey's marks.

"Never had you down as someone who played games, Taryn. As you can see, game's over. Get in the SUV while I have a talk with Coleman."

Taryn almost laughed. "You sound as though you honestly believe I will."

"Come now and we can avoid all this."

"I'd rather lie under an elephant suffering from diarrhea with my mouth open wide."

"You know what will happen if you persist with this. People are going to get hurt, namely Coleman. Do you really want that on your conscience?"

"Oh no, you don't get to turn this on me. If anyone gets hurt today, it's because you refuse to let go of something that was never yours to begin with." She would bet money that if she had been within reach, Roscoe would have slapped her for that.

"Don't be looking at Taryn, look at me." Trey's tone demanded attention. "I'm the one you should be worried about."

"You must have a death wish, Coleman," said Roscoe. "It's the only reason I can think of that would explain why you would kidnap my mate."

"Kidnap your mate," repeated Trey with a smile. "I think you'll find that Taryn's mine."

"She wears my mark."

"Not a mark, a wound—one that I very nicely covered with a mark of my own."

"She's mine," snarled Roscoe.

Growls of disagreement rumbled out of the throats of the seven males around her. Taryn couldn't help but notice that, by contrast, although Roscoe had a large crew, they didn't appear to be standing *with* him. There was no one flanking him or eyeing up the rest of Trey's pack, picking an opponent he wanted if it turned into an out-and-out fight. They were simply...there.

"Here's how it is, Roscoe. Taryn is my mate, I've claimed her, and I *will* kill anyone who tries to take her from me. If you can accept that, you can live and you can leave here peacefully. If you can't, well, you must want to die."

"Then it looks like we battle it out."

Taryn gaped. "You have got to be kidding me. Why would you bother? You can't tell me you're that obsessed with the idea of breaking my spirit until I'm some kind of slave."

"That's what he had planned?" Trey's wolf leaped for control, wanting to gut Roscoe.

Roscoe shrugged. "What male wouldn't want to be able to turn a dominant female like Taryn into a gorgeously submissive slave?"

"Well, they would be the sane males," said Taryn.

"Stand back, baby," ordered Trey as he removed his T-shirt and then tackled the fly of his jeans. "You heard him. He wants to battle it out."

She might have tried to calm the atmosphere if she hadn't known from experience that when two dominant male wolves agreed to battle, it meant the situation was past help. She had the strange urge to kiss Trey, but knew he didn't need to look weak right now.

"To the death," Trey said to Roscoe in a calm but icy tone. "We battle to the death." Having heard what Roscoe intended for Taryn, Trey's wolf wasn't going to be happy until he'd torn out his throat. There was no way Trey would stop him from going feral.

Roscoe, now naked, nodded. "To the death." Suddenly bones were popping and his body was altering and then, mere seconds later, he was a large, sandy, snarling wolf.

But Trey was larger, Taryn soon found out as she watched him shift into a seven-foot-long and approximately thirty-two-inch-high, gorgeous, silvery-gray wolf. He looked just as intimidating and overawing in wolf form, with his powerful build, his heavily muscled neck, and his robust limbs. His hackles were raised, his angry eyes were drilling into Roscoe, his ears were upright, and his lips were curled back, exposing fangs and gums. The growl emitting from him sounded more like a boat motor.

Abruptly the sandy wolf sprang from his crouched position and rushed forward at the gray wolf, coming up short, just to snap his teeth together. The gray wolf didn't move a muscle, just stood looking large and fearsome, making a clear point that he was the more dominant animal in this situation. The sandy wolf reversed slowly, only to rush forward aggressively and snap at the other once again.

Apparently, the gray wolf had decided that the other had had his chance to back down and he wasn't going to stand still any longer. Growling, he began circling the sandy wolf, who then copied the move so that they were circling each other. Maybe because he was stupid or maybe because he was just suicidal, the sandy wolf growled at Taryn. That was when her mate went feral.

The gray wolf lunged at the other wolf and they came together in a clash of claws and teeth. As shifters had superior speed and strength, it was like watching a recording in fast-forward motion. There was growling, there was body slamming, there was scratching, there was biting, and there were sideswipes as each wolf fought to pin the other to the ground.

Taryn winced when the gray wolf bit down hard on the other's hind leg, making him yelp loudly. The yelping faded to whimpering until the gray wolf yanked hard with his powerful jaws, snapping the sandy wolf's leg. *Damn, that had to hurt.* When the injured wolf tried scooping himself off the ground, the other wolf slammed into him and knocked him onto his back. Then, in a typical wolf shifter killing move, the gray wolf slashed open his opponent's midsection with his claws and simultaneously closed his jaws around his throat. With one sharp yank, he'd torn out his challenger's throat.

As much as it seemed like forever before it was over, it couldn't have taken more than a minute for the feral wolf to overpower the sandy wolf. *Overpower* was a mild word. Hell, the gray wolf had the other's lifeless body by the throat, shaking it like a rag doll while growling loudly.

Several more minutes went by and the gray wolf continued to attack the carcass, showing no signs of tiring or calming or any willingness to part with it. It was clear that he wasn't coming out of his feral state anytime soon.

"One of us is going to have to do something," said Taryn.

Dante shrugged. "When he gets like this, you just have to leave him to tire himself out."

Trick nodded. "At least he hasn't charged at any of us this time."

"But he's injured. I need to heal him and I can't while he's in wolf form." She was going to regret this, she knew she was. "Let me see if I can calm him down."

"Whoa, now, hang on a minute," began Dante, palms out to ward her off. "Taryn, you can see the state he's in, right? That's not Trey. He's buried way down deep, very much aware of what's going on, but with no way of taking control for as long as his wolf is feral. If you go near him, he'll see you as a threat and he'll attack you just as he would anyone else."

She rolled her eyes, implying he was being dramatic. In actuality, he was dead-on. "He won't hurt me. I know it's not Trey, I know his wolf is in control, but his wolf considers me his mate just as Trey does."

"She's got a point," said Trick, sighing. "She's the person he's least likely to hurt. He usually shows signs of calming by now."

"His mate was threatened. That's why he's like this." Marcus gestured at him, as anxious and fidgety as the others. Whenever an Alpha was unstable, it leaked out into the pack link.

"I can't just stand here." When Dante again blocked her path, she growled. "Move out of my way."

"Taryn, come on, I'm Beta. He'll kill me if something happens to you."

"And I'm temporarily Alpha female, which means I outrank you, but even if I wasn't Alpha, I'd still expect you to move the hell out of my way. So do it."

"What if he hurts you? It'll distress him to know he's harmed his mate. Have you thought about that?"

She huffed impatiently. "He won't hurt me."

"You're sure about that?"

Of course not. "Yes, I'm sure. Now move."

Finally he did, signaling for the others to give her some space, but without going too far. Very slowly she took a few steps toward the wolf. She knew there was no point in calling Trey's name and appealing for him to come back. The wolf wouldn't respond to the name, wouldn't understand the words. The only way that Trey could overcome his wolf was if his wolf came down from his feral state. And that wasn't going to happen until she got him away from that carcass. The smell of the blood would only be making him worse.

As she couldn't exactly go over there and snatch away his prize, she decided her best bet might be to distract him from it. As an idea formed in her mind, she removed her denim jacket and balled it up. Hoping like hell this worked and didn't just act like a red flag to a bull, she gently threw the jacket so that it landed to the side of the carcass. Instantly the feral wolf dived on the jacket, as though it was a rabbit or a hare. Picking it up with his jaws, he shook it just like he had the carcass.

And then he seemed to pause and his growling eased a little, as if he recognized the scent on the jacket. Hopefully, he recognized it as the scent of his mate and not another threat.

"Hey, Cujo," she called in a soothing voice. His head whipped around to face her and he snarled while at the same time standing over the carcass and flattening his ears outward, warning her away from his prize. There was no logic or rationality in those eyes. "Now that's not very nice," she said in the same gentling tone. She knew he wouldn't understand her, that the words would be indistinguishable, but her hope was that he might recognize her voice and find it calming.

His head extended toward her and his nostrils flared, scenting the air. He let loose a low whine, and she had the feeling that he acknowledged who she was but wasn't sure how to calm himself.

Feeling reassured by him recognizing her, she moved another step toward him but then halted; she wanted *him* to come *to* her so that he was away from the dead wolf. Easier said than done, of course. "Come on, big guy, you don't want to play with that nasty carcass. If you can hear what's going on, Trey, then let me just tell you that you'll be buying me a new jacket. This one's now covered in foam, fur, and blood."

Tao took a step toward her. "Taryn—"

"Don't," she ordered, but the gray wolf had already seen the male approaching his mate and he wasn't too pleased about it. With her jacket still in his mouth, he began to advance on Tao, who very smartly froze. "Cujo," she sang. "Hey, remember me?"

The wolf's gaze darted from her to the carcass to Tao repeatedly. Clearly he was torn on whether he wanted to continue playing with his new toy, go see his mate, or attack the male who dared talk to her.

Knowing she was about to make herself vulnerable to attack, but not sure what else to do, Taryn squatted and tapped the ground with her fingers. "Come here, come on." He took one tentative step toward her, but then glanced back at his carcass. "Seriously, you don't want to keep that. Come on." Again she tapped the ground, knowing he could feel the vibrations through it.

Flicking a disgruntled look at Tao, the wolf slowly took a few steps toward her before halting to whine at the carcass.

"No, we'll get you another toy. Get your furry ass over here." Still at a sluggish pace, he covered those last remaining steps between them and dropped the jacket at her feet. "Hey, there." The wolf rubbed his cheek along hers and buried his nose behind her ear to inhale her scent. Then he took to happily licking along her jaw. "Ew."

She now considered it a good thing that the foam and blood from his mouth had transferred to her jacket. Rather the jacket than her face. She winced when she saw that he was injured in several places. It was nothing fatal or even anything that would cause him much pain, but the healer in her wanted it fixed.

Allowing the wolf to continue rubbing himself against her, she turned her head toward the mass of wolves that Roscoe had brought along, all of whom were still waiting. Not even one of them appeared to have moved a muscle. Keeping her tone light, so as not to startle the animal, she asked, "So which one of you considers yourself Alpha now, because I'm pretty sure you all had this sorted out before you got here?"

They gave her "I'm not sure what you mean" looks.

"Come on, don't play dumb. Not one of you looks even the slightest bit bothered that your Alpha is dead. I really don't care one way or another how you feel about it. I just want to know who I should be talking to when I ask if we should be expecting retaliation over this." The challenge was fought fairly, but it wouldn't be the first time that someone who was sour about a loss decided to take revenge.

The three males at the front of the mass glanced at each other, and then the one in the center stepped forward, identifying himself as the Alpha. "There'll be no retaliation. We didn't agree with him coming here to try to separate mates, but he was set on having you."

"And you were following orders. Nothing wrong with that, just like there's nothing wrong with you not being prepared to die for an ill cause." The wolf, apparently not liking that he didn't have her full attention, nipped her chin. She rubbed her cheek against his reassuringly and then turned back to the new Alpha. "Now that Roscoe's gone and there's no animosity between the packs, I don't see a reason why there can't be an alliance."

The new Alpha's expression was a mixture of shock and eagerness. "An alliance would be acceptable," he said coolly, seemingly trying to hide his excitement and look the composed Alpha.

"We can't exactly discuss it properly now, for obvious reasons," she said, flicking a look at the Alpha male of her pack, who was still very much in wolf form. "We'll call it a temporary verbal contract, one that will expire in thirty days if you don't contact us to lay out the details with Trey."

Looking apprehensively at the gray wolf, the Alpha said, "You'll be there too, right?"

She smiled. "Don't worry, I won't let him eat you. Once we're inside, you can take Roscoe's body." At the Alpha's surprised look, she said, "We're not trophy killers here." His nod communicated respect.

With that, she slowly stood and began to walk toward the caves, signaling for the rest of the pack to keep a fair distance away so that Cujo didn't feel threatened and turn feral again. She didn't have to encourage him to follow her. He remained at her side the entire time, half companion, half guard.

Once they had passed through the main entrance of Bedrock, she went to the living area and sat down on the large rug. The wolf sat between her legs, closing his eyes as she ran her fingers through his fur.

"Trey, I need you to come back now or I can't heal you. I don't want to hear any macho shit about Alphas not needing healing. If you expect to have sex ever again, you won't fight me on this."

It was something like twenty seconds later when the change began, and suddenly Trey was back in his human form. Instantly he flopped onto his back, breathing hard.

"Someone get him a bottle of water," she called out as the living area filled with people.

"I'm okay," he wheezed.

"Sure you are, Flintstone." His wounds actually weren't that bad, but they were ugly and would most likely scar if she didn't heal them.

Greta appeared, growling. "Now, if you'd have just handed her over, Trey, you'd be fine."

"Not now, Wicked Witch of the East," groused Taryn.

"Here." Grace placed a bottle of water beside Taryn.

She offered Trey the bottle, but he shook his head. "You still have some blood on your mouth and I'm not going near said mouth to heal you until you've washed your face, at the very least."

"Why would you need to go near his mouth to heal him?" asked Rhett in that curious tone of his.

Turning to see that Trick was the one standing closest to the window, she asked, "Trick, would you open that for me?"

"Why?"

"So I can gaze lovingly at the sun. Will you just open it?"

Grunting, he did as she asked while Trey finally drank down some water and wiped his face.

"Now be still." She was pretty sure he only did it out of curiosity. Taryn placed her hand on his forehead and watched as several patches of his skin suddenly illuminated where there were scratches and bites. She heard a few gasps, a "Whoa," and a "Holy shit" coming from behind her, but ignored them.

Leaning down, she placed her mouth at Trey's and inhaled deeply, taking the foulness from him and then blowing it out of her mouth toward the window. She repeated the move over and over until, finally, the last luminous patch faded. "I'd say you're done." With that, she allowed herself to flop onto her back, much as Trey had five minutes ago. She almost laughed as she opened her eyes to see several faces, all peering down at her. Then suddenly she was snatched from the rug and cradled against Trey's chest.

"You shouldn't have done that; you look worse than I did."

"I'll be fine, you ungrateful asshole. I just need some water and maybe some sort of sugary food."

"You got it," said Grace as she dashed out of the room.

"You do know that was awesome, right?" Dante's smile was almost as wide as Marcus's clown grin.

"More like unnatural," muttered Greta.

"Did you just use the word *awesome*?" Dominic asked Dante, chuckling.

"Come on, she totally calmed a feral wolf and at the same time negotiated an alliance before doing some weird healing stuff. That's some seriously cool shit."

Trey strangely felt a twinge of pride for her, though he still wanted to spank her ass for going near his wolf while he was feral. "My wolf could have hurt you."

"Yeah, I know. Blame Dante, he told me I should go for it."

Dante spluttered. "That's not—I didn't—She—"

"You should see your face." Her chuckle was interrupted by a cough. Her throat always felt a little hoarse after she used her healing gift. At that moment Grace handed her a bottle of water and an energy bar. "Thanks."

"Never again are you allowed to use that gift," stated Trey firmly, not liking how pale she was. His wolf wasn't happy about it either.

"Don't be a goof. Of course I'm going to use it. I wouldn't be much of a healer if I didn't."

"You look like a corpse."

"*I'll be fine.* Just plunk me on that monstrosity of a sofa and let me have a twenty-minute nap and I'll be just as lively as I was before." She wouldn't have even needed the nap if Trey hadn't had so many bruises and wounds. "Just a little power nap and I'll be fine."

Trey couldn't help smiling at the way she curled up on the bulky sofa in a fetal position five minutes later. She looked even tinier than usual, but still not fragile. There was too much steel in her for that.

"Ryan just called," Tao informed him. "They've gone."

Trey nodded and then watched in surprise as some of his pack gathered around her. Dante, Grace, and Rhett sat on her left while Lydia, Marcus, and Cam sat on her right. Trick, Dominic, and Tao all sat on the floor with the backs of their heads resting against her legs. It was a gesture of support, comfort, and acceptance, as well as an indication that they intended to guard her as she slept. She had earned the respect of each of them in the short time that she had been here.

A strange pang struck his chest—unfamiliar and unnerving. "I'm going to take a shower. I'll be back in a few minutes." They nodded but were focused on Taryn, who had gone out like a light. He and his wolf were comforted by the knowledge that they would stay with her while Trey removed the streaks of blood and the lingering scent of the dead wolf from his body. The dead wolf who was now no longer a threat to his mate or their mating.

As Trey was showering he thought back to how he had felt when, forced to be nothing but an observer, he saw Taryn tentatively trying to gain his wolf's attention. The anger, the frustration, and the anxiety rushed back. There had been something else in that cocktail of emotions. Fear. Trey had actually felt fear.

It wasn't that he hadn't experienced that emotion before. Of course he had. Having an underdeveloped conscience and an explosive temper didn't mean he didn't know fear. What was bothering him right now was that he had felt such fear for Taryn, had feared she would be seriously hurt and would be taken from him just like that—and at his own hands. He couldn't even say it was his wolf's fear. His wolf had been going through his own shit right then. No, that had been *all* Trey.

It had to have been a direct consequence of the natural crazy possessiveness and crazy protectiveness that came with mating. It was obviously age-old instincts pushing to the forefront, taking over. Trey understood that the mating would be temporary, but his instincts to protect his mate were obviously going to override his thoughts. Obviously. Just like his instinct to mark his mate and make her submit to him had overridden his true indifference to those things.

Yeah, that was all it was, all it could be. Obviously. That didn't improve his mood any, because there was another issue that was bothering him. Taryn shouldn't have been able to calm his wolf.

When a wolf shifter went into feral mode, he behaved a lot like a rabid animal. He attacked senselessly, he felt no emotional attachments, he lost all sense of reason and logic. And yet her scent and voice had reached his wolf even through that fog.

Trey had felt how quickly his wolf had recognized her as his mate, how quickly he had switched from wanting to kill to wanting to protect. The only reason his wolf had been reluctant to leave the carcass was because he still hadn't been stable enough to understand that the sandy wolf was dead and no longer a danger to Taryn.

If his wolf was this attached to Taryn now, what would he be like in three months? What would happen when she left? Trey's wolf growled his objection, confirming Trey's suspicion that his eventual separation from her could be more problematic and uncomfortable than he had anticipated, even though they hadn't imprinted.

Unlike with true mates, a relationship between imprinted mates could wither over time. For an unhappy imprinted couple it wasn't simple for them to shake hands and go their separate ways, because of the metaphysical bond that existed between them. The pain of that kind of separation was on a psychic level just as much as a physical one.

For most wolves it meant constant migraines, a lingering sense of emptiness, and slipping in and out of depressive states for a few years, if not longer. Some wolves even retreated within their human halves completely, unable to function without their mates. The worst-case scenario for any wolf separated from his mate was that he turned rogue, remaining in wolf form and turning completely feral, attacking anyone he came into contact with—like Trey's mother had.

After his dad had banished him, his mom—who had been a submissive wolf—had for the first time in her life rebelled against Rick's authority. When Rick refused to reconsider the banishment, Louisa left with Trey and the others, believing that she would cope with the separation because her bond with his father had been through imprinting as opposed to them being true mates. The separation had proven too difficult for her, however, most likely because she had been a submissive wolf. Within six months she had turned rogue...and Trey had been the one to kill her.

There was no way he was prepared to go through something like that again. As long as he and Taryn didn't imprint, there was no risk of either of them suffering any of those effects when they separated, but it was obvious that his wolf was already becoming attached to her. And that spooked the hell out of Trey. So instead of going straight to Taryn to check on her like he wanted to, he shut himself in his office.

Another thing that spooked him was the knowledge that if she hadn't been with him in that mediation meeting, if she hadn't kept him calm with her touch, he would have most definitely lost it and gone for Darryl's throat. Never had he been able to truly rely on another person. Never had there been someone for him to draw strength from. But that had been okay, because he hadn't wanted to need anyone. He hadn't been the type of kid who craved physical affection—which had been a damn good thing, since he'd never gotten it.

He had always prided himself on not having that weakness of needing anyone or anything. Having a mate, having a connection that came with mating, was fucking with that. Not that he believed for even one minute that the mating connection could override the way he functioned and had always functioned, but he didn't have any interest in encouraging the cravings for his mate by feeding them.

Maybe if he distanced himself from her, spent little time with her, didn't touch her, it would ease the matter and ease his wolf's attachment to her. He needed to ignore these urges he had to be with her, to touch her, to mark her entire body, to ensure his scent was all over her. Those urges had nothing to do with Taryn as a person and everything to do with the fact that she was the one he had mated. If she had been someone else, things would still have been the same.

Would they really though? questioned a voice in his head, a part of him that thought he was talking out of his ass.

Of course it would. That wasn't to say that he didn't like Taryn. He did. And he respected her, which said a lot. And yeah, okay, there was that weird thing between them, that primal hunger. And she made him laugh, and she was refreshing because she wasn't afraid of him or to speak her mind in front of him, and she—

Dammit, no! No, the attraction was mostly just due to their mating. It was just his instincts driving him, not his regard for Taryn. Trey wasn't at the mercy of those instincts or his wolf. He had a mind of his own and that mind was going to rule how he behaved from here on out.

Unless the situation required him to touch her—like when they were posing as mates—he would resist doing so. It would probably be best not to have sex with her again, given that he could never resist the urge to mark her whenever he was inside her, but he couldn't guarantee that sex wouldn't happen— if she made advances, he very much doubted he'd be able to ignore them.

To satisfy his overprotectiveness, he would allocate her a bodyguard. No, his wolf wouldn't like her spending large amounts of time with another male, but his wolf would just have to deal with it, because Trey *was* going to get a handle on this situation and he was going to start now.

Taryn jerked awake at the sound of laughing. Three heads that had been leaning against her legs swerved around.

"Oh, sorry," said Tao, "it's just that this episode of *Friends* is hilarious."

"They're all hilarious," she mumbled as she sat upright. Trick and Tao each scooted over a little so that she had room to stretch her legs out.

"How are you feeling?" asked a voice to her right as a finger trailed down her cheek.

She looked up to see Grace. "Fine, thanks." It was only then that she realized that they were all gathered around her. She understood what this meant. Not only had they been offering her comfort, they accepted her as a member of the pack. *Temporary* member of the pack, she reminded herself.

"You look better," said Tao.

"How long was I out?" she asked no one in particular as she stretched her arms, which were a little stiff from her fetal position.

"About an hour," replied Dante.

"You should have woken me. I didn't need to sleep that long."

Tao, who was rubbing his jaw against her knee, asked, "Do you always need sleep after you use your gift?"

She shook her head. "I was just tired because Trey had so many injuries, even though they weren't life-threatening. Where is Flintstone, anyway?"

Dante suddenly seemed a little uncomfortable. "He went to have a shower and um...he's probably making some calls or something in his office."

In other words, he hadn't reappeared to check on her. Why should he though?

"You need anything?" asked Grace. "Coffee or something?" Taryn waved her hand. "I can get it, I'm fine."

"No," they all said in unison before Grace rushed from the room.

She rolled her eyes. "I'm not an invalid."

"No," agreed Lydia, "but you're our Alpha female which means we look out for you."

"Come on, you know it's only temporary. You don't need to take things so far."

"Then let us just do it temporarily."

"Is there anything else you want?" Grace asked as she handed her a huge mug of coffee.

Taryn took the mug gratefully and sipped from it. "Actually, I was wondering if any of you have a computer I could use once I've had a shower."

"I do," said Rhett. "It's in my room."

"Then, let's go." Seeing that they were all ready to object to her moving just yet, she held up her hand. "I said I'm fine. As much as I appreciate the concern, I'm going to need you all to stop fussing." Wearing petulant expressions, they gave her space to rise and leave.

A shower and a change of clothes later, she was in Rhett's bedroom. It was smaller than Trey's and had quite a geeky feel to it. He led her to his "IT Corner" and introduced her to his amazingly high-tech contraption. He had almost every program she could think of, thousands of games, access to all kinds of confidential shit, and a mind that worked just as fast as that piece of technology. She didn't know whether to be impressed or freaked out. "So, in short, you're a hacker. I can just about manage e-mailing."

"Hacking's not as hard as you might think. It's pretty much like sex—you want to get in and out, leaving little trace of you ever having been there. So, what do you need?"

"I just need access to the Internet. I've probably been disconnected from my old pack web, so I'll need to join yours."

"Your what?"

"You don't have a pack web?" Taryn was surprised, considering he seemed to have everything else.

He shook his head. "What is it?"

"It's kind of like a social network, but it's exclusive to whoever is in your pack."

"A little like Facebook and Twitter?"

"Exactly, only it's not so much to encourage social interaction as it is to showcase your pack. Let me show you."

After typing in the address, Taryn took them to the homepage of USA Pack Webs. Entering her name and password, she was immediately transferred to a visual of what was termed the Onyx Pack Web—her old pack. It was a little like looking at an image of the solar system, only instead of the sun being in the center it was a photo of the Alpha, her dad. And instead of planets dotted around the eight circles surrounding the sun, individual photos of each pack member were randomly dotted around the circles. Her own photo was set aside, as if free-floating in space. Oh yeah, she'd been disconnected, all right.

"Because we're not part of the pack, we don't have access to this web, which means we can't see the public blog and add to it, but watch this." Using the mouse, she moved the arrow to point on one of the photos. Instantly the photo enlarged and a little personal information on that pack member came up; it was like looking at a baseball card, only it was referred to as an information card.

Rhett read it aloud. "Full Name: Shaya Critchley. Gender: Female. Age: Twenty-three. Status: Unmated. Rank: Subordinate. Challenges: Four. Challenges Won: Two."

"That's all you can know unless you were to gain permission from the Alpha to browse through the pack web."

He turned to look at her. "Every pack has one?"

She shook her head. "Not every pack. They're a good thing to have, because not only is it a good way for all pack members to interact no matter where they are, but it means that other packs can get a vague idea of how powerful yours is. Look at this." Taryn pointed the cursor at Lance and instantly a photo popped up with a small amount of personal information underneath.

Again Rhett read it aloud. "Full Name: Lance Kai Warner. Gender: Male. Age: Forty-three. Status: Mate Deceased. Rank: Pack Alpha. Challenges: Twelve. Challenges Won: Twelve. Number of Alliances: Thirty-two. Total Number of Wolves: Twenty-six." He seemed lost in thought for a moment, before turning his attention back to Taryn. "So we could create our own web?"

She nodded. "Easy. First you just need to sign up to USA Pack Webs. You know, this would be a good way to form alliances. Other Alphas now have a way of getting in touch with Trey without risking turning up, only to get their head chewed off."

"How could they contact him?"

"See the option on the top right of the information card, Send Message? The same option is on everybody's information card. Speaking of which, let me just check to see if I have any." She double-clicked on her own card and saw a notice that she had fifty-seven messages.

"Fifty-seven?"

"It'll just be people wanting to know if the mating's kosher and all that. All I'm interested in is whether Shaya and Caleb have been in touch." It turned out that they had both contacted her. Again they'd both expressed concern about her safety and tried convincing her that she was wrong about Trey being her true mate, asking to meet up with her so they could all talk. "I think that's exactly what I'm going to have to do."

"What?"

"Meet up with them. They're not buying that the mating is real. If they hear it from my mouth, if I can convince them that

I'm fine and Trey doesn't intend to hurt me, then maybe they'll accept it. They're both tenacious bastards; they won't let this go."

Rhett sighed. "I doubt Trey will let you leave the property."

Let her leave? Snort. She leaned back in her chair and folded her arms. "Actually, I was thinking that if they see me here in this setting, it might be more believable for them."

"You're probably right there. Okay, you got time to help me with this before you go ask Trey?"

"Sure."

Trey looked up from an old photograph of his dead mother when he heard the knock on his office door. "Come in." As he expected, Tao strolled inside. He had also anticipated Dante tagging along, since he was a nosy bastard. Both wolves took the seats in front of Trey's thick, oak desk. Shoving the photo underneath the sheaf of papers beside it, he focused his attention on Tao.

"I'm electing you as Taryn's personal bodyguard." The Head Enforcer nodded agreeably, which sort of stunned Trey. "You know what this means, don't you? I'll need to pull you away from your usual duties, because your main priority will be Taryn's safety."

"Someone else will become Head Enforcer, I know," said Tao with a nod.

"I was sort of expecting a protest."

Tao shrugged. "I considered it an honor when I was made Head Enforcer and I enjoy that position, but it will be just as much an honor to be my Alpha female's bodyguard. Besides, Taryn's interesting to be around," he added with a smile.

Trey arched a brow. "I hope that's all you find her to be."

"Isn't it going to be a bad idea for you to have someone else looking out for her?" Dante asked rhetorically.

"Why would it be?"

He sighed. "Because it's your job as her mate to be her protector, and it will nettle your protective instincts—not to mention your wolf—if you ignore that."

"I'm not ignoring it. I'm assigning someone to watch over her, which means I'm addressing the issue of her safety. Protective instinct covered." Trey had kept his tone aloof and cool, but the way Dante narrowed his eyes told him that he was seeing more than Trey wanted him to.

"Speaking of Taryn, you might want to come see what she and Rhett set up."

"Set up?"

"On the computer. Come see."

Minutes later many of the pack were crowded into Rhett's bedroom as he showed them their pack web and explained everything about how it worked and how it would benefit the pack. He showed the others how to use it and introduced them to the public blog.

"Well, what do you think?" asked Rhett.

"This was your idea?" Trey asked Taryn, impressed.

"And Rhett's. It was a joint project."

"I had no idea other packs had this kind of stuff," said Dante, sounding a little awed. "How long ago did your dad set his web up?"

Taryn jiggled her head as she thought on it. "Five years ago, maybe?"

"It's good," said Trey, "really good."

Tao draped an arm over her shoulders. "Guess who's been assigned to you as your bodyguard?"

"I need a bodyguard?"

"No, but most Alphas have them. In reality, bodyguards are more like hovering slaves."

"And you're happy to be a hovering slave?"

"I'm happy to be *your* hovering slave."

At that moment Trey was very much regretting having made Tao her bodyguard. He didn't like Tao's flirtatiousness, didn't like how easily Taryn had taken to the other male's touch. He wanted to grab Taryn and pull her to him, wanted to lick over his mark to remind her she was claimed. Claimed by Trey.

Rhett's voice broke into his thoughts. "I checked to see if Darryl had set one up, but he hasn't. Shame. We could have gotten an idea of who has what position within the pack nowadays."

"By the way," Taryn began as she went to stand directly in front of Trey. "Remember the female who kept trying to get me to walk away from you while we were in the club?"

"Yeah," he replied, hiding how content he was that she was away from Tao. It was a struggle not to touch her, but he wouldn't let those instincts rule him.

"Her name's Shaya, she's my best friend. Well, her and Caleb."

"Caleb?"

Rolling her eyes at the amount of jealousy coating that one word, she continued, "I'm going to need to meet up with them. They're not buying that this mating's real. They need to hear it from me, face-to-face."

"Then we'll meet up with them somewhere public, like—"

"No, no, no, you can't be there when we talk."

"What do you mean I can't be there?" He had meant to sound affronted, but it came out petulant.

"Not the whole time anyway. They're worried about me; they think you might be hurting me or that you're forcing me to stay. It's why they're so desperate to speak to me alone. I want to see if I can get them to come here, to see that I'm alive and fine and that you and I are 'happily' mated."

He folded his arms across his chest to stop himself from reaching out to her. "Why exactly weren't they so worried when Roscoe forced his claim on you?"

"That was different. Unlike you, Roscoe wrapped his meanness up in charm and managed to fool a lot of people with it."

"You're saying I have no charm?"

She gave him a bright, mocking smile. "Why, of course you have charm. You practically ooze it. Ego better now?"

He sighed. "Call them, invite them to come here sometime this week."

"The weekend would be better, because they work through the week. I'm thinking Saturday morning."

"Fine."

The way he so abruptly left the room had Taryn frowning. It was as though the guy was desperate to get away from her or something. It wasn't until later that evening, when she found herself lying in bed very alone, that she began to think on it a little more.

Trey had been different with her since the confrontation with Roscoe that morning. Or, more accurately, he had been *in* different. There had been no more heated looks, no more whispered promises, no more licking the marks on her neck, no more taking the odd moment to inhale her scent. But it wasn't just that. He was barely speaking to her.

And now here she was, alone, because he had "things to do" in his office.

Well, it seemed like the very sexual male from the past two days had retreated, or had retreated from her, at least. It occurred to her then that maybe it had only been his wolf's insecurity in the mating that had been behind his fevered urge to be inside her and mark her. Maybe now that the threat of Roscoe was gone and his wolf was more settled, Trey would no longer have that urge. Hell, maybe without the mating urges he would never have wanted her at all. The idea shouldn't have sparked a dull ache in her chest and it shouldn't have made her suddenly desire to cuddle herself. Yet it did.

But what had she expected? Trey was a big guy with a lot of pride and probably didn't have a thing for tiny females who would challenge his dominance. Her body wasn't exactly model material, and then there was the fact that she was latent. He acted as though it didn't bother him, but it was likely that in truth he saw the latency as a weakness, and it made her very unattractive to him.

A noise penetrated her thoughts and she realized that someone had entered the room. The scent flowed over her, stroking her senses and stirring her wolf, who was anxious for some contact with her mate. But Taryn hadn't begged for scraps from her dad's table and she wouldn't be begging for scraps from Trey's table either. So she remained on her side facing the wall, faking sleep, ignoring her wolf's growling protests.

Trey took one look at Taryn's still form and sighed in relief. She was asleep. He hadn't woken her. He had been fighting his wolf—hell, he'd been fighting himself—for hours on the subject of going to Taryn, of getting in some physical contact, social or sexual. He was literally starving for it. Had he known that mating would be this bad, with all its urges, instincts, and needs, he probably wouldn't have mated at all.

After quietly using the bathroom and stripping down to his boxers, he slipped beneath the covers and resisted the desire to snuggle into her. Instead, he rolled to his side so that his back was to hers and there was enough space between them in the large bed to fit another person. His wolf growled at that idea, but Trey ignored him and ignored his instincts. And he closed his eyes, completely oblivious to the fact that the eyes of the woman behind him had opened and had a haunted look in them at the realization that she'd bound herself to a wolf who now had no interest in her.

CHAPTER SEVEN

Just as she had each morning over the past week, Taryn was perched on the kitchen counter sipping her coffee while engaged in a staring contest with dear old Greta. It was practically ritualistic for them to partake in a battle of wills whenever they were in the same room. Each time, Taryn would leave the room smiling, leaving Greta purple in the face and growling. Once Greta had realized that she wasn't going to scare Taryn off, she had taken to simply insulting her and generally being difficult. In truth, Taryn found the whole thing just as entertaining as everyone else did. As usual, they were all eating quietly as they waited for the verbal spar to begin.

"What are you looking at, hussy?" Greta finally spat.

"I haven't figured that out yet."

Huffing, Greta drank down more of her weird green herbal tea. "I hope you're not getting comfortable. You won't be here for much longer."

"So you've said. Repeatedly."

"You might have some of the others fooled, but I see you for what you are."

"Is that right?"

"I warned my boys all about females like you."

"Oh, come on, your imagination was never this good."

Hand over her heart, Greta said with fake misery, "My daughter is probably turning in her grave now. You've got tattoos, for God's sake!" A cruel smirk suddenly curved her lips. "I suppose I shouldn't have expected much better, what with your wolf basically being disabled. What does it feel like to be latent? To know your wolf will forever be trapped?"

"I don't know. What does it feel like to be so old that your birth certificate is in Roman numerals?" The smirk quickly fell from the crone's face and Taryn smiled.

Entering the kitchen, Trey wasn't surprised to find his mate and his grandmother glaring at each other. Neither even spared him a glance. Given that Taryn seemed cheery, while Greta looked like she was chewing a wasp, Trey could guess who was on top of the situation. His grandmother was doing her best to intimidate Taryn; however, his little mate was holding her own, making it clear that she didn't take any shit from anyone, especially one who was "old and senile."

His wolf didn't like that Taryn's attention hadn't immediately shot to him, and before Trey knew it he'd yanked gently on her hair to make her look at him. Restraining himself from nipping her lower lip, he simply gave her a nod. A growl of approval built in his chest as he saw that she was wearing a black, tight-fitting T-shirt that showed off some of his marks—marks that were fading, he then noticed. His wolf growled angrily inside his head.

"Morning, son. Come sit down and get something to eat." Greta's voice was now sugary-sweet.

"How long before your friends get here?" he asked Taryn as he took his seat.

"They should be here any minute now. Remember what you promised."

"I'll give you some time to talk with them alone," he assured her, though it would nettle his wolf to know there was a strange male wolf around her. He told himself it wouldn't bother Trey the man so much, and if his wolf could have snorted, he would have. "At some point I'll come over there so we can act the mated couple, totally devoted to one another and completely smitten and all that."

Again Taryn was struck by the feeling of how unfair it was that she would never have that, especially that she would never have it with Joey. And now here she was, about to commit the ultimate blasphemy again and claim that the one person created for her had never been her true mate at all. God, this sucked big-time.

At least she and Trey were exchanging a few words. Occasionally he wouldn't speak to her at all. Or there were the times when she would enter a room and he would immediately leave it. He spent most of his time cooped up in his office. She knew he had to keep an eye on his investments—he actually had a pretty good head for business—but surely he didn't *need* to spend that much time in there. Making the whole thing even more annoying was that Selma had picked up on the huge divide between them and tried clinging to him as much as she could— just as she was doing right now at the table. The only thing preventing Taryn from reacting was that Trey was growling, warning the female away from him. Still, it pissed her off to no end, but damned if she would let either of them know that.

"Morning," drawled Tao as he strolled into the room. He play-punched her shoulder before joining the others at the table.

"Ass," she snapped, smiling.

Trey knew he shouldn't have the urge to growl at his ex–Head Enforcer. It was just a play punch—it wasn't sexual, it hadn't hurt her, and it had only been the briefest touch. But Trey was honestly considering stabbing the wolf with his fork. It might not have annoyed him so much if Tao wasn't always touching her. The guy had taken his role as bodyguard a little too literally. Trey couldn't understand how he hadn't noticed before the way Tao looked at her—mixed in with admiration and respect was a deep longing. And Trey didn't like it one bit.

His wolf was urging him to take a swipe at his enforcer and warn him off. Perversely, Trey the man liked that others wanted what was his, and that gave him strength against his wolf's drive to separate her from the other male. Also, Trey knew that no matter how much Tao might want Taryn, he would never encroach—he was too good a guy for that. Nonetheless, his wolf wasn't particularly interested in whether or not Tao was a good guy. He didn't want him around Taryn so much.

Trey inhaled deeply, reminding himself that *he* was in control—not his wolf, not those primal instincts. The smile on Dante's face said he knew what inner struggle Trey had been going through. The ringing of his cell phone distracted Trey from thoughts of flicking scrambled egg at his Beta. "That was Kirk," he announced on ending the call. "They're here. He just let them through the gate. Should only be a minute before their SUV pulls up outside."

Taryn hopped down from the counter and stretched. "Time for Scene One: The Alpha Pair's Welcome. Make it good, Flintstone. These guys won't be easy to convince."

"I noticed that at the club."

"They won't be trying to separate the two of you like they did that night," stated Dante.

Hearing the fierceness in his tone and watching the way his body language became confrontational, Taryn pointed hard at him. "You are not going to spend the next few hours trying to intimidate them. They're already scared half to death by Trey."

"Are you going to tell me they won't try to convince you to leave with them?"

"Of course they will."

"Let's hope our luck stretches that far," muttered Selma. Hope chuckled. Everyone else ignored them.

"They won't dare ask you to leave if a few of us are sitting with you," said Dante.

Taryn shook her head. "Not a chance, Barney Rubble. You all stay the hell away and give us some privacy."

"It'll only be until Trey comes over."

"No, I'm not having any of you hovering around us like parental supervisors. Not even Tao."

Tao frowned. "But I'm your bodyguard."

"They're not a threat to me." As all three males opened their mouths to say something, she held up her hand. "I don't want to hear it. Now let's do this."

Seeing the resolve in her expression, Trey sighed and took her soft hand in his large, callused one as they walked together to the main door. Marcus was holding it open, watching with his usual grin as their visitors hesitantly exited the SUV and, with slow, nervous strides, made their way up the stairs.

Trey locked his arms around Taryn's waist, keeping her back against his chest, and allowed himself the luxury of burying his face in her neck to drown in that scent that could so easily make his cock hard. He shouldn't have been surprised when he woke up that morning and found himself curled around her with his face nestled in the crook of her neck, taking comfort in the exotic smell of his mate as he slept. At some point in his sleep he had covered that huge space between them and fed the hunger that he had ignored for the past week. Then he had sneaked out of bed before she realized. Had she not been such a deep sleeper, he would never have gotten away with it.

As Shaya and Caleb finally came to stand in front of them, shuffling from foot to foot and completely avoiding eye contact with Trey, Taryn had to refrain from groaning. She knew he had an intimidating presence, but she didn't think he was *that* bad. Okay, maybe he was. "Thanks for coming."

"It's been weird not seeing you every day," said Shaya.

Taryn discreetly pinched Trey's arm, urging him to do his part.

Flinching a little, he said, "Welcome. I have a few things to do, but Taryn will take you down to the lake, won't you, baby?"

"Yep."

Four days ago Greta had come to him complaining that Taryn had taken their deck chairs and barbecue from storage and set them up near the lake as an area where she could go and relax. Well, she hadn't taken the items personally—more like she had turned into Captain von Trapp and had his enforcers virtually marching as they followed her every command. He had to admit it was a nice little setup, and he was surprised no one had thought to do it before.

"Great, thanks," said Caleb, his eyes still lowered.

A few minutes later Taryn was sitting by the lake at the patio table, trying her best not to laugh at the way Shaya and Caleb were glancing around nervously, as if they were expecting Trey to jump out and pounce on them.

"They're all very protective," noted Caleb, referring to the pack.

And wasn't that an understatement. It was laughable the way the males were hanging around, trying to look as though they weren't there to keep an eye on her and ensure she wasn't kidnapped. Like that would ever happen. Marcus and Trick were lazing in the lake as if it wasn't a chilly day, Tao sat against a nearby tree reading a book that was upside down, and Dante and Ryan were cleaning a barbecue that was already spick-and-span. All were occasionally sneaking covert looks at Taryn and her friends—at least they thought they were being subtle anyway. Apparently, she should have better defined "*the hell away*," because they didn't appear to have gotten the idea.

"Yeah," she agreed.

"Which means you must have proven your worth as an Alpha female, so I'm guessing that tale about you calming a feral Trey was true."

The emphasis on the word *feral* irritated Taryn. "He hasn't hurt me and he's not going to."

"Taryn, have you seen yourself in a mirror? You're covered in marks." Most of which were fading, thankfully. "Someone that possessive isn't balanced."

"I know Trey's a few fries short of a Happy Meal, but it doesn't mean he'll hurt me."

"How can you be sure of that? His wolf goes feral, for God's sake."

"But even feral he doesn't hurt me."

"And you expect us to believe that's because he's your true mate, right?" Caleb snickered. "There's no way I can believe that."

Shaya appealed to her with a look. "Taryn, we watched you, at nine years old, slip into a state of depression. It was like being around a zombie. You existed but you didn't live. It was all just mechanical. And we understood why—you had just lost the other half of your soul. It was a shock that you even survived it; no one thought you would. I mean, I know you two hadn't mated, but you had still formed a connection, and you were so young."

"It hasn't occurred to you that maybe the reason I lived was because that connection—solid and true though it was—just wasn't the connection between true mates? That maybe the reason I reacted so badly was because I'd just lost my best friend *and* my mom in the same accident?"

Caleb lowered his voice as he spoke. "Look, if your dad's right and you did this to get away from Roscoe…well, he's dead now. You don't have to keep this up. God, you could have come to me, I'd have mated you. I still will if it's what you want."

Taryn smiled. "Caleb, that's sweet and all, but do you really think I'd ask you to enter a permanent mating with someone you thought of as nothing but a friend—an annoying friend at that— ending any chance of you having a life with your true mate?"

He shrugged, suddenly seeming uncomfortable. His voice was even quieter when he spoke again. "Who says I see you as nothing but a friend? Maybe I just hadn't acted on what I felt because it would have felt like I was betraying Joey."

Taryn rolled her eyes. "Yeah. Right."

"So you hadn't wanted to mate with Roscoe?" asked Shaya.

"Not particularly, no. I thought he was kind of vain and overly flirtatious—you know how stuff like that annoys me. I don't know how my dad or anyone else can claim that me mating with Trey—someone who had been a stranger to me before that day—has anything to do with that. Maybe if I had the power of mind control and could hypnotize him to believe and claim that I was his true mate, then yeah, sure."

"Obviously you guys believe you're true mates; I saw for myself what happened," said Shaya. "But isn't it possible that it was just a really strong case of lust at first sight? 'Cause, you know, I've been there—it's powerful."

A loud, sharp, metallic *tock* sound had Taryn looking up. She smiled at her relatively new friend, who was perched on a branch high in the tree to her left. "Hey, big guy. Come on down here."

"Oh no, Taryn please don't," Shaya whined. But it was too late. The huge, glossy black raven was already on the table.

Caleb frowned. "What is it with you and birds? Why do they always like you?"

Taryn shrugged one shoulder. "Isn't he gorgeous?"

"I don't like crows," whined Shaya, leaning back in her seat.

"It's a raven."

"Well, then, I don't like ravens."

"How can you not like them? They're so intelligent and beautiful. Look at the way his feathers shine a kind of metallic violet in the light." He made a series of guttural croaks that had Shaya flinching.

"Aren't ravens an omen of death and disease?"

Taryn rolled her eyes at the nervousness in her friend's voice. "For God's sake, Shaya, it's only a bird."

"And a scavenger, did you forget that part? Wait, does it only have one leg? And hang on, did it just *bark*?"

Taryn chuckled. "Ravens can imitate a whole variety sounds, even a human voice." As if to back her up, he made a series of gurgling and croaking noises, followed by another bark. "See, LJ's cool."

Caleb made a choking noise. "LJ?"

"Yeah, as in Long John...Long John Silver, the sailor cook with the one leg?"

"Oh. Right."

"Ravens only have one mate too, you know," she said as she watched him return to the tree.

Caleb sighed. "I don't care what you say, Taryn, there's no way I'll believe Joey wasn't your true mate."

Of course he wouldn't, the opinionated SOB. "Just because I'm mated now doesn't mean Joey means any less to me than he did before. That bond we had doesn't mean any less because he once filled a place inside me. It's not that Trey's replaced him, because Trey has his own place." Not one word of that had been a lie. Now that she'd mated with Trey, he did have his own place. He just wasn't filling it.

Shaya ran her hand through her hair, sighing. "I want you to have this, Taryn, I really do want you to have this. I'm just worried that somewhere along the way you'll think, 'Hey, I was wrong, he's not my true mate at all.' Then you'll have lost two mates. Where would that leave you? I don't want to see you in that state ever again. And, well...for God's sake, Taryn, how can you *not* be petrified of him?"

"He's a walking time bomb, Taryn, he's—"

Taryn held up her hand. "Look, Caleb, if you're here to try to turn me against my own mate, then you might as well save your breath to blow up your doll."

Grinning, he shook his head and took the hand that Taryn had held up. "I want to say I'm happy for you but...well, I'd be lying. I don't want you mated to a psycho. Just swear to me that you're happy here. At the end of the day, that's all that really matters."

In some ways, Taryn was happy. These people—with the exception of Greta, Kirk, Brock, Selma, and Hope—didn't treat her like she was inferior just because she was latent. She didn't feel like an outsider or someone who needed to be constantly on the defensive. The atmosphere here was the total opposite of the one she had grown up in, and she found it refreshing.

She had become close friends with Lydia, as she spent a lot of time helping with her graphic design business. She was a great person to be around—she entertained Taryn nonstop with her little eccentricities and her habit of saying whatever the hell she thought. Taryn wouldn't have thought that someone like that could be so suited to the very sensitive Cam, and yet Lydia was.

When she wasn't with Lydia she was often with Grace, who was helping her improve her cooking skills, or sometimes Rhett, who was teaching her how to hack. Tao was of course often there, but as her friend just as much as her bodyguard. He was very easy to be around; he wasn't complicated, he didn't brood, and he didn't blow hot and cold. Trey could learn a few things from him.

She also found that she got along pretty well with Marcus, which kind of surprised her, because ordinarily she tired of flirtatious people. And Marcus was *extremely* flirtatious. When he turned the full force of his huge, impish grin on her, there was no holding back a blush. Maybe it was because he gave some fantastic shoulder massages that the flirtatiousness didn't bother her...? Very possible.

She hadn't known that he and Trick scratched each other's itch from time to time until she stumbled upon them having some fun at the lake. Damn, that had been hot, and it had taken all her self-control to leave rather than stay and watch. Apparently, they had known she was there, as Trick later teased her about it and still continued to do so on occasion. Trick was a tease in general. He seemed to get his kicks from making people blush or feel uncomfortable, but since he targeted Selma and Kirk a lot, Taryn was totally fine with it.

Although Ryan didn't talk much and mostly communicated through grunts, Taryn rather liked him. Unlike everyone else, she spoke to him as though she actually expected him to respond until eventually he began to talk to her a little. She wasn't surprised to find that Ryan was quite intelligent, even more so than Rhett. He was very big-brotherly with her, as opposed to Dominic, who often asked her what color her underwear was and tried to look down her shirt. He was the worst perv ever and constantly hit her with dirty chat-up lines that he didn't need to use—just one look at him had females drooling. He just seemed to enjoy being a perv, and yet it was impossible not to like him. Dante was another person who was impossible to dislike, but behind his laid-back "I don't take life seriously" attitude was an astute, diplomatic, extremely observant person.

Trey's withdrawal from her, however, tainted her otherwise happy state. She knew it was a good thing that they didn't spend much time together. She knew it was best that she didn't find herself happy here when she had every intention of leaving. Still, it stung, because she got the feeling that Trey's withdrawal had nothing to do with that and everything to do with the simple fact that he didn't desire her.

Seriously, who would want to lie in the same bed each night with someone who purposely left enough room between them to fit an elephant? Worse, she couldn't argue with the fact that she still belonged to him in a sense. Who would want to belong to someone who didn't want her?

She was considering moving into one of the guest rooms, but she suspected that if she increased the distance between them, it would only make her wolf worse. Her wolf was restless and miserable enough after going a week with only minimum contact with her mate. What Taryn was thankful for was that she and her wolf were in perfect accord on one thing—there would be no begging her mate for more, no matter how bad things were.

Taryn consoled herself with the reminder that this would all be over in just over ten weeks and then, with any luck, she might be able to switch to her uncle's pack. She had been delighted when she discovered that his pack was signed up to the USA Pack Webs. She had sent him a nice, friendly message, asking how he was doing and stuff—of course not mentioning that she and Trey weren't true mates. Only when Darryl's challenge was over would she let the information loose. Her hope was that she might first be able to forge an alliance between Trey and her uncle's Alpha. Not only would this benefit Trey, but it might also increase her chances of the Alpha agreeing to let her join his pack at a later date.

Taryn was snapped out of her thoughts as Caleb abruptly dropped her hand and his gaze was drawn to something over her shoulder. She turned to see Trey strolling toward her, looking as sexy and intimidating as always. *Time for Scene Two: Looking Lovey-Dovey.* She hadn't expected that it would be so hard emotionally to fake intimacy with a person, but it felt weird and uncomfortable because it wasn't real. On the plus side, some physical contact with him would calm her wolf a little.

Trey grabbed the chair beside Taryn, turned it to face her, and then sat before lifting her from her own seat and placing her on his lap, straddling him. He couldn't help marveling over how well she fit there, and at the same time being annoyed about it. His cock wasn't annoyed; it was quickly rising to attention—especially as she was wearing those "bend me over and fuck me now" knee boots. "Hey." After skimming his nose along the crook of her neck to again take her scent deep into him, he gave her a lingering kiss. He'd missed her taste. "How's my girl doing?"

"Fine." She almost purred as he ran his hands up and down her back. Her wolf was lazing, content, within her. It didn't matter to her wolf that the entire thing was an act. All that mattered was that she was having physical contact with her mate.

Unable to resist, Trey licked over his mark and smiled as she quivered. "I know you wanted some time with your friends, but I don't like it when you're out of my sight for too long." It was a pain in the ass that that was the truth. Although he spent little time with her, he would still seek her out several times a day—usually every few hours—just to check on her.

"That's okay, I missed you." She brushed her lips against his and then gestured to her edgy-looking friends. "And Shaya and Caleb don't mind."

He gave them a simple nod of acknowledgment, which they returned with shaky smiles. His attention quickly returned to Taryn as he drank in the sight of her in a way that he usually did only when no one was watching.

"Have you noticed my surveillance team?"

Trey smiled. "I noticed. I approve."

"I'll bet you do," she grumbled.

He shrugged unrepentantly as he spoke against those luscious lips. "I like knowing you're safe."

"And yet you haven't thrown out your inherently evil grandmother."

Chuckling, he shaped her waist with his hands. "I know she's being a little difficult right now, but she's one of those people who grow on you."

"No, she's one of those people who are like Slinkys."

"Slinkys?"

"Yeah. Basically useless, but they make you smile when you push them down the stairs."

He laughed before nibbling and sucking on her earlobe. "She'll come around."

A shiver racked Taryn's body as he grazed his teeth over his mark. "Trey, you can't do that in public. It has an embarrassing effect." His totally wicked laugh made her nervous. Of course the bastard nipped at her mark. Deciding some retaliation wouldn't be such a bad thing, she squirmed slightly against his very hard cock—he might not particularly desire her, but his body would still react to his mate's scent. He groaned against her neck.

Trey knew he could leave now. They had done enough touchy-feely stuff and she probably still had things to talk about with her friends. In fact, he *should* leave—her friends were anxious and uncomfortable when he was around, as though they expected him to lunge at them or something. But he couldn't bring himself to break the contact with Taryn. Instead, he lazed back into his seat and pulled her forward so that she was draped across his chest. "Don't mind me, you carry on talking. I won't even be listening, I'm too distracted by your scent." Another truth.

As he looked over her shoulder, he saw that Tao was looking at them with envy in his expression—envy that he wasn't bothering to conceal. Holding Tao's gaze, Trey knotted a hand in Taryn's hair—a gesture of possessiveness, a reminder that she was his. Tao lowered his eyes and continued staring at his book. Did he know it was upside down?

"How's my dad?" Taryn asked Shaya, groaning as Trey began gently massaging her back.

"Feel good, baby?" he asked. She nodded against his chest.

"Alternating from being angry with you to wondering if just maybe this mating could be more beneficial than the one with Roscoe would have been," Shaya replied to Taryn's question, her expression studious as she observed Taryn and Trey together.

"Thought as much," grumbled Taryn before groaning again. "Trey, your hands are magical."

"You already knew that." He groaned again as her body shook against his chest as she laughed, sending all kinds of interesting vibrations through him and his very hard cock. He combed his fingers through her hair. "I love the way it has all those different shades of blonde in it and even a little bit of red." Another truth.

"It annoys me. It can't seem to decide what color it wants to be."

"It has me curious."

She lifted her head, resting her chin on his chest. "About?"

In a voice too low for anyone else to hear, he said, "Well, as much as I like you bald down there, I wouldn't mind knowing if the color of the carpet matches the curtains."

She slapped his chest. "Trey!"

"Oh, look," snickered a familiar, annoying, witchy voice. Greta. "Not only is she lounging all over you like a slut, but she's flashing her underwear to all and sundry."

Glancing back, Taryn saw that the top of her red, lacy thong had ridden above her jeans. "Do you like it? I quite like your blouse, Greta. Wouldn't you like to slip into something more comfortable though? Perhaps a coma?"

"Didn't anyone ever tell you sarcasm's the lowest form of wit?" Greta turned to Shaya and Caleb. "Do us all a favor and take this hussy with you when you leave."

Taryn sighed. "How about we play fetch with a twist, Greta—I'll throw the ball for you, but just don't come back. What do you think?"

Huffing, the old woman marched off. Taryn smiled at a chuckling Trey before laying her head back on his chest, facing Shaya and Caleb. She wondered what their odd expressions meant. She finally found out an hour later as she walked them to Shaya's SUV.

"I told you that what really matters is that you're happy," said Caleb. "And it seems like you are."

"Is that your way of saying that I have your blessing?"

"I'm still having trouble getting my head around him being your true mate, but…well, you act like true mates and he obviously adores you. That's enough for me. I have to admit I'm kind of jealous that everyone around us seems to have mated."

She patted his arm. "Don't worry, I'm sure your own true mate is somewhere just waiting for you to find her, and I'm sure she's the next model up from the inflatable one you already have."

"Bitch," he said affectionately.

Shaya had her palm pressed against her forehead, looking stressed and confused. "I don't know how anyone can *not* be terrified of that wolf...but his true mate wouldn't be. Mates never fear each other. And clearly you don't, so...Look, just promise me that if you suddenly think you've made a mistake or if he ever hurts you, you'll call me and get out of here."

Taryn smiled. "Aw, Shaya, if he ever hurt me, he'd be dead before I made that call."

A grin spread across Shaya's elfin face. "That's my girl."

It hadn't been a surprise to discover that Trey had disappeared into his office before the car had even moved out of sight—acting time was over. She turned to Tao, who had been waiting a few feet behind her. "Hey, fancy going out somewhere?"

"Where?" He sounded a little suspicious.

"I've gone twelve whole days without pizza, and that's just not right."

He grinned. "Pizza definitely sounds good. Let me just tell Dante we'll be out for a while."

She hadn't realized just how much she had missed her Hyundai until she was driving it to town five minutes later. Tao, apparently not content with being her bodyguard, had wanted to play chauffeur too, but she easily got her way because he was smart enough to know that she wouldn't give in.

"Did your friends buy the act?" Tao asked about fifteen minutes into the journey.

She shrugged. "They've accepted it, but I don't think anything will ever completely convince them."

"They don't think you and Trey fit?"

"It's not so much that. They saw how close Joey and I were, and then they watched me deal with his death pretty badly. For

me to suddenly claim that Joey was nothing but my best friend…"
She let the sentence trail off, knowing he'd see her point. "I think
if it had been anyone other than Trey, I might have had more luck
with getting them to accept it."

"Trey's not your type?"

"I meant because he's psychotic. Although it's true that I've
never been with a guy built like a highlander before, but I don't
really have a type. I either like someone or I don't."

"And you like Trey."

"To an extent," she said with a smile. "Selma made it clear
that I'm not his type."

"Trey's always gone for, what do you females call them?
Hourglass figures or something like that?"

Noticing he hadn't sounded so fond of them, she prodded,
"You're not such a fan?"

He shrugged. "I wouldn't say no to one. Plenty of times Trey
and I have shared one of his women—"

"Really?"

"—but I prefer my women to be more…athletic, I guess. And
I have a thing for blondes."

"Ooh, please don't say that line—that was the first thing
Roscoe ever said to me. Makes me shiver even now."

His words were both consoling and sympathetic. "It has to
have pissed you off that you had two guys wanting to mate with
you, but neither really wanted you for you."

"Yeah, but I don't think I'll make a good mate anyway."

"Why?"

"My natural reaction is to hold back from people, especially
guys. It's something I honestly can't control. When Joey and my
mom died, I had this big hole and it's as if when I taped it up, I
did it too tight. I don't know if I could ever really make myself
completely vulnerable to another person again. And when you
mate with someone, *really* mate with someone, there can't be
protective walls."

Tao's smile was a little sad. "The right wolf will hammer them down."

"It might take more than a hammer. Anyway, let's talk about something more interesting. What's this thing about you and Trey sharing women?" Ménages weren't exactly unusual among shifters, but she wouldn't have had Trey down for someone who shared.

"Before you, Trey's never been possessive with women. Plenty of times we've shared. The invite was always open to our Beta too, but Dante just likes to watch with Marcus, Trick, Ryan, and Dominic."

"They watch?" She chuckled, not finding it difficult to believe, especially since many shifters had voyeuristic tendencies.

"Oh, yeah, if Trey's in a good mood, he doesn't mind. You ever participated in a ménage?"

She snorted. It was hard enough making things work out with one guy, let alone two. "Having a sex life isn't as easy for an alpha female as you might think."

"In what way?"

"Guys say they like a woman who'll take charge in the bedroom, but most of the time they're talking out of their ass." Finally they pulled up in the parking lot of the pizza place, and Taryn couldn't stop a joyous smile from taking over her face. She really had missed the taste of pepperoni pizza.

"But most alpha males would be hard at just the thought of battling an alpha female for dominance in the bedroom."

"Yeah, but that erection often disappears when the male realizes it's not as easy as he thought to win that battle. Most of the time they think that if they just chase us around and tire us out, we'll surrender or something. Then there are the males who confuse dominance with bullying. When it comes to alpha females, submission has to be earned, not taken. You've never been with an alpha female?"

"Not yet." Most likely in response to her baffled expression, he said, "What's wrong?"

She gestured to the pizza delivery guy, who was exiting the restaurant with a pile of boxes. "I've just never worked out why they put pizza in a square box."

Intending to seem as though he was leaving his office only to refill his coffee mug, Trey left the room and began walking toward the kitchen, wanting to discreetly check on Taryn. Two things quickly became apparent. One, it was a lot quieter than usual. Two, although Taryn's scent was everywhere he turned, it was faint…as if it was simply what lingered in the air.

In the kitchen Dante, Greta, Marcus, Trick, Grace, Lydia, Selma, and Hope sat at the table, laughing and joking. It looked as though Selma and Hope were having a separate conversation, unsurprisingly. They had made themselves pretty unpopular with their refusal to accept Taryn. After refilling his mug, Trey asked, ensuring his voice was casual, "Where's Taryn?"

"Out," replied Dante.

"On another run with Tao?" Although she was latent, she was just as fast as any shifter.

"No, she went into town."

Trey had to have heard wrong. "What was that?"

"She went into town."

Dumping his mug on the counter, uncaring of the scalding hot coffee that had splashed on his fingers, he demanded, "Where? With who?"

"She and Tao went for pizza," said Greta, her voice full of implications.

Selma dived on that. "He's a very attentive bodyguard, isn't he? You have to admit they look real cute together. Right, Hope?"

"Oh, yeah, real cute."

"Shut it," snapped Trey, surprising most people in the room.

"She didn't tell you she was going out?" asked Marcus.

"No, she didn't," Trey managed to grit out, pissed off that she had ventured out without a word and jealous that she had asked Tao to go with her rather than him. He switched his attention back to Dante. "Why didn't you stop her from going?"

"Why would I have stopped my Alpha female from leaving pack territory? And *how*, exactly, would you have expected me to stop Taryn from doing that or anything else?"

"When did she leave?"

"Calm down, Trey. What's the problem?" But Dante knew exactly what the problem was—he always saw too much.

As the sound of laughing coming from outside the caves met their ears, Marcus nodded. "That's probably them now."

Trey stalked toward the main door, clenching his fists. Almost yanking the damn thing off, he opened it to find Taryn and Tao practically stumbling up the stairs as they laughed so hard at something they were keeled over. The sight of them looking so happy and comfortable with each other sent another surge of jealousy rushing through him.

Eventually they looked up and saw him. He could guess that his expression was thunderous, because Tao immediately lowered his eyes. Taryn, on the other hand, presented him with a smile.

"Well, hello," Taryn said brightly as she went right on past the ass she had mated with and strode into Bedrock.

"What the hell did you think you were doing, leaving pack territory without telling me!" he bellowed as he followed behind her. Slowly she turned and appraised him from head to toe. Not with fear or even apprehension, but like someone would scrutinize a bug.

"Did you forget to take your pills again?"

"I've been in my office believing you're safe, and you've been in town hanging out with Tao!"

"Yes, and we had a lovely time, thanks."

"If you'd have said you wanted to go somewhere, I'd have taken you! Why sneak off?" When she just stared blankly instead of answering him, he persisted, "Taryn?"

"Oh, sorry, I was just busy picturing a gag in your mouth."

"This is serious! The new Alpha of Roscoe's pack hasn't been here to finalize an alliance, which means there's still a possibility of retaliation over his death. Then there's the fact that although your dad might not come here and challenge me, you can bet your little ass he'll take you, given half the chance."

"Did the UFOs tell you that when you removed your foil hat?"

"I'm not being paranoid!"

Taryn snickered. "What you're being is an overprotective asshole who didn't like it that his mate didn't say 'pretty, pretty please, Master' before leaving pack territory." Fed up with him, she retreated to the living area and, sighing, plunked herself onto the reclining corner of the sectional sofa. "I am so stuffed."

"You won't want coffee, then?" said Grace with a smile.

"I'm not that stuffed."

One by one, people began to pile in—other than Trey, who stood near the door, arms folded, snarling. "I think I prefer him in Cujo mode," she muttered to Tao, who was beside her on the sofa.

"Been out all afternoon with another male," drawled Greta. "Didn't I tell you she was a hussy, Trey?"

"Hey, there, Mistress of the Dark Arts, how are you?"

"If I'd known you guys were going for pizza, I'd have asked to go along," said Cam.

Taryn smiled. "Not to tease you or anything, but it was absolutely gorgeous. Deep-dish, extra cheese, pepperoni—"

"Now that's not fair."

"You know," began Dominic, wearing that impish smile that meant he was about to deliver another of his cheesy lines, "I'm a lot like Domino's Pizza. If you don't come in thirty minutes, the next one's free." Everyone groaned, trying to hold back smiles.

"Here you go," said Grace as she handed Taryn a mug of coffee.

"Oh, you're a gem." She sighed dreamily as Marcus leaned over the back of the sofa and began massaging her shoulders.

"I take it this is what everyone means about it being uncomfortable when newly made mates are separated for a while?" prodded Trick.

Taryn sighed inwardly when she saw that Trey hadn't moved from the doorway or dropped his scowl. He looked unbelievably pissed, but he also looked a little lonely. As much as he had annoyed the hell out of her, Taryn had the urge to soothe him. Extending her hand, she said, "Come on, Flintstone."

He looked at her hand, looked at her face, and then stormed off. With a sigh, she dropped her hand and shrugged. But she wasn't as aloof about it as she appeared to be. Would it really have been that horrible to sit with her for a while, to spend a teeny-weeny amount of time with her and his pack? Apparently, yes, it would have. And apparently, she hadn't played the aloof female as well as she thought.

"How many times in your head have you killed him?" asked Grace when they were alone in the kitchen preparing dinner.

Taryn sighed. "Honestly? Too many to count. I've even dug the grave and hidden the body."

"You know, I can't understand why he's acting so shitty. I know he was never overly attentive or anything, but it was obvious he liked having you around, and then all of a sudden he turned indifferent. At first I thought you guys had just had a fight or something."

"No. It was after I calmed his wolf. In fact—no, he was okay right up until I had that nap after healing him. When I woke up, he was all weird, and he's been that way ever since."

"Do you think maybe he just doesn't want to look weak in front of the others by being all affectionate and shit? You know guys can be weird like that, and he's the Alpha, so there's that pressure there to look as though he has no weaknesses."

"But if it was that, he'd be okay when other people aren't around."

"You guys aren't fucking?"

Taryn shook her head. "Not since the morning before Roscoe's visit and subsequent demise. If it was just sex he was being weird about, I'd have thought he might be getting it elsewhere. Selma isn't exactly shy about her eagerness to have him. But he barely speaks to me, even when we're alone, so there's a bigger issue at play here. I just don't know what it is."

"It's not that he doesn't want you," Grace insisted. "I've seen the way he looks at you. It's not just with lust either. That's what makes this shit all the more confusing."

"If he wanted me, he wouldn't hold back. It's not in Trey's nature to hold back when he wants something."

"Don't worry, honey, we'll find out what's going on in that weird head of his eventually."

"I'll have killed and buried him for real by then." She frowned as the sudden sounds of cursing and raised voices drifted into the room. Both females immediately stopped what they were doing and headed through the tunnels to find out what the fuss was all about.

Arriving at the main junction, Taryn saw many of the pack had gathered and were looking as defensive as they were confused. Marcus and Trick appeared to be interrogating them. Seeing her there, everyone fell silent, and a chill ran down her spine. "What is it?"

Marcus went to speak, but then swallowed hard and looked at Trick, as if hoping he would answer.

"What's going on?"

"Follow us," said Marcus as he and Trick made their way out the main door and down the flights of stairs. On reaching the bottom, they led her into the concealed parking lot, where she stopped dead. She couldn't see what the problem was, but she knew what Trey, Dante, Tao, Ryan, and Dominic were gathered around. She shrugged her way through them and gasped. The doors and windows of her Hyundai were covered in red spray paint. Worse, the red paint very clearly said, "Go Home Warner Slut."

"Who. Did. This?" Her voice was dead, toneless.

"We don't know," replied Trey, his own voice thick with anger. His mate's car. Someone had dared to do this to his mate's property. His wolf wanted to surface so that he could hunt them down. "Almost every pack member's scent is in this lot, because everyone uses it. If we had gotten to it when the paint was still wet, then maybe the culprit's scent would be heavier in the air than the rest, but…"

An arm curled supportively around her and she turned her head to see Tao looking down at her, wearing a sympathetic expression. "It's okay," Tao assured her. "We will find out who did it, somehow. In the meantime, someone will clean it."

She shook her head. "I'll do it."

"No," they all objected at once.

"It's my car." Hers, it was her baby…and someone had vandalized it. Sure, it was only a little paint, but dammit, that wasn't the point. Her territorial shifter nature made it even harder for her to keep calm. Rage was coursing through her, making her grind her teeth and ball her hands into tight little fists. "I'm going to kill them."

"Get in line," said Ryan.

Tao took one of her fists and uncurled it. "Come on, come inside."

"Go," said Trey. "We'll take care of this. Go inside." He knew he'd probably sounded a little sharp with her, but he didn't like seeing another male's arm around her. In fact, he wanted to snap it off.

She sighed. "I—"

"No."

Her wolf calmed a little when he came close, but he didn't touch her, even though she needed it, even though he would feel that she needed it. "It's my car," she repeated, knowing that it didn't really have any bearing on the matter of who cleaned it. She was simply too pissed off to think right.

"You don't need to see this. Whoever did this did it to upset you. Don't give them what they want."

"Says the world's worst brooder," she couldn't help muttering through clenched teeth.

"Taryn, we'll take care of it." He raised his hand to touch her face, but then he dropped it again. More than anything he wanted to comfort and calm her with his touch, and that was exactly why he didn't. "Go," he urged softly.

Relenting, she allowed Tao to lead her inside, but she didn't go into the living area to relax the way everybody was advising her to. No, she went straight back to the kitchen and over to the onions to continue dicing them. Grace opened her mouth as though to object, but a warning look from Taryn kept her quiet. Taryn didn't want to relax, didn't want to talk, didn't want to be alone with her thoughts and her anger. She just wanted a distraction.

While she and Grace worked on the evening meal, Marcus and Trick spoke to every member of the pack, trying to establish each person's whereabouts over the past few hours. Cam, Rhett, and Brock were the only ones who didn't have alibis, Marcus informed her as they ate the evening meal. Of course everyone was straining to listen to their conversation, and she got the feeling that that was the whole idea—that the guys were closely monitoring the expressions of the others as Marcus told her everything they knew. Taryn still wasn't convinced that Selma hadn't had something to do with it, but apparently Kirk and Hope stated that she had been with them the whole time. She wouldn't put it past Kirk and Hope to lie for Selma though.

It wasn't a surprise that Trey barely spoke to her, let alone touched her, through the evening meal, even though he had to sense how much her wolf was craving comfort from her mate. Nor was it a surprise when she went to bed alone or when he didn't lie beside her when he finally did join her. But it still burned. Not just in a physical sense, but in an emotional sense. She hated herself for that. Herself and him, in fact.

Instead of the burning easing over the next few days as she resigned herself to the way her mating with Trey was going to be, it only worsened. It wasn't just because of her wolf's hunger for contact with her mate. Taryn the woman wanted Trey the man, which made absolutely no sense, given that they barely interacted or touched. But when they did interact and they did touch… Ah, hell.

None of this was good. Not a damn thing about this mating—other than her having escaped Roscoe—was good, but she wouldn't back out on a deal. That wasn't who Taryn was. It wasn't like she had anywhere to go even if she did leave. Her uncle still hadn't gotten back to her, if he even intended to.

And so the burning stayed and worsened as more days and nights passed with absolutely no change. Sure, there had been moments when she had been tempted just to jump on him and be done with it, but she didn't want scraps and neither did her wolf.

It was extremely annoying that Trey didn't appear to be going through the same struggle, but she ignored that annoyance, she ignored her urges, she ignored her wolf's pining, and she continued on as usual. But then one really shitty day came a few weeks later and she was seriously at risk of exploding with it all…The anniversary of her deceased mother's birthday.

CHAPTER EIGHT

Trey jumped to his feet as the door to his office suddenly burst open. Thinking that there must be some sort of emergency—and feeling a spike of fear that something might have happened to Taryn—he walked around the desk toward where Dante, Marcus, and Trick stood, scowling. His wolf had snapped to alertness and was pacing within him.

"What the hell did you do?" demanded Marcus.

Surprised by not only the question but by Marcus's insubordinate behavior, Trey frowned. "What the hell are you talking about?"

"Taryn. What did you do to her?"

His wolf went still. "What about Taryn?"

"You've been holed up in here all morning, so you wouldn't be aware that she's got the personality of a zombie right now. We can barely get any conversation out of her. She's not even responding to Greta's taunts—just looks through her like she's not even there. That's not Taryn."

No, it wasn't, and he had the sudden urge to go see her and find out what was wrong. Instead, he simply shrugged. "She seemed kind of quiet earlier, but other than that..."

"Yeah? Well, now she's really quiet. As in mute. That's when she's not telling us to get out of her way while she cleans every room."

"Cleaning?"

"Like Mary Poppins on crack. You know, the way women do that fast-forward cleaning when they're pissed off."

"It's not just that," said Trick, looking more worried than agitated. "It's like, I don't know…like one wrong word would break her. I'm not sure if she's angry or just trying to distract herself from something."

"What did you do to her?" repeated Marcus. "What did you say to her?"

"Maybe it's what he *hasn't* done or said," said Dante as he folded his arms across his broad chest.

Trey glared at him. "What's that supposed to mean?"

"You don't talk to her, Trey. In fact, you don't bother with her at all. You claimed her, brought her here, solidified the mating, and then handed her safety over to Tao. Look, I get that this is only supposed to be a temporary thing and so there's no need for you both to build a bond, but it's more than that. You purposely avoid her. You never touch her—don't try to tell me that's not driving your wolf crazy. And unless my hearing's suddenly gone to shit, you're not sleeping with her either."

"That's none of your business," snapped Trey.

Dante held up a placating hand. "With all due respect, this is our business because you're our Alpha male and, whether it's temporary or not, she's our Alpha female. Your relationship affects the rest of the pack. *And* we like her, we respect her, it's in our nature to protect our females. Right now there's something wrong with Taryn and you need to do something."

"You know, I hear you all whining, but look who's *not* here. Taryn. If she had a problem with me, I'd know about it. If her wolf was riding her too hard, she'd have come to me whether she wanted to or not."

Dante laughed, but there was no humor in it. "Is that what you think? She's not like the women you're used to, Trey. She's an Alpha. Her wolf's probably going just as crazy as yours is, but neither Taryn nor her wolf will ever come to you begging for some attention. Not ever."

"Maybe this isn't about you," said Trick. "Maybe it's something else eating at her; we don't know. We're worried about her and thought you might have some luck reaching her."

The urge to find her was fierce now, but again Trey shrugged. "She could be just having a rough day—"

"Christ, Trey," interrupted Dante. "She was there for you when you were in a bad state. She reached you while your wolf was feral, and you're going to ignore this?" He waved his hand dismissively at Trey and headed for the door. "Forget it. Hide some more, whatever."

Looking both disappointed and disgusted, the three males walked out of his office and left Trey alone with his thoughts, thoughts that revolved around Taryn. He had noticed that she seemed off—her odd mood had unnerved his wolf and had him clawing at Trey, wanting to get to her. But, as always, Trey had acted against his wolf's wishes and his own instincts and simply shrugged off his concern.

He wanted to do the same thing again now, but one thing was stopping him; as he had reached out through the pack link to sense her emotions, he'd hit a wall. She had somehow erected a big enough barrier around her that her own mate couldn't reach her. A person didn't do that unless a strong emotion was eating at her and she was trying desperately to hold herself together.

With a determined stride, he strolled out of the office and made his way to the living area, where the majority of the noise was coming from. The fact that her scent was stronger the closer he got told him that was where she was.

He entered the room. And stopped dead in his tracks. Across the room was Taryn, balancing on one of the dining chairs as she used a feather duster to tackle nonexistent cobwebs. But it wasn't Taryn. Taryn was life and fire and sensuality and adorable sarcasm. She was not quiet or expressionless or withdrawn or robotic.

Most of the pack, even Greta, was gathered in the room on the sofa facing the TV, but all eyes were fixed on Taryn. And all, even Greta, appeared concerned. So concerned that they only spared him a brief glance before turning their attention back to her.

Slowly he covered the space between them until he was beside the chair she was balanced on. She didn't look at him. But she wasn't ignoring him, he quickly realized. She was simply elsewhere in her mind. "Taryn?" he said softly. "Taryn, baby... you okay?" She double-blinked, as if snapping out of a daze, and then peered down at him. "Everything okay?" he asked again, really not liking the vacant look on her face.

Taryn nodded. "Fine." Why, of all the times, did he want to speak to her now—now, when he was the last person she needed to be around? The answer instantly came to her: because someone had sent for him—if they hadn't, he wouldn't have bothered with her.

She went back to her dusting and Trey realized he had just been dismissed. "Come on, baby, come down from there." No response. "I think we can safely say there isn't a speck of dust left up there." Nothing. Not even a sarcastic comment. His wolf was pacing again, not liking that she was obviously hurting. "How about you get down and we'll go get a cup of coffee?"

Taryn wanted to hit him. Why was he talking to her like she was an insane person having an episode? A better question would be, *Why won't he just leave?* And, as it happened, there was actually plenty of dust up here.

"Taryn, how—"

"Don't you have something to do in your office?"

Trey winced. He deserved that, he knew he did. "I'm not moving from this spot until you tell me what's wrong, baby," he told her gently.

"Good," she said as she hopped down from the chair. "That means you'll be a long way away from me, because I'm about to leave the room." She picked up the chair and carried it through the tunnel toward the kitchen, deliberately ignoring Trey as he trailed behind her. Tao wasn't far behind him. She returned the chair to the dining table and put the duster back in the cupboard before going to the sink to wash her hands. Noticing there were a few mugs and dishes on the counter, she stacked them into the sink and filled it with hot, soapy water.

"What is it, baby? Tell me what's wrong."

That was now the fourth time he had called her *baby*. Cheeky bastard. If he thought he could block out her existence but then still expect her to confide in him, he was seriously mistaken. Taryn would have told him that, but she didn't want to argue with him; she just wanted him to go back to his hidey-hole and leave her to grieve her mother in peace.

Taryn knew that her method of grieving wasn't normal, that shutting off from the world around you while your body went on autopilot and you disappeared in your thoughts and memories was not good. It was the same state she had slipped into when her mom and Joey were in the accident. Although she had eventually dug her way out of it, she always tended to retreat on the anniversary of their deaths or either of their birthdays. It was just how she coped. The only way she could cope without screaming.

But having Trey around her—someone who frustrated and annoyed the hell out of her and had her wolf all messed up—was threatening the stability of her seemingly indifferent state. All that frustration and annoyance that she had been shoving aside was at risk of bursting out of her. If that happened, she would break. She couldn't afford to do that.

"Come on, leave those and come sit with me."

Ignoring him in the hope that he would go away, Taryn continued scrubbing the dishes.

"Taryn, you can't tell me you're not upset about something."

Realizing he was closer now, she warned in a low voice, "Back off, Trey."

"Back off?"

"Yes."

"You want me to back off?" It was one thing when Trey assumed she just didn't want to talk about whatever it was that was bugging her, but it was another thing altogether for her to want to freeze him out.

"Yes, I want you to leave me alone. It shouldn't be too hard. You do it easily enough any other time."

"Is that what this is about? You're mad at me for not spending time with you?"

A short, humorless laugh escaped her. "Yes, because the world revolves around you."

"Then what is it?"

"Like I said, just back off."

"I won't back off. Not until you tell me what's wrong."

Deep breaths, she told herself. And those deep breaths actually worked. The tension didn't leave her body, but it eased a little. Until hands wrapped around her middle and a large body pressed against her back. Making it even worse, he whispered into her ear, "What's wrong, baby?"

There was that word again! Something inside her snapped. Abruptly she spun, splashing water everywhere. Shocked, Trey jumped back out of the way. "Didn't I tell you to back off? I'm pretty sure that's what I said."

He held his hands up in a calming gesture. "Taryn—"

"Just stay away from me. That's all I'm asking you to do. It's something you do every single fucking day, so *why*, on this one day that I really need a little alone time, am I suddenly of interest to you?"

"I just want to know what's wrong."

"Well, that's tough shit, psycho boy, because I don't want to talk to you!" Seeing that people were starting to gather was only making her worse. She suddenly felt like a cornered animal, like everyone was taking up her breathing space. Growling, she wiped her hands on the hand towel and then stalked toward the door. The crowd quickly parted, apparently not daring to intervene.

"Where're you going?"

"Away from you!"

Trey jogged down the tunnel after her. "Oh no, you don't get to shut me out like this. You're my mate."

She pivoted on the spot. "No, I'm not."

"What did you just say?" he asked softly, but in a very dangerous tone.

"We don't count as mates if you only act like it when it suits you. But, hey, don't get me wrong—if putting on an act for other people is as far as it goes for you, then that's fine. But don't you *dare* throw that 'you're my mate' shit at me when I won't do what you want!"

He knew she was right, but the denial was automatic. "You *are* my mate, Taryn."

"Is it fun in La La Land? It must be, because you go there a lot." Out of patience, she spun and began stalking away.

"For God's sake, Taryn, will you stop walking away from me?" Trey honestly wasn't sure what happened…He'd reached out and placed his hand on her shoulder and the next thing he knew he was flat on his back on the ground and Taryn was snarling down at him. Damn, the woman knew some good moves.

"*Back. Off,*" she growled. She looked up at the others, who were slowly edging toward them, their expressions unsure. "*All* of you back off! I want to be *alone!*" Then she was striding out the main door, down the mountain, across the small, open field, and into the forest.

Many times she had gone on a leisurely walk or a run through here with Tao, but never had she gone as far as she intended to go today. Plenty of times she had heard the sound of the river in the distance, had known it was there and known that one day she would really need to go there for some alone time.

The River Kids—that was what her mom and Joey's mom had called them. Some kids liked beaches, some kids liked swing parks, and she and Joey had liked rivers. No, they'd loved rivers. Loved the sounds, loved the surrounding wildlife, loved paddling in the shallow water and balancing on old tree branches that crossed the expanse of the river. There was something calming about them, she thought. Right now, she needed to calm the hell down.

On eventually reaching the river, she found a boulder to perch herself on and took a deep, cleansing, calming breath. Again and again she filled her lungs with the fresh, crisp forest air, letting it relax her. The familiar smells of wet earth and pine made her wolf ease a little within her. It was amazing how a place could relax you even as a barrage of sad memories hit you, Taryn mused.

A familiar guttural *tock* sound snagged her attention and made her look to the tree beside her. "Hey, LJ," she said around the frog in her throat. Why the bird followed her around sometimes she had no idea, but that had been another thing that she and Joey used to marvel at together—the way birds were so at ease with her, almost attracted to her.

Hey, Joe. I know that I shouldn't always come to you whenever I need to talk to someone, that I should actually try confiding in people who are alive...but they'd be able to tell me to shut up. And in truth, you're all I have.

As much as I really like these people here—with the exception of a few, including the evil and very senile version of Yoda—I still don't feel like I can really talk to them. Not even to say, "Hey, I miss my mom." Actually, no, it's not that I don't feel like I can talk to them, it's that I don't want to start opening up to them and getting too comfortable here. Snort. Not that there's really much chance of me getting comfortable with psycho boy around.

You know, I used to look at mated couples and I'd think how amazing it must be, that once you mated you'd never feel alone ever again, because that person would become a part of you. I mean, I know that my mating with Trey doesn't count in an emotional sense, but I still didn't expect this feeling of being...trapped. I'm bound to someone who won't even touch me socially, who deliberately avoids me—unless I want to be left alone; apparently, I'm interesting to him then—and he has my wolf enthralled. And how is it that he's able to get my wolf so enthralled with him anyway? That shouldn't be possible. She's such a traitor sometimes.

It's freaking shit, the lot of it. I should be able to turn around to the person I'm mated to, even if it's only temporary, and say, "You know what, it's my mom's birthday today and I miss her," but I don't even feel like I can talk to him like that. See, you really are all I have.

A noise in the distance pulled her from her conversation with Joey. So she hadn't been left alone after all, and they'd apparently thought she wouldn't realize it. The bastards.

So this was what Taryn had been feeling like, mused Trey as he sat at the kitchen table tapping his fingers on the surface. It hadn't occurred to him that establishing a distance between them could actually be a bad thing, that it could actually hurt her. But the way Taryn had frozen him out, walked away from him, pulled away from his touch...it hurt.

She was his mate. No, not of the soul or heart, but she was still his mate and she had ordered him away from her. She had rejected his comfort. Generally he wasn't a guy who offered comfort, but this was his mate. And she didn't want him. A part of him knew that it shouldn't hurt this much, but he didn't want to think on that or he would have to address the question of why it hurt like this.

What bothered him more than any of that was that she was clearly nursing some sort of emotional ache. One strong enough to make her withdraw from everyone and everything around her. His strong Taryn was close to breaking, and he couldn't do a damn thing about it. That sense of helplessness was eating at both him and his wolf, increasing his need to find her and soothe her.

Suddenly Tao appeared, panting. "Trey, we got a problem."

Instantly he was on his feet. "What?"

"Taryn. I can't find her."

"What do you mean you can't find her?"

"I did what you said—I stayed a good distance away but was close enough to hear if there was a problem. Maybe she heard me and got pissed off that someone had followed her. I don't know, but I can't find her."

"Shit." So a large party of them searched. Searched every single inch of the forest, checked every tree, even the river. But there was no sign of her. It was obvious she had stopped at the river for a while, but then she seemed to have taken off while covering her tracks. And damn if she wasn't good at covering her tracks.

With each minute Trey became more concerned and his wolf grew more restless, understanding that his mate was hurting and missing. For a split second, Trey wondered if she'd done something stupid while so emotional, but the thought left his head instantly. Taryn would never take the coward's way out of anything.

"Okay," said Dante as they came to a halt outside the forest. "Let's put ourselves in Taryn's shoes. She wanted to be alone. Nothing more than that, right?"

"Yes, so she came out here," said Trick.

"But we wouldn't let her be. And I doubt that while she was in that foul mood she was too pleased about her simple wish being ignored like that."

"Definitely not," agreed Marcus, "but she didn't come and verbally kick our asses, and that doesn't sound like her."

"It's worth pointing out that she wasn't at all herself," Dominic said with a shrug.

"But she *will* have been utterly pissed and insulted by the idea that we thought we could still follow her and think she wouldn't know," said Tao.

"Do you think maybe she's been teaching us a little lesson about how *not* stupid she is?" asked Ryan.

It fell into place suddenly. Trey smiled. "Something like that. She's been leading us on a merry chase. I know where she is."

Everyone's expressions begged, *Where?*

"She's back inside the caves. I'll put money on it. She'll have known that if she made it look as though she was missing, we'd come out searching for her."

"Leaving the caves empty apart from a few," said Ryan.

"And giving her what she wanted," finished Trey, "the simple chance to be alone." It was a brilliant plan, he had to admit. She had totally played them, and played them well.

"Shit," cursed Trick. "I can't believe we've been out here for hours and she's been in the house all along. You're sure?"

"It sounds like something she'd do," said Marcus.

It turned out that was exactly what she'd done, although at first Trey had wondered if he'd been wrong, as she wasn't in the kitchen or living area or in their bedroom. If he hadn't picked up her scent in the second-floor tunnels, he might have ended up back on that merry chase.

Following her scent, he soon found himself outside one of the guest bedrooms—not that they ever had guests. There were no sounds coming from inside, but he was certain that she was in there. Slowly and quietly he turned the doorknob and opened the door. His chest tightened at the sight before him. Taryn was curled up on the bed, asleep, with dried tears on her red cheeks. She was cuddling something, he noticed a few seconds later.

As he carefully closed the door and crept closer, he realized that it was a shoe box. One that she had had for a while, if the bad state of the cardboard was anything to go by. Curious, he sat beside her and gently took the faded white box from between her now limp arms. As he removed the lid, his chest tightened again. Inside were inconsequential little things—a net bag of marbles, a large, shiny stone, a plastic engagement-type ring, a miniature plush bear, and some homemade Christmas and birthday cards and other bits and pieces. But these little things meant everything to Taryn, because they had obviously either belonged to her true mate or been given to her by him.

Spotting a little velvet book, he flipped it open and realized it was actually a photo album. Even when she was a little girl, Taryn's hair had had all those different shades running through it. She looked just as fiery and energetic. The kid who Trey guessed was Joey had clearly been besotted with her. In every picture he was standing protectively close to her, hugging her or holding her hand. Trey wasn't proud of the twinge of jealousy he felt at how the little kid had been more or less born with rights to her.

Inside the final two photo sleeves were small, laminated cards. One had a picture of the kid on it, along with his date of birth and the date he had died with a small sort of "rest in peace" type of message. On the other was a picture of a woman who looked uncannily like Taryn. Her mom, he quickly realized, noting that the date of her death matched the date of the kid's. And then something else registered in his brain. Her mother's birthday...it would have been today.

Well, shit. He bowed his head and squeezed his eyes shut as it dawned on him. She had been grieving her mom today, had been probably screaming inside as the agony tormented her, but instead of coming to him—her mate—for any kind of comfort or even to just confide in him or cry on his shoulder, she had retreated within herself.

Because she hadn't felt like she could come to him, had probably thought that he wouldn't want her to.

Then when he, like a bastard, refused to give her the space she needed, she had finally sought comfort. The fact that the only place she thought she could find it was a shoe box filled with memories of her dead true mate was like a blow to Trey's gut. A blow he deserved.

Guilt knifed through him as he thought about how much of a prick he had been to Taryn. Dante was right. Although this mating was temporary, that didn't mean that Trey should be able to just cast her aside. She had become his responsibility the second he claimed her, but all he'd done was try to escape that responsibility when he got a little spooked by his wolf and some primal instincts. He had frozen her out, just as she had done to him today. The feelings of rejection, anger, and desolation he had experienced earlier were things that she had obviously been suffering with all this time. In total silence.

Shit, she hadn't deserved that, hadn't deserved his cold shoulder, especially when she was being so loyal to their deal.

It was a wonder that she hadn't left—it wasn't as if she couldn't have sneaked off. It was clear by the way she had led them on a merry chase and covered her tracks so well that she had the ability at least to try to make a run for it. It wasn't as though fear of him kept her here. She hadn't once expressed any fear of him, not even when his wolf had gone feral. Although Roscoe was dead and she didn't need Trey anymore, she had stayed to fulfill her end of the deal. Even though he'd been a total ass. Even though his grandmother constantly strove to make her feel unwelcome. Even though it meant having to lie to her friends and repeatedly claim that her true mate had been nothing but a good friend.

One thing was for sure—she was a better person than he would ever be. She was someone who any male would be proud to have as his mate, temporary or not.

He wished she was his true mate, even though that made him an absolute bastard as far his actual true mate was concerned. But Summer had just been a baby. A tiny, screaming baby who had been dumped in his arms while her mom rooted through her handbag for keys. The second she had landed in his arms she had stopped wailing and looked up at him. The next thing he knew, her mom was flapping excitedly, saying stuff like "instant connection" and "true mate."

Instead of being happy, he'd been scared. At fourteen years old, it had felt too damn weird to him to be told he had a strong bond to a tiny little baby. It had even made him feel a little ill. The fact that he hadn't felt the tug of the bond made the whole thing worse, reminding him just how closed-off he actually was. So he had stayed away from Summer and kept totally quiet about it. Her mom had promised to give him time to get used to the idea before telling anyone. But then two months later she'd fallen asleep in her cradle and hadn't woken up.

Unlike Taryn, he'd never had a chance to know his true mate. The only picture he had of her was the one in his mind, and that image was of a little baby with the same features that most babies had. He had been disloyal to that little girl from the second he found her. He didn't have anything at all that had once belonged to her, didn't even have any memories of her. Taryn, on the other hand...She had kept her true mate's memory alive as best she could. But for Trey and for the deal she had made with him, she had publicly renounced that kid whom she'd adored and who had obviously adored her in return.

And Trey had trampled all over her and her feelings, being as neglectful to her as he had been of his true mate.

Well, enough of that shit. The mating might be temporary, but for as long as this female was here she was his to respect and care for and protect—especially to protect from himself and his asshole ways. It was the least she deserved, but more than that, it was what he wanted. He knew that even if—by some miracle—he was to mate with someone permanently in the future, this temporary mating he had with Taryn would probably be the closest he would ever get to having a true mate, because she was everything he would have wanted. He doubted he would ever meet anyone else like her.

Placing the shoe box on the floor, Trey carefully lay down behind her and locked his arm around her waist as he curled his body around hers. His wolf released a rumbly growl of contentedness, but right now Trey wasn't doing this to appease his wolf or feed a hunger. He was doing it because Trey the man wanted to hold her.

If it hadn't been for the hunger pang in her stomach, Taryn probably wouldn't have woken. Not while she was so comfortable and warm and relaxed. And certainly not while her wolf was so at ease, having Trey snuggling up to her. Wait, what? Instantly her eyes shot open and she tensed.

"You wouldn't believe how many times I've woken up to find myself curled around you like this."

She would have told him to fuck off and give her the breathing room she had asked for—no, demanded—but there was something different about his voice. The gruffness she had gotten used to was gone. There was a new softness to his tone, a tenderness she hadn't heard before. Both of which she had to be imagining, along with the hand that was affectionately fondling her hair.

"I'm really sorry about your mom."

She stiffened even more. "You went through the shoe box." Through her very personal things. She was just getting ready to snap at him for it when he surprised her by brushing her hair aside so he could kiss along her neck. Damned if her neck wasn't hypersensitive.

"You look a lot like her." He kissed his way up the curve of her neck and grazed his teeth over her ear before sucking the lobe into his mouth, eliciting a gasp from her. "I love how responsive you are."

"Okay, this is where you explain to me what the hell you're doing." She had meant to sound abrupt and firm, but the words had come out kind of breathy. "I asked to be alone."

"And I don't blame you. I wouldn't want to be around me either." Wanting her soft and relaxed so that she didn't bolt before he had a chance to talk to her—and just because he liked to taste and touch her skin—he continued to kiss her neck and ear while at the same time snaking his fingers beneath her sweater to caress her stomach. "You have the softest skin."

"Now I'm really confused. What is this? Your idea of comforting me?" She didn't want him touching her because he felt sorry for her. In fact, she didn't want him touching her at all, or at least that was what she told herself.

"This is me saying I realize I've been a prick and it's going to stop."

"What?"

As he swiped his tongue over his mark, she shuddered, deeply satisfying both him and his wolf. "I shouldn't have kept my distance from you the way I did. I shouldn't have frozen you out."

"No, you've been doing the right thing by trying to keep a distance. We don't want to imprint." It was getting hard to follow the conversation now that his touch was becoming less gentle and more seductive.

"Just because we don't want to imprint on each other doesn't mean I should be delegating you to someone else like you're a duty. There is a halfway measure between keeping a distance and imprinting."

"And what's that?"

"Fun." He slid his hand over her jeans and rubbed against her clit, relishing her moan. "We can have that, can't we?"

"I take it by fun, you mean sex." Surprising her, he flipped her around to face him and cupped her face. His expression was serious.

"I'm not just talking about that. I'm talking about us spending time with each other the same way people who are in a casual relationship do."

"What's brought all this on?"

Unable to resist those lips, he leaned forward and nipped at them. "When you froze me out earlier, it hurt, but I realized I deserved it. I got to thinking about the way I've been acting, and the way I *haven't* been acting. Like I told you that first night, I claimed you and you're my mate, whether this is short-term or not. It's time I started treating you like it." He licked his tongue along the seam of her mouth, tempting her to open for him. The little witch didn't. Obviously his explanation wasn't good enough. "I'm not much good at verbal apologies, baby, but I am good at oral ones."

"Oral ones?" His meaning became clear as he gently pushed her onto her back and began sliding down her body. She gripped him by the head, keeping him still—which happened to place his mouth level with her breasts. So he grazed one of the nipples poking through her sweater with his teeth. "Where do you think you're going?"

"I need to apologize. It's really very important."

She wouldn't laugh, she wouldn't. "Look, as much as it would be nicer if we could actually interact, that doesn't mean that sex has to enter the equation."

He stiffened. "Are you saying you don't want me?"

"I'm saying I don't want someone who doesn't want me."

"Where the hell did you get the idea that I don't want you?"

"I'm not your type. Don't even dare lie and say that I am."

"I admit you're not the type I've gone for in the past, but I've realized it's been a mistake to overlook slender blondes with heart-shaped asses and breasts like these." Leaning up on his elbows, he bunched up her sweater and cupped her bra-clad breasts. "See how perfectly they fit in my hands."

He sounded awfully pleased about that, enthralled by the idea. "Trey, I—"

"Just this once, baby, don't fight me. I'm not saying submit," he added quickly before she snapped his neck. "I'm just asking you to lie back and let me make you come. This isn't foreplay; this is me wanting to make you feel good. Me apologizing."

"You don't want anything in return?" she asked, doubt clear in her voice.

He shook his head. "No sexual favors for me, no fucking. Just me making you come. In a way, I'm sort of being your slave right now. You might want to make the most of that, because it won't happen again."

Was he really suppressing his need to dominate—a need she knew was intense? Was he seriously offering to make this all about her? It wasn't sympathy driving him, she could see that. He was genuinely contrite and genuinely wanted simply to give her pleasure with no demands attached. "Then get to it," she said with a smile.

Returning her smile, Trey tackled the front clasp of her bra and brushed both cups aside so that they framed those breasts he'd missed. He latched on to her nipple and sucked hard, making her gasp and moan. At the same time he shaped her ribs, the flat of her stomach, and her hips with his hands.

God, he loved her body, loved the way his large hands could span her waist. She fit his body in a way that no woman ever had. It still amazed him that the difference in their sizes didn't make things awkward. Instead, it was as though his body had a perfect groove for her slender form to fit into, and that only increased his possessiveness.

When he transferred his attention to her other breast and closed his mouth over her neglected nipple, Taryn moaned again and clutched his head to her. She knew that her grip on his head had to be causing him some pain, but she couldn't quite let go of him. The pleasure was building the friction within her, and he was the only anchor she had to keep her from going mindless.

A part of her thought she'd given in too easily to him, that she should have told him to go shove his apology up his ass. But one thing she knew about Trey was that, like all Alphas, he had a lot of pride, and one thing that was hard for him to do was admit he was wrong. Not only had he done that, but he had apologized. And now he was reaffirming that apology in the only way a highly sexual being in unfamiliar territory knew how.

Releasing the taut bud with a pop, he told her, "I'm going to taste you now." Trey could smell the mouthwatering scent of her arousal from where he was—enticing him and luring him. He began to nip and suck and kiss his way down her body. He couldn't hold back a growl as he saw that most of his marks had completely faded. The only one that would never fade was his claiming mark, and Trey told himself and his wolf that that was enough.

Ignoring the urge to replace his marks, he tackled the buttons of her jeans and peeled both them and her black, lacy thong from her body. Then he settled himself between the V of her thighs, inhaling deeply to take that feminine scent inside him. Satisfaction flooded him at how wet her pussy was. Gently pulling her glistening, slippery folds apart, he bent his head and swept his tongue between them. And groaned. *Fuck.* Her spicy, seductive taste burst on his tongue, urging him to feast on her. So he did.

Taryn writhed and moaned as he worked her into a frenzy, using long sensual licks. His tongue constantly teased her opening, but never delved inside. It was torture and it was pleasure and it was goddamn unfair.

Frustrated, she was helplessly squirming and arching. If he was hoping she would beg, he was in for a disappointment. She had warned him in the beginning that she never begged, not for anyone. But she couldn't take any more teasing, she couldn't. She tried escaping his hold, but his hands tightened on her thighs, claws digging warningly into her skin, and he growled. The rumble sent vibrations shooting up her core and through her body, sizzling all the way to her extremities.

She was ready to smack him over the head when she suddenly felt the lash of his tongue to her clit. Then his tongue was swirling around it as a finger speared inside her and she groaned, melting into the mattress. He growled again—this one was approving.

Trey knew that Taryn wouldn't last much longer, that she really needed to come, but he couldn't bring himself to part with her taste. It was like an aphrodisiac to him, because it was creamy and zesty and *his*. For as long as she was mated to him, every part of her was his; this pussy that he loved feeling around his cock was his, and he needed to hear her say it.

Abruptly he shoved another finger inside her, making her cry out and buck. "Who does this pussy belong to?" he gritted out as he curved his fingers inside her while pressing his thumb on her clit so that his hand was clamped around her. Eyes glazed with lust met his.

"Shut the fuck up, Trey, and make me come."

He thrust his fingers deep and again she bucked and cried out. "Whose is it, Taryn?"

"As I'm the one who cleans it, waxes it, keeps it tidy, and has it medically checked, I'd say it's mine. But you can borrow it if you like."

He couldn't hold back a smile. "If you want to come, you better be careful, baby, or I might just stop."

"That's fine. You've laid the foundations. My vibrator will take care of the rest."

"No fake cocks. This"—a thrust of his fingers—"is mine. The only cock that goes inside here is mine. Nothing else, no one else. Say it."

"I would," she rasped, "but I don't believe in telling lies."

"I mean it, Taryn. Nothing and no one goes inside you except me." He flicked her clit with his tongue. "I don't share what's mine."

"Now that's a lie, because I've heard that you and Tao have double-teamed some of your girlfriends in the past."

It surprised him that Tao had told her. "That was different." He suckled gently on her clit, smiling at how close she was to coming. He wouldn't let her until he'd heard what he wanted to hear. Needed to hear.

"Yeah?" she breathed.

"Yeah, I didn't consider them mine. I didn't mark them as mine. And if you don't tell me right now that this hot little pussy here is mine, I'll keep you hanging like this."

"You motherfucking, ass-licking, son of a goddamn cock-sucking bitch!"

It took effort not to laugh. "All the teasing will be over the second you tell me what I want to hear." Instead, she shook her head, growling. He rose to his knees and gripped his cock through his jeans with his free hand. "See this, baby? This is yours. I'll give you as much cock as you want, whenever you want. It's yours. And this"—he plunged his fingers hard inside her—"is all mine. No other cock except mine. Say it."

Again she growled, clawing his pectorals enough to tear his T-shirt but not enough to draw blood. "Just make me come, you miserable bastard!"

He slashed his claws in a diagonal line from her breast to her hip. "Fucking say it."

Taryn kicked at him but he didn't remove his hand, only cupped her harder. She could see by the tight line of his lips that he wasn't going to drop this. "No other cock except yours. There, I said it!"

"And why is that, Taryn? Why does nothing or no one go inside this tight pussy except me?"

"Because it's yours," she growled.

"That's my good girl." In one quick movement, he withdrew his fingers, gripped her ass, curled her hips, and stabbed his tongue inside her. Her back arched as she gave a loud cry. Her fingers threaded through his hair, tugging painfully, but he didn't give a shit. Not while her taste was in his mouth and her perfect ass was in his hands and she was making those goddamn noises.

He continued fucking her relentlessly with his tongue and then, when he sensed her orgasm was close, he pulled her ass cheeks apart and plunged one wet finger into her ass. She screamed as her release hit and, unable to help himself, Trey moved his mouth to her inner thigh and bit down hard, sucking and licking and marking. Quickly he realized that he hadn't bitten her to placate his wolf. He'd done it because Trey the man wanted to mark her.

CHAPTER NINE

Taryn was still panting and vibrating with aftershocks when Trey kissed his way up her body and lay down beside her, gathering her against him. Although his eyes had darkened with lust, he wasn't making any moves on her. In fact, he seemed pretty content just to play with her hair. As much as she appreciated his selflessness, a part of her wanted him to be a little selfish right about now, because she really wanted his cock inside her.

"Tell me about your mom."

There went her arousal. When she hesitated answering, he gave her a reprimanding look. He didn't want to be frozen out again.

"She was—this is going to sound mean. She was dizzy."

"Dizzy?"

"Yeah," she chuckled. "Wherever she went she'd leave something behind. The worst part was she wouldn't even realize she'd left anything until someone asked her if it was hers. Common sense was something she lacked, but that was one of the things that everyone loved about her, because she could always make them laugh. Oddly enough though, she was good with money. You'd have thought that her dopiness would have interfered with her money-management skills, but no, she was great with numbers."

"You two were close?"

She nodded. "I think one of the reasons she doted on me so much was that I was her only child. She and my dad tried for more, but for whatever reason, she never got pregnant again. I knew she felt guilty about that, like she'd let my dad down."

"Was your dad just as doting until he realized you were latent?"

"No. As a female, I was already a disappointment to him."

Trey made a derogative snort. "That guy really is an asshole." He gentled his voice as he asked, "How did she die?"

Again she hesitated and again he gave her that look. "My mom and Joey's mom were close friends. Every Sunday they'd go to the market in town and take me and Joey with them. On this one day, I couldn't go because I was in the basement—"

"The basement?" There was something in the sound of her voice that had his hackles rising.

"It was my dad's version of a punishment."

"He used to *confine* you?" Hell, that would be bad for any kid, but for a shifter…

"It's all part of that 'him being an asshole' thing. Anyway, on the way into town, some totally blitzed guy in a banged-up Chevy crashed into them, sent them toppling over…It was thought that the three of them were unconscious when it went up in flames. The drunken bastard was fine."

Trey held her tightly to him and kissed her hair. "It's weird just how similar our situations are."

Taryn pulled back to meet his gaze. "What do you mean?"

"Both of us lost our mothers and true mates. Both of us were lumbered with assholes for fathers. Both of us have to deal with bold inner wolves."

"How did they die?" When he just stared at her, she growled. "Wait, I'm supposed to lay it all out, but you get to remain a closed book? I don't think so, Flintstone. Get talking."

Not wanting to, but knowing she was right, he sighed and nodded. "There weren't just the sixteen of us when I left the pack. My mom came. The separation from my dad—she wasn't strong enough to deal with it and she turned rogue. Then I killed her. She'd attacked Marcus…"

When he paused midsentence and Taryn saw the pain in his eyes, she couldn't help but stroke his chest and snuggle closer. He shot her one of those macho "I don't need comfort" looks. "I'm not sympathizing with you, I'm just cold."

"As for my true mate…Her name was Summer." That was the first time he'd spoken her name in a very long time. "She was two months old when she died in her sleep."

Taryn's heart clenched at the idea. "You said when we first met that you hadn't acknowledged her?"

"I was fourteen, she was a baby…It felt weird and I acted like a dumb shit. Then when I heard she was dead…Let's just say I didn't take it too well and I made a mess of my room. My dad put two and two together and teased me about it."

"*Teased* you?" Rage and protectiveness surged through her, making her wish the bastard was alive so she could kick his ass.

"He thought the whole thing was funny, because something had finally gotten an emotional reaction from me. He wanted me to cry. See, I'd never cried, no matter what he did to me, and he hated that. I'd always stay stoic and take every punch, refusing to give him the reaction he wanted. Even as he teased me about Summer, I couldn't cry. It's just not in me to do that, I guess."

"You're right, he was an asshole. So am I right in thinking that it was the teasing that made you lose it and beat him up so bad you almost killed him?"

He nodded. "I'd put up with his shit for years, but everyone has a limit, and that day he found mine and pushed it. I'm not sorry. Not even now that he's dead. If he was here right now, I'd do it all over again, and I'd enjoy it." He wanted her to know who he was, what he was capable of. He wanted to know if she could handle it. She didn't disappoint him.

"And I'd be cheering you on."

Sliding his hand to her nape, he brought her face to his and kissed her hungrily, lashing her tongue with his and nibbling on her lips. The urge to plunge inside her and take her over was eating at him. Making it worse was that the scent of her arousal still flavored the air. Shit, he deserved a goddamn award for his restraint.

The sound of her stomach rumbling had Taryn chuckling into Trey's mouth. "I need feeding."

"I've already eaten," he said with a wicked smirk. He tapped her bare ass lightly. "Come on, let's get you some food."

Five minutes later Taryn was fully clothed again and accepting a piggyback ride from Trey, who rushed her into the kitchen. The entire pack was there, other than Cam, who was on guard duty. All were smiling, with the exception of Greta, Kirk, Selma, and Hope. Taryn could only assume they had overheard her and Trey having some quality time together, or had guessed by the sight of his slashed T-shirt, which he had purposely left on.

There was someone else who wasn't smiling, she suddenly realized. Tao's expression was carefully blank. Before she had the chance to wonder on that, Grace came and handed Taryn— who was seated on the counter with Trey standing beside her—a plate with a few slices of watermelon, and also a candy bar, just because she was an angel. "It's good to have you back."

She took the plate gratefully. Grace always took care of her. Then she topped it off by handing her a mug of coffee. "I think I love you."

"So the hussy's back, is she?" sneered Greta, glaring at Taryn like she was a giant turd.

Taryn only smiled. "Is there no way you could just pull your bottom lip over your head and swallow?"

Dante's drink sprayed out of his mouth as he went into a fit of coughing.

"I'd have shoved this piece of watermelon in your mouth if I didn't like it so much." Taryn saw Dominic biting his bottom lip and just *knew* he was doing his best to bite back a dirty chat-up line. Perv.

"While you and Taryn were, um, busy," Rhett said to Trey, "I checked our pack web for messages. Turns out there're a lot of Alphas interested in discussing an alliance with you, Trey. The new Alpha of Roscoe's pack included."

Taryn laughed. "I had a feeling he might get in touch through the pack web. He seemed too terrified of Trey to come back here."

"There was someone else too." He looked at Taryn then. "Your dad. Only he wants to set up a meeting to discuss it in person. Any idea why?"

"My dad likes to name-drop."

"Name-drop?" echoed Trick.

"There are different levels to an alliance. Most simply want the association with that pack, want to build the number of associations to look impressive."

"A little like people on social networks wanting to have a massive friends list?"

"Exactly. Others want an assurance that if they ever need to call on the pack in an emergency for backup of some kind, they'll get it. Then there are some who are a lot like people who enjoy boasting about all the important or influential people they know—like to drop names into conversations and claim that person is a close acquaintance in order to look impressive to others."

Trey folded his arms across his chest. "So, basically, your dad wants to be able to throw my name around to deter others from fucking with him, and maybe even call on me for protection?"

"Yep."

"Cheeky bastard. A basic alliance, sure. But the right to use me on a protective level? Hell no." After the way he'd treated Taryn, the man was lucky to still be breathing.

"The whole point of mating with me was to get an alliance with my dad. You can't let the fact that he's an asshole get in the way of your big plan."

Yeah, but Trey couldn't agree to this alliance without feeling as though he was being disloyal to his mate. God knew he'd hurt her enough already. "Rhett said a number of other Alphas are willing to discuss alliances. Maybe I won't need your dad."

"You've never needed him; you've never needed this mating," stated Kirk.

"I agree," said Selma, crossing her arms over her chest, accentuating her cleavage. "*She* has no place here."

"No Warner will ever have a place here."

Taryn shook her head. "This stuff is getting real old."

"Isn't that right, Hope?" pressed Selma, ignoring Taryn.

Hope gulped and nodded. "You've no place here."

"Why won't you listen to us, Trey?" Kirk sounded genuinely confused. "Darryl will never go through with this challenge—you have to know that."

"Son, why not just calm down," said Brock.

"Are you telling me that you support her being here? Support having a Warner around?"

Brock sighed. "No, I don't support it, and I don't think we'll get anything out of her being here. Nonetheless, we don't question our Alpha, you know that."

Sharply, Kirk stood and stalked out of the room. Selma and Hope followed closely behind him.

"Their lack of support isn't exactly a shock," said Dante, shrugging as if their input meant jack shit.

Trey nodded his agreement, then stood between Taryn's swinging legs and pulled her flush against him. "You're sure you'll be okay with me meeting up with your dad to sort out an alliance?"

"Do you honestly think I'd keep my mouth shut if I wasn't?"

He smiled. "Good point. All right, Rhett, set a meeting up for this weekend, somewhere that's neutral territory."

"You do know I'm coming, right?" said Taryn. Seeing that he was about to argue, she placed her index finger over his mouth. "I don't mind if you want to start ranting, just as long as you understand I'll be ignoring every word and I fully intend to be there. Any Alpha pair would go together to a meeting with another Alpha, you know that."

He nipped her finger, making her snatch it back and scowl. "This isn't just any Alpha. This is the asshole who was a complete and utter bastard to you throughout your entire life."

"I'm not sure why you'd want to be in the same room with him ever again after the way he just tossed you aside because of the latency," Ryan said, clearly in protective mode.

Taking in the sympathetic faces, Taryn sighed. "I take it this means you all know about my relationship—or lack thereof—with my dad."

Rhett pointed at Marcus. "It was him who told us all."

"Only because you were all talking about her like she was Warner's golden girl. His treatment was far from golden."

"Which is why I don't want you near him," Trey said to Taryn. His wolf was in full agreement.

She smiled sweetly and scraped her nails lightly down the column of his throat. "As cute as that is, it doesn't make an ounce of difference."

Again he wanted to argue with her, wanted to protect her from harm just as his wolf did, but now that Trey had come to know more about Taryn, he understood that how he handled this now would be very important. Throughout her entire life, people had seen it as their right to undermine her and disrespect her. If the male she had mated did that, it would hurt her deeply. Even his wolf understood that part of his job as protector was to protect her emotionally—something he hadn't been doing very well so far. So, groaning, he nodded and didn't let it show that her beaming smile had any effect on him.

"It's good to see you're starting to understand that I have a will of iron." Seeing Dominic's face scrunched up in agony, indicating that it was obviously killing him to hold back, she sighed tiredly. "Whatever the dirty line is, get it out of your system now."

Dominic shrugged innocently. "You like watermelon. It got me wondering...If *I* were a watermelon, would you spit or swallow my seed?" Some chuckled, some groaned, and Trey scowled at him.

"Okay, okay, I got a better one. If your left leg is Thanksgiving, and your right leg is Christmas, can I visit you between the holidays?" More people chuckled than groaned at him this time. Trey, of course, growled.

"Where do you hear these lines?"

"Some I've heard from other guys. Some I've read on the Internet or heard on TV."

Trey glared at him. "Well, you can stop using them on my mate."

Dominic gave him an apologetic look that couldn't have been more false. "I can't help it, she's like a dictionary—she brings meaning into my life." This time everyone groaned. "Oh, come on, that wasn't that bad."

The next few hours went as usual for the pack of an evening—they ate together in the kitchen, they watched TV together, Taryn and Greta exchanged more insults. But there were two major differences. One, Trey stayed with Taryn, as opposed to closing himself in his office. Two, for some unknown reason, Tao didn't appear to be talking to her.

It wasn't until just before she was ready to head to her room that she managed to catch a moment alone with Tao in the living area. "Would you like to tell me why you won't even look at me?"

As if she hadn't spoken, he rose from his seat on the sofa and started to leave the room.

She jumped up and placed herself in front of him. "Oh no, there'll be no walking away. You tell me what it is I've done."

Sighing, he ran his hand through his hair. She didn't think he was going to answer, but then he abruptly snapped, "You shut me out, Taryn." Gentling his tone, he continued, "I thought we were close. Close friends, I mean. And you totally shut me out. What's worse is that the person you opened up to is the one person who didn't deserve to have you confide in him like that."

She could understand why he might feel a little hurt. They had become good friends. Her wolf wasn't so understanding about his tone and was growling inside Taryn's head. "Today is my deceased mom's birthday." His mouth dropped open. "I actually hadn't told Trey. He found my box of memories and realized for himself."

"But he was still the person who brought you out of that daze. *Him.* Or do you just like being eaten out so much?"

Hands on her hips, she invaded his personal space. "Who do you think you are, speaking to me that way?"

He stepped back and raised his hands. "I'm sorry. I just don't understand why you'd let him use you. All he's done since the beginning is brush you off and now that he's decided he'll treat you like a mate, you're just going to give in to him, just like that? You deserve better than that."

"You're making him sound cruel, Tao. He was trying to avoid imprinting—"

"Yeah, I know, but I still think you deserve better. *I'd* never have hurt you like that, Taryn. Never."

As the meaning of his words registered, it was *her* mouth that dropped open as her hands slipped down from her hips.

"Yeah, that's right. Don't worry, I'd never poach—that's not who I am. Maybe once the battle's over and you're leaving"—he paused, shrugging—"maybe you'll think more about me then."

This time she didn't try to stop him from leaving the room. She didn't do anything, just stood there, frozen with shock. Should she have known this was how Tao felt? Sure, she'd noticed he was always around her a lot, but he was her bodyguard. He was supposed to be. And yeah, okay, he touched her a lot, but Marcus gave her shoulders a massage every single day and there was nothing going on there.

Why did it have to mean something if a guy was friendly? Couldn't platonic friendships between a male and a female exist anymore? This was so shit.

The sound of soft footsteps had her turning to see Dante entering the room. His expression was sympathetic. "You heard that." He nodded. There was no surprise on his face. "You already knew." He nodded again. "Everybody knows." Another nod. "Even Trey?"

"I'm not sure if he knows that Tao is prepared to leave the pack with you, but he knows Tao wants you."

"It hasn't caused any bad feelings between them, has it?" She'd leave before she came between two close friends. Her wolf growled at the idea of her leaving, but Taryn ignored her.

"No. Like Tao said, he'd never poach, and Trey knows that." He cocked his head and pursed his lips. "Would Tao have a chance with you if you left here?"

"There's no *if* I left here about it, Dante. Trey only wants this to be short-term, you know that."

"I'm not so sure about that. I've seen Trey with women. He's never treated any of them the way he treats you."

She snickered. "What, you mean totally shoving them aside?"

"As much as Trey's tough, we're all scared of something. And he's terrified of imprinting, Taryn. He saw firsthand what happens when a wolf turns rogue. He had to kill that wolf. As long as you don't imprint on each other, there's no chance of that happening to either of you if you separate."

She noticed he had again used the word *if,* but she didn't comment.

"When he made that deal with you, he hadn't considered that he might just come to like you in more than a physical sense. You brought out things in him that he wasn't prepared for, and it knocked him for a loop."

She shook her head. "That's just his wolf, Dante. Just his mating instincts. It's not Trey."

"He knew in advance that his wolf would be possessive, he knew his instincts would ride him hard—he'd been ready for all that. He hadn't been ready for how it would be if he himself felt those same things."

"You're wrong." The denial was automatic. Automatic because she'd come to the conclusion a long time ago that she could only ever rely on herself, that she would never have that total acceptance that came from a mate. She was defiant, sarcastic, snappy, contrary, stubborn, and strong-willed—not an attractive combination to male wolves, in her opinion. When she'd lost Joey, she'd also lost that one chance of being cared for exactly as she was, latency and all. Besides, this was Trey they were talking about, for God's sake! "There's no danger of us imprinting."

"I agree. There's something a lot bigger than that going on here."

"What's that supposed to mean?"

"That's something you both need to figure out on your own, but I'm not convinced either of you is ready to accept it yet."

Not liking that smug, all-knowing look on his face, she pushed past him and jogged to her room. In under a minute, she was stripped of her clothes and stood under the soothing, hot spray of the shower. There was no denying that this day had been one of the strangest of her life. On the plus side, at least it wasn't possible that it could get any stranger. But she didn't want to think about anything. Not her mom, not Joey, not Tao's confession, not Dante's dumb theory. All she wanted was to just forget about it all, just for a little while. She would decide what to do about Tao tomorrow, she really would, but right now she just needed to relax.

Finished in his office and ready to head to his room, Trey swung the office door open and frowned at the sight of Dante standing there with his hand ready to knock.

"Hey," said his Beta, dropping his hand. "I'm just passing on a message from Rhett. The meeting with Warner is scheduled for next Saturday morning at ten at Mo's Diner."

"Good."

"You don't sound all that excited."

"I don't?" asked Trey, hoping to sound aloof, as he stepped out of the office and closed the door behind him. In truth, the idea of making any kind of agreement with Lance Warner irritated both him and his wolf.

Dante sighed, rubbing his nape. "I don't like it either. Taryn might say it doesn't bother her, but it's got to piss her off a little."

"She's always known I wanted the alliance; she's never forgotten why she's here," Trey said a little defensively.

"Yeah. Would have been a lot easier using her like this if she was an evil heifer though." As Trey shrugged past him, Dante added, "I wouldn't expect her to be in a great mood when you see her."

Trey swerved. "Why's that?"

"Tao just dropped a bomb on her."

He didn't have to say anything more for Trey to understand. "I didn't think he'd tell her. Little fucker."

"Trey, come on, he's just overheard her screaming from an orgasm *you* were giving her, and he feels like you're treating her like a toy you can pick up when you feel like it."

"A toy? She's my mate." He would admit he'd been an ass to her, but never had he thought of her as a toy. Never had he disrespected her in his thoughts like that.

"I know that. Tao would never trespass on your territory and if you had mated with Taryn for life, then I doubt he would have said a word. Not that I'm making excuses for him. I'm not. It was a totally uncool thing to do, especially on a day when she's feeling so raw."

"She didn't know, did she?"

Dante shook his head. "She seemed a little worried that it might cause trouble between you and him, but I made sure she knew that wouldn't happen. I don't think it's a good idea to keep him as her bodyguard though."

"She won't need one. She has me." Trey was surprised his voice sounded human, considering that he was fighting his wolf from surfacing. His wolf wanted to hunt down the male who not only coveted his mate but had made it damn clear that he wanted her.

Dante grinned. "I like that answer."

Trey gave him a small nod and turned to leave, but then he spoke again.

"There's something else. Telling you probably isn't a good thing, but keeping it from you would be worse—you're my Alpha, and my friend. And I'd hate to see you throw something away without first realizing how important it is to you."

"Dante, English."

"Well, Tao basically indicated that if she was agreeable, he'd leave the pack with her when this was over and mate with her."

"What was that?" he growled. His wolf bucked and clawed at Trey, wanting to get out and rid the world of this male. Tao had to be having suicidal thoughts—that was all Trey could conclude from that. "I'm going to kill him."

In a blink Dante was directly in front of him, blocking his path. "No, no, no—Trey, man, just listen. I know Tao crossed a boundary by suggesting that to her while she's still mated to you, but he wasn't thinking right. He was jealous and hurt."

None of that meant jack shit to Trey or his wolf. Shoving his Beta aside, he stalked down the hallway in pursuit of his prey.

"If you go kick Tao's ass now, Taryn will leave."

His wolf snapped to attention at that and Trey halted in his tracks. No other words would have gotten through to him. His wolf didn't understand all the details around this matter, but he did understand cause and effect. If Trey acted on his anger and hurt Tao, his mate would leave.

"She won't stick around even one hour longer if she thinks she's coming between the two of you. I know you can't just switch off the anger, but man, you've got to choose which is more important—venting that anger, or making sure Taryn stays."

He was right. Trey knew he was right. But he was also right about something else. Trey couldn't switch off the anger just like that. "Dante…" The word was guttural.

"She'll leave, Trey. You touch Tao, she'll leave right now."

And Tao might leave with her. "What did she say when he told her?"

"He didn't give her a chance to say anything, just left the room. You can't really blame him for feeling that way about her."

"I don't. But what he did crossed a line."

"Yeah, and imagine how that's made her feel. She thought Tao was her friend and she's already had enough going on in her head today. Go to her. Make sure she's okay. Tao's suffering enough just by having to see you guys together." When Trey continued to hesitate, Dante sighed. "Tao or Taryn. Decide."

It was as she was rinsing the conditioner from her hair that Taryn felt a chill on her back, followed by the presence of a warm, muscular body behind her. Trey's scent swirled around her, comforting both her and her wolf. Without saying a word, he took the soapy sponge from the shelf, tipped her head forward, and washed every inch of her back. Then he moved on to her arms, her ass, her legs. Never was his touch anything but gentle. Then he turned her to face him and washed the front of her body in much the same way. At no point was his touch seductive, but somehow she was as turned on as all hell by the time he'd reached her thighs.

Abruptly Taryn knotted her hands in his hair and tugged his head down as she mashed her lips to his. He didn't require any coaxing. Groaning, he plunged his tongue into her mouth and made the kiss his own. There was nothing gentle about it; the selflessness of earlier had gone. He took, he dominated, he devoured, he conquered. She had never felt so taken in her entire life, and he was only kissing her.

Trey honestly hadn't joined her in the shower with the intention of seducing her. Not today, when her head was full with all kinds of crap. All he'd meant was to offer her some kind of comfort, to make sure she didn't feel alone, to ensure that she knew she wasn't alone. Any other day he might have had a little willpower, but not today, not when his own mind was all messed up.

The second she'd joined her lips to his, all his good intentions left him. All his pent-up arousal escaped into the kiss, into the way that he clutched her to him, into his groans and growls. The flirty scent of her arousal washed over him, luring him and urging him to taste her.

His entire body clenched as one of her hands trailed down his body and her soft fingers curled around him. She swiped her thumb over the head, smearing the drop of pre-come as she did. He sucked in a breath as she began to pump. Her grip was just how he liked it, firm and sure. Every wicked stroke intensified his need for her, his need to taste and fuck his mate—the same mate who was sneakily attempting to dominate him, to control the situation. His wolf approved of her attempt, of her feistiness, but just like Trey, he wasn't going to allow her to have the control.

A shudder ran through Taryn as a powerful fist tangled in her hair and snatched her head back before sharp teeth raked down her throat. The move was dominant and possessive and much approved of by her wolf, who quivered at each demonstration of his strength. Her back arched and her breasts pushed out, pressing her hard nipples against his chest and making her inhale sharply.

Looming over her, Trey seized her gaze. "I need your taste in my mouth, Taryn." He really did need it. Needed his senses to be full of her, his mate. His mate, who was there with him, not with Tao or anyone else, but him. He watched as defiance flashed on her face and she growled. Trey gripped her wrists, backed her into the tiled wall, and pinned her there with his body, keeping her hands high above her head. His rebellious little mate struggled just like he knew she would. "Yeah, baby, fight me. Fight me all you want, but you're not going to get dominance here."

Trey was coming to understand a few things about Taryn. He was learning that her problem with submitting went a lot deeper than just being an alpha female. She didn't want another person to have any power over her, didn't want to be vulnerable to anyone who could hurt her the way everyone else had. The only two people who had ever protected her in any way had been the same two people who were taken from her when she was just a kid. She hadn't been safe in a very long time. Hell, her own dad hadn't even protected her.

Trey's theory was that if he could get her to understand that he wouldn't abuse any power she ever gave him over her, then just maybe she wouldn't fight him so hard. Oh, she'd still be fiery and obstinate and spit strings of profanities at him, but she might just be more accepting of his dominance.

"Move, you piece of shit!" she growled as she squirmed wildly, snapping her teeth at him. She met his gaze boldly and unflinchingly, trying to stare him down.

"Keep fighting, baby. Shall I tell you what's going to happen when you stop? Shall I tell you how I'm going to reward you when you submit?" His voice was low and calm; he spoke at a slow and steady pace. "I'm going to carry you to the counter and sit you on the edge. Then I'm going to tell you to spread your legs. And you will. You will because you know how good it will feel when I taste you and fuck you with my tongue. Would you like to know what's going to happen after that?"

No, Taryn didn't want to know, because she could feel his sensual voice, full of temptation, beginning to weave a spell around her, and she didn't trust herself not to succumb to his wicked promises. His tone was deep, commanding, controlled, and dominant, much like that of a hypnotist. And it was making her wet. Her body was such a traitor sometimes.

Although she was still writhing, she had stopped snapping those teeth. Even better, Trey knew he had her full attention. "I'm going to slowly sink my cock into you, fill you up, and then I'm going to fuck you raw." Moving his mouth to her ear, he spoke in the same low, calm voice. "It'll feel so good, Taryn. It's okay to submit to me, because I'll respect that submission. I won't hurt you. You're safe with me." Instantly she froze and he guessed he'd surprised her. "You know that. You can feel it. Your wolf knows it."

Okay, so it turned out that it *was* possible for something to shock Taryn more than anything else that had happened today. The amount of assurance in those few words, *You're safe with me*, told her that Trey was fully aware of just how much her resistance to submitting was fueled by self-protection. He was right—she did believe she was safe with him, just as her wolf did. She was confident that he would never physically hurt her. It gave her a thrill to know that this strong, powerful male could easily hurt her, but he didn't.

"I don't want you to be a submissive wolf, baby. That's not what this is about. You're an Alpha female; I acknowledge that and I respect it. But I need you to respect that I'm an Alpha male. A very dominant Alpha male who wants you to submit to him— not become submissive, just submit to him in this."

Again he had surprised Taryn. He didn't want to change her, wasn't disregarding her own strength the way others had before him. Instead of making their battle for dominance all about physical strength and proving his will was stronger, he was promising to give her what she'd missed from her life since it became apparent that she was latent—respect and protection.

She knew he couldn't offer her the one other thing she was missing—just plain old someone to care about her—but he could give her those other things if she would trust her safety to him. And with that acknowledgment of who she was and what she needed, he had just earned her and her wolf's submission in a whole other way.

For a moment Tao's words came back to her, his implication that by giving in to Trey she was allowing him to use her. They were already using each other in a sense though, weren't they? Their mating was based on a mutually beneficial deal. Would it really be such a huge thing to include sex in the mix? Sex that just happened to be the best she'd ever had. Was it really so bad that she wanted to lose herself in Trey for a little while? Not lose herself in the mating and forget it wasn't real, no, never that. She just wanted to enjoy this mating bond that she might never have again.

Trey felt as the rigidness slowly began to leave her body, but he sensed that her defenses weren't down yet. "You can do this, baby, I know you can. I know you're strong enough to let me lead here." She swallowed hard and her jaw lost its tenseness. Almost there. "It's okay, baby. You're safe, I swear. It's okay." When she inhaled deeply and the spark of defiance left her eyes, triumph shot through him and his wolf. "That's a good girl. My good girl."

So damn turned on it wasn't even funny, Trey ravished that carnal mouth, drinking her in. Having this strong Alpha female submit to him like that sent a ravenous hunger like nothing he had ever known before blasting through his system. And not just any strong female, but Taryn.

Surely it was wrong that even though Taryn was imprisoned between him and the wall and could barely move, she was so unbelievably close to climaxing. His implacable voice that oozed supreme confidence hadn't helped, and now she was writhing and whimpering as she ground against him. Suddenly he cupped her ass and hoisted her up, urging her to curl her legs around him. Keeping her pinned to the wall, he rubbed his cock against her clit, making her groan into his mouth.

"Is this what you need?" he asked.

"Not enough. Want you inside."

"Not yet, baby. You can have my cock a little later."

Not liking the teasing expression on his face, she kicked her legs wildly, trying to escape his hold. He only pinned her more firmly against the wall. "You said it was mine. You said I could have it whenever I wanted it."

"And you can. Just as soon as I've tasted you I'll give you what you want." He turned off the spray, carried her out of the shower, and slid her down his body to stand on the mat. Then he curled a towel around her and began to rub her dry before drying himself, never once moving his gaze from hers. Gripping her by her waist, he lifted her and placed her on the counter near the basin before uncurling the towel.

"Spread your legs and lean back, baby. I want to see how wet you are." Unsurprisingly, she stared at him uncertainly, not finding it easy to submit totally. "Taryn," he growled, "spread your legs and lean back." Still staring hard at him, she slowly did as he'd asked. "Very good." He swallowed at the sight of her pink, swollen, glistening folds. Her scent urged him closer like a magnet, luring him to glut himself on her, to take what was his.

Hands abruptly slid under her thighs to cup her ass and cock her hips as his mouth closed over her clit. Taryn cried out and thrashed as he suckled hard and pleasure rushed through her like a scorching-hot wind. She practically melted when his tongue swiped through her folds and circled her clit before he flicked it with the tip of his tongue. He was merciless in his assault. He licked, nibbled, sucked, and bit, wringing moans and whimpers from her. He groaned and growled against her flesh, intensifying the pleasure until it was too much and she tried to wriggle free. "No more."

Growling, he grazed her inner thigh warningly with his claws, making it clear that he wasn't willing to part with her taste yet. Bastard. Then he nestled his tongue inside her, swirling and stabbing and sending sparks of agonizing bliss zinging through her. With each thrust of his tongue, the friction built within her, threatening to shatter her. She wanted him to stop. She wanted him to keep going. Then a finger drove inside her as he bit down gently on her clit and she virtually imploded, moaning and shuddering.

When Taryn was able to lift her head and open her eyes, it was to see him staring at her, licking her juices from his bottom lip. "You're a teasing bastard." Her voice was hoarse. Wearing a very boyish smile, he gently but firmly collared her throat with his hand and urged her to sit upright. Then his lips ravaged hers as his tongue drove into her mouth, forcing her to taste herself.

"Now I have the taste of you on my tongue, I want the feel of that tight pussy around my cock. Do you want me inside you?" She nodded. "Tell me. I want to hear you say it."

Hadn't he made her wait long enough? Asshole. "I want you," she said sharply and begrudgingly. "Now do it."

Trey pulled her to the edge of the counter and angled her just how he wanted her. Then he locked his hands onto her hips and began to work his cock inside her. He groaned as her muscles tightened around him, trying to drag him deeper. His wolf wanted him to ram into her, to fuck her hard and fill her with his come, but Trey simply eased himself slowly inside, controlled and smooth. He stopped after only feeding her a few inches. Her lust-dazed eyes slammed to his. "Do you like that? Shall I give you more?" She nodded. "I want the words, Taryn."

"I'm pretty sure you promised to fuck me raw."

"My little bitch is getting impatient, is she?" he asked with a smile. "Then tell me, do you want more?"

"Yes, dammit," she growled.

He gave her another couple of inches, then stilled again. "More?"

Taryn wanted to wipe that superior look from his face. Even her wolf didn't like it. "If you want someone who'll make all the right noises and say all the right words when you tell her to, then go find someone else!"

Trey nipped her lip. "I don't want anyone else, baby. I just want to hear my Taryn telling me she wants me. Shall I tell you how much I want to fuck this hot little body? How I've wanted to fuck you since the second I saw you? That's right, baby, I wanted you before we mated. What I want to do right now is make you come so hard you scream." At a sluggish pace, he withdrew and then slowly sank back in, but he didn't go any deeper than before. She moaned irritably. "If you want more, all you have to do is say so. Come on, give me the words, baby. Give me what I want."

After a lengthy pause, she said, "I want more." Abruptly he slammed into her, forcing her to take all of him, and she very nearly screamed. The sensation of his size stretching her was incredible. It was pleasure, it was pain, and nothing had ever felt better.

"So tight," he groaned. "God, that feels so fucking good." As he waited for her body to adjust, he ravished her lips, knotting his tongue with hers over and over. "I love your mouth. One of these days, I'm going to have those lips of yours wrapped around my cock while I fuck your mouth."

"No way, asshole."

"And that's another thing I'll be doing very soon. Fucking your sweet little ass."

"Could you come back from La La Land? At least till we're done here with the whole fucking me raw thing?"

Hearing the impatience in her tone, he said, "Don't worry, baby, I'll give you the hard fuck you want. Even if you didn't want it, I'd make you take it." He reared back and then began ruthlessly pounding into her at a furious pace. Her head dropped back and those husky sounds he loved began pouring out of her.

A growl rumbled up Trey's chest as her claws pressed into the flesh of his back. She wasn't breaking the skin though, wasn't marking him. He knew that she wanted to leave her mark on him—she was clenching her jaw against the urge to bite him, just as he had done that first night. Unlike her, he had no interest in holding back. He liked seeing his brand on her body and liked knowing that others would see it.

Trey leaned forward and bit down hard at the juncture of her neck, groaning as her muscles tightened around him, just as they always did when he marked her. Unable to help himself, he swooped down and took a nipple into his mouth, sucking hard and then biting down to leave another mark.

Her head snapped up as she growled. "Stop branding me!"

He smiled. "Why would I want to do that, baby?" Without warning, he dragged her from the counter, keeping her legs wrapped around his waist, and slammed her back against the wall. Then he plunged a finger into her ass and she cried out. "That's where I'm going to be soon, Taryn," he promised as he continued fucking her feverishly.

"No," she bit out, ignoring the carnal bliss of the double assault to her body.

"Oh yeah, your ass is going to squeeze me so tight, just like this sweet little pussy I'm fucking."

She kicked and scratched even as she groaned and whimpered.

"That's it, baby, scratch me. Mark me. Your wolf needs it, doesn't she?"

The traitorous bitch did, but Taryn was resolute that she might scratch him, but she wouldn't break the skin, wouldn't mark him. She wasn't going to make the eventual separation more difficult for her wolf. It appeared that he, on the other hand, wasn't interested in exercising any restraint. He bit her earlobe, her throat, her shoulder, and the hollow beneath her ear. The worst part about it was that it had her groaning every time. At this point she was making noises that were somewhere between moans and sobs.

"Louder, Taryn. I want every person in these caves to know that I'm fucking you right now. I want them to know that I own you." When defiance again flashed on her face, he thrust the finger in her ass hard. "Don't you tell me no. You belong to me."

"Then you belong to me!"

"You're right, baby, I do." Sensing she was close, Trey reached a hand between them and parted her folds, exposing her clit to the feverish motion of his pelvis as he repeatedly hammered into her. "Let me hear you scream, Taryn," he demanded. "Let them all hear you scream. Now!" He locked his teeth over his mark and plunged a second finger into her ass. She jolted and screamed as her climax tore through her, making her muscles close down on his cock and milk him as he forcefully exploded inside her. "Fuuuuuuck!"

This female was going to kill him.

Not sure how much longer his legs would hold him, but not wanting to leave her body just yet, Trey turned and slid down the wall until his ass met the floor with a thump. She collapsed across his chest, panting and quivering with the aftershocks. "It's not normal to come that hard." He hadn't realized he'd said that aloud until she spoke.

"I was just thinking the same thing."

Obviously, it was only due to their partially developed mating link and the temporary connection between their wolves. Ignoring that part of himself that insisted what was between them was more than that, he let his head fall back against the wall. He grinned as his cock began hardening inside her. This was going to be a long night. He had weeks to make up for.

CHAPTER TEN

———◆———

Taryn wasn't oblivious to the looks she was getting from the people in the diner. As this was a place where powerful Alphas—the kind who saw latency as a weakness—tended to congregate, the door had never been open to her. It was kind of like a school situation, where only the popular kids got to hang out in a particular crowd. That wasn't why people kept looking at her though. It was because she was sitting next to a hulking great Alpha male who was known for being a violent bastard but was toying with her hair with the lightest touch as she ate her breakfast. The same hulking great Alpha male who had a tendency to turn feral in his wolf form.

Their expressions ranged from curious to awed, probably due to the rumor that she had calmed him when he was feral, or maybe just because she was sitting with the local psychotic shifter. Of course, they were quick to look away if Trey shot them a scowl, but he seemed to like the idea that other males might want her. Weird bastard.

Smiling at the sight of his tiny mate practically attacking a plate of bacon, scrambled eggs, toast, tomatoes, and baked beans,

Trey massaged her nape. "Enjoying that, baby?" Apparently too engrossed to give him any attention, she simply nodded.

He hadn't ordered anything for himself other than coffee, as he wasn't particularly hungry, but the smell of meat so close was too much to resist. He took a slice of bacon from her plate and bit a chunk from it. She froze, then slowly swerved her head to face him, snarling. He knew why. He'd learned early that his mate was territorial over her food, but needling her was always fun. Surprising him, she abruptly leaned forward and snatched the bacon from his hand with her teeth, making him think of a chameleon catching a fly with its tongue. His chuckle quickly died as the door of the diner opened and a familiar scent reached his nose.

Taryn looked up to see Lance Warner walking toward them, flanked by Oscar and Perry. All three looked relatively nervous, even though the meeting had been set up by Trey via Rhett. As Trey was convinced that forming an alliance with her father would upset her, he had earlier that morning offered to cancel the meeting. However, she had encouraged him to go. It seemed dumb for him to have mated with her for this alliance, only then to refuse even to meet with her father to discuss the issue. As she always did when Lance was around, her wolf flexed her claws and growled—although she recognized this wolf as her father, she didn't like him.

As Lance stopped before their table, it was Trey's cue to stand, but he didn't—something that conveyed a lack of respect and made it clear that he didn't trust Lance. The older Alpha had the option of leaving, refusing to sit with someone who would show disrespect, or he could sit down and attempt to earn that respect. Trey guessed that Lance would want an alliance too much to just walk out. He was right.

The three wolves joined their table, sliding onto the bench opposite theirs, with Lance in the middle. The older man folded his arms across his broad chest. He was in good shape for his age, Trey thought. But both of them knew Trey could take him easily.

Lance's gaze finally flicked to Taryn, who, apparently uninterested in waiting for her own father to acknowledge her, was focused on her half-finished meal. "I'm sure you'll remember Oscar and Perry, so I don't need to introduce them. A few of my other enforcers are outside."

Trey heard the "I'm not defenseless" warning within that sentence. "If you look behind me, you should see my Beta and a few of my own enforcers." He heard Dante say, "Hi there." He imagined that Tao, Dominic, and Ryan would be giving Lance looks that said they hoped he gave them a reason to pounce on him. Each one of them despised the old Alpha for his treatment of Taryn.

Lance exhaled heavily. "It's fair to say we got off on the wrong foot."

"Are you referring to how you tried to take my mate from me?" Trey's wolf growled at the memory.

"I had every reason to believe that she wasn't your true mate. Considering that she's my daughter, taking her with me wouldn't exactly have been kidnapping her."

"Your daughter, huh? Biologically, maybe. In practice, not so much."

Again Lance's gaze darted briefly to an otherwise occupied Taryn. "I heard about what happened with Roscoe."

"Yes, it was all very sad."

"I also heard that you went feral and that Taryn managed to calm you down and bring you back from that." Lance's gaze focused solely on her and he seemed to be looking at her through new eyes. Almost done with her meal, she was eating what was left of her toast. Damn, she ate fast. It always brought a smile to Trey. Not right now though, because she was being ogled by her father's enforcer, who didn't think Trey would notice.

He knew she was a very sensual creature, and sometimes it gave him a kick to know that others wanted what was his, but not when those males were obviously daydreaming about that fantasy mouth of hers. "If you keep staring at my mate, I'll rip your fucking throat out." Oscar double-blinked, then quickly lowered his eyes. That didn't placate Trey or his wolf. As if Taryn sensed that, she rubbed her jaw against his shoulder and briefly patted his thigh. He calmed slightly at the bodily contact and, needing more, resumed massaging her nape.

Lance frowned, watching them closely.

"It was wise that you didn't come along with Roscoe. I'll tear anyone apart who tries to take her from me, I don't give a shit who they are or how many alliances they have." The look on Lance's face said he believed him. So he should. Trey decided not to think about the fact that it was more than his wolf's possessiveness and his mating instincts that drove him to make that very truthful statement.

Sighing happily now that she had demolished her meal, Taryn leaned back in her seat and rubbed her bloated stomach. "I'm stuffed."

"Not too stuffed for coffee, right?" said Trey.

"Never too stuffed for coffee." She reached out and gripped her cup, only then meeting her dad's eyes. "Well, hello, Daddy Dearest."

"Nice of you to finally acknowledge me."

"Really? I wasn't aware you'd give a shit."

Puffing up his chest a little, Lance said, "All right, let's talk alliances."

Trey held up a hand. "Firstly, let me be clear on a few things. I might agree to an alliance with you, but I'll never like you. You judged Taryn's worth on whether she could shift—something that has to do with her genetics. Instead of protecting her as you should have, you *literally* threw her to the wolves and she spent her life fighting off assholes. You were even prepared to force her into a mating, at which point I would have lost her. So, yeah, we can talk alliances, but I wouldn't bother continuing this discussion if you're hoping for my permission to use me as protection."

Lance narrowed his eyes. "I won't have your support in the event of another Alpha making a challenge against my pack?"

"I didn't say that. But, see, Taryn's told me all about how you like to name-drop." When Lance's gaze moved to her, she gave him the sweetest smile. "If there are incidences when you need to call on your alliances for backup, well, that's one thing. What I won't have is you throwing my name at people whenever you feel threatened. Understand?"

"If you're going to restrict the alliance to such a degree, I'm not sure there's any point to this conversation."

Recognizing that Lance was calling his bluff, Trey smirked. "Don't play games with me, Warner. You want this alliance more than I do. If you don't like my terms, feel free to go."

"You have very few alliances. You would benefit more from this than I would."

"I didn't say I wouldn't benefit more from this than you, I just said I didn't want it as much as you do. As my history shows, collecting alliances has never been a particular interest of mine."

"Until now."

"Until Taryn. Things change when you mate."

"Yes, they do," he allowed. "I have a condition of my own. I want to be able to call on Taryn whenever I need a healer."

Uh-oh, thought Taryn as she felt Trey's body tense.

Both incredulous and irate, Trey leaned forward. Whatever the males saw on his face made them lean back. "You honestly think I'll agree to you *using* her the way you have been all these years?" Lance had spoken about her like she was an object or tool that he would like to pick up when he felt like it—of course, that was how he had always seen her and treated her. A growl built in the back of Trey's throat and sent vibrations down his chest.

Lance swallowed hard in a nervous movement. "She's a powerful healer."

"She's also a person. My mate. *No one* uses Taryn like that. Not anymore."

The appearance of a tall brunette halted the conversation. Trey heard Taryn groan and guessed this wasn't a friend of hers. He couldn't help noticing that everything about the female appeared to be false.

"Alpha," she said respectfully to Lance with a nod by way of greeting.

Oscar cleared his throat. "We're a little busy here, Brodie."

She waved her hand. "That's fine, I was just coming to say hi." Then her eyes landed on Taryn and she smirked evilly. "I'm guessing you must be lost to be in this place."

Taryn smiled, though it wasn't pleasant. "Hating me won't make you pretty, Brodie." Anyone else might have been very careful how they spoke to the mate of someone like Trey Coleman, but one thing Brodie always loved to do was make herself look the big, strong female in front of big, bad Alphas. There were plenty of those in this place, and for some reason this woman still hadn't realized that Taryn wasn't quite the easy target that Brodie thought she was. "I see your nose healed a little crooked. Shame, that."

"You broke her nose, baby?" Although Trey really didn't like that this female was confronting his mate, he knew not to interfere. To do that would be to undermine her own ability to take care of herself.

"She wouldn't let me pass and then she called me a freak. What was I supposed to do? Yeah, okay, I suppose I could've just ignored her, but there wouldn't have been any fun in that."

Brodie snickered. "You only hurt me because I didn't fight back," she stated loudly, drawing the attention of everyone in the diner as they recognized her confrontational posture. "It would be like picking on a disabled person, and I was raised not to do that."

Taryn glanced around at all the onlookers and sighed. "So you've decided to schedule some time to make a spectacle of yourself."

"Honey, the person who should be embarrassed here is you. You're nothing but vapor to people like us. It's laughable that you even walked through the door."

"You know, Brodie, you're like an STD: no one wants you, everybody hates you, and you're a reminder of the devastating consequences of not using protection during sex."

Brodie's over-tanned face flushed. "Very funny, aren't you, little freak."

"As it happens, I have my moments."

"Want to know what's even funnier?"

"Not really."

"The idea of you as an Alpha female of a pack. I honestly don't think I've heard anything as ridiculous as a latent running a pack. Except maybe for this rumor of you calming a feral wolf. We all know that was a nice little story you spread just to make others think your own strength matched that of your mate—if he even is your mate, which I'm not buying *at all*."

A growl escaped Taryn, which had Brodie jumping in surprise. "Frankly, I couldn't give a shit what you think, but disputing my claim to Trey—that I won't tolerate." Her wolf was in full agreement.

"Won't tolerate?" said Brodie, sounding amused. "What're you going to do? Insult me to death?"

"Too slow a method. Challenge me to a woman-to-woman fight, Brodie, I dare you."

"You don't know what you're asking, latent. How about I give you a taste of what you're dealing with." She flung her alpha vibes at Taryn, intending for them to oppress and intimidate her. Instead of lowering her gaze submissively, Taryn retaliated by clotting the air with her own.

As Taryn's Alpha vibes smothered them all like humidity in summertime, Trey realized something. That night when she had hit his grandmother with them, she had held back. All she'd been doing was giving Greta a small demonstration of her strength, just to shut the woman up. This demonstration here and now was different. She was unleashing the full force of her wolf's Alpha strength on Brodie, making it perfectly clear that although she couldn't shift, her dominance, strength, speed, and power exceeded Brodie's. In a woman-to-woman fight, Brodie would be overpowered within seconds. Shit, if Trey wasn't hard as a rock right now at her display of dominance.

"Come on, Brodie, challenge me," urged Taryn. "You've always liked an audience. Shall I kick your ass in front of one?" The terribly fake female let loose a low whine as she ducked her head, averting her gaze as a gesture of submission. "No? Then it might be best if you back the fuck off and scamper, don't you think?" Taryn's wolf was extremely disappointed when Brodie did exactly that.

Trey kissed her temple and ran his hand through her hair, hoping to soothe her wolf. "I'm surprised you didn't throw her at the wall like you did Selma."

Reining in her Alpha vibes, she smiled at Trey. "Brodie isn't one of your mistakes, so she gets to walk away without a cracked skull."

"How did I miss it?" asked Lance.

Taryn arched a brow. "You mean the fact that the female you've been sleeping with is about as smart as your toenail?"

He cast an annoyed look in Brodie's direction, obviously unhappy about her making their sex life common knowledge. "How did I miss how strong your wolf is? Or I suppose a better question would be, why did you hide it?"

"I didn't hide it, I just didn't care to show you." He seemed genuinely confused that she hadn't wanted to impress him. "I'm not interested in having the approval of people I don't respect. And I'll never beg for scraps from anyone's table. You just never got that."

For the first time ever, there was an element of respect in Lance's eyes as he regarded her. "But you're not going to fight this alliance?"

"This here and now isn't about making friends or building bridges. This is politics, pure and simple. Us being related by blood has no relevance because, as unfortunate as it is, there's just no emotional bond there." It was a sad, simple truth, delivered with a shrug. It hurt more than she would ever admit or let him see.

"I underestimated you quite a bit, it seems. You two suit well. You make a good Alpha pair." After a heavy sigh, he asked irritably, "Okay, Coleman, what exactly *are* you willing to agree to?"

"Like I said, if there's a situation that requires you to call on your alliances, then you'll have my support. In other words, I don't mind being part of a solution to your problems, but I won't have you doing your name-dropping thing and using me as a deterrent to the beginning of any problems. And there'll be no using Taryn."

"Out of curiosity, if you didn't consider me such an awful protector where Taryn's concerned...?"

"Then we wouldn't even be having this conversation. My allegiance would be automatic and have no limits." And Trey sincerely meant that.

Maybe it was petty of Taryn to be enjoying that, for just once in her life, her dad was regretting his treatment of her. Not because he cared about her, true, but because it had cost him in a political sense—something more important to Lance Warner than anything else. "How's that karma tasting, Daddy Dearest? A little sour, I'll bet."

Lance simply gave her an impatient look. "I'll agree to your terms," he said to Trey, albeit a little begrudgingly.

Trey looked at Taryn. "All of that okay with you, baby?" He knew he'd surprised her by asking for her input, but she didn't let it show on her face.

"One last thing," she said to Lance. "Because of your attitude toward me growing up, a lot of people saw it as their right to target me just for fun. Don't think that if they decide to do it again, like Brodie, I'll back down just because of the alliance. They shouldn't challenge me unless they're damn positive they can take me. I'm an Alpha female of a pack, which means any attack on me is an attack on the pack. And I won't ignore one."

Lance gave her a sharp nod. "I'll make sure the pack understands this."

"Good." After draining the last of the coffee from her cup, Taryn said, "Shall we go, then, Trey?"

"Sure, baby." They all rose, and then Trey took the hand that Lance extended and shook it once. "Until we next meet…"

"Oh, wait." Lance gave Perry a subtle signal and the enforcer dug a bulging sports bag from under the table and handed it to Taryn. She didn't take it, just raised a brow at Lance, hoping for an explanation. "You know what your mother was like for saving money. She began a fund to give you a kick-start when you mated. Obviously, there would have been more in it, had she not died."

Tentatively she took the bag. "There's money in here?"

"Twenty-five thousand dollars."

"Twenty-five thousand dollars," she echoed quietly, more than a little stunned. It struck her that he could have just kept the money for himself, knowing she'd be none the wiser. "Why are you giving me this?" It sure wasn't because he cared for her.

"I'd never ignore the wishes of my mate."

"Come on, baby." Giving a slight nod to Lance, Trey draped his arm over her shoulder and kept her close to him as they walked side by side from the diner, with Dante and his enforcers trailing behind them.

Trey kept her just as close when they slid into the backseat of the Toyota, sensing that she was feeling a little off-kilter due to the bag, which she was staring at as if it were a ticking bomb. He gave her the comfort she needed and would probably never have asked for—running the tips of his fingers along her bare upper arm and rubbing his jaw along her temple.

"Well, does it feel good to finally have the alliance you've been wanting so badly?" she asked, forcing her gaze away from the bag. She wouldn't have thought being given a gift from her mom would have made her feel anything but incredibly happy, but this particular gift had had a purpose. Her mom had been starting a fund for her so that when Taryn and Joey were ready to begin their life together they would have some money to help them along. And that was why Taryn was—as unreasonable as it might be—feeling guilty for taking it.

Her mom hadn't scrimped and saved this large amount of money to help Taryn along with a fake mating while she declared to all who'd listen that Joey hadn't been her true mate. The woman had been a hopeless romantic and wouldn't have seen Taryn's mating with Trey as resourceful. She would have viewed a mating based around a deal that brought mutual benefit to both parties as a mockery of what mating was all about. She would have been right.

"Yes," Trey answered carefully, hearing a difference in her tone that told him she'd withdrawn a little. His wolf growled, not liking it any more than Trey did. He nuzzled her hair and cuddled her closer. She didn't resist him, but she didn't melt into him either. He nipped the tip of her ear. She jolted and scowled at him. "Don't freeze me out," he insisted in a low, calm voice.

She sighed. "It feels like I've accepted it under false pretenses. Hell, I have."

"Not exactly. Your mom may have intended to give it to you and your true mate, but I don't think she'd begrudge you having it just because you mated with someone else."

"Of course she wouldn't have...*if* the mating had been real."

"This is real, Taryn," he growled.

"Yeah, I know. I mean, *if* we'd mated with the intention of actually staying together, if we had feelings for each other. Now that's something she would have understood, because she was all about love and romance and all that stuff. Not this though. She wouldn't have understood this. She would have mated with Roscoe before renouncing her true mate."

"The fact that you didn't doesn't make you a coward, Taryn," he firmly stated, knowing that was where her thoughts had taken her. "Like you said, she was one of those romantic people. You're more of a practical thinker, like me. Practical thinkers aren't so much into self-sacrifices. They prefer solutions. And you're not someone who's prepared to wait around with the belief that life will hand you a solution—you go looking for one." She smiled a little, but still looked troubled. "You don't have to spend it. You don't even have to open the bag. Put it away with your shoe box. She'd be happy enough about that, right?" Her smile widened then and he felt a pang in his chest. Nodding, she finally relaxed into him, pleasing both him and his wolf. As with all those other chest pangs he'd been feeling recently around her, he automatically ignored it.

"Ah, come on, Taryn, don't get all glum on us," pleaded Dominic. "I tell you what, why don't you come here and let me give you a great big hug. You can sit on my lap and we'll talk about the first thing that pops up." Ignoring Trey's growl, the gorgeous blond pervert added, "I'll even let you rub my lucky scrotum. Ow!" He still had the nerve to chuckle when Trey smacked him over the head.

When they returned to pack territory, they found everyone waiting in the living area for news of how the meeting went. "Well?" prodded Trick.

"We got the alliance." Trey winced at the loud celebratory noises.

"I checked the pack web earlier," said Rhett. "You've got more Alphas requesting basic alliances. It really was a great idea to set up a pack web."

"Yep, which means if it wasn't for Taryn, we probably wouldn't have any of those alliances," said Marcus. He grinned as she flopped into the recliner and wiggled her shoulders, hinting for him to give her the usual massage. As always, he obliged her.

Greta snorted. "I still say you don't need them. Or the hussy."

Taryn looked at her with mock pity. "Isn't it time for your nap yet, Old Mother Hubbard?"

"Listen to her. She's never shown me any respect from day one. All common and no manners."

"I just thought it was important that you felt comfortable around me."

"Trey, you're going to be the laughingstock of all the other packs, having a latent as an Alpha female. Can't you see that? I'll bet she can, but she's got it good here so she'll drag this out as long as she can. Won't you?"

Taryn simply smiled. "I'd tell you to stop having a hissy fit and act your age, but then you'd die, so…Actually, maybe I *should* just—"

"Oh, yes, make your smart remarks now, but it won't be long until it's time for you to go and then Trey will mate with a real Alpha female. One who's not common and sarcastic, or disrespectful and slutty."

"Come on, you have to admit I keep life interesting." Taryn thought she had hidden pretty well just how Greta's last statement had stung. It was only the truth though. Taryn *would* leave, Trey probably *would* mate again, and the female he mated with for real *would* most likely be better suited to be an Alpha female. And what would Taryn be doing? Trying her hardest to find a pack that would take in a common, disrespectful, sarcastic, latent female.

Hoping against hope that her uncle might have replied to her message, she excused herself and went up to Rhett's room to check her messages on the pack web. Her hoping paid off. Smiling, she skipped down the stairs and reentered the living room. "Hey, guess what? My uncle's been in touch through the pack web."

Trey frowned. "Uncle?"

"The one whose pack I was planning to seek refuge at if all else failed."

"Oh. Right."

"He's invited us to a mating ceremony that's taking place for someone in his pack a few weeks from now." That was a hell of a lot more than Taryn had hoped for. She'd thought it might take a few web conversations before her uncle would be interested in them meeting up. An invite to a mating ceremony had definitely been unexpected.

"Wait, start again. How does he know about us? Had he just noticed you on the pack web?"

"No, I got in touch with him."

Trey did a double take. "What was that?"

"It seemed like a good idea to get to know him before I ask his Alpha to take me in when our deal's over. Maybe if my uncle and I somehow bond I'll have more of a chance." The way Trey's eyes had seemed to ice over and his face had darkened to a purplish shade had her frowning. "Why are you looking at me like I strolled into your house on your birthday and shat on all the gifts?"

"Oh, I don't know, *maybe* because no one's supposed to know that we're not true mates."

Taryn's mouth dropped open. "You think I *told* him? You think I went back on our deal and told him all about it?" A deathly silence filled the room, because everyone knew that questioning Taryn's integrity was a very bad thing.

"Awkward," muttered Dominic.

"Seriously, you think I would actually do that?"

No, actually, Trey didn't think she'd do something like that, but he tended to say stupid shit when he was pissed off, and hearing that she had been in touch with her uncle when he knew she was hoping to join the guy's pack had made his blood boil.

It shouldn't have made his blood boil, because it shouldn't bother him that she would soon be leaving his pack, yet it did. "It just seemed unlikely that you'd try to fool him if you're planning to later ask him for a place in his pack. You think he'll actually take you in when he realizes you lied to him right to his face about us?"

"No, doofus," she spat in a goofy voice. "That's why I'm planning to say to him what I'll say to everyone else—that I was wrong about us and that Joey was actually my true mate after all. Sure, it's going to make me seem a little nutty that I could mix up something like that, but it's a better fate than a life with Roscoe ever would have been. I figured that this might be good for you too, that maybe you could get an alliance with my uncle's Alpha out of this. He must be at least willing to consider it or he wouldn't have given my uncle permission to invite us to this mating ceremony. I've told him to expect us."

Everything in Trey rebelled against the idea of Taryn going to that ceremony, of her building a bond with her uncle so she could leave. He knew she needed to leave his pack eventually. Logic even told him that the sooner she left, the better, because their separation would become harder the longer that they were mated. But logic wasn't ruling just then. It was being overshadowed by a tangle of intense emotions that Trey didn't understand, all of which drove him to do one thing: try to stop her from going to meet the other pack.

"Look, Taryn, I'm going to have a lot of stuff going on in the next couple of weeks. I can't shove it all aside just to go to some mating ceremony of people I don't even know."

She stared at him for a minute. "Fine. I'll take Dante or Marcus with me."

"You don't think it would look both weird and disrespectful that I didn't go with you?"

"Of course it would. I'm still going."

"Taryn, listen—"

She took a step toward him. "No, you listen, Flintstone. We made a deal and I will live up to my part of it. At the end of this, you'll walk away with tons of alliances. Me? I'll have nothing, because I walked away from everything for this deal we made. I need to have somewhere to go. I'm *not* going to live the lone wolf lifestyle. My best bet is to get a place in my uncle's pack— even if it's only temporary, at least it'll be something. If you don't want to come with me to this ceremony and maybe try and get yourself an alliance out of this, then fine. But I *will* be going in the hope of increasing my odds of getting a place in that pack, because the alternative is taking a chance being out there on my own, and that's not acceptable to me."

He could tell her the truth of why he didn't want her to go to the ceremony, he could, but now wasn't the time or the place. All right, that was, in fact, an excuse, but it was an excuse he was sticking to. Rather than piss her off any further, he went to her and tugged her to him. "I didn't think of it that way. If you want us to go, we'll go."

"Really?" she drawled, suspicion dripping from the word.

"Really."

A nod. "Okay." She squealed as he suddenly scooped her up and began strolling out of the room. "What the hell are you doing?"

"No more talking. Really need to fuck."

And he really did need it. He needed to be buried deep inside her body, needed to be swimming in her scent, and needed the taste of her in his mouth. Only then would he be able to calm himself and his wolf.

The thought of being separated from his mate had sent his wolf pacing and growling, fighting for supremacy. It had nettled

Trey's mating instincts, playing on his protectiveness and possessiveness until all he wanted was to pin her down and bite her, remind her that she belonged to him.

As for Trey the man...equal measures of infuriation and angst had shot through his blood, making anxiety curdle in his stomach. He told himself that if he hadn't mated with her, there would be no such anxiety whatsoever, that the separation wouldn't particularly bother him. In truth, he wasn't so sure that the man in him was still detached from the mating, or even if he ever had been.

Now this was one of the things Taryn would really miss about Bedrock, she thought with a smile as she sank into the luxurious bath. There was a brief stinging sensation as the hot water made contact with the fresh scratches and bites now coating her body, but it passed pretty quickly. Damn the bastard for branding her so thoroughly! How in the hell was she supposed to move on after this mating when his marks were all over her, serving as constant reminders of him? Maybe that was what he wanted— to make sure that she wouldn't be able to forget him. He might not particularly care about her, but the possessiveness that came with the mating was probably messing with his mind.

She had no intention of telling him that he didn't need to brand her so completely to ensure that she remembered him. As much as it pissed her off, she couldn't change that she sort of, well...she really liked him. A voice in her mind insisted that was an understatement, but Taryn ignored it. She didn't understand how she could like him so much. The guy could be so tactless and impatient, so remote and unapproachable. He was unbalanced. He had shitty communication skills. He thought apologies went in the form of oral sex, and he could brood with the best of them.

And yet, she truly liked the guy. Naturally, her wolf was very pleased about that.

Well, enough thinking about him. All she wanted to do right now was relax and soothe those aches that always came with the rough fuckings he gave her. She had a strong feeling that her manly mate wasn't going to be too happy about the smell of jasmine that now filled his bathroom, thanks to the soap Lydia had given her. Just the thought of that made her smile—simple pleasures and all that stuff.

She was so relaxed that she was beginning to wonder if she had entered subspace, so the little tapping sounds were just background noise to her at first. Soon though, they penetrated her daze, pissing her off. The noises reminded her of when Shaya used to throw stones at her window at night when they were teenagers, hoping to get her attention. She tried to ignore the incessant tapping. After a short while though, they began to grate on her nerves.

"Trey?" she called out, hoping to have him check out the noise. "Anyone?" Nothing, which meant she was going to have to see what the fuck it was herself. Fabulous.

Muttering curses, she stepped out of the bath, wrapped a white fluffy towel around herself, and made her way into the bedroom. As she had suspected, something seemed to be tapping against the window. Still muttering curses, she stalked over to the window and pulled aside the curtain. And jerked back. "What the fuck?" Oh no, that wasn't what she thought it was. It couldn't be. It just couldn't be.

Having sensed her alarm and anxiety through the pack link, Trey came dashing into the room. "What is it? What's wrong?" And then he saw it. Slowly he went to her. "Is that—is that the raven you always talk to?"

Grinding her jaw, she nodded, close to tears at the sight of the beautiful bird now dead. Not just dead, but hanging upside down by some kind of string, his beak repeatedly tapping against the window as his body blew with the wind. "I heard the tapping."

"Baby, come here." Not giving her a choice, he pulled her to him and enfolded her in his arms.

"Somebody did that," she said through her teeth as shock and rage flooded her veins.

"I know," he said, working to keep his voice soft or else his rage might feed her own.

"Somebody killed him and then hung him there, like that, for me to find."

"What happened?" asked Dante as he, Tao, Marcus, and Trick came dashing into the room after having sensed their Alphas' alarm. "Shit!"

"Is it dead?" asked Trick. "Why would someone—Shit, Taryn, is that your crow?"

Marcus supportively squeezed her shoulder as he moved toward the window. "Looks like someone snapped its neck."

"Who the hell would do something like that?" Dante shook his head, sickened.

"Maybe the same person who vandalized her car," suggested Tao. "Maybe not, but it wouldn't surprise me."

Leaving Trey's arms, Taryn demanded, "Out. Everyone out. Now!"

Dante nodded. "I'll go…get him down." He gestured to the enforcers to follow him out of the room. Casting her sympathetic smiles, they reluctantly went.

"Baby, what're you doing?" Trey asked as he watched her snatch clothes out of the wardrobe in a rush. She didn't answer, just began pulling on a blue cashmere sweater and tight-fitting jeans. "Taryn—"

"Someone did that to hurt me. They went to the trouble of hunting him down, catching him, *killing* him, and creeping around outside our cave to hang him upside down like that where I'd find him. I want to know who the sicko is, and I want to kick his ass." Having slipped on her knee-high boots, she headed for the door.

Understanding her need to retaliate but not liking her hurting so bad, he dashed after her and wrapped both arms around her front, bringing her to a halt. Nuzzling her neck, he rocked her from side to side. "Let me deal with this, baby. I promise you, as soon as I find out who's responsible, they're all yours."

Her voice came out flat. "Let go of me, Trey."

"Come on, you're upset and in shock. Let me deal with this for you."

She could sense that he was just as infuriated as she was, yet he was containing it all in the hope of easing her anger and hurt. It was sweet, but there was just no way anything could soothe her right now. "Let go."

Dabbing a soft kiss to her neck, he slowly released her. Before he could say anything, she was marching through the tunnels. He stayed at her heels as, to his surprise, she headed outside and down the flights of stairs.

"Stay back," she told him as they reached the bottom.

Seeing that she was close to snapping, he stopped still and held up his hands in a white-flag gesture. He had thought she intended to head to the river, as she had the last time she was upset. Instead, she paced a short distance away from him and looked up at the crowd that had gathered at the mouth of the caves.

"So which one of you was it, huh?" she shouted, enraged beyond belief. "Which one of you was it?" No answer. They each looked from one to the other, but didn't move from where they were. "You have a problem with me, then come down here! Come on! You and me, let's go!" Still, nobody moved. Pacing back and forth, she continued to shout. "I'm latent, *remember*? I can't possibly win! You think killing a *bird*, a small creature that couldn't even fight back, is brave? It's sick and it's cowardly! If it's me you want, then get the fuck down here! I *dare* you! No, I *challenge* you!" Still, not one person moved from where they were. "*Come on!*"

"It's okay, baby," Trey said softly when no one spoke or reacted in any way. "You know they won't come. Whoever it is knows they can't take you. Come here. It's okay."

"No, it's not!"

Slowly he closed the distance between them and pulled her into the cradle of his shoulder. "Shh, let's go inside. The coward's not going to own up to it."

"When I find out who it is, there's a good chance I'll kill him."

"I know, baby. And I'll be cheering you on," he said, using the supportive words she had once given him.

CHAPTER ELEVEN

◆

Taryn's uncle and his mate were a lot warmer toward her than Trey had been expecting. They seemed pleased to see her and they were happy and relieved to know that she was away from Lance. If her uncle had anything to do with it, she would definitely be welcome here if she asked to join the pack.

In fact, the damn Alpha would probably be just as welcoming. He had been staring at Taryn for most of the evening and it was seriously beginning to piss Trey off. Had she not made Trey promise to behave, he would have threatened to gut the ogling bastard. Even his promise to her wouldn't have stopped him if the Alpha hadn't been so careful not to cross any lines.

It was only then, as he sat lounging on one of the reclined deck chairs, sipping beer and watching her play with some of the pups, that Trey realized he had secretly hoped that they would all be assholes who didn't care to know her. Without anyone to turn to, she could have been persuaded to stay with him a little longer, even after the battle with his uncle. Although he still had just over a month left with her, it didn't seem enough.

For the past few weeks he had tried convincing himself that it wasn't the man in him who wanted to prolong her stay, it was

231

just his wolf or his mating instincts or maybe a mixture of both. Only a moron would continue to deny the truth, and Trey was a lot of things, but he'd like to think a moron wasn't one of them. The truth was that this wasn't about their wolves, this was about Trey and Taryn. And Trey wanted Taryn to stay a little longer.

Of course he hadn't told her that. He wouldn't tell her, because naturally the question she would ask would be "For how long?" Unless his answer was going to be "permanently," there was no reason for her to stay longer, because it would only make their separation worse. Where was the sense in that? There was none. Yet even as he acknowledged that, he couldn't change that he wanted more time with her.

How could he not? Who wouldn't want more time with a woman who was so sensual and gorgeous? The quirkiness she had brought to his pack and his life was something he wouldn't have originally thought he'd want, but he knew that when it was gone he would miss it. Just as he would miss their bedroom battles. She was so responsive, so challenging, and so damn receptive to everything they did. Each morning he would wake Taryn by gorging himself on her taste, and each night he would bury his cock deep inside her and fuck them both to sleep. Then he'd wake up sometime during the night and fuck her again. What guy in his right mind wouldn't want more of that?

He grinned as his little vixen suddenly looked up and met his gaze. He didn't get his usual "come get me" smile; it was more of a "please rescue me" expression—which had a lot to do with the crowd of kids still hovering around her. With all her energy and sparkle, she was like some sort of kid magnet.

He might have gone to her—that was all it would have taken to make the pups scatter—if the Alpha, Nick, hadn't chosen that moment to sit on the deck chair beside him.

"I think you might end up with a houseful of pups."

Trey winced inwardly at the feel of one of those damn chest pangs. Ignoring it, he forced out a response. "You might be right."

"You know, you're very intense with Taryn. I don't think you've moved your eyes from her for more than a few seconds since you got here."

"Neither have you."

Nick smiled unrepentantly. "Don't worry, she spent the entire time we spoke talking about you and your pack. Apparently, she has even developed a fondness for your grandmother, though she says she would still like to gag the senile old crone."

Trey was pretty sure that both women actually liked each other, although neither would ever admit it, because they enjoyed the battles of wills they engaged in too much.

"I've always been very selective in who I form alliances with."

Trey grunted. "I don't believe I asked you for one." All he really wanted was to punch the arrogant asshole for ogling Taryn. His wolf liked that idea.

Nick only smiled. "The rumors about you are...worrying."

"Then why invite us here?"

"Her uncle wasn't convinced that you're true mates. He believes her true mate died when they were pups. Don was worried that she had gotten herself into something dangerous and was looking for a way out."

"Is that a fact?" Trey bit out. "Well, hear me when I say this. Taryn's my mate, she's mine, and I'll kill her interfering bastard of an uncle if he tries to take her from me. So either get out of our business or ask us to leave. Either one will please me just fine."

The weird prick smiled again. "I didn't say I agreed with him. If I hadn't seen you interact with Taryn the way you have tonight, I'm not sure I'd have been interested in forming an alliance between our packs." Most likely in response to Trey's questioning look, he added, "Maybe you don't realize just how different you are with Taryn than anyone else. And she you. You're both much calmer when you're together. It's the way of it with mates. That's why I've no intention of interfering, in spite of her uncle's concerns, and it's also why I believe you're not quite the rabid shifter everyone makes you out to be."

"Hey, Nick," purred a husky voice that promised sex. Both males looked up to see a curvy, dark-skinned female standing before them wearing…practically nothing. Once upon a time she might have interested Trey. Right now she did nothing at all for him. He never would have thought he would have described breasts as too big, but they were. Not like Taryn's, which fit just right in his hands, like they were made just for him.

"Is it time for the ceremony to start?" asked Nick.

"Almost." Her eyes focused on Trey and she grinned wickedly. "I'm Glory. And you are?"

"Mated," snapped another female voice. "So move your ass very far away."

A smile curved Trey's mouth at the sight of Taryn approaching, sneering and emitting a sexy low growl. He loved seeing her in possessive mode. He didn't blame Glory for her fast departure. Even he wouldn't be interested in fucking with Taryn right now. He'd happily fuck her though, especially while she was wearing that little black dress that clung to her like a second skin.

"I'd say I'm sorry for upsetting one of your wolves, but lying's a sin," Taryn told Nick, who just smiled. Damn if the guy wasn't hot with his short, silky butterscotch hair, sensual mouth, and that set of piercing, dusky-green eyes. Still, she preferred the dark, broody psycho beside him. "Hey, Flintstone."

Trey gave her a lopsided smirk as he appraised her for like the hundredth time. "Come here."

She cocked her head. "If I don't?"

"I'll chase you, catch you, and spank you in front of everybody."

"Was that supposed to be a deterrent?"

Nick now forgotten, Trey reached out and snatched her arm, pulling her on top of him. He licked her lips and she immediately opened up for him, flicking his tongue lightly with her own and conjuring images in his mind of her flicking her tongue along the head of his cock. Her sly grin told him she'd known exactly what she was doing. "Careful," he warned.

"Where would the fun in that be?"

Quietly, he replied, "You're right. Fun would be if I forced you to get down on your knees and then shoved my cock in your mouth."

"You could try, but I'd just bite it off. Maybe I'd heal it, I don't know."

He chuckled, running his hands along her back. "Such a snippy little bitch, aren't you?"

"I am, yes."

"Wrong. You're *my* snippy little bitch." Brushing her hair from her face, he frowned. "You look tired."

"I'm not surprised. I didn't get much sleep."

He heard the implication in her voice. "I'd say I'm sorry, but I'm not."

"You never are," she grumbled, still smiling. "So what have you been doing all the way over here while I was practically attacked by a swarm of pups?"

"I've been busy enjoying myself watching some gorgeous female."

"Oh, is that so? You'll have to describe this female to me so I can go kick her ass."

Collaring her throat with his hand, he guided her head backward and slid his hand away so he could kiss and nibble at her neck. "You can't miss her. She has all different shades of blonde in her hair."

"Poor girl."

"And the cutest ass"—he tapped it lightly—"and a hot little body"—he smoothed the palm of his hand up and down her spine—"and a very sharp tongue. Oh, and she has a wicked mouth that was made to take my cock."

"Stop kissing my very sensitive neck so I can think straight and respond with a sarcastic comment." She wouldn't let him know that, in truth, she had thought about it several times. Had wondered what it would feel like to take him in her mouth, how he would taste. But—and maybe she was alone in this—that one sexual act felt like an extremely submissive one. She was working on letting him lead in bed, but she wasn't sure she was ready to get on her knees before him and do what seemed like the ultimate surrender.

It wasn't that she had never done it before. It was just that whenever she had done it in the past, it had been while she was the dominant figure in the relationship. Giving a guy a blow job when she was supposed to be mostly submissive seemed like something else altogether, in which case it surprised her that she was even considering it. Just as it surprised her that, as much as the wolves in Nick's pack were great and as much as she could see herself being happy here if they accepted her, that didn't make her feel as relieved and excited as it should. No, because she would miss Trey and his pack.

She really had thought she was being careful not to get comfortable in the pack, knowing that her stay would be a short one. But with them being so warm and fun—with the exception of a few—and seeing her as more than a healer who was rather inconveniently latent, it was damn hard to keep an emotional distance from these people and the situation itself.

If she were honest with herself—which she really didn't want to be—she had also stupidly gotten a little too comfortable in her temporary mating with Trey. His heavy masculinity gave the impression of a hard individual, but she had come to see that there was more to him than that. Sure, he could be aggressive, sullen, and psychotic, but he had demonstrated that he could also be attentive, reassuring, gentle, and even indulgent—or at least he could be with her. Not to mention how his sexual appetites matched her own. Without realizing it, she had somehow fallen a little into the fantasy of their mating, even though she had resisted the urge to mark him. How shitty was that?

"It's almost midnight," announced Nick as he stood. "Ceremony's about to start."

Taryn frowned when she noticed how Trey was scowling at the Alpha. Sure, Trey was pretty antisocial with 99 percent of the population—she was working on that with him—but when he scowled at someone like that, it usually meant they had pissed him off.

Making a mental note to ask Trey about it later, she rose to her feet and pulled him with her to join the loose circle that the pack had made around the mated pair in the clearing. She snuggled into Trey as he pressed against her back and locked his arms around her. As always, she never felt squashed or suffocated by his huge body. He made her feel safe and protected.

At exactly midnight, Nick began to speak the ritual words that called to the full moon to bless the mating. She had been a witness at several of these ceremonies in the past, and the intensity of the sacred event never failed to amaze her. Although the ritual words didn't hold any particular power, and the ceremony was a case of the mates demonstrating to each other just how committed they were and wanting to celebrate that, the whole thing still gave her goose bumps and stirred her wolf.

What affected Taryn most, however, was witnessing the succession of intense emotions that flittered across the mated pair's faces. To be loved, adored, and worshipped like that by the person you loved in turn had to be the most amazing thing in the world. And it was something she would never have. She only ever experienced the tiniest twinge of jealousy. It was impossible not to be happy for those people who had found it. For a moment she wondered what it would be like to have that with Trey, but quickly dismissed the dumb thought.

"What do you think they'll do?" he whispered into her ear.

She knew what he was asking. It was traditional that mates celebrated the ceremony by having sex, and whereas most preferred to do so in the privacy of their home after the party, there were some who gave in to their exhibitionistic urges and had sex beneath the full moon, regardless of who might be there to watch.

She whispered her response. "Well, I spoke to Lena only a couple of times, but she seems pretty shy, so I can't see her wanting to get down and dirty with her mate in front of everyone. Then again, it's the quiet ones you have to look out for." Knowing how dominant and possessive his wolf was, she said, "I don't have to ask what you'd prefer."

"Oh?"

"You'd love the idea of everyone watching. You're quite the exhibitionist, even for a shifter."

Trey merely shrugged. "We all have our kinks."

"And so," said Nick, "do you, Robert, and you, Lena, enter this mating with your body, mind, heart, and soul?"

"I do," they said in unison.

Nick then blessed the mating, using a string of Latin words that Trey didn't have a hope of understanding. He couldn't help frowning as Lena kissed her mate before biting his unmarked shoulder, branding him for all to see. The one thing that his own little mate had never done—though she'd have every right, considering how many damn times he had done it to her—was leave her brand on him. Although she had scratched him and nipped him plenty of times, she had never marked him. His wolf keenly felt the absence of that mark; he didn't understand why she hadn't branded him. Neither did Trey.

He knew that she wanted to, knew that her wolf was pushing her to act on the basic urge to mark her male. Taryn's resistance had to be pissing her wolf off and making her feel insecure in the mating. Yet Taryn was fighting her. Much like he'd been fighting his own wolf from the beginning, he mused. So maybe he wasn't the only one of them who had been battling emotions he didn't understand. Or maybe he had found his way into La La Land.

"I was right," whispered Taryn, "she's too shy to have an audience. Come on, let's eat. I'm starving."

Shoving his thoughts aside, Trey allowed her to lead him to the large table beneath the canopy, where a huge feast was set out. Although the ceremonies were considered to be sacred and solemn, the after-party was always jubilant and lively—the general plan being to dance, eat, and get ridiculously drunk. Since neither he nor Taryn was particularly good at dancing, they stuck to stuffing their faces with food and gulping down plenty of beer—though not too much, considering Trey needed to drive them home.

He really didn't want to like these people who would soon take Taryn away from him—or at least that was how he saw it—but a part of him could admit that they seemed to be pretty okay people. If he was going to lose her to another pack, then this was a fairly decent one for her to join. The only wolf he couldn't be too sure about was her uncle. The tall, bald guy had purposely avoided Trey the entire time they were there. Several times Taryn had tried to introduce him, but Don always managed to artfully dodge her. Trey didn't particularly care, though he didn't like that it was upsetting Taryn.

That meant that when the party ended at six in the morning and Don finally approached him while Taryn was saying goodbye to the pups, Trey really wasn't in the mood to take any shit. And of course Don happened to have some shit to throw at him.

"You seem fond of my niece," said Don, squinting, as he crossed his arms over his chest in a very confrontational posture. "And you're certainly possessive of her. Still, I'm not buying the true mate thing. Nor am I buying that you've mated with her because you care for her. Being fond of her and wanting her with you for life are two very different things. Don't get me wrong, I'm grateful that you got her away from her father, who was a bastard to her. My issue is that I've heard all about your reputation, Coleman, and I promise you now, if I find out you've got my niece involved in anything dangerous, you'll have me to deal with."

Resisting the urge to grip him by the throat, Trey took a threatening step toward him and cocked his head. It pleased his wolf when the other male backed up a little. "You know what pisses me off most about what you just said? That you think you have the right to act the caring uncle *now*. Where were you when she was growing up? Like you just said, Lance was always a bastard to her, and yet you left her there with him, believing that there would never be a true mate to come along and take her away. You didn't even keep in touch with her, did you? No. So don't think you get to stand here and be all high and mighty with me or that being my mate's uncle will save you. Taryn might care about you, but I don't, and I sure as shit won't have anyone saying she's not my mate."

"You're right," he conceded, surprising Trey, "I wasn't there for her. I will be from here on out though. I want her to be happy. I want her to have the kind of mating you've seen tonight and I'm not sure you can give her that. I don't see how you'll bring anything to her life other than danger and trouble."

He was right, of course, and that only nettled Trey's agitated state. "As Taryn would say, if I wanted to hear from an ass, I'd fart."

"Trey," said Taryn cautiously as she approached and took in the tension, "everything okay?" Slipping a slender arm between the two male bodies that were almost pressed together, she stroked Trey's chest.

"Fine, baby," he replied, using her closeness to calm him. "I'm just getting an idea of what it's like for you when you have to listen to my grandmother's shit."

Rolling her eyes and groaning, Taryn looked at Don. "I really hope you haven't just done the man-to-man talk when you've only been back in my life five minutes."

Don sighed. "That's pretty much what he just said. I just want you to be happy and—"

"Well, I was, until you put Trey in a bad mood."

"I know you, Taryn. Beneath that hard exterior, you're not so different from your mom. You want kids and commitment and a happily ever after—he can't give you that."

"If I was pining for the pitter-patter of tiny little feet, I'd buy a kitten and put slippers on it. And what do you know about what Trey can or can't give me? You don't even know him."

"I know this mating isn't real—"

"Watch what you say," she snapped. Her wolf growled inside her head, just as incensed as she was by those words. A much louder growl was coming from Trey.

"You deserve better, you can have better—plenty of wolves would be happy to mate with you. Hell, there are wolves here who'd be happy to mate with you."

Taryn wasn't in the least bit surprised when Trey's eyes flashed wolf and he made a move toward Don. Quickly she placed herself in front of him and wrapped both arms tightly around his waist. "It's okay, it's okay," she whispered. He halted but released a chilling growl.

Don was quieter as he said in a shaky voice, "He's not good for you."

"If that's how you feel, then I guess we part here."

"Taryn—"

"No. We're leaving." Rubbing her chin on Trey's chest she said, "Come on, Flintstone, let's go." But his entire focus was on Don.

Don tried again. "Taryn, I—"

"I said *no*. You insulted my mate. If you were anyone else, I'd go for your throat. Now back off."

"Let them be, Don," ordered Nick, who was walking up behind them. He nodded respectfully at Taryn and Trey.

"Thank you for inviting us, Nick," she said quietly. Pressing her body weight against Trey, she tried urging him to move. No effect, unsurprisingly. "Come on. Let's go home." The word *home* seemed to penetrate his "must kill Don" haze, because a little of the tension left his body and he gave her a very slight nod. Mute and Terminator-stiff, he walked her to the car and had them out of Nick's territory in seconds.

When, minutes later, he showed no signs of calming or becoming less robotic, she was tempted to try to talk to him. However, she somehow sensed that, for whatever reason, Trey needed to be alone with his thoughts right now. Going with that instinct, she turned her focus to the view ahead and said nothing.

Trey had thought that the farther he got from that other pack, the more he would calm. That just wasn't happening. Maybe it was Don's claim that Trey wasn't good for Taryn that was agitating him. Or maybe his claim that she wanted things that Trey couldn't give her. Or maybe even Don's suggestion that she stay with his pack and mate with another wolf. But no, as much as all that had seriously pissed him off, none of those accusations were responsible for his mood. What had him as annoyed as fuck right now was that Taryn had defended him.

No female other than his mother or Greta had ever defended him. Not only had Taryn done that, she had basically chosen him over her uncle. It pissed him off that it meant something to him when it shouldn't have. What annoyed him more was that he couldn't be sure if that had been real or if she had just been sticking with their true mates act. He tried telling himself that it didn't matter, tried telling himself that it wasn't relevant, but it goddamn was to him.

He was sick of her doing things that touched him like that and then left him sitting there wondering if he was looking too deep into things or if she was having the same inner struggle as he was.

Like the way she snapped if anyone questioned their mating, as she had with Brodie and her uncle. Was it because her sense of possessiveness now ran bone-deep, just as his did, or was it just her wolf? Like how she held back from marking him. Was that because she was already finding it hard to remain detached, or was it only her wolf finding it hard? And like how she had repeatedly tried so hard to help him form so many alliances, when he had never asked that of her. Was it because she cared for him in some way and wanted to help him, or was it that she just wanted to help the pack as a whole?

He didn't want to be going through this weird inner struggle on his own and, as idiotic as it was, he wanted her to care about him. Mostly because he was afraid that he just might care about her.

And so his bad mood remained with him throughout the long journey home and was still there hours later while he sat on one of the chairs by the lake, soaking up the midday sun. He knew Taryn wouldn't let him brood in peace much longer, so it wasn't a surprise when he heard footsteps. Unfortunately, it turned out that those footsteps didn't belong to Taryn.

"Hey," Dante called out in his usual gruff voice.

"What do you want?"

"Yes, I will have a seat, thank you, Alpha."

"No one likes a smart-ass."

He took the chair opposite Trey's and straddled it. "I take it things didn't go well with her uncle."

Trey sighed. "Actually, he was happy to see her. All of them were pretty hospitable."

"Well, I can understand why that might piss *you* off since— though you'll never admit it—you don't want her to leave, and nor do you seem ready to face just why that might be. But I don't see why it would have Taryn all irritated."

He chose to ignore the first half of what Dante had said. "Her uncle didn't believe we were true mates, said the mating wasn't real."

Dante winced. "Ooh, yeah, that'll do it. She might know this mating's temporary, but she sure doesn't like anyone saying it's not real."

"He also said I was bad for her. Said I couldn't give her those things a woman wants. Then he suggested she stay there and mate with another wolf."

"Prick."

After a pause, Trey said, "She defended me, you know."

"Of course she did. You're her mate. Mates don't stand for that shit."

"Yeah. Her wolf wouldn't want anyone insulting her mate, would she?"

Dante snickered. "You're one blind bastard."

"Blind?"

"Or maybe just dumb." Shaking his head, he looked away and sighed. When he looked at Trey again, there was a mischievous glint in his eyes. "Well...I don't see what you've got to be pissed about. Her uncle's an ass, but he's right. You *are* bad for her. You *can't* give her the things a female wants, because the mating's temporary. And, yeah, there's a good chance she'll go and mate with another wolf when she leaves." When Trey growled warningly, Dante's face took on a superior, smug, know-it-all look. "You know, you could just ask her to stay for good."

At that moment, Trey hated him. Hated him for seeing far more than he should. Hated him for making Trey see exactly how much he wanted that—which seriously scared the shit out of him. He hated his wolf too. Hated him for constantly fighting Trey over the idea of Taryn leaving, for being so unreasonably possessive of her. He also hated Tao for wanting Taryn, he hated the wolf she might one day mate with, and he hated her uncle for speaking the truth he'd been trying to ignore. Mostly, he hated him-fucking-self for caring about a female who didn't even care enough to mark him. "Why would I do that?"

"The two of you are good together. You actually laugh these days. You behave a lot like true mates do."

"Look, Dante, I'll admit I like her—she's fun to have around and she knows what she's doing in the bedroom—but it wouldn't have mattered if I hadn't liked her or if she was someone else, we still would have mated and fucked. This is about a deal, that's all." Trey was aware that he'd sounded pretty harsh. He was also aware by the scent that suddenly flavored the air that Taryn had heard him. *Shit.*

Taryn had been following Trey's scent, hoping to hunt him down and get him to stop brooding, when she heard Dante's words: *"You know, you could just ask her to stay for good."* It was said that eavesdroppers tended to hear things they didn't like. In this case, the saying had proven to be true. It wasn't as though she'd thought things were any different than what Trey firmly stated to Dante, and it wasn't as though she'd thought he cared for her. Yet the effect was still like a hot lance slicing through her. Why? For the same reason that a dull pain had struck her chest and her windpipe had begun to ache...She loved Trey Coleman. The realization punched the breath from her lungs.

God, how horrible was this? She loved a guy to whom she was basically a faceless fuck. She could be anyone to him. In other words, she was no one and nothing to him. Her wolf—who was already insecure in the mating due to not having marked Trey—was tempted to curl up and whine. Taryn was tempted to punch the ass right in the face. Overruling all that was an uncharacteristic urge to flee. To run far and fast. To get away from this person who had so much power over her. To find somewhere to be alone while she faced her pain.

As the conversation abruptly came to a halt and awkwardness filled the air, Taryn knew they had sensed her presence. There went the option of retreating as if she hadn't overheard. Although the urge to lunge at Trey was great, Taryn had been dealing with asshole Alphas long enough to know that it was imperative that they didn't believe they had the power to hurt you. They would stomp all over you if they spotted a weakness, just like her dad and Roscoe. She couldn't afford for Trey to know that she felt anything for him.

Pasting an easy smile on her face, she walked out of the trees and over to the patio table, examining Trey's cautious expression as well as Dante's apologetic one. "Hell, Dante, was it really necessary to needle him when he was already in a bad mood?" she said playfully.

"I, um, we just—"

She rolled her eyes and waved away his attempt to explain himself. "I just came to see if Trey had stopped with the whole brooding thing, but I see he hasn't, so I'll leave him to sulk some more."

Feeling like absolute shit, Trey said, "Taryn, wait—"

"I promised Shaya I'd call her, so I'll see you guys later."

"Taryn, wait." He reached out and caged her wrist with his hand, but when he tried tugging her to him, she shook him off like he was a spider.

"I said I'll see you later."

"Look, what I said—" Words completely failed him because, as he'd told her before, he wasn't good with apologies. He wasn't good with words at all.

"Trey, it doesn't matter."

"Yes, it does." It especially mattered because he could sense her hurt, could *feel* it.

"You only said the truth. It wasn't anything I didn't already know."

Trey growled, pissed at himself for saying dumb shit and pissed at her for walking away from him. "Taryn?" His call went unanswered.

Dante sighed. "You fucked that one up."

For the rest of the day, Taryn kept herself thoroughly occupied. She called Shaya. She went shopping with Grace for groceries. She did a run around the border of pack territory. She showered. She did some laundry. She beat Trick's ass at Mario

Kart. Hell, she even watched a TV program about knitting with Greta, during which they engaged in a battle of wills. Anything so that she didn't have to think about Trey or what he'd said or, more importantly, the fact that she...cared about him. She wouldn't say the *L* word. It was officially banned from her vocabulary.

She tried throughout the evening meal to appear normal, but she was pretty sure that no one bought it, because the guys had crowded around her supportively while shooting scowls at Trey. Still, she had persisted with the act. When Trey spoke to her, she replied, and when he pulled her onto his lap, she let him. There was a sort of desperation in the way he held her so tightly, yet gently. Like the way a person would try to hold a butterfly—careful because it was small and delicate but on guard because it was flighty. None of his touches were seductive or teasing. All were soft and soothing, kind of apologetic. But it didn't ease her hurt or make her relax. How could she be relaxed by the touch of a guy she...cared for, when to him she could be anyone?

After the meal, Taryn had done as she usually did—she lay down on what was, hands down, the most comfortable sofa in the world, to watch some TV. When the time she normally went to bed arrived, she hadn't been able to move.

Maybe it was dumb that she had originally thought that if she just had a little time physically away from him she could somehow build some mental walls that would freeze him out again. Could freeze out the pain. But even as she lay there reminding herself that none of this was real, that Trey wasn't important, that soon her part of the deal would be over, another part of her was considering just flipping him the finger and leaving. She wasn't sure she could bear being around him every day knowing he thought so little of her.

Then she took in the wolves in the room and realized that she couldn't run. This whole thing was about more than just Trey. They didn't deserve to suffer just because of one asshole. She had always dealt with assholes. What was one more to throw into the mix? He wouldn't even be the first asshole she cared about who felt nothing for her.

Still, even though the constricting sensation around her chest seemed to ease, she knew there was no way she could lie beside him tonight, knowing that he would snuggle into her and then try to bring her to orgasm as she woke. Not tonight. Tonight was a night for rebuilding her walls, and to do that she needed distance. So instead of saying her good nights and making her way to bed, she let her eyes drift shut and took comfort in the scents and voices around her until they lulled her to sleep.

It should have sent him into threatening mode to have other males giving him looks that warned him away from his mate. *His mate.* But Trey honestly didn't blame them for the way they were crowding Taryn's sleeping form and regarding him like he was a threat. He'd fucked up. Just like Dante had said. Whether he'd meant for Taryn to hear those cruel words or not, he had hurt her and there was now a gulf a mile wide between them. And he didn't know how to close it.

She was now uneasy around him and emotionally wary of him again, both of which were like blows to his system. He wanted her to know that he was sorry, that he hadn't meant what he had said, that he would never purposely hurt her, but each time he tried to get her alone, she had managed to slip away. She was freezing him out again. It burned even more this time than it had the first time. His wolf also sensed her withdrawal as well as her pain, and both ate at him.

As Trey stared down at her, he promised both himself and his wolf that he *would* fix this. He refused to believe what Dante had said—that he might have broken something that couldn't be mended. No, he refused to believe that. He couldn't accept that. Feeling the sting of her withdrawal had given him a taste of what it would be like without her, and although Trey still wasn't sure about those chest pangs or the emotions that tormented him or the extreme sense of possessiveness, he now knew that he couldn't be without her.

Despite his low, "move out of my way" growl, none of the males moved even an inch from their positions. Tao, Trick, Dominic, and Ryan remained sitting on the floor with their backs against the sofa, while Dante was sitting on it with her feet on his lap and Marcus was beside her head stroking her hair. Trey had to admire their loyalty to their Alpha female, and that was a good thing, considering that she wasn't going anywhere, but no one kept him from his mate. His wolf was in full agreement with him on that.

He released another menacing growl, letting his eyes flash wolf. Reluctantly the males on the floor shuffled along to make room for him. Trey bent and gently scooped her up to cradle her against his chest. She fussed a little in her sleep but didn't wake. He held her tighter against him, stilling her movements, and strode out of the room through the tunnels.

In the bedroom, he placed her gently on the bed and then carefully removed her clothes. Once he'd removed his own he slid under the covers and held her possessively to him, wanting his skin against hers. As she always did, she wriggled a little until she found that groove that seemed to have been made just for her. Then instantly she settled and her expression melted into that sinful-angel look she had when sleeping.

Cupping her face and breezing his thumb along her cheekbone, he whispered, "I'm sorry, baby." Then he nuzzled his face into her hair and closed his eyes, feeling a strange kind of peace now that he was no longer at war with himself and had made the decision to do whatever it took to keep her.

CHAPTER TWELVE

Ordinarily Trey's trigger for waking was either a hunger pang in his stomach or a full bladder. This morning it was something else. As he lay there with his eyes closed, he felt something nagging at him. Something was different, wrong, something that agitated his wolf and had him reaching for the surface, annoyed with his human side for not realizing the problem.

Taking a deep breath, Trey scrubbed at his eyes. He hadn't had to open them to know what was disturbing his wolf. Taryn's exotic scent had instantly shot up his nostrils, but it was too faint. Which meant that she wasn't there.

As his lids flipped open, his eyes confirmed it. The rest of his senses told him she wasn't in the en-suite bathroom, which meant that she had woken before him and sneaked out of the room—there had to have been sneaking and creeping involved, or else he would have easily woken. Unlike Taryn, he was a light sleeper.

Not since the morning after the anniversary of her mom's birthday had Taryn left the room before him. They always had a little play in the mornings before going for breakfast together. It seemed that she was establishing a distance between them, and apparently, it wasn't just going to be an emotional one.

Well, fuck that!

Yeah, he had messed up. Yeah, he had said shit he shouldn't have. And yeah, he had hurt her. But he was still her mate, and if she had just given him five minutes of her time, she would know that he was sorry. Okay, maybe she would never have mated with him if it wasn't for their deal, but their mating had created a connection between them. It was a connection that wouldn't allow for distances—something that he had discovered the hard way. So now his wolf was highly agitated and fighting for control of the situation. His wolf wanted to hunt her down and show her just what he thought of this distance she wanted.

In fact, Trey didn't think that was such a bad idea at all.

Within minutes he was washed, dressed, and storming his way through the tunnels. He found the little witch in the kitchen, sitting on the counter, nibbling on a slice of toast while reading a magazine. She didn't even look up as he entered. He noticed she was alone and wondered if the others had cleared out, suspecting this might happen.

In three long strides, he was in front of her, placing a hand on the counter on either side of her to cage her in. Slowly she raised her head and arched a brow questioningly, as if she couldn't possibly imagine what his problem was.

"You weren't there when I woke up." The words rumbled out of him.

"True. And?" Taryn hadn't actually expected him to react so badly. She had considered that his wolf might feel cheated out of what had become his morning ritual and maybe she'd end up with a nipped lip—that seemed to be his favorite thing to do when she annoyed him—but it wasn't his wolf looking back at her. It was Trey. With his mouth a harsh line and his eyes smoldering, he looked incensed, determined, and pretty damn horny.

Her traitorous body responded to that lust. There was something else there too…If she didn't know any better she'd have thought it was hurt.

"I like making you come in the morning, hearing you moan, having your taste on my tongue. This morning you weren't there."

"Huh. Well, my aim in life isn't to please you, so—"

He placed his face closer to hers. "Spread your legs."

Her stomach clenched. "What?"

"I want my morning taste of you. So spread your legs like a good girl."

"Not a chance, asshole."

The fire in her eyes had his already-hard cock aching painfully. "Don't talk about assholes unless you want me to fuck yours. You know exactly what my problem is, so stop playing dumb. You snuck out of my arms and out of our bed—*snuck* being the key word. Believe me when I tell you that it's in your best interest to not push me any further, because I'm seriously pissed off."

She cocked her head. "Do I get extra points if I fake giving a shit?"

Growling, Trey tangled his hand in her hair and mashed his lips to hers, thrusting his tongue inside and exploring her mouth. It was a hard, possessive, punishing kiss, but of course, his little mate wasn't prepared to take that punishment. She bit his tongue and pulled away.

"Go force your will on someone who'll bow down at the wonder that is you."

Out of patience, Trey gripped her ass and tugged her to the edge of the counter as he boldly cupped her and leaned forward to lick over his mark. As always, she shuddered. "That's it, baby, relax for me. That's my good girl." He unsnapped the top button of her jeans and went for her zipper. Shocking him to complete stillness, she slapped a slice of toast onto his face.

Before he could react, Taryn slipped off the counter, ducked under his arm, and was running out the door. *Bitch*. Amusement and anger warred within him for supremacy. He chased after her through the tunnels, out the main door, down the narrow flights of stairs, and into the forest. He was stunned by just how much distance she had been able to place between them. Christ, she was fast. And so unbelievably agile.

Knowing she was nearing a pond and would soon need to turn left, Trey detoured through the trees and came at her from the front, springing in front of her. She froze and smirked smugly, further inciting his wolf. He was insisting that Trey take her, take her now. Liking that idea, Trey stripped off his clothes, holding her gaze the entire time.

Helpless to resist the effect the naked body of her mate had on her, Taryn licked her lips as she ran her gaze along Trey. He was so gloriously male. His form seemed designed to seduce, seemed created especially to deliver raw, carnal pleasure. And Taryn was eager for it. Eager to feel that long, thick shaft tunneling in and out of her. A wave of savage need had her stomach clenching and her body quivering. Afraid that she would end up giving him exactly what that hard-on said he wanted, she backed away. His cautioning growl made her halt.

"Is this your new thing, Taryn—putting space between us?" He shook his head, tsking. "It won't work. We're mates."

"Wrong. We might have *mated*, but we didn't do it because we chose each other and wanted to have that bond. We came together for a deal. That makes it an arrangement, not a mating."

"I don't much care what you want to call it, Taryn. The point is that because I've claimed you we have a connection you can't ignore, that neither of us can ignore."

"And this connection means I'm supposed to give you whatever you want?" She snorted derisively. "Well, fuck you."

"I know you're upset with me, baby, but did you give me a chance to apologize? Or did you try to freeze me out again?"

It startled her that he sounded genuinely hurt by that. In fact, he looked it too. "Who said I was upset?"

"If you're not upset, then prove it. Come here so I can give you what both of us want. I can smell your arousal, Taryn." He fisted his cock. "You want this."

He was right, the bastard. She couldn't help being annoyed with her body—it didn't care that he had hurt her. No, it was responding to him as it always did—like the goddamn hussy Greta described! Even now, as she was considering a good place to bury his body, she couldn't move her eyes from the sight of him stroking himself.

Not trusting that she could keep resisting him, she snarled and sprang upward, grabbing onto the branch above her head. She hauled herself up and stood perfectly balanced. He didn't look impressed.

"Get your pretty little ass down here now and I might not spank it."

She snorted. "You say that as if you think I'd let you spank me."

"Now, Taryn," he drawled.

Instead, she shot him a challenging look. As she expected, he began climbing his way up the tree, reaching for her. She sprang to the next tree, then swung from that tree to the next, and the next, and the next before finally jumping to the ground and dashing away. She could hear him hot on her heels but she didn't once look back.

Moments later a set of powerful arms locked around her and tackled her to the ground. At the last second, he spun, taking the brunt of the fall before then rolling her onto her stomach.

"Caught. Trapped. And soon to be mounted."

Taryn struggled. "Oh, I don't think so!" He grunted as she reared back and slammed her elbow into his ribs. Although she managed to scramble from beneath him, he grabbed her feet and dragged her back to him.

"Tricky little bitch," he said with a smile. "*My* tricky little bitch."

"No."

He draped himself over her and placed his mouth at her ear. "Oh yes, baby, your ass is definitely mine. And if you keep struggling, I swear I'll fuck it."

Instantly she stilled, but then, as she felt his arrogant smile at her neck, a surge of anger hit her. She sank her hand into the soil and hurled a handful of it at his face. He coughed and spat, cursing. As the pressure of his body left her, she managed to crawl from beneath him and was almost on her feet when he again clamped his arms around her and pinned her to the ground.

Harder than he'd ever been in his life, Trey tore her jeans from her body and then gripped her arms and locked them behind her back, trapping them there with one hand. He curled his other arm around her waist and pulled her ass in the air. "God, you've no idea how hot you look right now. Totally submissive." Without any preamble, he plunged two fingers inside her. "You're so wet for me. See, baby, your body knows it belongs to me."

She hated herself for the moan that escaped her. Not prepared to let him win, she continued struggling, but stopped and gasped in outrage when he spanked her ass. What pissed her off even more was that she liked it. "You do that again and you'll find out what your right testicle tastes like!" She fought against his hold, but he didn't even loosen it.

"You don't really want to get away, Taryn. What you want is me inside you."

Again, he was right. "Goddamn caveman bastard!"

Aligning his cock to her entrance, he told her, "I'm going to fuck you. Because I can, because you belong to me, because this body is mine to fuck whenever I want." And then he slammed into her and she cried out. He groaned as her muscles clamped down on him like a vise. She was so hot and tight and felt as good around him as she always did. After giving her a moment to adjust, Trey blanketed her body with his and grazed his teeth over the mark on her neck. "I'm going to fuck you hard and deep now, Taryn. Fuck you until you're dripping with my come. And you're going to take it like a good girl."

"You cock-smoking shitfaced motherfucking piece of monkey shit," she growled, squirming again as she tried to free herself, only to have him lock his teeth on her shoulder in warning. He rested more of his weight on her then, pinning her still.

"You know I won't force you, baby. I'd never hurt you. If you want me to stop"—he began to slowly drag his cock out of her body, wanting her to feel every inch of him—"all you have to do is say so." He paused when there was only the head of his cock lodged inside her. "Is that what you want? Do you want me to stop?" When she only growled, he smiled, adding, "Or do you want me to fuck you until you come so hard it hurts?" He gave a very slow yet deep thrust, loving the long, drawn-out groan that escaped her. "Shall I stop?"

"Just do it!"

"Do what, baby? Stop, or fuck you? Be very clear."

"Fuck me!"

"Whatever you want." He closed his teeth over her nape and rammed his cock into her, growling.

Taryn decided it was very possible that Trey could fuck her into unconsciousness. He was pounding into her at a frenzied pace, like fucking her was the last thing he would do before he died. Pinned as she was, all she could do was take everything he had to give. It should have infuriated her that his huge, powerful body was like a cage around her, leaving her unable to move. But, strangely, she found that she kind of liked it. It was sheer male domination, but it wasn't threatening or painful.

Her wolf approved of her male's dominance, believed him to be worthy of her surrender. The pleasure had swept Taryn under and she couldn't even find it in herself to care that she was still hurt by his words or that her heart was a mess. Her body was winding tighter and tighter, making her moan and groan and whimper.

A voice inside Trey whispered that he was being too rough, but he was too far gone to heed it. Lust had consumed his blood. *She* had consumed his blood. Every sound she made had his body burning hotter and hotter, had him heading closer and closer to his climax. He could already feel the telling tingle in his spine, but no way would he come until she had found her own release.

Just then, a hint of a familiar scent drifted to him and he almost smiled. Tao was obviously on a run in his wolf form and had wandered close. Trey removed his teeth from her nape and whispered in Taryn's ear, loudly enough for only her to hear, "You know Tao's out there, don't you? I'm glad he's watching. I want him to see my cock thrusting in and out of you, *owning* you. I want him to remember that it's me who fucks you—not him, not anyone else."

"No one owns me," Taryn somehow managed to growl even as she was still moaning and whimpering. She flexed the hands he had pinned behind her back, clawing his stomach in retaliation.

He groaned. "Yeah, baby, scratch me. You know I like it. Do you know what else I like? Feeling your hot little pussy squeeze my cock while you come all over me. Make that happen for me, Taryn. I want it, *now*." With that, he upped the speed of his thrusts and sank his teeth over his mark. Instantly she screamed and her muscles bitingly clamped down on his cock, milking him as he growled her name and exploded inside her. Completely sated, he released her arms and they both sank down to the ground, him still atop her and still inside her.

"I swear to God I'm going to rip your spine out of your ass," she panted. "As soon as I can move, I'm going to do it."

He chuckled and licked his mark, liking the shudder that ran through her. Movement in his peripheral vision snatched his attention and he looked to see Tao again. Most likely sensing that Trey's wolf saw him as intruding and wanted to attack, Tao turned and trotted away.

Only when he was satisfied the other wolf was a fair distance away did Trey return his focus to Taryn, nuzzling her hair. "I'm sorry for what I said, baby. I was in a shitty mood. I took it out on Dante."

Just like that, all the emotional torment that she had pushed aside came flooding back. She swallowed hard. "Like I said, it wasn't anything I didn't already know. You only said the truth."

"No." He withdrew, gently flipped her over, and then slid back inside. They both groaned. He kept his thrusts slow and sensual as he spoke. "I just say stupid things when I'm pissed. I didn't mean any of it."

"Then why say it?"

"I don't know. I'm not good with this stuff, baby. Things weren't supposed to be like this. It was only supposed to be about a deal."

He sounded so lost and confused that it prickled at Taryn's protective instincts. Before she thought better of it, she was curling her arms around his neck.

"When Dante talked about you staying and I realized how much I wanted you to, it spooked the hell out of me and stupid shit starting coming out of my mouth."

She could understand him being spooked. When she realized she cared for Trey, she'd freaked out. Even now, she didn't want to use the *L* word, even though she knew it was what she felt.

"All I know is that I don't want you to leave. If you do, I'll hunt you down and bring you back, Taryn, I shit you not, I will. Not because of our deal or my wolf, but because I want you here with me." Then abruptly he reared back and began hammering into her, capturing her cries with his mouth as he crushed her lips with his. He groaned when she began sucking on his tongue, thinking of something else he'd like her to suck. Of course, she was well aware of that. "If you do that again, I'll pull out and shove my cock in your mouth."

She beat his back with her legs. "I'll bite it off and shove it up your ass!"

"Then who would fuck you like this?" Drawn to one of his marks on her neck, he bent down and sucked at it, loving how her muscles tightened around his cock and how her nails pressed into his back. But like always, they never broke the skin. "You know what I want, Taryn," he growled as he leaned over her, curling his hips as he increased the pace of his pounding. "Give it to me."

Taryn knew what he meant, but she clamped her mouth shut and shook her head.

His eyes flashed wolf. "Bite me, mark me, now."

"No!"

He tangled both hands in her hair and tugged hard. "Do it, Taryn. Put your fucking brand on me."

She writhed beneath him, growling, "Fuck you!"

He gentled his voice a little and pinned her gaze with his. "Why fight it? Why?"

"This isn't real," she almost sobbed.

"Wrong, baby. This is as real as it gets."

"I told you, I won't always placate your wolf!"

"He needs it, baby. *I* want it. *I* need it."

Taryn shook her head again, knowing he couldn't realize what he was asking, couldn't realize what might happen. Nor could he realize that she was fighting herself just as much as she was fighting him. "It'll never fade!"

"I don't want it to. I want to look in the mirror and see it there. I want everyone else to see it there."

"You want me to mark you so another female can cover it with hers? Fuck that!"

He arched a brow tauntingly. "You don't like the idea of another female marking me? Then leave your brand there, warn them off. Show them who I belong to."

"It might start the imprinting! You don't want that!" It surprised her that his expression suddenly softened.

"You're not listening to anything I'm saying, baby. I'm not giving you up. Even if we don't imprint, I'm not giving you up, I can't. If another man touches you, I'll kill him. I will. I'll rip his fucking throat out and I won't even care. You're mine, Taryn, and you're not going anywhere. I need you here with me, and I need your brand on me. Do it, Taryn! Give it to me!"

Whining in defeat, Taryn lifted her head and sank her teeth into the juncture of his neck and shoulder.

It took everything Trey had not to come there and then. "Fuck, yeah. More!"

She raked her claws down his back, just like she and her wolf had wanted to from the beginning.

"Again, Taryn!" This time she bit down on his shoulder but she didn't release him, and he loved the possessiveness of that act. Pounding into her even harder, he demanded, "Come for me, Taryn." He clamped his teeth over his claiming mark and she screamed around the flesh of his shoulder as her climax tore into her. That together with her muscles closing around his cock had him erupting inside her once again.

And that was when it happened. Taryn released his shoulder with a gasp as her entire body clenched. Suddenly she was struck by something that felt like an ice-cream headache. Seconds later it eased and a feeling of warmth washed over her, like how she felt when she was wrapped up in a blanket with a hot-water bottle under her feet and a mug of hot chocolate in her hands—snug, contented, and sheltered.

She lifted her head and rested her chin on his chest, only then realizing he had rolled them over and she was lazed over him. "I—" Nothing more came out. Shock had apparently taken away her ability to speak. She could have told herself that what was happening was the imprinting bond beginning to develop, but she knew it would be a lie. She knew that what was happening was more than that, knew it as surely as she knew that she needed oxygen to survive—it was a knowing that basic and primitive. A bond was developing between them all right. A true mate bond.

Should she really be so surprised? Wasn't this what her wolf and her body had hinted at all along? There had been plenty of signs. Like the way her wolf reacted to Trey's scent—hell, she'd even been calm when he kidnapped her—and constantly craved his company and touch. Like the way her body had from the very beginning reacted rather enthusiastically to him. Like the way she had somehow been positive that he would never hurt her—for God's sake, the psycho actually made her feel safe.

She realized then that, on some level, she had known she was speaking the truth when she told Shaya that the awful state she had slipped into after Joey's death had been because of the double blow of losing her mom at the very same time. After spending her entire life believing Joey had been her true mate, it had never occurred to her on a more conscious level that she could have been wrong—especially when Trey had also always believed that his own true mate had been another shifter. Apparently, fate liked to play jokes.

Considering how long Trey had been imprint-phobic, he would have expected to shit his pants if he somehow discovered that his true mate hadn't died at all, that he had found her. Instead, he found himself strangely at peace. Another strange thing was that he wasn't so shocked to find out that Summer hadn't been his mate. Thinking back, he realized that it had been her mom who had spoken the words "true mates." Trey himself had never claimed that, never felt the tugging of that bond. He had taken what she said as truth, because he hadn't known any better—he was fourteen, he knew nothing of mating bonds and wasn't all that familiar with feelings. As he gazed up at Taryn, he marveled at just how…happy…he was to have been wrong about Summer.

It made sense that the bond had never clicked into place before now, he mused. Both he and Taryn had held back from each other all this time. Now that he had come to accept he couldn't be without her and she had finally branded him, there was a bridge between them that enabled the bond to exist. It wasn't fully developed yet, as it was only in its early stages, but it was enough that he could *feel* her and what she was feeling.

So this was what Dante had meant each time he spoke to him of a truth that Trey wasn't yet ready to accept. Dante had obviously suspected for a while that they were true mates. He was going to be so smug about this. "You know this is more than imprinting, don't you?" he said softly.

She nodded. "Are you scared?" she asked quietly, dreading the answer.

Trey shook his head. "No." He wanted her bound to him in every possible way. "Are you?"

Not wanting to lie, and thinking he would probably sense it if she did, she nodded again.

He stroked her hair gently. "Why?"

"I don't know if I've just claimed someone who doesn't care for me."

"Feel what I feel."

Closing her eyes, Taryn found their connection instantly. She didn't feel it in her head as she had thought mates did; she felt it everywhere, felt Trey everywhere. It was like he was a shadow— something insubstantial that was forever just behind her but that she couldn't touch. Yet, like with her shadow, although she couldn't touch it or even feel it, she knew it was there—close and a part of her. She *knew* that he was genuinely happy that they had bonded, *knew* that he had been serious when he said he wouldn't have let her leave, no matter what.

And beneath all that, there was something else. God, it was as if he had this knot inside him that chafed and nettled—threads of protectiveness, possessiveness, adoration, respect, desire, and loyalty, all twisted and matted with disorientation, panic, incredulity, and even fear. With all these feelings, he was in totally unfamiliar territory and couldn't make sense of anything, but he was sure that he cared about her and couldn't be without her.

Hell, it had been a lot more than she ever expected to find. She would have thought that anything he felt for her would be based on a primal need for sex and the instincts that came with his wolf and their mating, but it wasn't that at all. This was about Trey and Taryn, the man and the woman. When she opened her eyes, it was to see him looking at her with confusion in his eyes.

"You think you love me," he practically whispered. He hated that he couldn't say it back, knowing it would hurt her. Stroking her hair again he said, "I don't know what that is, baby."

Taryn's heart literally ached for him. He was telling the truth; he didn't know what it was. He had never had any real examples of love in his life, and he was convinced from the things he had done and was capable of doing that he wouldn't be able to feel an emotion like that. He'd been only a child when he'd closed himself off—a child who didn't want his dad's words or treatment to be able to hurt him anymore. Closing himself off so early like that had stunted his development and he was, in a way, emotionally immature. That's what was stopping him from untangling that knot.

It was like a kid with a complex math formula—too many factors and variables and unfamiliar terms for him to work out what it all meant. "Love is giving someone the power to completely destroy you, and hoping that they won't."

Trey framed her face with his hands, brushing his thumb over her bottom lip. "I'd never purposely hurt you. Never. I'm a man, which means I'll fuck up. Regularly. I'm not good with words, I spout crap when I'm angry, and I'm about as romantic as a pebble. But…See, I'm not good with words. All I can say is you're important to me in a way I can't explain or understand. More important to me than anything else."

And Taryn could work with that because he did care for her, and that was more than she would have hoped for. "Same here."

Gently he brought her face to his and ravished her mouth, gliding his tongue against hers and drinking her into him. "My wolf's feeling pretty smug about this."

She smiled. "So is mine. Think the rest of the pack will be okay about it?"

"Let's go find out." Although it had been hot at the time to tear her jeans from her body, Trey was regretting it as he walked back toward the house with a half-naked Taryn. Shifters were pretty easy about nakedness, since they had to strip in front of each other a lot for shifting, but it wasn't something they did so casually under other circumstances. When they reached the spot where he'd thrown his clothes, he gave Taryn his T-shirt to wear. A smile spread over his face at the sight of her practically drowning in it.

"Did it ever occur to you that I'm not too small and you're just ridiculously big?"

Zipping his fly, he shrugged. "You like how big I am."

As usual, he was referring to the bulge in his jeans. She snorted. "It's a wonder that *thing* even fits inside me."

"Thing?" He pulled her to him and kissed her forehead. "Of course it fits. It belongs there." Swatting her ass, he added, "Now come on."

Strolling through the tunnels toward the living area, they passed Greta. As she took in Taryn's appearance, she huffed. "Hussy."

"Prude," Taryn shot back without breaking stride as she and Trey walked hand in hand into the living area. Cam, Rhett, Grace, Lydia, Trick, Marcus, and Dante all looked up, saw their clothes—or lack thereof—and grinned.

"So you've kissed, bitten, and made up?" asked Dante.

"Get the entire pack together," ordered Trey. "We'll be back in a few minutes."

Exactly ten minutes later both Taryn and Trey were back in the living area, washed and dressed in fresh clothes. Taryn was surprised at how nervous she was about the pack's reaction. She knew that most of them liked her and respected her and even viewed her as their Alpha female to an extent. However, this would no longer be a temporary thing. They would now have to accept her as their true Alpha female, latency and all. She hadn't had to care before about what they thought of her, but now it mattered.

She was certain that Kirk, Selma, Hope, and Greta wouldn't be pleased about it, and she suspected that Tao might not be so happy either. Even though he was reasonably friendly, he didn't spend time with her the way he used to and envy wafted from him whenever she and Trey were together around him. He could very well decide that he wasn't going to stick around and watch her and Trey be mated.

Taryn was quite sure that the others would be okay with her staying. Brock she couldn't be too sure about because he didn't talk much, but she suspected that if Tao threatened to leave and some of the others got upset then Brock would want her gone— which wasn't going to happen, no matter what any of them thought. God, this was nerve-racking.

Sensing—no, feeling—Taryn's anxiety, Trey took her hand and tugged her closer to his side. "You should all know that Taryn is now officially your Alpha female."

"You're staying?" asked Marcus, leaning forward in his seat, wide-eyed.

Rhett frowned at Taryn's nod. "What about imprinting?"

Trey smiled crookedly. "We haven't imprinted. We've bonded." As he'd expected, Dante smiled smugly.

"Are you saying you're true mates?" asked Trick. Surprisingly, he didn't look all that shocked. "Well, that explains a lot."

"Oh, that's all we need," griped Greta. "A midget with a sharp, sarcastic tongue for an Alpha."

Taryn sighed and smiled. "In a perfect world I would be taller, you would be alive, and chickens could cross the road without being the subject of a joke. Guess you'll just have to deal."

Tao puffed, shaking his head in disbelief. "Well, that was the last thing I'd have expected. After what Trey said last night, I thought you'd have headed for the hills." He flinched when Dante jammed his elbow into his ribs.

"We all knew he didn't really mean what he said," Dante growled at Tao.

"Tell me this is a joke!" demanded Selma.

"For God's sake, Trey, she's latent," said Kirk, red in the face. "And a Warner."

"Your point being what, exactly?" asked Dominic.

"I'm not bowing down to a Warner!"

"*I'm* not bowing down to a latent!" Selma practically screeched.

"Well, I'm happy for you guys," said Marcus, grinning.

"Me too," said Ryan.

Dominic winked. "And me."

Grace did a little jump. "Oh my God, this is great!" Most of the others nodded their agreement, smiling.

"How can you all accept her as your Alpha?" demanded Kirk, his gaze drilling into everyone.

Taryn sighed. "Kirk, if you're going to act like an asshole, then go do it somewhere else."

"I have the right to have an opinion!"

"Yeah, but I still have the right to think you're a stupid prick."

Panting like a raging bull, Kirk shook his head. "I can't support this." He stalked out of the room and was followed closely by Selma and Hope—although Hope seemed to be leaving just because Selma was.

Dante sank back into the chair with his hands clasped behind his head, looking kind of smug. "I said at the start that you two would imprint. When I saw you covered in bites, I made the others a bet that you'd end up staying here. Unfortunately, no one bet against me, so then we just made bets on how soon imprinting would start. I was closest."

"I was furthest," admitted Trick. "I thought you would need to leave before Trey snapped out of his state of denial."

"But it didn't take long for me to see there was more to it than that. I've been wondering how long it'd take for you to realize that you're true mates." The impatience in Dante's tone indicated that the wait had been killing him.

Trey searched all their faces. "I take it this means none of you are opposed to this. Not that it'll make any difference, but I'd prefer if you were all good with it."

Dante stood and then dropped to one knee, head bowed. Marcus copied the move. Then Ryan, Trick, Dominic, Grace, Lydia, Cam, Rhett, Tao, and finally Brock.

"No, guys, please don't," said Taryn. But they remained where they were, like white knights, and it freaked her out. "Come on, get up." She nudged Trey. "Tell them to get up."

"They're acknowledging us as their Alpha pair, offering us their loyalty."

"Well, they can be loyal standing up."

Trey turned to his grandmother, who looked like a sulking child. "Greta?"

"This sort of thing wouldn't have happened in my day," said Greta. "When I met your grandfather, we were both virgins. You can't tell me *she* was one."

Taryn smiled. "Well, of course you were. It was expected back in 1465."

"And it's not natural how much…um…intimate relations you have. We might be shifters, but we're not animals. It's disgusting."

Trey groaned. "How about we skip the insults and just get to the point."

"I'm not getting down on one knee," she spat.

"But you accept this? We have your loyalty as your Alpha pair?" he pressed.

She gave him a tiny nod, then hissed at Taryn. "But she's still a hussy. And just you remember, hussy, he's *my grandson*."

With that, she marched out of the room, mumbling about latent wolves, sarcastic females, and men who were led around by their penises.

"Right," began Trey as he picked Taryn up, wrapping her legs around his waist, "then we'll see you guys later, because we have some celebratory sex to do."

"Okay, but, Taryn," said Dominic, "if it doesn't work out with him, well…I'm no Fred Flintstone, but I sure can make your bed rock." He chuckled at everyone's groans.

Trey, of course, growled and then strode out of the living area with wide, determined steps.

"We've just done the deed twice outside!" she reminded him.

"You know I'm always good to go again when it comes to you, baby."

"It'll only ever be me from now on, got that?"

"Same goes for you. I told you, there'll be no other cocks inside you but mine."

"Glad we understand each other."

Finally in the bedroom, he literally dumped her on the bed and then tackled his fly. "I have a feeling the sex will be even better now that we're partially bonded. Let's find out."

It turned out that it *was* even better. Trey had felt her pleasure, sensed as it rose, which had then intensified and amplified his own until he came so hard he almost passed out. What made it even better was that he not only knew but could feel that it was more than sex for her, could feel how much she cared for him.

He'd never thought of himself as a lovable person, and yet this amazing female actually loved him. She didn't say it aloud for the same reason that she never begged—she feared being completely vulnerable to him. Similarly, he feared being completely vulnerable to her. He suspected that for as long as that fear existed for both of them, the bond wouldn't be complete.

At one time, he would have thought that wouldn't be such a bad thing—if their relationship fucked up and they separated, it would be easier for both of them if they weren't completely tied to one another. But he had no plans to ever let this female leave him, and he wanted all of her even as he feared giving her the same. Yeah, that was bad, and if he'd had a fully developed conscience, then maybe he would have felt shitty about it. Or maybe he would always be unapologetically selfish where Taryn was concerned. As he looked at her, lying beside him, shuddering, panting, and totally naked, he figured yeah, he would.

Later that evening, they all decided to go for a run as a pack. Well, all except for Greta, Kirk, Selma, and Hope, who were still sulking. Taryn smiled at the feeling of the cool night air on her face as she accompanied the wolves as they loped through the woods, enjoying the sense of belonging and closeness that could only come from running with the pack. Eventually they reached a small clearing, where some of the wolves lay down to relax.

The wolf with the salt-and-pepper fur—Dominic—had other ideas. Cautiously he approached the only jet-black wolf—Tao—and bowed down, sticking his rear in the air and wagging his tail, inviting the black wolf to play. The second Tao got close, Dominic bounded away. They playfully growled and released high-pitched, dog-like barks as they tussled and chased one another. A gray-black wolf with a white undercoat—Dante—quickly joined the fun, followed by two gray-brown-yellow wolves—Trick and Marcus.

There was a lot of mock fighting, shouldering one another, pouncing, ambushing, bumping bodies together, jaw wrestling, and attempting to grab each other by the scruff of the neck. From where she was lying on her side on the ground beside two white-gray wolves—Grace and Rhett—Taryn rolled her eyes at the sight of Cujo and another wolf peeing on rocks and trees. It was typical of Trey and Ryan to not join in the fun and instead spend the time leaving scent markers to warn away strange wolves.

She doubted either of the oh-so-serious males even knew how to enjoy himself.

It wasn't long before said serious males trotted over to her. Ryan was beautiful as a wolf. His fur was predominantly black, but his face, neck, and the insides of his ears were all a creamy blond. His posture and tail were low as he approached and licked her jaw. Then he loped off, leaving her with Cujo, who rubbed his cheeks against hers and then repeatedly licked her face. When she ran her fingers through his dense, coarse fur, he settled down beside her to enjoy the contact further.

She couldn't help smiling at the sight of her mate, her pack, her wolves—things she hadn't really expected to ever have. Finally, she had a place where she belonged, where she could be happy, and where she had the feeling that she fit. Now all she had to do was make sure that asshole Darryl Coleman didn't take it all away from her.

CHAPTER THIRTEEN

The one thing Taryn had always known would be annoying about being mated was that having such an intense connection to someone meant there were no secrets. Not that Taryn had any huge, dark secrets or anything, but there were little itty-bitty ones that she would have preferred to keep to herself.

Like this, for example—Taryn had to come to love waking up with Trey's big body practically cocooning her. It made her feel safe, sheltered, secure. It also made her feel a little dumb and feeble. She was an Alpha, for God's sake, and yet she loved being cuddled and protected. It felt like a weakness. If Trey woke up now and tapped into what she was feeling, he would know that. By God, if he teased her about it, she'd kick his balls so hard they ended up in his throat.

It was still hard getting her head around the fact that they were true mates, although it wasn't so much that. It was just the way everything seemed to have happened at once; realizing she loved him, hearing he cared about her, and then suddenly discovering that what she'd grown up believing was bullshit and that she and Trey were true mates—all in the space of twenty-four hours.

And now she was mated. Now she had that deep connection to someone that she had always dreamed of having—that every shifter dreamed of having. Casting a shadow over that, however, was the heavy sensation that was saddling her chest—guilt. Guilt that she could be so happy to be wrong about Joey.

She had sensed that Trey wasn't experiencing that guilt. Finding out that Taryn was his true mate had brought him nothing but masculine satisfaction and a sense of peace. She knew what she needed to do if she was to have that same peace, and she planned to do it after breakfast. The feeling of him nuzzling her hair broke into her thoughts.

"Hey, baby," he greeted in a sleep-croaky voice. Without having to look, Trey had *known* she was awake. Just like he had known she enjoyed his body crowding her but would never admit it. Just like he had known she was feeling slightly guilty. "Do you wish I wasn't your mate?" It startled him just how much it would pain him if she said yes.

Taryn shook her head. "No. Look deeper, behind the guilt. I'm happy about it, about you. Really, I am."

He relaxed a little when he sensed it was the truth.

"Then why the guilt?"

It wasn't an emotion he'd had an awful lot of experience with, and it had never made much sense to him even when he did. It seemed dumb that you could feel a rush of happiness but that a negative emotion would be attached to it. Wasn't happiness supposed to be just that, happiness?

"When I think about it, I'm not sure I know how to think about Joey without having guilt ruling me. Guilt that I should have been in that car and died in the accident with him and our mothers, but didn't. Guilt that I survived losing him when most people expected me not to. Guilt that I wasn't spending every single day grieving him. Guilt that I could be attracted to other guys and still want to mate with somebody someday. Hell, when I lost my virginity, I cried the whole time." She twisted in Trey's arms so that she was facing him. "And now I find out that this person was never my true mate at all, and a part of me thinks I should be lamenting that. But I don't. I can't. It makes me feel guilty that I'm glad I was wrong."

He sighed. "I get what you mean, but I can't say I feel the same. I don't feel any guilt whatsoever to know that Summer wasn't my true mate. If that makes me a bad person, well, that's because I am a bad person."

"You're not a bad person. You're just an ass." She smiled when he chuckled. "I'm sorry if I'm hurting you with the guilt thing. I don't mean to."

He ran his fingers through her hair. "It's okay, you can make it up to me."

When he rolled Taryn onto her back and began sliding down her body, she knew exactly what his intention was—the same intention he had every single morning. This was Trey's version of breakfast. Being the kind, generous mate that she was, she lay still and let him feast.

It always felt so good when he tasted her, but it was so much more amazing having him do it while the mating bond was partially formed. She could feel that although it gave him a bone-deep satisfaction that she belonged to him, he wasn't just trying to answer his possessive urges by carrying her taste in his mouth. He was completely engrossed. The combination of her taste, the moans she made, and the knowledge that he was pleasuring his mate all had him totally gripped. As usual, when she came in his mouth, he didn't let a single drop of it go to waste. Then he swatted her ass and, whistling, strolled into the en-suite bathroom. Cocky bastard.

Rather than waiting for him as she always did, she dressed quickly and made her way to the kitchen. Yesterday most people had seemed accepting enough of their mating, but she couldn't help wondering if their acceptance and offers of loyalty were for Trey's benefit. As such, she wanted to go alone for breakfast this morning to see if their attitudes were different while he wasn't around. That plan pretty much flopped, since the only person in the kitchen was Grace. The second she saw Taryn, a beaming smile took over her face.

"So...you're true mates after all," she drawled, handing Taryn a mug of coffee. "I'm so thrilled. I must say, you look just as shocked this morning as you did yesterday."

As usual, Taryn settled on the counter. "Yeah. I knew I'd come to care for him, but I didn't expect him to feel the same. I certainly didn't expect all this."

"He's cared about you from the beginning. He's just not good with showing he cares."

"Well, he never had many examples of it." She hated that he'd had such an awful childhood.

"That's true. Louisa...she was a good person, but she wasn't affectionate. It wasn't part of who she was, like Greta. Kids...they need hugs, kisses, praise, and words of love. She never gave him that. His dad gave him pretty much the opposite."

"It's no wonder he doesn't know what love is."

Most likely in response to Taryn's sudden frown, Grace asked, "What is it?"

"Nothing." At Grace's "tell me now" expression, she sighed. "It's just...I can't help feeling a little hurt that he doesn't care about me as much as I do him. I know it should be enough to be mated to someone I love even if he doesn't love me back—especially when I'd never thought I'd have the mating bond at all. But the idea of spending my life with someone I love who doesn't feel the same...I'm worried it'll eat away at me over time."

"Of course it hurts. You want to be the center of his everything, just like he's the center of yours. But, honey, I'm pretty sure you already are. He cares about you about as much as he's capable of doing. It's up to you to show him what love is, to wrap him up in it until he comes to recognize it and feel it himself."

"I don't know if that's possible. Trey...he's so guarded. Hell, we both are. I'm not sure that the mating bond will ever be fully complete."

Grace gave her a gentle smile. "You know what the answer is, don't you? Chocolate. It's always the answer, no matter the question."

Taryn's chuckle died as Selma entered the room, wearing what might as well have been a tissue. Clearly the female was set on continuing to flaunt herself in front of Trey. "He's not here yet."

Scowling, Selma took a seat at the table and, naturally, the tissue rode up her thighs to the point of indecency. "I'll bet you're feeling very smug. Well, be as smug as you want, but I have to say I feel kind of sorry for you if you think this is over. He's still not yours. The mating bond is only in the early stages. The link can be broken quite easily."

"So can your nose. Don't test me, Selma. Right now I don't have the patience required to deal with people whose IQ lands on the right side of the decimal point. Trey didn't want to mate with you before I was here, and even if I left he still wouldn't want you as his mate."

"Oh, he wanted me just fine all those times he had me in his bed. Just think...Those silk sheets you sleep on at night—he fucked me on those."

Grace snorted. "Oh, have some pride, Selma. It happened all of *one* time and that was years ago *in your room*! If it's really that important to you to be some guy's Alpha female then go seduce one at a club or something."

"Trey's mine! This pack is mine!" Her eyes flashed wolf as her attention turned back to Taryn. "You'll never be accepted here as Alpha female. Never. You might have gotten most of them to pledge their loyalty to you, but you're naive if you think they all meant it."

"Amen," muttered a witchy voice.

Taryn returned Greta's glare. "Hey, Old Mother Hubbard. Still alive? Hmm. Guess those voodoo dolls don't work after all."

"Yes, yes, make your jokes, hussy."

"Who said I was joking?"

A cruel smirk played around the edges of Selma's mouth. "I'll bet it hurts knowing you'll never run together with Trey in your wolf form."

It did, actually, but Taryn wouldn't let her see that her hit had met its target. "You know, I can't understand why you'd spoil such gorgeous blonde hair by dyeing your roots black." Selma's smirk died and was replaced by a snarl. She probably would have said more if Trey, Dante, and Tao hadn't then entered the kitchen. Dante and Tao both greeted Taryn with smiles and respectful nods of the head.

"Hey, why didn't you wait for me?" Trey asked against her lips as he stepped between her legs. He heard Selma—a mostly naked Selma, his peripheral vision informed him—call his name, but he didn't pay her any attention. He wasn't stupid.

"I needed caffeine." Taryn gratefully accepted the plate of food Grace handed her. Trey frowned when Grace didn't present him with a plate of his own.

"You don't have to start running round after her just because she's officially your Alpha female," Greta told Grace.

Trey groaned. The woman never let up.

Unable to resist needling her, Taryn said, "You know, Greta, you and I will get on a whole lot better once you accept that I'm a goddess."

At that moment, Marcus entered and, obviously having heard her comment, bowed to her. "Oh beautiful goddess, how may I serve thee?" Trey slapped him lightly over the head.

"A goddess? *Hmph.* I gave you my loyalty because I'd never do anything to upset my grandson, but I'll never see you as my Alpha female."

"Yeah? Watch me pretend to care." In actuality, she could demand Greta's complete submission and even punish her for her disrespect, but Taryn wasn't interested in being one of those Alphas who were so damn strict that they basically prevented the members from having minds of their own. She didn't want the loyalty of her pack out of fear, but out of respect.

If a few members weren't prepared to give her that, then fine, whatever. Besides, she was so used to her relationship with Greta being like this that it would feel kind of weird if it was any different. And it was way too much fun to battle with her.

By the time Taryn had downed her breakfast and morning coffee, Trey had gone to his office as usual to check his e-mails and do whatever else he did in there. Taking advantage of his absence, Taryn went outside to the small clearing and then made her way into the forest, headed for the river. She hadn't been there since the anniversary of her mom's birthday, nor had she felt a need to. Until now.

On finally coming to the river, she sat on the same boulder as on the previous visit, again enjoying the fresh, crisp air and the various comforting smells. She wasn't sure how long she sat there trying to pluck up the courage to speak, to find the right words. Finally, she took a deep breath, swallowed hard, and straightened her posture.

Hey, Joe. God, where do I start? Last time I was pretty miserable, huh? Remember I told you all about how the Alpha I'd mated with was basically ignoring my existence? His name's Trey—I don't think I ever told you that. Well, things are kind of totally the opposite now.

We've, um, well we've sort of…We sort of discovered that… It turns out we're true mates. I bit him yesterday and the bond clicked into place. I feel awful for saying this, but…well, I'm happy about it. I'm so sorry if that makes you hate me, but I'd rather not lie to you.

You don't mean any less to me than you did before. It's like I said to Shaya—you have your own space inside me, and now so does Trey. And now he's filling it. And...and I love him. I'd like to think you can be happy for me, that you wouldn't want me being alone. I know I'd feel that way if the positions were reversed—although I admit I'm petty enough that I'd have been a little jealous. But I wouldn't have wanted you to be lonely or to never find someone who cared for you. And that's what I have. Not love, no, I'm not sure I'll ever have that, so I'm not even sure our mating bond will ever be fully formed. But I'm actually happy. I hope you can be glad for me.

With tears clouding her vision, she rose and smiled. *Love you, miss you.*

Although her heart felt as heavy as it usually did after talking to Joey, she wasn't filled with that old sense of hopelessness or plagued by a feeling of loneliness. Yes, she missed Joey, there was no way she couldn't, but now she knew that it wasn't because he had been her mate, but because of what close friends they had been. Now she had something good to go back to, someone who had gotten rid of that emptiness she had once felt. Someone she loved. Her mate.

She had taken approximately ten steps when she realized she was no longer alone. Looking to her right, she saw a very familiar, whopping-big gray wolf. "Hey there, Cujo." She knew that although the wolf would have picked up on her surface emotions, he wouldn't quite understand what her pain meant or what she had been doing by the river, but there was a strong possibility that Trey did.

She walked to the wolf and squatted beside him. He rubbed his jaw against hers and licked her ear. "I had to explain to him, Trey," she said, knowing he would hear her. "And I needed to find that peace. You get it, right?" For a split second the wolf's eyes flashed Trey's arctic blue, and she knew he was letting her know he had heard. Smiling, she shook his muzzle and pushed him away from her. "Fancy a race?" Then she was gone.

She and the wolf played for something like an hour, tagging and chasing each other, wrestling, mock fighting, and ambushing one another. Although he didn't hold back with those teeth or claws, he didn't once draw blood. Finally, they collapsed near the lake beside Trey's discarded clothes, panting and huddled together. She hadn't meant to doze off, but it wasn't a great surprise that she did.

She woke to the telling sound of popping and snapping. Opening her eyes, she saw Trey beside her in his human form once again. His sharp eyes were glinting with a lightheartedness she had never seen there before. His usual scowl had all but disappeared and he wore a beaming smile.

Knowing she was wondering at his uncharacteristic cheeriness, he explained, "I never really made time for playing and fooling around. I became Alpha when I was just a teenager, remember. Had to grow up pretty quickly. There wasn't really fun or quirkiness in my life until you got here." He clipped her hair behind her ear and kissed her lightly before sucking her bottom lip into his mouth.

"So you never really went out and had fun with the guys?"

"Not really. There I was, suddenly responsible for all these wolves, and I wasn't in a great frame of mind after everything that had happened." He exhaled heavily. "I wasn't in control of my emotions. Hell, I didn't even know what the emotions were. There we were with no territory, no home, no money. I knew I needed to gain control fast or I'd never keep the pack alive."

"So you bottled it all up," she said in a whisper. "Turned yourself into a robot."

"I guess I did. It wasn't hard to rein it all in. I'd always been good at that."

It tugged at her heart to know that he had basically missed out on his youth. Teenage years were about personal growth and fun and finding your identity. Trey had missed all that, and that was just unacceptable to Taryn. "Well, now that I'm around, you'll be expected to have fun occasionally—know that right now."

"We have plenty of fun." He grinned wickedly and licked over his mark while his hand cupped her breast.

"Not that kind of fun," she said a little breathlessly as he sucked and nibbled her neck. "But we'll do lots of that too." And they did do lots of that. In fact, they spent the next hour doing plenty of it.

"Have I ever told you that you have an epic ass?" she said, thanking God for the creation of Levi's as she watched him walk ahead of her toward the caves.

He laughed. "The one with the epic rear is you, baby. I should know, I've bitten your ass often enough."

She snickered. "Where on my body *haven't* you bitten?"

Again he laughed. "If I think of a place, I'll correct the oversight."

"Maybe I'll retaliate."

"Oh, I really hope you do."

"Great. How about now in your office?"

"Baby, does the word *nympho* mean anything to you?" At that second, the cell phone in his jeans pocket beeped. "It's a text from Brock," he told her. "Apparently, Ryan's been trying to call me from the security shack and hasn't been able to get through."

"Is the signal crap?"

"Doesn't seem to be. I'll go see Ryan, find out what he wants." He smacked a hard kiss on her lips. "See you at dinner, if not before."

She released a dreamy sigh at the sight of his butt as he walked away at a leisurely pace. It was odd to see him do that—usually he was always marching or running, too intense to be in any way relaxed. With his newfound sense of peace, however, that had changed. Not his personality, no, that hadn't changed. He would always be intense and menacing, and much too serious. But she loved him anyway.

She turned toward the stairs and ran her fingers idly along the mountain wall as she took each step. It tore at her to know that his life had always been so serious. He'd had so much responsibility, so much weight on his shoulders, from such a young age. The thought of him watching as all the others got to relax and have fun, of him always feeling on the outside, made her chest ache.

She could tell through their link that he hadn't realized how much it had actually bothered him until they had bonded and suddenly he had someone who was his. As Alpha, he had always been slightly apart from the others. Now he had an equal, someone whom he could share everything with, and who was held to him by more than just pack loyalty.

Someone who was also going to ensure that he learned how to have fun, whether he liked it or not. She would bet he had never set foot in a bowling alley or a cinema. Well, he would soon. And she knew that he would grumble the entire journey there. Still, she was set on him—

Shit! Abruptly she felt a sharp tug on her ankle and suddenly she lost her footing, hit the ground hard, and struck the right side of her forehead on the stone step. *Motherfucker.* Then it was as if she was floating, as spots began to dance before her eyes, and there was a deafening, high-pitched ringing in her ears. Everything was suddenly so distant and foggy, and it felt as though she was falling into a dream. She might have completely fallen into it right that second if there hadn't been a sensation of two hands grabbing her ankles from behind and beginning to drag her down the stairs.

She wanted to fight against that unseen force, she wanted to gain some purchase with her hands, but it was as if her body was disconnected from her somehow, like her limbs weren't there at all. Her vision had gone blurry, everything seemed to be spinning, and she felt as though she was slipping away.

Distantly, she realized that there was a voice shouting something—her name? Abruptly her ankles were released and she heard the sound of footsteps running away from her. There was more shouting and she recognized the voice. Trey, it was Trey. She tried calling his name; although her mouth formed the word, no sound came out at all. The shouting was nearer now, but she couldn't focus on the words, couldn't make out what they were— she was slipping away again. Her wolf was howling, panicky and scared, and urging Taryn to fight that dreamy state. She tried, she really, really did, but things just became foggier and foggier. Then the blackness came.

Trey reached Taryn just before her body turned limp. He'd felt it the second she'd hit her head, felt just a hint of the pain, and he'd sensed it as the dizziness rushed over her and almost took her under. Instinctively, he had rocketed through the forest and taken the steps three at a time to get to her. Panic speared him as he called her name over and over but received no response.

"What happened?" asked Dante as he rushed over with the enforcers, apparently having sensed his anxiety and Taryn's pain through the pack link.

"I don't know. Looks like she fell, hit her head, and passed out."

"Is she breathing?" asked Marcus.

Trey placed an ear to her lips. "Yeah, she's breathing."

"Nothing's blocking her airway?"

He swept his finger into her mouth and shook his head. "No."

"Good. Everyone move so he can take her inside."

Dante winced. "Going by that bump on her head, she smacked the ground damn hard."

Tao pursed his lips and narrowed his eyes. "But did she pass out, hit the ground, *then* bump her head, or did the crack to the head cause her to pass out?"

Trey shrugged. "How the hell would I know? I wasn't here." He'd walked off toward the security shack and left her to make her way back to the caves by herself. The rational part of his brain told him that it wouldn't have made any difference if he had been there. If she was going to fall, then she was going to fall and that was that. But all he could think was that his mate was hurt and he hadn't been with her.

At the door of the living area was a frantic Grace. "Lay her down and use something to elevate her legs so they're above the level of her heart. It'll help restore blood flow to the brain."

With Tao's help, Trey carefully placed Taryn on her back on the rug and then gently rested her legs on the sofa. Ignoring Dominic's suggestion that he slap her to wake her up, Trey stroked a hand through her hair, *willing* her to wake. His wolf was growling and pacing, just as anxious and fretful as Trey was. If she had been anyone else, he would have said it was only a bump, calm the fuck down. But this was his mate, and bumps and blackouts were just unacceptable where she was concerned.

Quickly Grace came into the room with a bottle of spring water. "Dab some of that on her lips." Then she handed him an ice pack. "And place that over that ugly bump on her head."

"It's bruising already," commented Trick. "She's gonna be pissed, walking around with that egg on her head."

"Is she all right?" asked Greta. She shrugged when all eyes widened and focused on her. "Not that I care. I'm just wondering."

"Hi there, gorgeous, you're awake," crooned Marcus. Instantly, everyone crowded around the sofa.

Too distracted by the realization that Taryn had come around, Trey didn't even shoot his enforcer a scowl for using an endearment with his mate. "Hey, baby, you okay? You scared twenty years off my life."

Damn, that light was bright. Taryn groaned as sharp, icy pains began shooting rhythmically through her head. Oh God, she wasn't going to throw up, was she? She sure felt like it. Confused and dazed, she peered around her to see the entire pack hovering.

Grace pushed her way through the enforcers. "How're you feeling?"

"Like my head has been stomped on. Repeatedly. By a giant." Tentatively, she brought her hand to her forehead and moaned at the feeling of the bump. Realizing she was on the floor, she tried pulling herself up, but her body was like Jell-O and her elbows gave out. She slipped onto her back again, but that was okay because she didn't feel like doing anything.

Carefully, Trey scooped her up and held her against his chest. Begrudgingly he allowed the stubborn woman to take over holding the ice pack to her head. "You really fucking scared me."

"Do you feel dizzy, honey? Disorientated?" asked Grace, biting her lower lip.

Was she kidding? "I blacked out, of course I do."

"What about headaches? Do you have one? These are all signs of concussion."

"A headache?" Trey pointed to the bump on her head. "What do you think?"

Grace rolled her eyes. "All right, fine. Keep that ice pack on that bump."

"Can't you heal it?" asked Trick.

Taryn shook her head. "Healers can't heal themselves."

"That's okay," said Grace. "I know a remedy that'll clear that right up. Ice, egg whites, and chocolate."

"Huh?"

"I told you, chocolate is the answer, no matter the question."

Dominic frowned. "I thought that was sex."

Dante bumped Grace aside, startling a *hmph* sound from her. She kicked him in the shin and then left the room—presumably heading to the kitchen to mix up her weird concoction. Dante didn't even flinch at the kick. "So what happened? Did you fall?"

She frowned. Now that the haze had begun to clear, a very important detail struck her. "Someone—"

"Someone what?" pressed Trey, breezing his thumb along her jaw.

"It felt like someone grabbed my ankle."

"There was no one there when I got there."

"Someone grabbed my ankle," she said with more conviction. "They grabbed it, and they pulled it to make me fall. Then I was being dragged down the steps." She lifted her hands and stared at the burning abrasions on her palms. If the same burning and tingling coming from her elbows and knees were anything to go by, she had similar abrasions there.

"That's probably just from when you placed your hands out to break your fall."

Dante took a closer look and shook his head. "No, those are scrapes...You can see where the skin was peeling, like her hands were dragging along the floor."

"Okay, well, maybe she slipped down a few steps."

"I didn't *slip*."

Not liking what this could mean, Trey shook his head. He didn't want to believe it. "Baby...No one here would hurt you."

Her brow arched. "Oh, really?"

"Spray-painting your car is one thing—"

"What about LJ?"

"Who?"

"The raven. Someone killed him and hung him upside down outside my window. That someone is not balanced."

Dante winced. "Yeah, that was some sick shit."

"Killing a bird and trying to seriously hurt you are two very different things." He kissed the uninjured side of her forehead and scanned the room for Rhett, intending to tell him to go ask Grace to make Taryn a coffee. That was when he noticed Ryan. "Ryan, what're you doing over here? Have you left the gate unguarded?"

He frowned. "I'm not on guard duty this morning."

"You're not?"

"No."

"Cam is the one on duty," Trick informed him.

Trey's frown now matched Ryan's. "Brock said you've been trying to call me from the security shack."

"I haven't tried calling you at all."

An uneasy feeling came over Trey. "Where's Brock?" Looking confused and defensive, the guy stepped forward. "Why did you say Ryan wanted to talk to me?"

Brock double-blinked. "I didn't. I haven't spoken to you all morning."

"But you sent a message to my cell phone."

"No."

"Where is it?" demanded Dante. "Where's your cell?"

Brock dug his hand into his empty pockets and shrugged. "I must have left it in my room or in the kitchen."

"Well, that's convenient." Dante marched out of the room with Marcus and Trick on his heels.

Trey switched his attention back to Taryn. Suspicion was written all over her face. "They pledged their loyalty to you," he reminded her, or maybe himself.

"Not all of them."

She was right, and he knew Selma and Kirk disliked her enough to hurt her. He just didn't believe for one minute that they had the guts to do it. Not only would they be very much aware that there was a strong chance Taryn would kick their ass, but they would then be branded traitors and exiled. Selma and Kirk didn't have the nerve to take that kind of risk—which was partly why they acted so big and bad. As for Hope…he suspected that the only reason she hadn't offered her loyalty to Taryn was because she was following Selma's lead, just like always.

Dante's reentry brought him out of his thoughts. "You have the phone?"

His Beta nodded. "The message is right there."

Brock spluttered. "What do you mean the message is there? I didn't send him any message, dammit."

"Well, it's right there in your Sent box," said Dominic.

Brock snatched the phone, read the message, and his face reddened. "Then someone else must have sent it. I didn't. Why would I? Why would anyone even lie to you about Ryan wanting to talk to you?"

"Maybe you wanted Trey out of the way so you had a chance to snatch Taryn. You would have known that he would feel her panic and help her...unless he was far enough away that he wouldn't reach her in time. Just what were you planning to do with her? Or *to* her?"

"I didn't send that message!"

"If my dad says he didn't do it, then he didn't do it," said Kirk as he stood beside him, folding his arms across his chest. "I'm not disputing that someone tried to pull you away from Taryn," he told Trey. "But whoever it was used my dad's phone, most likely to implicate him and shift the blame. It wasn't him."

Taryn groaned. "I can't deal with all this yelling."

"Come on, baby." Trey rose with her in his arms and carried her out of the room, through the tunnels and into their bedroom. He placed her gently on the bed and lay down next to her.

"Now do you believe me?" She sighed when he didn't answer. "I don't care what you say, *someone grabbed me.* If you don't want to face the fact that someone in your pack—the people you've grown up with—could do that, then I can understand that. I really can. But it doesn't change that I'm right. Like it or not, you have someone in your pack who would willingly hurt your mate, because I'm not lying."

Angry with himself for hurting her, he stroked a hand through her hair. "Hey, I never thought you were lying, baby. Not that. Just that maybe you tripped."

"Oh, I tripped. With help."

CHAPTER FOURTEEN

There was being possessive, there was being crazily possessive, and there was this: being a total shithead. Taryn groaned and slapped her hands over her face. All she wanted was to go shopping with Lydia. It wasn't like she was planning to go shopping on a whole other continent or that she would be walking around naked the entire time. Trey, however, was totally opposed to the idea of her going without him.

When attempting to bully her into taking him along hadn't worked, he had switched to trying to manipulate her with a little reverse psychology. When that failed, he introduced some seriously good bribes. As she had still refused, he was now trying his hand at emotional blackmail.

Releasing her face, she looked at her mate, who sat at the kitchen table wearing a kicked-puppy expression. "For God's sake, Trey, I'll only be gone a few hours. I'm pretty sure you'll cope without me."

"Yeah, but I like being with you."

That should have sounded corny or pathetic, but it had managed to sound sweet and cutely protective. Oh, he was so good at this. She had learned over the past few weeks that although Trey was mostly hard and antisocial, when he really wanted something, he was more than capable of a little charm. He had a way of totally focusing on her in a manner that she would have expected to freak her out, but instead it made her feel adored and safe.

What made it better for Taryn was that he was completely unashamed of how much he liked having her near him all the time. He didn't hold back—except in a sexual sense—in front of other people. Maybe that was why they didn't make fun of him for it. Maybe his complete conviction that it was normal, reasonable, and his right to act that way rubbed off on others, so that they too saw it as natural and expected.

They didn't even poke fun at him when he agreed to let Taryn take him places he otherwise would never have bothered his ass with, like the beach, the cinema, the bowling alley, and even a skating rink. "You can be with me as much as you want when I get back."

"Why is it you're so set on me not going?"

Because it was his birthday in a few days and she wanted to get him a decent gift as a surprise, but he didn't have to know that. Just as he didn't have to know that they were all planning a surprise party, or he would probably hide. According to Dante, Trey didn't like to celebrate his birthday—something about him not liking that kind of attention. Well, that was just tough shit; it was time for him to stop being so serious. "You already know that it was Lydia who organized the trip. How can I justify taking you along when she won't even let Cam come along? Besides, you hate shopping."

"No, I don't."

"It's not like we're only visiting one store. There's going to be a lot of browsing around shoe stores and boutiques and going bag-hunting in the mall. You wouldn't last five minutes in that jungle."

"Hey, I wear clothes, I've seen women's clothes. I'm pretty sure I could cope in a mall."

"Trey, let me cast your mind back to the time when as a pun-ishment for being a bastard I took you to Victoria's Secret and tried on a load of lingerie for you, but then never bought any." His pained expression made her smile. "You remember how you were sweating and huffing and puffing and asking how long before we could go home?"

"That was because you'd just made me watch you model all kinds of kinky shit, got me hard as a rock, and then expected me to walk without being in agony."

"No, Trey, that was *before* we even got into the store. You're not cut out for this sort of thing. Leave it to the experts."

Taking her by the wrist, Trey pulled her onto his lap to straddle him. It probably wasn't a good idea, since that position sparked off some really dirty thoughts, and quickly his cock began to harden. Then again, when was it ever limp when Taryn was around? The fact that she soon *wouldn't* be around—even if it would only be for a few hours—was enough to cause his surge of lust to wane and to perturb his wolf.

When she was there, he was content and relaxed in a way he had never been before. She made him laugh and gave him a feel-ing of being anchored, of having perfect equilibrium. When she wasn't there, he missed her and didn't think about much but her anyway, so he didn't see the logic in her not being with him. It was really that simple to him.

Of course he was aware of just how possessive and greedy he was being, but he also knew that Taryn would never let him steamroll her. If she thought he was taking it too far, she would let him know about it in a way that would make him seriously hesitate doing it in the future. Brushing his lips against hers, he asked, "Is it really so bad that I just want to spend time with you?"

"That's not going to work, Trey. Especially since I know that this isn't only about you wanting the pleasure of my company."

"Okay, I'll rephrase. Is it really so bad that I just want to spend time with you and have you in my sight at all times?"

Taryn sighed. As they were mates with an incomplete bond, no, it wasn't bad—it was normal. For wolves that hadn't completely bonded, the possessiveness and protectiveness hit extreme levels, because there was a lingering insecurity for both of them. Had it only been that, Taryn could have easily waved away his behavior. The problem was she knew from their connection that he wasn't dishing out bullshit. He *did* like being with her, he *did* want to spend time with her…and now he was kissing her neck. "Trey—"

"Is it really that bad?" he prodded gently.

"No, but—"

"Is it really so awful that I like having you close so I can reach out and touch you whenever I want? Play with your hair, feel your skin, taste your lips, inhale your scent. Is it really so awful?" He briefly paused kissing her neck to lick over his mark.

"Not awful," she replied breathlessly, shuddering, "but—"

"It makes perfect sense for me to come and—ow! Son of a bitch!"

Regaining her mental composure, Taryn jumped to her feet, frowning down at her mate, who was rubbing the sensitive tip of his ear where she had bitten him, hard. "That was for trying to manipulate me *again*."

As Lydia and Cam entered and took in her frown and Trey's face creased in pain, Lydia arched a brow. "Have we walked in on a domestic argument?"

"Trey's just sulking because I'm not taking him shopping."

Cam scratched his nape. "You know what I don't get? How women can spend the majority of their lives in shopping malls but still say they have nothing to wear."

Lydia snorted. "You know what *I* don't get? How men can spend the majority of their lives playing sports where they're being trampled on and listening to noisy mobs, yet they're put off by shopping, when it's no different." Both males tilted their heads, conceding that.

"At least let me give you some—"

Holding up her hand, she said, "No, Trey, I have my own money."

He curled an arm around her waist and drew her close. "But I know you don't want to touch that fund."

Combing her fingers through his hair, she smiled. "Back then I didn't. Things were different then. Our mating was only about a deal." She adored him for being so sensitive about it.

Rhett walked in and looked from her to Trey. "You asked her yet?"

"I nearly forgot. Don sent me a message over the pack web." He smiled at her low growl. "It wasn't to dish out more insults. He was apologizing for his 'despicable behavior' at the mating ceremony. He wants to come visit and apologize in person."

Taryn huffed. "I hope you told him you'd rather cram your cock in the ass of a bear with inflamed hemorrhoids than ever be in his company again."

He chuckled. "I figured I'd talk to you about it. He's a prick, but he's still your uncle. I want you to have people from your family in your life."

"No, you don't." She could feel that what he really wanted was to be the only person she ever needed, wanted to be everything to her. But since he thought that he *should* want her to have family in her life, he had made the suggestion. "Yeah, he's my uncle, but you're my mate and he insulted you. Badly. So he can go ride a donkey naked through the desert with snapping turtles attached to his nipples, for all I care. Anyway, *you're* my family. You and the pack."

An intense pang struck Trey's chest. He tightened his arm around her, barely resisting the urge to take her upstairs and bury himself deep inside her body. Not so he could take her hard and fast, but soft and slow.

"You might feel that way about your uncle now while you're still angry with him," said Lydia, "but you might regret it later if you don't at least give him a chance."

Taryn cursed, hating that Lydia was right. She would feel like she had let down her mom if she didn't give the woman's baby brother one more shot. Sighing, she nodded. "Fine. I'll give him a chance."

"He asked in the message if he could come tomorrow afternoon. That too soon?"

Trey shook his head. Taryn just shrugged.

"Then I'll confirm the arrangements."

"What arrangement?" asked Dominic as he strolled into the room.

"Taryn's uncle Don's coming to visit tomorrow afternoon," explained Trey. "Apparently, he wants to apologize."

What in that sentence sparked Dominic to think of a chat-up line, she had no idea, but she could tell by the smirk on his face that one was coming. She shook her head at him. "No, no more!"

He frowned. "Oh, come on, it's a good one. I suppose it must make you feel uncomfortable since you're obviously attracted to me." She snorted. "You're denying it? Okay then, fine, let's settle this once and for all. Smile if you want to sleep with me."

She tried her hardest to hold back a smile, she really, really did, but there was no way of doing it. Of course he laughed, smug as all shit. She growled. "You're a pain in the ass."

"Sorry, honey, we'll use more lubricant next time." He flinched when Trey smacked him over the head.

Glancing at the clock on the wall, Taryn saw it was time to go. Guzzling down the last of her coffee, she gave Trey a kiss on his very inactive lips, which were stuck in a sulky pout. "A few hours and I'll be back." The ass followed her and Lydia to the main door, wearing that kicked-puppy look. It was clearly one last-ditch attempt at making her feel bad. Of course it didn't work, because she didn't want him there when she bought him a gift. So she smiled, waved, and left.

Well, it was worth a shot, Trey thought, sighing, as he watched Taryn's car leave pack territory in spite of his efforts—or ploys—to make her take him with her. His wolf wasn't happy about it and was snarling his disapproval.

As he turned to go back inside, he noticed Tao stood not far away, staring in the direction Taryn had headed. He didn't look at her with the same coveting look that he used to wear, as if he had come to accept that she was unobtainable. He now looked at her the way the others did. Like she was truly his Alpha female—someone whom he revered, respected, prized, trusted, and looked to when in need of something, yet he still regarded her as being of senior rank and Trey's co-leader. However, there was something that was still irritating Trey and he thought it was about time that he addressed it.

Slowly Trey strode toward him, noticing how Tao stiffened as he sensed his approach, but he didn't look at him. A month ago, Trey's irritation would have been due to Tao's attraction to Taryn, but even though he still wanted to kick the shit out of Tao for it, his main problem with Tao now was that he was still distant with Taryn, and it troubled her.

She had never said this aloud, but she didn't need to, not now that they were partly bonded. Trey didn't want anything making her feel uncomfortable in her own home, her own pack. Also, he was pretty sure that the slight longing in Tao's gaze when he looked at her wasn't for her as a mate, but for the friendship they had once had.

Finally, he came to stand before Tao, but the wolf kept his gaze ahead. "So when are you going to pull your head out of your ass and stop moping?"

Tao looked at him curiously, obviously surprised that Trey would even bring it up. Until now, they had never spoken of it. "I'm surprised you've never punched me."

Trey shrugged. "I thought about it. A lot. You've made things awkward for Taryn. She feels like she lost her friend and that she's come between us. It didn't need to be that way."

"You're a lucky bastard, you know."

"I know. Fix the mess, Tao." He went to leave, but Tao spoke again.

"Wait, why are you asking me to sort things out with her? It's got to be easier for your wolf this way. You should be thrilled that I'm hardly around her."

"Why would I be thrilled about anything that hurts her? Fix it, Tao. And soon." At that, he turned away and went inside.

Taryn hadn't been lying when she said that she and Lydia would be visiting dozens of stores. Lydia was the type who was easily drawn in by something in the display window. She had practically raided the clothes stores, hunting down dresses, shoes, and accessories. Taryn bought a few items, but only casual wear— mostly she was just replacing the things that Trey had torn from her body like the dirty bastard he was.

Once they had picked up a few birthday gifts for Trey, they went for a light lunch, which left them with only one place left to go: Victoria's Secret. Taryn had decided to buy a kinky outfit to wear on the night of Trey's birthday, even though there was a good chance he would tear it off her, and she convinced Lydia to do the same for Cam. The girls had plenty of laughs browsing the store and choosing outfits. Lydia selected a leopard-print slip while Taryn picked a sparkly black-lace flyaway baby-doll.

Finally, after four and a half hours of shopping, the girls were ready to go. It was as Taryn was closing the trunk of the car after placing the bags inside that she suddenly felt two unfamiliar presences at her back. Male wolf shifters.

Before she could react, she was abruptly grabbed by the hair and swung around. A hand wrapped around her neck and slammed her back into the brick wall that was behind her car. Distantly she heard Lydia shout in alarm from the passenger seat, but Taryn knew that, as a submissive wolf, she wouldn't exit the car. Thank God. Taryn didn't intend to let the two bulky shitheads hurt her and it would be a lot harder to defend both of them than it would be to take care of herself.

What she wanted to do was scream, *Let me go, you son of a bitch*, but she knew from experience that letting an attacker think she was scared and that he was in control was often the best tactic. Resisting her wolf's desire to claw at the hand around her neck, she asked, "Who are you?"

The dark wolf with the cockeye appraised her slowly. "They weren't lying when they said you were dinty, were they?"

"I think you mean *dainty*," said Taryn.

"They were right about that ass too." The other wolf flicked his mousy hair from his face before offering her a slimy grin. "A very fine ass."

Cockeye nodded. "They also said you were a mad bitch."

"And that you were always late."

Both Cockeye and Taryn looked at Mousy, baffled. "Always late?" she said.

"They said she was *latent*," snapped Cockeye.

Mousey straightened and shrugged. "Right. I knew that."

Taryn rolled her eyes. Great, she was being assailed by Dumb and Dumber. She suddenly felt like the kid in *Home Alone*, facing Harry and Marv. "Is there any chance either of you could tell me why I'm being pinned against a wall?"

Cockeye puffed up. Maybe he thought it made him look impressive or intimidating. "We have a message for you."

"Oh yeah?"

"From Darryl. Tell your mate that his uncle feels it would be in your best interest if he agrees to unite the packs. He only has seven days left before the twelve weeks are up, so if he's wise, he'll give in to Darryl's request quickly."

Anger rushed through her veins and her wolf began pacing and flexing her claws. "Darryl," she growled with an involuntary snap of the teeth that had both wolves jerking in surprise. "If Trey doesn't...?"

"Next time what we do to you will be much worse than what we're about to do. In other words, we might not let you live next time. We may even have some fun with your little friend there after we're done here."

"Oh. And what is it you think you're going to do to me now?"

Mousy smirked. "I'm thinking that I'd like to fuck that mouth of yours."

"Sorry. I was raised to never put small objects in my mouth or I might choke."

Cockeye burst out laughing. "She got you there."

"I'm thinking I'm not your type either," she said to Cockeye. "What with me not being inflatable and all."

"Cheeky bitch. You should watch how you talk to us, little girl. There's pain and there's *pain*."

"You do know that you're signing your death warrants, don't you? Trey will kill you." And Darryl had to know that...which meant this was probably a trap to enrage Trey. Having grown up with Lance as a father, she knew all about Alpha games and could spot one a mile away. It was pretty damn possible that Darryl was thinking that if he could make Trey go against protocol and attempt to attack him before the twelve weeks were up, Darryl could appeal to the council to agree to his request. *Fuck. That.*

She made a *C* with the fingers and thumb of one hand and abruptly struck Cockeye in the throat with the web of her hand. He made a choking sound and instantly released her, backing away slightly as he struggled for breath. She followed that up with a sharp kick to his groin that had him falling to his knees.

"Shit," cursed Mousy in surprise, before his hand shot out and shackled her wrist as he tried to pull her to him.

Knowing that the weakest point of his hold was where his fingers and thumb met, Taryn twisted her wrist so the thumb side of her forearm was at that weak point and yanked herself free. Before he made to grab her again, she delivered a head butt to his nose that had him stumbling backward as blood poured from his nostrils.

Wanting him down on the floor with Cockeye, she quickly grabbed his testicles, squeezed, twisted them sharply, and then jerked so hard she was surprised they didn't come off in her hand. He fell to his knees with one hand cupping his nose and the other cupping his balls.

Both peered up at her, wearing looks of total astonishment, which satisfied her wolf. "Yeah, I see you had low expectations of me. It happens a lot."

"You broke my nose and nearly ripped off my ball sack, you crazy bitch!"

"Crazy bitch? Oh no, honey, I'm an angel, I swear. The horns are only there to hold up the halo. But all the same, I think it's best that you don't come at me again until you've at least learned how to wipe your ass."

Cockeye spat what she suspected was supposed to be an insult, but it was garbled—because of the pain from the throat strike or the groin kick, or maybe both.

"Now, let's chat. You can thank Uncle Darryl for getting in touch and inform him that he shouldn't expect his little plot to work. You know, I'm curious. Why would you let him use you as bait?"

The wolves exchanged a confused glance that had Taryn groaning.

"I can only assume that Darryl is just as dumb as you to not only think his little plot would work, but to send two guys who'd be out of their depth in a puddle. Now, if I were you, I'd get out of here as quick as I could. I've no doubt that my friend called her mate who will have told Trey what's going on, so he's most likely on his way here." They hadn't even been smart enough to think of that. She was kind of insulted that Darryl thought these two were a match for her.

"You're letting us go?" said Mousy.

She shrugged. "I'd be playing into Darryl's hands if I didn't. Besides, it would be like handing over two mentally handicapped kids to a sociopath. But before you go, you can help me out with one thing. How did you guys know where to find me? I know I wasn't being followed; I'd have sensed you long ago." Unless of course they were good at what they did, and Twit and Twat here certainly weren't.

Cockeye's face instantly closed down. Apparently, she wasn't getting any information from that corner. Mousy, on the other hand, shrugged as if the answer was simple. "Darryl's informant from your pack told him you'd be—Ow!" He scowled at Cockeye, rubbing the spot on his head where Cockeye had hit him. "Hey, what did you do that for?"

"You just don't know when to shut up. Idiot."

Their arguing faded into the background as the implications of what Mousy had said finally settled into her brain. Sure, she'd known she wasn't liked by everyone in the pack, and she'd known that one of them hated her enough to vandalize her property, kill her bird, and even cause her to have a bad fall. But for one of them to be an informant for Darryl, for someone to betray Trey so completely...She was surprised by just how much it hurt.

Turning her attention back to the idiots at her feet, she gestured with her hand as she ordered, "Go, get out of here." She watched as they hobbled away, constantly casting her suspicious glances. Her wolf growled her disappointment, wanting to rip out both their throats for daring to touch her.

Only after Taryn saw them drive off in a transit van did she get into her own car. Lydia was trembling and panting. "You okay?"

"You fought them," said Lydia, wide-eyed. "I can't believe you fought them. I was expecting you to trick them and get away, not to—"

"Did you call anyone?"

Lydia double-blinked, shaking her head as if to clear it. "Um. Yeah. Cam."

"Which means Trey and some of the pack will probably be on their way here."

"Why did you let those two guys go?"

Taryn glanced at her face in the mirror of the sun visor and cursed. As she'd suspected, there was a small cut on her forehead from when she'd butted Mousy. This was going to make Trey's reaction so much worse. Jamming the keys in the ignition, she threw the car into gear and reversed from the parking space. "Call Cam. Tell him we're making our way back."

Nodding, a still shaky Lydia fished her cell from her pocket. "Cam, it's me, we're—No, she's fine. She, well, she kicked their asses. We're just on our way back to—No, they, um, got away. Taryn can explain—Really, I swear, she's fine." Taryn and Lydia both winced as they heard Trey yelling in the background. "Taryn, Trey wants to talk to you. I'm going to put him on speakerphone."

"Taryn, tell me you're okay, baby," he demanded through his teeth.

"I'm fine, really, we're—"

"What the hell happened? Where're the bastards? Did they touch you, Taryn? Tell me they didn't touch you. I swear to God I'll—"

Knowing what he meant by "touch," she quickly assured him, "No, they didn't touch me."

"Who the hell were they?"

"Um…we'll talk about that when I get home." She knew for a fact that if she mentioned Darryl, the guys would drive straight to his territory, playing into his hands. "We're about ten minutes from Bedrock. Where are you?"

"I don't know, five minutes away from the mall maybe."

She had thought about asking him to turn back and she'd meet him at home, but hearing how frantic he sounded, she knew that the sooner he saw her safe and unharmed, the better. "Then we'll probably come across each other soon enough. We'll keep a lookout for you."

Approximately three minutes later the two cars were parking on the side of the road. She hadn't even had a chance to switch off the engine before the door was quickly yanked open and she was practically snatched from her seat.

As soon as Trey had her in his arms, with her limbs all curled around him, the constricting sensation in his chest began to ebb slightly. She was safe. She was there. She was okay.

When Cam had burst into his office and told him about Lydia's call, Trey was pretty sure his heart had stopped for a moment. Fear for Taryn's safety had instantly blasted through him, galvanizing him into action while at the same time completely fucking up his thought processes. His wolf had howled inside his head, fought for supremacy with such strength that Trey had been wincing in pain. Had the other males of his pack not been there to keep him calm, he might have shifted right there in the car as he drove like a man possessed.

Trey buried his face in the crook of her neck and swam in her exotic scent...and that was when he smelled the scent of the other male.

Taryn gasped as Trey pulled back and she saw his eyes flash wolf. "Trey—"

"I can smell him on you." Trey trailed his finger over her neck. "He had his hand here." His gaze landed on the tiny wound on her forehead and a long, chilling growl spilled from his throat. "He hurt you."

She framed his face with her hands, capturing his gaze. "No, I got that teensy little cut when I head-butted him and broke his nose. I'm fine."

"What the hell happened?" asked Dante as he hurried to their side with the enforcers on his heels.

Ignoring them in favor of keeping her mate calm, she lightly dabbed a kiss on Trey's lips, then one on each cheek and another on his lips. "I'm okay." With each soft kiss, the tension ruling his body began to lessen, but only ever so slightly. He was nowhere near calm, and it wouldn't take much for him to leap to an irrational state. "Can we talk about this on the way home?" She tried to sound a little vulnerable and shaken in the hope that it might shift him from needing revenge to needing to comfort her.

Good ole Cam—not at all aware of her plan—suddenly approached and said, "Lydia's just told me they said something about Darryl. That true?"

Fan-fricking-tastic. Just like that, Trey's body stiffened and his arms fell to his sides, making her slide down his body.

He stepped away, panting and growling. "My uncle?"

Taryn shot Cam an annoyed glare. Looking nervous, he took Lydia by the arm and led her to Taryn's Hyundai—a good thing, since she didn't want to mention the informant in front of anyone other than Trey, Dante, and the enforcers. It wasn't that she suspected Lydia or Cam, but she wasn't sure she could trust them not to panic or to keep quiet about it. She returned her focus to Trey. "It was just a pathetic attempt at making you agree to unite the packs."

"So he set that up. He ordered them to hurt you."

"I'm surprised you didn't sense them following you," said Dante.

Anger flashed across her face and Trey tensed. "What? Tell me."

She sighed. "Apparently...someone from our pack told Darryl where I'd be." She winced as his face turned purple. Then he was striding purposely toward his Toyota. No prizes for guessing where he was going. She dashed after him and leaped onto his back, locking her arms around his neck and her legs around his middle. "Trey, no, listen to me. You can't go after him, it's what he wants." He continued onward as if she wasn't even there, completely undeterred by her weight—though it was fair to say she didn't weigh that much. Deserting her plan to placate him, she took another approach. She kicked her legs madly and bit his ear. "Trey, don't do this! For God's sake, will you just listen!"

Trey halted abruptly and shifted her so that she was once again wrapped around his front. He held her gaze as he growled, "Don't, Taryn. Don't ask me to ignore this. You're my mate and he sent two wolves after you. It doesn't matter that you kicked their asses, *he wanted you beaten—maybe even worse.* To add to that, he has one of my own wolves betraying me, betraying you."

"I know, I know it's bad, but—"

"You've always known who and what I am. You've always known what I'm capable of. Don't ask me to ignore what he did to you, don't ask me to be something I'm not."

"That's not what I'm doing. I know you want to shred the bastard into tiny pieces—you're not alone there. All I'm asking you to do is put a pin in it. Just delay it for a while. You have to see that it's a trap."

"A trap?" asked Ryan.

"No shifter would dare harm another shifter's mate unless he was hoping to die a long, painful death. He will have known that Trey would react ten times worse and most likely go feral. He's probably getting desperate now—the twelve weeks are almost up. If he could get you to go against council protocol and attack within the next seven days…" She didn't need to say more, knowing he would see her point.

"Makes sense," Tao said after a minute. The other males nodded. Other than Trey.

Taryn dabbed another kiss on Trey's lips. "He thinks he's got you all figured out. But he hasn't. You might be the wolf shifter version of the black mamba snake and have homicidal urges from time to time, but you're also smart. Smart enough to know that if you go to him now and react like he wants, you're giving him power over you. Smart enough to know that the important thing now is to figure out who his informant is before they feed him more information."

Trick stepped forward. "She's right, Trey. I say we let Darryl sweat. He'll know he's not going to get away with it. Leave him to sit and wonder what you'll do and when you're going to do it."

Trey snarled at the suggestion. "And what if he goes after her again? Huh? What if I put a fucking pin in it, and then he sends more wolves after her in the meantime? He'd most likely send an even larger number the next time just to be sure she gets the beating he ordered."

Growling, Taryn gripped his head and turned it sharply so that she could stare into his eyes. "You listen to me, psycho boy. You might be happy to give your uncle the satisfaction of falling into his trap, but I'm not. Here's what's going to happen. We're all going to calm down and drive back to Bedrock and you're not going to give me any shit about it or, so help me God, I'll beat you so bad you'll have to put toothpaste in your ass to brush your teeth!"

There was a moment of quiet before some of the guys chuckled and others just smiled.

"I think she's having caffeine withdrawal," said Dante.

Trey sighed in frustration. Why did she have to be right? All he wanted was revenge. Was that really that bad? He didn't think so. Nor did his wolf. But, as Taryn had pointed out, that was what his uncle was counting on. Well, if Trey was going to do something totally out of character and delay his revenge, then there were going to have to be a few changes around here. He pinned his little mate with a look. "No more telling me to stay behind. If you leave pack territory, I'm right there with you."

Not liking his tone, but recognizing how hard it was for him to back down, Taryn nodded. "Got it."

"And if he comes after you again, don't expect me to play the waiting game any longer."

"Sure thing, Flintstone. Now let's go home." Apparently not willing to part with her just yet, he ordered Tao to drive her car home while he pulled Taryn on his lap in the backseat of the Toyota. He didn't say a word during the entire journey, not even to contribute to the "We hate Darryl" chat that Dante, Trick, and Marcus began. She could tell that the guys were eager to discuss whom the informant might be, but they knew their Alpha well enough to know that he needed time to calm the hell down before having any discussion.

Knowing how much he liked it, Taryn snuggled into his arms and melted against his chest, but not even that or her featherlight kisses to his neck or her soft petting of his chest were able to ease the tension from his body. His rigid body barely moved other than to run his hand gently through her hair. When they arrived home, he did what he always did when things didn't go his way—brooded. And Taryn did what she always did when he brooded—left him to get on with it alone.

After stashing Trey's gifts in the bedroom and hanging up her new clothes, she took the groceries she'd bought to the kitchen and helped Grace with getting started on dinner—chicken curry. It wasn't exactly a surprise when Trey didn't appear for dinner. When he sulked, he did it good.

Greta was the last to take a seat at the table, and her grim expression had Taryn smiling. "I bet you wish Darryl's wolves had given me a good beating."

Greta harrumphed. "There's no such luck." After swallowing a mouthful, she whispered—loudly and very much for Taryn's benefit—to Cam, "Does this taste funny to you?" How he managed to keep his expression neutral, Taryn wasn't sure.

"I've got no complaints," he replied before shoveling a chunk of curried chicken in his mouth.

"Dinner always seems to have a funny taste when *she* helps."

"Oh, that's just the poison, Greta," said Taryn. The old woman made a face, but, of course, continued to eat the meal—like she hadn't eaten in a week.

"How much longer do you think the brooding will go on for?" asked Dominic.

Trick shrugged. "Maybe a day or so."

"Give the guy a break," chastised Dante. "He got a scare."

"So you're not hurt or anything?" asked Kirk, sounding awkward. "Other than the gash on your head, I mean."

Taryn shook her head, wondering at his sudden concern. Or *apparent* concern.

"You should have seen the way she took those guys out," said Lydia, still a little shaken but refusing to admit it. "It was absolutely awesome."

"Well, if she hadn't gone out all day shopping for herself, none of it would've happened." Greta gave Taryn a withering look. "That would never have happened in my day. No. The women stayed at home and took care of their mates. If I *did* go out, my Arthur came with me."

Taryn just smiled. "Well, I suppose it was better that you didn't venture out alone, in case a T. rex got hold of you, huh." The muffled laughs coming from some of the pack had Greta growling.

"I'll never know what he sees in you. Selma's so much prettier." More laughing from some of the pack, as it was well known that Greta disliked Selma even more than she did Taryn. Even Selma herself looked surprised. "Such beautiful long hair. Not like yours."

"Speaking of hair, your mustache needs a trim."

That shut Greta up and the conversation turned to lighter, general things; although Taryn chatted away to the others, it was forever on her mind that Trey was outside somewhere, hungry, pissed, and unable to calm himself. She knew this because she could feel it through their mating link, but she could also feel that he wanted to be alone. So she didn't do what she wanted to do—track him down and force some food down his throat. Instead, she watched some TV with the others, hoping that Trey might turn up at some point. Unfortunately, it had been a pointless hope.

She rose from her seat on the sofa. "I'm heading to bed. Can't stay awake any longer. Good night." She had only taken two steps toward the door when Dominic called her name. She turned and raised a brow questioningly. He motioned with one finger for her to go to where he was on the end of the chaise. Rolling her eyes, she walked over and sighed.

He smiled. "I just made you come with one finger. Imagine what I could do with my whole hand." Everyone groaned. "What? That was a good one."

Shaking her head and chuckling, Taryn left the room and was making her way through the tunnels when Tao suddenly caught up with her.

"Um, Taryn, I just wondered if we could talk for a minute. Here, alone."

Surprised that he had gone out of his way to speak to her, when usually he only did if she asked him a question, she shrugged. "Sure. What's up?"

For a minute he didn't say anything, just fidgeted and ran a hand through his hair and repeatedly cleared his throat. "I'm sorry," he finally burst out. "You've no idea how sorry I am."

"For what?"

"Maybe if I hadn't been such an idiot I still would've been your bodyguard and then I'd have been there today and—"

"No, Tao, don't do that. Don't even think like that. The second I officially became the Alpha female of the pack, I would have insisted on not having a bodyguard. I know some Alpha pairs have them, but Trey doesn't and it would have made me look weak to have a bodyguard when he didn't."

He nodded a little. "I'm still sorry. I've been an ass and I know it. Look, I'd really like it if we could be friends again. I get that you're with Trey. I look at you both now and…you make sense—if that makes sense. You suit each other. The jealousy…it isn't there anymore. You're my Alpha female and I respect that. And I'd really like it if we could go back to being friends."

Pleasantly shocked, she smiled. "I'd like that. Good night."

Feeling a little lighter, she made her way to her room. Once she had taken a quick shower, being sure to wash away the scents of the strange males, she threw on one of Trey's old T-shirts and hopped into bed. She had planned to lie awake so that they could talk when he finally joined her, but she must have nodded off at some point, because she woke abruptly some time later to a light touch on the tiny wound on her forehead.

Opening her eyes, she saw Trey sitting beside her, his back against the headboard and his legs crossed at the ankles. "Hey there, Flintstone," she said in a voice gone husky from sleep.

"Sorry. Didn't mean to wake you."

Even if she hadn't been able to feel it through their link, the deep crease between his eyebrows would have told her that he was still pretty pissed. "You know I was right, Trey," she said in a low voice.

He turned his head away and sighed. "I know. It doesn't mean I have to like it."

"And stop torturing yourself about not having been there."

"I'm your mate, Taryn. It's my job to protect you."

"I was the one who insisted you didn't come with me."

"Something that won't be happening again," he reminded her.

She drew circles on his bicep with her fingertip as she asked, "Does that mean you're done now?"

"With what?"

"Sulking."

One brow lifted. "Sulking?"

"Yeah." She climbed onto his lap and straddled him. "Sulking because you can't go kill the sly wolf."

"He ordered an attack on you, Taryn. He wanted the shit knocked out of you." If he knew Darryl like he thought he did, then the asshole would have ordered that she be sexually assaulted and then beaten almost to death—assurance that Trey would come for him. The drive to do just that was still hounding both him and his wolf. Moreover, he had the painful knowledge that someone within his pack had betrayed them.

She massaged his shoulders and brushed his nose with hers. "Darryl didn't get what he wanted though. I'm fine."

The way she said it, as though that made everything okay, had Trey shaking his head incredulously. She thought that what he'd been doing all this time was pouting about not getting his revenge and torturing himself about not having protected her. If she had looked deeper, she would have seen what was tormenting him most, would have known that the terror he had experienced earlier on hearing she was being attacked was still coursing through his veins.

He had envisioned all kinds of fucked-up scenarios as he drove like a crazy person to get to her, had imagined finally arriving only to find her dead. Her strong personality always made her seem inches taller than she was, but in reality she was just a tiny little thing. So easily breakable. He could snap her neck right now with minimal effort—and those wolves who'd tried to attack her could have done the same, even if they hadn't meant to.

Trey took her face in his hands, fighting to keep his touch gentle while anger and fear was still stabbing at him. "You just don't get it, do you? You have no idea how important you are to me. I need you to be okay, Taryn. I can't be without you; you have to be here and okay or I won't be able to fucking function."

Taryn doubted he could have known how much those words meant to her, especially when she knew just how hard he found it to articulate himself like that. Even now, he looked as though he wasn't sure if what he'd said had made any sense. She could feel his need to assure himself that she was with him, safe and alive, in the most basic way—by possessing her body. He was restraining himself though, because he didn't trust that he wouldn't hurt her while his blood was still boiling. Well, then, she'd provide him with the assurance he needed, if he wasn't going to take it for himself.

Leaning forward, Taryn licked along the seam of his lips, wanting admission, as she raked her claws down his chest—not enough to tear his T-shirt, but enough that it sent a shudder through him. "Kiss me." Sliding one hand to her nape, he gave her what she wanted, possessing her mouth, owning it. She ground herself against his cock and he groaned into her mouth, but then he tore his lips away.

"Baby, not tonight." Shit, he deserved a medal for holding back. Knowing that she was naked beneath his old T-shirt was killing him. He could smell her arousal, knew she was wet and primed for him. "My head's not in a good place."

"Shh—"

"I'm too wound up—"

"I said shh." She took his arms and draped them over the headboard. "Keep them there."

There was an edge of dominance to her tone that he hadn't heard before. It intrigued his wolf. Trey narrowed his eyes and went to question her, but she raised a brow and shook her head. Then, surprising the hell out of him, she tore the T-shirt he was wearing right down the middle. He might have made a comment about it if she hadn't then swirled her tongue in the hollow of his throat and sucked at the patch of skin the way he liked.

She explored his chest with her lips and tongue, occasionally using teeth. He loved those little bites she did, loved that she had the urge to leave marks of possession on his body. He hadn't realized his eyes had drifted shut until she tackled the buttons of his fly and his lids flipped open. "Taryn—"

"Didn't I tell you to shush?" she said, sitting up again and straddling his thighs. She was pretty sure he would have snapped at her for that comment if she hadn't curled her hand around the base of his cock. She stroked upward and ran her thumb over the silky head, sweeping up the pearl of pre-come there. Holding his eyes, she brought her thumb to her mouth and sucked it clean, smiling as he groaned.

Trey's entire body clenched as she began working her soft little hand up and down his length, her eyes never leaving his. "Taryn, I'm not in the mood to be teased."

"Are you in the mood to be sucked off?" She smiled inwardly as shock stiffened his body while his dick jerked in her hand. "Because that's what I have every intention of doing." Leaning forward, she asked against his lips in a wickedly submissive tone, "Can I? Can I suck your cock? Please?"

"You're a witch." For so long he'd dreamed of this, but he wasn't sure that now was the time. "Be certain you want to do this, Taryn. I'm not in control, baby. I'm not going to be able to keep my hands up here and just let you play."

"I'm certain."

He bit her bottom lip hard. "Then suck that cock until I tell you to stop."

"Yes, sir," said Taryn in a mockingly submissive tone, but he still growled in approval. Again she kissed and nipped his chest as she crawled backward until she was settled between the invitation of his slightly spread thighs. He hissed as she ran her tongue along his cock from base to tip, lapping up the drop of pre-come from the slit. Several times she licked his length, laving it and teasing him in the process until he bucked slightly, hinting for more. Smiling, she swirled her tongue around the head and took him into her mouth.

Trey shuddered and groaned as she sucked hard on the head of his cock, flicking the sensitive part underneath with the tip of her tongue. Then she took more of him, swallowing, and the feel of her throat constricting around him had him groaning again. "Oh yeah, suck it. Like that, baby, yes. Take more. *Fuuuuck.*" Each time she took him deeper, sucking so hard her cheeks hollowed. Then she was doing some wicked thing with her tongue, swirling it around his cock before grazing him with her teeth.

Better than all of that, Trey could feel that she was enjoying pleasuring him like this. Knowing that, he couldn't stay still any longer. He tangled a hand in her hair and began pumping his hips, fucking her mouth, but she didn't fight him. Instead, she began playing with his balls and making moaning sounds in the back of her throat that were eating at what little control he had.

So many times he'd imagined this, imagined her deep-throating him and then swallowing his come, but right now the desire to come in her mouth was being overruled by the need to have her come apart around his cock. Another need was eating at him. The need to take, to dominate, to remind her that she belonged to him.

Both needs were so violent that he was scared he'd hurt her. Even now his hold on her hair had to be causing her some pain; although he stopped fucking her mouth, he couldn't make himself totally release her. "Taryn, tell me I'm hurting you, tell me you need me to stay in control."

She shook her head. "I like it when you're out of control."

"Not like this, baby, you don't want me like this. Tell me to ease off."

"Why would I do that? I don't want you being someone you're not."

With that his last thread of control snapped and lust hazed his brain. He tightened his grip on her hair, yanked her upright, and then plunged a finger inside her. Her muscles gripped it tight and moisture swamped his finger. "So wet. I think my little bitch got off on sucking my cock. Did you, baby?" She only nodded. "I can't hear you."

"Yes."

Trey withdrew his finger and sucked it clean, groaning at her taste. He roughly dragged her to him and gathered up the T-shirt she was wearing and pushed it up and over her head. Then he was shaping her body with his hands, thumbing her taut nipples and pinching them hard. She jerked when he stabbed two fingers inside her and flicked her clit with his thumb. A hint of the pleasure she was feeling reached him through their bond. Snaking his free hand around her throat in a possessive grip, he growled harshly, "Who was this pussy made for, Taryn? Huh? Tell me who."

Instinctively Taryn wanted to fight his dominance, but the look in his eyes stopped her. It wasn't just the determined, demanding glint there, but the lingering anxiety she had sensed earlier. Taryn knew that with an Alpha for a mate, there were times to push and times to submit. Right now, Trey needed the latter. Something had happened today that left him feeling helpless, left him feeling out of control. She needed to give that control back to him, even if it meant squashing her instincts to fight him. It wasn't hard to do when his dominant vibes were clogging the air and quashing her own, impressing her wolf.

As Trey felt the defiance leave her body and watched her go slightly slack in his hold, he groaned. There was nothing sexier to him or his wolf than Taryn submitting to him. "Tell me who," he repeated.

"You," she finally replied in a moan as he thrust his fingers deeper.

"That's my good girl. One day I'm going to tie you up while I fuck you. I'm going to have my gorgeous, dominant mate all tied up for me."

"No way." She ignored that the idea excited her, not wanting to acknowledge that apparently she had a tiny submissive streak. "That's where I draw the line."

He tsked, withdrew his fingers, and slapped her clit with his cock. "There are no lines, baby. You belong to me. I own this body. I can do whatever I want with it. I can use it however I want. Right now, I want you to ride me." He positioned his cock at her entrance and she placed her hands on his shoulders as she began to slowly sink down onto him. "You like that, baby? You like my cock filling you and stretching you?"

"Yes." She bore down harder, wanting those last few inches.

"Oh yeah, that's it, take all of it." Finally, he was buried balls-deep inside her and he groaned as her muscles tightened around him. As she took a minute to adjust, he licked and raked his teeth over his mark until she was moaning and squirming.

With one hand collaring her neck, Trey slowly guided her body upward, loving how she didn't fight him but gave him complete control. Then, just as slowly, he impaled her on himself again. He knew his Taryn, knew how she loved it hard, so he teasingly kept the movements agonizingly slow and gentle as he impaled her on himself over and over. Soon enough she was squirming again. "What's the matter, baby? You want more?" She nodded. "Then take it."

So wound up with the need to come, Taryn didn't hesitate; she began riding him hard and fast like a woman possessed, oddly liking the friction from the denim of his jeans against her ass. There was just something about fucking a guy when she was totally naked and he was still partially dressed that got Taryn going. She probably shouldn't have enjoyed the way he was gripping her throat, but she did. It was possessive and dominant and a reminder of how much stronger he was, how easily he could hurt her, but that he never would.

Sparks of bliss were shooting through Trey's body with each of her downward thrusts. He had to wonder if she'd taken horse-riding lessons growing up, because, shit, she had some strength in those thighs and abs. He tugged her face closer and closed his mouth over hers, kissing her with a desperate hunger that matched her pace. He swallowed every moan, groan, and whimper she made, eager for more. Knowing what she liked, he used his free hand to tweak and pluck at her hard nipples and to mold and squeeze those breasts that were bouncing as she rode him, drawing his gaze.

"Trey, I need to come."

"No. You don't get to come until I say." He wasn't ready to leave her body yet. "Do you have any idea how hot it was having you suck my cock, how long I've imagined you doing that? Since the day I had you drugged and brought here. You've been mine since that day, Taryn. You always will be. Do you hear me?" She nodded. "Nothing can ever happen to you, *nothing*, understand?" He'd never get through it if he lost her. Never.

The anxiety in his voice tugged at her heart. "It's okay. I'm fine. Fine. Here. Yours."

A growl escaped his lips. "Always mine. Say it."

"Always yours."

"Louder."

"Always yours!"

"Good girl." With the hand clasping her throat, he urged her to go faster as he began punching his hips up to meet her downward thrusts. "Bite me." He groaned and shuddered as she bit his chest, sucking and branding him. "I love it when you mark me." He moved his hand from her throat to her hair and snatched her head back as he began punching his hips harder. "Come. Now." He sank his teeth into her neck and slipped his thumb between them to circle her clit. Just like that, she shattered.

An intensely powerful orgasm ripped through Taryn, wrenching a scream from her lungs. Her muscles closed around his cock and he punched into her one final time, growling her name, as his own release hit and his cock pulsed deep inside her. Totally replete, she collapsed against him, gasping for breath. He held her close as the aftershocks racked their bodies—it was a hold so tight that it was almost desperate. "I'm not going anywhere, Trey," she assured him softly.

He grunted. "You say that as if you have a choice."

"Ass," she chuckled.

"I mean it, Taryn. I won't ever let you leave. I'll never give you up. I'll never let anyone take you from me."

She lifted her head and smiled at him. "Then it's a good thing I'm planning on staying."

The sight of her warm, reassuring smile triggered another of those strange pangs in his chest. Trey meshed his lips to hers, indulging in a long, thorough tasting of her mouth. Then, content, he nuzzled her neck and breathed in deep. And froze.

"What's wrong?"

"You smell different."

"What? How?"

"Our scents. They've mixed." A smug grin spread across his face. "It's the mating bond. It's advancing." That meant that whatever it was they were doing, they were doing it right. It also meant that any shifter who picked up her scent would know she was a mated female before even seeing her mark—or marks.

Although she rolled her eyes at his self-satisfaction, he could feel that she too was glad about it and liked the knowledge that it would instantly be clear to everyone that he was taken. He also felt her concern that maybe this was the most they would have, that the bond would never be complete, because they might never feel they could be totally naked to each other.

What caused him the most unease was that beneath all that was her fear that he might never come to feel for her what she felt for him, that she would forever be in a mating with someone who couldn't love her. It made Trey want to kick his own ass.

He wondered if she was able to sense just how much he wished he could give her those words she wanted. It amazed him how there could be so much power in three little words. To him they didn't have any true meaning or hold the same power, because they had never been part of his vocabulary. It wouldn't have been any different than someone reciting an unfamiliar Japanese phrase and expecting him not to only repeat it but also to understand what it meant. His mom had been a good mother, but she hadn't been what anyone might call tender or loving. His dad had been far from it. Even Greta, the person who had played the most part in his upbringing, had never used those words, though he believed she cared for him.

Trey knew though that even if he had heard the words every day of his life, there was still a possibility he couldn't have repeated them to Taryn. Considering the things he had done in his life and how fucked-up his conscience was, it was possible that love wasn't something a person like him could feel, that it was reserved for good people like Taryn. It made him wish that he were a better person. There was no denying that Taryn deserved a better mate. Even with that in mind though, he couldn't give her up. Wouldn't.

He hadn't thought of his life as something that was dark or empty until she came here and suddenly lit it up and filled it. Even when he had been doing his level best to avoid her, he had been simultaneously drinking in her presence in his life. It pained both him and his wolf that he couldn't give her—his mate—what she needed. What he did know was that if it were possible for someone like him to experience an emotion so strong, then Trey would feel it for Taryn.

CHAPTER FIFTEEN

"So...who do we think the informant is?"
Everyone at the patio table looked at Dante, but no one answered him. No one wanted to actually face the fact that one of their own had betrayed them. Trey had secretly arranged for him, Taryn, Dante, and his enforcers to meet at the lake this morning to discuss the issue in private. As sad as it was, he felt that these were the only members of his pack he could truly trust. Well, them and Greta. However, he didn't trust Greta to keep the issue of the informant to herself. She would most likely begin confronting and interrogating everyone, and he didn't want the informant to know that they were aware of his betrayal yet. Taryn very much doubted that Darryl's two thugs would own up to him that they'd told her about the informant, so if Trey played dumb, they might just get to the bottom of the matter before anything else happened.

"Personally, I don't think it's a stretch to conclude that it's the same person who vandalized Taryn's car, killed the bird, and left her with that bump a few weeks back." Tao shrugged.

"Then we need to look at people who aren't particularly happy about her being here," said Trick around a mouthful of chewing gum.

"Most of us weren't happy at the beginning, including me," Dominic admitted before offering her an apologetic smile—a smile that quickly turned impish, warning her of what was to come. "Of course, I love you now. If I had a star for every time you brightened my day, I'd have a galaxy in my hand." As usual, some groaned, some chuckled, and Trey hit him.

Taryn shook her head. "You just can't help yourself, can you?" Dominic winked.

"Getting back to the shitty subject at hand, the obvious suspects would be Selma and Hope," said Trey, massaging Taryn's nape. "Although I think Hope would have only been involved if Selma was."

Tao cocked his head. "What about Kirk? He's sure pissed about her being here."

"I don't get why he's so hateful about it though," said Taryn. "I mean, I know he doesn't like me, but if he is responsible for all this, then it seems a bit of an overreaction to disliking me."

"Kirk's always been hateful. He has issues. Mommy issues."

"Care to elaborate?"

It was Marcus who explained. "His mom was human. She wasn't Brock's true mate. Apparently, Brock found his true mate, but she was already shacked up with another guy. He got involved with this human female—not telling her he was a shifter. When she realized what Brock was and that their son was half shifter, she freaked and deserted them both. Kirk was only a toddler at the time."

Taryn couldn't help feeling a pang of sympathy for both Kirk and Brock. "There's always the senile old crone," she said with a smile.

"Greta might call you every name under the blue moon, baby, but I know for sure she likes you in her own way," Trey assured her.

She snorted. "If you say so. Maybe it's not about someone liking or disliking me."

"What do you mean?"

"Well, if we're assuming that the informant has been in contact with Darryl from the beginning, we have to assume that they told him our mating was all about a deal to get you plenty of alliances. Darryl wouldn't have liked that, so he would have wanted me out of the equation. A good way to do that would be by trying to make me feel unwelcome, damaging my car, killing my raven."

Marcus nodded a few times. "If you think about it, it wasn't until you both discovered that you were true mates that anyone tried to actually hurt you."

"It would make sense for him to want you hurt, as is evident from last night," said Ryan. "A shifter whose mate is hurting isn't in the best frame of mind, and it would make you, Trey, more easily provoked into breaking the agreement with Darryl."

Trey wanted to punch something. The betrayal cut deeper than he would have thought possible. Apparently, he wasn't as guarded as he'd always thought himself to be, or maybe his mating with Taryn had changed that. "Why would someone help Darryl? What could they possibly gain from it? If they weren't happy here and wanted to join his pack, they could have left. I wouldn't have stopped them. What they've done is punishable by death."

"Then the question is," began Trick, "who would be prepared to take that risk?"

After a long silence, Trey sighed and got to his feet. "I need to go for a run. My wolf's restless and pissed, and I can't think straight when he's fighting for supremacy so hard."

Tao shrugged. "Then let's all go for a run together."

Trey held out his hand to Taryn. "Come on, baby."

Many days a week, she and Trey would go play in the forest while he was in Cujo form and then lie near the lake while she read the newspaper, all the while running her fingers through his coarse fur. Occasionally some of the pack would join in on their play in their wolf forms and then collapse beside her and Cujo, enjoying the close contact with their Alpha pair.

Taryn wouldn't have thought such a thing could be peaceful. She was drained, dirty, and currently had seven wolves all pressed against her. But always there was that sense of peace, belonging, and family. She could only assume that the wolves felt it too, as they always seemed content just to laze there, all sprawled out with their eyes closed and their breathing even. So when each one of them suddenly jerked upright and went on the alert, Taryn knew something had to be wrong.

She thought of the male wolves who had attacked her the day before, wondering if they would be dumb enough to try to creep around Phoenix Pack territory to finish the job they had barely begun. There was no question that they would be dumb enough, but the wolves didn't dart off in various directions to hunt down any intruders, as she would have thought. They remained there, crowding her, protecting her.

A howl in the distance received an immediate response from the wolves around her—it was a familiar howl. Kirk, she thought. The wolves all seemed to relax slightly, as if the possibility of danger no longer worried them, but they didn't seem happy, and Cujo was emitting a low growl.

Before Taryn could think on it any further, there was the sound of a car approaching. She attempted to stand and see whom the car belonged to, but Cujo growled and licked her jaw and she got the distinct impression that he wanted her to remain where she was. Soon there were footsteps and the sound of Greta speaking ever so sweetly. Voices—familiar voices—responded just as pleasantly, so that everything made perfect sense.

A minute later, three male wolf shifters appeared with Greta. Instantly, Cujo was on his feet, his attention solely on the male in front, but he didn't move from Taryn's side.

Taryn groaned and shot Greta, who was smirking mischievously, an accusatory look. "You knew he was in his wolf form. It didn't bother you that he might have attacked my uncle?" Taryn had forgotten all about their visit.

Greta huffed. "After the things he said to my grandson, no. I hope Trey rips out his throat." She snarled at Don, Nick, and another male wolf—all of whom were staring at the old woman in amazement as she made the transformation from gracious, welcoming host to an agent of the Axis of Evil. Oh, she knew how to play the frail, saintly old woman.

Taryn sat up and wrapped her arms around the neck of a growling Cujo, who clearly remembered Don and was in an overly crazy, protective state after her being attacked. Her own wolf wasn't too happy to see him either. "Trey," she whispered into the wolf's ear, knowing Trey would be aware of what was happening and would hear her. "I need you to come back to me now." Unfortunately, Cujo wasn't in any rush to retreat and let his human half have control. Had she recalled arranging her uncle's visit, she would have postponed it for another time. Too late now.

Looking up at Don, she said, "If you could all just take a seat over there at the patio table, we'll be over in a sec." Turning to the six wolves around her, she ordered, "Change." Not looking all that happy about it, they shifted back to their human forms and—not moving their gazes from their visitors—each retrieved his jeans and T-shirt from the ones that were scattered around. Dante then brought over Trey's clothes and handed them to her. Focusing back on Cujo, she whispered, "Come on, Trey. Come back."

Seconds later the change began and Trey sat in front of her, his gaze still drilling into her uncle. She handed him his clothes and, without a word, he stood and pulled them on. Obviously sensing the precariousness of the situation, each of the visitors had his head lowered slightly, communicating that they had no intention of challenging him, that they were no threat.

Once Trey was dressed, he held his hand out to Taryn and gently pulled her to her feet. He kissed her softly, letting her touch and closeness reassure his wolf. Never had his wolf liked strange wolves around his mate—hell, he'd never liked any males around her—but as their mating bond hadn't fully clicked into place, his wolf was even worse. The fact that she had been attacked yesterday and that one of the males here had once wanted to take her from him worsened his mood.

"Okay?" she asked, combing her fingers through his hair.

He nodded and nipped at her mouth. "Just stay close." If his wolf felt confident that Taryn was nearby, safe, and protected, they might just get through this without him going for Don's throat.

As Trey and Taryn approached the patio table, the visitors lifted their heads to reveal nervous expressions. Trey gave them a nod of greeting and took a seat opposite them, pulling Taryn onto his lap. She snuggled into him the way he liked. Dante and Tao took seats on either side of him and Taryn. He knew without looking that both their gazes were on a gulping Don.

Nick broke the silence. "Thank you for granting us permission to visit. You already know Don. This"—he gestured to the stocky wolf on his right, who was stroking his goatee—"is my bodyguard, Derren. I asked my Beta and my enforcers to remain in the car." Well, that had been wise of him. If Nick had arrived at the lake surrounded by a large number of strange wolves, Cujo would have pounced on them without a doubt.

Trey nodded curtly. "On my left is Tao, my Head Enforcer. On my right is Dante, my Beta. Behind us are Trick, Marcus, Dominic, and Ryan. And you've met my grandmother, Greta."

Nick smiled. "Yes. She's, um, charming. She has good reason to be unhappy to see us."

Don cleared his throat. "Yes. I realize I was very rude at the mating ceremony. And, well, I made judgments about you based on what I'd heard from others. It's simply that—"

"No," interrupted Taryn. "There are no excuses. An apology we can work with. Excuses—hell, no."

"Fair enough."

Hearing her defend him again caused another pang in Trey's chest. Massaging her nape, he said, "That's not to say you weren't right about me. I'm not a good person. If I thought someone deserved it, I'd kill them without blinking and I'd think nothing of it. I am, by my own admission, a hard, selfish, ruthless bastard. There's only one person in this world who's guaranteed to come to no harm from me, and that's Taryn."

After a moment of silence, Don nodded once.

"Dominic," drawled Taryn in her sweetest voice. "Is there any chance you could go ask Grace to fix us all some coffees?"

With the offer of hospitality, the visitors visibly seemed to relax and Don exhaled a sigh of relief—probably relieved that he was still alive. "How've you been, Taryn?"

"Fine, thanks," she practically purred. She loved it when Trey kneaded her nape, even though she knew he was mainly doing it to take comfort in touching her. Her wolf was just as contented. "How're the pups?"

"Still little beasts. They wanted to come and see you, but, well…"

But, well, Don wasn't sure if things would be amicable or if Nick would be scooping him from the floor with a spoon. "Next time, make sure you bring them."

Don smiled a little as he asked, hopefully, "There'll be a next time?"

"If you're good."

"She doesn't give an inch, does she," he said to Trey.

Trey smiled down at his mate. "I kind of like that about her."

Greta harrumphed, hands on hips. "Dante, shove over, son."

Grinning in amusement, Dante shuffled along to the next chair so that she could take his. Her posture was both regal and confrontational.

Nick folded his arms across his chest, but not in a manner that was confrontational. "Well, I hope—in spite of what happened—you enjoyed the mating ceremony."

"It was real nice," said Taryn. "It's been awhile since I went to one."

"You and Trey haven't had one?" asked Don, surprised.

Not liking this subject, because she knew full well that Trey wouldn't want one, she simply gave her uncle a bored look and a dismissive wave of the hand.

"You're not one of those girls who dreamed about it all your life? Wow, my Ana already has hers planned and she hasn't even found her mate yet. Not to mention she's only seven." Don turned to Trey. "What about you, Trey? Don't you want a mating ceremony?"

Being the least romantic person alive, Trey hadn't even thought about it before now. He'd never even wondered if Taryn would want something like that—which she did. And she didn't. He couldn't sense any more than that, so he wasn't sure what was behind her indecision, but it was something they would definitely be discussing in private. He just shrugged. "If Taryn wants one, we'll have one. If she doesn't, we won't."

Nick tutted. "You don't want to be giving your mate her own way all the time."

"Yes, he does," Taryn stated.

Greta huffed at Taryn. "In my day mates weren't allowed to live together until after the mating ceremony."

"In your day a guy named Noah was building an ark."

"And they had more self-control than to fornicate twenty-three hours of every day." Greta didn't enunciate the word *fornicate* properly, as though she thought even talking about it was immoral and would get her sent straight to hell.

"There's nothing depraved about sex. Of course with a little creativity, some toys, and a whole lot of dirty talk, you can change that."

Trey laughed into Taryn's hair as he saw the horrified look on his grandmother's face. God, he really did love his mate's spunk. Greta looked at him expectantly, obviously wanting him to berate Taryn for talking to her about—heaven forbid—*intimate relations.*

Although shifters were easy about sex, Greta had always been, as his mate often called her, a prude. It was obvious, however, that the real reason she was berating Taryn was because she got a kick from it, and that was why Trey would never interfere on Greta's behalf. Well, *that* and the fact that he liked sex with Taryn too much to risk angering her.

"You shouldn't be using that word in front of your own uncle," chastised Greta.

Taryn played dumb. "What? Oh, you mean sex? Well, I suppose there are other terms I could use. Trey likes to call it 'Burying the Bishop,' but I prefer 'Hiding Pedro.' "

"Enough, enough, enough," insisted Greta, but she was barely audible over the laughter that spread around the table.

"So sorry, my halo slipped for a second there."

Conversation seemed to flow a lot easier after that. However, even though the atmosphere became more relaxed, Trey still had to concentrate hard on keeping his wolf suppressed. Although Don had apologized, that didn't matter to his wolf. Nor had he been satisfied by Don's submissive behavior. His wolf didn't want his submission; he wanted Don to challenge him so he could attack and rip his throat out. Maybe he wouldn't have been as overprotective and prickly if Taryn hadn't been attacked only yesterday, or maybe he would always be that way where his mate was concerned.

Sensing that Trey's wolf was far from at ease, Taryn snuggled deeper into Trey's arms and began to pat his chest softly, scratching him lightly with her nails through his T-shirt. A growl of contentment rumbled up his chest and he curled his arm tight around her.

They sat that way for the next few hours, chatting and laughing with everyone. Don and Taryn even did a little reminiscing, talking about her mom and sharing some of the many stories that perfectly demonstrated just how dizzy the woman had actually been. Even Greta had laughed.

It was because the atmosphere was so cheery and relaxed that Taryn sensed the change the second it happened. "What is it?" she asked Trey, who was speaking to Kirk—who was on guard duty—on his cell.

"*What*?" he snapped into the cell. "I'll be right there." Flipping his cell closed, he stood upright and then placed her on the chair. "Stay here, Taryn."

"What? Why?"

"Baby, just stay here for me."

He didn't say *please*, but Taryn heard it in his tone. If he was so wary about a situation that he was pleading with her as opposed to barking at her, it couldn't be good. She nodded once and he kissed her quickly before disappearing into the forest. Dante and the enforcers followed him.

"What's going on?" asked Greta.

"No idea."

Nick's Alpha instincts kicked in and he straightened in his seat. "Maybe Don, Derren, and I should go see if—"

"No, when Trey's wolf goes on high alert, he sees anyone outside his pack as intruders—he'll just think of your behavior as interference."

Greta huffed. "So, what, we just sit here while there's obviously trouble going on?"

"I didn't say that." Taryn stood and pointed hard at the others. "Stay here."

Of course they didn't, and she wasn't exactly in a position to preach at them. Taking the same route Trey had, she traipsed through the forest toward the front gate. As she stepped out of the trees near the security shack, two things made her halt. One, there was a group of approximately ten people—all wolf shifters, her nose told her—standing near the front gate. Two, although the gate had been opened to allow them through,

Trey and the guys had formed a protective wall in front of the shack—a warning that the newcomers weren't to move any farther. Despite there being only eight Phoenix Pack wolves, it was a pretty impressive and intimidating display, and it was working.

The eyes of every stranger moved to Taryn, scrutinizing her intently. There was nothing confrontational in their posture or manner, but that didn't ease her tension. "Who are these people?"

Trey replied without turning his head, not wanting to move his gaze from the wolves in front of him. He wasn't one little bit surprised that Taryn had disobeyed his order. It wasn't in her nature to sit around twiddling her thumbs when there was trouble, just as it wasn't in his. "These are some of the wolves from my old pack." He felt her confusion, knew she was wondering why he wouldn't be at least a little glad to see them. Simple: he didn't trust anyone from his old pack around her right now.

For all Trey knew, in spite of what they said, they were in league with Darryl. Even his wolf, who recognized their scents, wasn't comfortable with their presence at all. When Taryn came to stand beside him, he lifted his arm to create a barrier, wanting her to remain slightly behind him. "Apparently, they're here to see you."

Taryn frowned, both at his words and how he seemed to be shielding her. Only the fact that she could sense his distrust and apprehension kept her from stepping around his arm. It wouldn't be a good idea to distract him if he truly had a good reason to be suspicious. "Why is that?"

"This is your mate?" asked a tall male—who Taryn thought had a slight resemblance to Ryan—in an extremely deep voice. She had to roll her eyes at the surprise in his tone. Okay, so she was small and Trey was big—it wasn't *that* odd a match.

Trey responded with a curt nod.

"But...I thought healers couldn't heal themselves."

Disliking that he wasn't addressing her directly, as though she didn't count, Taryn answered, "They can't."

"I don't understand. You look…fine."

"Why wouldn't I?"

Trey explained. "It would seem that Martin overheard Darryl talking to the wolves who attempted to attack you yesterday. Everyone you see here knows Darryl ordered it done. What they don't know is that the wolves were lying their asses off when they assured Darryl that you were in a bad physical state."

"So the guys who interfered in the attack stopped it before it even started," presumed Martin.

Taryn frowned. "What guys?"

A smile curved Trey's mouth. "The ones who supposedly stumbled upon you being attacked and kicked the wolves' asses."

She laughed. "I can't say I blame them for that sweet little lie."

Martin's brows pulled together. "Then who was responsible for their injuries?"

"Oh, that would be Taryn," replied Dante, his pride in his Alpha female clear in his voice and his grin. The other males wore similar smiles of pride.

A curvaceous, peroxide-blonde female, who Taryn noticed was eyeing up Trey like he was a snack, snickered. "*She* did it? Her?" Her voice rang with skepticism.

Taryn felt a spike of anger. "*Her* is standing right here and is Alpha female of this pack. I'm also very, very close to wiping the floor with your face for ogling my mate. Would you like that?"

Trey doubted that he would ever find it any less amusing to watch the shock on people's faces when his little mate let her bitchy attitude come out to play. Quickly the blonde averted her gaze and edged closer to Martin. Each of the wolves of Trey's old pack once again appraised his mate, seeing not the delicate tiny female she appeared to be at first glance, but the tough, strong, powerful Alpha that she truly was.

"Well, well, well…This is quite a turnout." Greta came to stand beside Taryn, her arms folded and her expression judgmental and suspicious. Don, Nick, and Derren were now behind them. "Shame none of you bothered to visit us sooner. Like fifteen years ago, when a teenage boy was banished instead of being given his place as Alpha."

Some of the wolves looked a little shamefaced, but not enough to satisfy Taryn.

A male who was basically an ancient version of Cam stepped forward, staring at Greta adoringly—Taryn smiled, brows raised, as the old woman blushed. "You look well, Greta. We just wanted you all to know that it wasn't the pack as a unit acting against you or your mate, Trey. Not all of us agree with Darryl's challenge. Of course we'd love for the pack to be whole again, but not for it to happen like this."

A roundish, graying woman spoke in a placatory tone. "We might not have been much help to you all those years ago, but we wouldn't wish you harm." Her gaze settled on Dominic. "I certainly wouldn't want anything for my nephew other than happiness."

The other wolves here, including Trick's parents, who were staring at their son with glittering eyes, nodded in agreement. Trey was surprised to see them, given that they had been loud supporters of his banishment—an attitude that had backfired when their son left along with him. Even with their seemingly harmless behavior, however, neither he nor his wolf was happy about them being around Taryn. "Well, you've seen that she's alive and well. Now you can go."

Dante's older brother, Josh, who ironically was much smaller than Dante, spoke up. "I was sort of hoping I could talk to my bro, you know. It's been awhile."

"Whose fault is that?" said Dante, sounding deceptively aloof.

Trey looked at Josh incredulously. "You don't honestly think I'd allow anyone from the Bjorn Pack near Taryn after what happened yesterday, do you?"

"Trey, come on, man, you can't think we'd hurt your mate."

"I take it that redheaded female you're holding is your mate?" Josh nodded. "Yeah. We mated a few months ago."

"Then you should have a pretty good idea of how I'm feeling right about now."

"None of the wolves you see here would hurt her, Trey," Martin vowed.

"I won't take chances where my mate's concerned. Her safety is my first priority, and right now, my intention is to be more vigilant than ever. Fortunately, Darryl greatly underestimated Taryn and she was unharmed despite his efforts. If there's a next time, he won't underestimate her, and I don't intend for there to be a next time."

"Trey?" It was spoken in a low, gentle, appealing tone by a very thin, dark, middle-aged woman, who was gazing at him in a motherly way, surprising Taryn. "I can understand you being a little surprised by us showing up like this, but you know that I'd never do anything that would hurt you or yours. You trust that, don't you?"

It was clear to Taryn that the woman was very much expecting the answer to be yes, and she wondered why.

Trey narrowed his eyes at the woman. The affectionate way Viv was looking at him was making him uncomfortable. "No. The only people in this world I trust never to betray me are those you see standing with me here. If any of you take offense to my not welcoming you all into my home with open arms, I don't much care. I'm extremely protective of what's mine, but I won't let Darryl trick me into losing control and attacking him for going after Taryn—you might want to pass that on."

Martin seemed to think on that for a moment, and then nodded. "Going by the fact that you didn't lose control...Does this mean you're not as, um...impulsive...as you once were?"

Trey had to smile. *Impulsive* wasn't the right word, but he knew what Martin was getting at. He went with the truth. "No, it doesn't mean that at all. It just means that Taryn keeps me calm."

"Why did you do it, Trey?" Trick's dad's tone was soft, not condemning. "Why did you almost kill your father, your Alpha?"

Trey simply shrugged, not willing to explain himself to any of them. "Because he deserved it. Deserved it so much that I'd do it again if he was alive." Oddly, that seemed to be a good enough answer for Michael.

Uma, Trick's mom, on the other hand, wasn't so satisfied. "You owe us more than that. You owe us an explanation as to why we missed our son growing up."

Oh, she did not just say that! Without conscious thought, Taryn sprang forward, growling. If Trey hadn't looped one arm around her and pulled her back against him, she would have been on that bitch—who had wisely backed up—in a blink. "Trey doesn't owe you *anything*. In fact, *you* owe *him* an explanation—an explanation as to why you didn't give a fourteen-year-old boy a chance to tell you what his asshole of a dad did. And don't tell me that you weren't aware he'd been an asshole. Didn't it ever occur to you that Trey could've easily finished off the job? He didn't though, did he? No. But your tiny little brain didn't even consider that. If you missed that time with Trick, it was your own goddamn fault. So if I were you, I'd exercise that right you have to remain silent, or you'll find yourself strung up like a piñata while I beat the freaking shit out of you!"

Smiling at the almost feral protectiveness in her manner, Trey kissed his mark and rubbed his cheek against hers. He wasn't the only one smiling. Yes, she had been offensive and threatening, but wolves respected that kind of strength. And no one much liked Uma anyway.

"I'm prepared to go to the council and tell them what I overheard Darryl saying," Martin offered.

Trey shook his head. "I'd much rather you didn't."

"Why?"

Smirks identical to Trey's surfaced on the faces of each of his pack. It was Tao who explained. "We deal with things our own way." Nothing more needed to be said for anybody to understand.

"If what you say about being concerned for Taryn's welfare is true, then I thank you for coming."

Understanding they had been effectively dismissed, the wolves all as one turned and made their way back to their vehicles—with the exception of one female, who began to slowly and cautiously approach Trey.

"Who's that?" asked Taryn in a whisper.

He sighed. "Viv. Summer's mom."

"*Oh.*" Well, that would certainly explain the motherly behavior. "I'll give you two a few minutes alone."

Surprised, he turned her to face him. "Baby, you don't have to do that. There's nothing for me to say to her now that I know Summer was never my mate."

"But *she* doesn't know that, does she? If you don't want to tell her, then don't."

"You would be okay with me letting her believe you're not who you are to me?"

She sighed. "No, I wouldn't *like* it, but that woman has already been through a lot. She probably sees you as her last link to her daughter. Someone else who saw her in the special way that she did."

"But I didn't. Not even when I thought we were mates." He released a long breath. "I'm going to tell her the truth. It's the right thing to do, for everyone."

Dante called, "Trey, Viv's asking to talk to you."

Trey turned his head to see that Tao and Dante stood in front of her, blocking her access to their Alpha pair.

Taryn nipped his chin. "Go on. I'll wait back at Bedrock. I'll have you a coffee waiting on the table. Of course you understand that Grace will make it, but the thought is all mine."

He smiled and bit her lip. "I'll just be a few minutes."

It wasn't until she was heading back through the forest—having rounded up the others like sheep and shoved them ahead of her, including her uncle, Nick, and Derren—that he went to where Viv was waiting. He signaled with an incline of his head for Dante and Tao to give them a moment alone.

"Thank you for speaking with me," said Viv, swallowing hard. "Trey, I—I just—I'm glad you're…happy. I always worried about you, wondered if you would survive the banishment. Your mate is very protective of you. You obviously care for each other. I didn't expect to ever see you imprint."

If he wasn't mistaken, she wasn't happy about it at all, despite what she claimed. It occurred to him that she might feel as though he had betrayed her daughter's memory in some way. Damn, she wasn't going to like what he had to say. He took a deep breath. "We didn't imprint."

"Oh, you're not mates?"

"Oh, we're mates. True mates."

Frowning, Viv shook her head. "No, that…that can't be. Summer was your true mate."

"Viv—"

"I saw the way she looked up at you that day—so adoringly, so focused on you. She used to cry all the time with those colic pains, but she calmed down as soon as you held her."

"And you mistook that for a true mate bond. I'm sorry if that's not what you want to hear, but I'm not going to lie to you."

She shook her head again. "You reacted so badly to her death. What you did…That was grief—"

"That was me attacking my father for teasing me about her death."

"He did that?"

"Don't kid yourself that I was someone who deserved your daughter and lost control in a moment of despair, that I'm just terribly misunderstood. When I heard she was dead, I felt guilty and angry with myself, but it could never have touched me the way it touched you. We weren't mates, Viv."

The hopeful gleam didn't leave her eyes. "I can't accept that. Maybe once all this is over with Darryl, you could come with me to visit her grave and—"

He held up his hand. "Viv, I get that you might wish you could have someone to sit there and grieve with you for your daughter, who saw her as special and who you can share stories with, but…I can't be that someone."

"Maybe if I showed you some of her pictures and—"

"Viv, you're not listening to me."

"Because you're wrong."

"No, I'm not. Taryn is my true mate." He didn't like the way she snarled at Taryn's name, nor did his wolf. "Don't you do that. I get that you're upset, but Taryn's my mate and I won't have you disrespect her in any way, just as you wouldn't with your mate."

The stiffness left her spine and she sighed. "I'm sorry, that was disrespectful. She seems like quite a character."

"She is."

"And you're happy with her? She cares for you?"

He nodded. "Even though I'm about as emotional as a broomstick, even though I'm not giving her what she needs. She doesn't judge me for being the way I am. She's so different from me it's not even funny. Taryn's *it* for me."

Viv's expression softened. "Then I'm happy for you. I won't lie and say I'm glad Summer wasn't your true mate, but that's because I selfishly wish I had some sort of connection left to her. What you have is what's best for you, and that's what I should be thinking about, not me."

"Then you're okay?"

She nodded, a half smile now on her face. "I'm okay." She bowed her head respectfully. "Take care, Trey. I really am glad you're happy." With that, she strolled over to the waiting vehicles and hopped into the backseat of one. Then the cars were beeping in good-bye and driving off.

"I wouldn't be surprised if at least one of them can't resist taunting Darryl over his failed attack on Taryn," said Dante as he and Tao came to stand beside Trey.

"Hearing Taryn wasn't hurt and you're onto his little tricks will make him unbelievably pissed," said Tao.

Trey nodded, sighing. "It's a satisfying thought." But he couldn't smile about it like Dante and Tao were. Although he was pleased to know that not all of his old pack was against him, the overriding issue for him was that there was still a threat to his mate walking the earth. That was unacceptable to him and his wolf.

He wondered if Taryn had any real idea of just how difficult it was for him to simply sit back and wait to go after Darryl. The need to avenge pecked at him constantly, demanding he go dish out his own personal brand of justice. The whole thing was making him restless, giving him that nagging feeling, like the kind he got when there was something he'd forgotten to do. Only this time he knew *exactly* what he needed to do, and it went totally against his very nature to ignore it.

Now that their cars were no longer in sight, Trey headed back to the caves.

Dante sighed. "I've got a feeling that Don will want to know everything that's going on—he'll be pissed to hear his niece was attacked."

"Do you think Nick will be willing to join us for the battle?" Tao asked Trey.

"There's only one way to find out." As Trey was making his way to the kitchen, he heard the words *hussy, disrespectful,* and *common*—clearly Greta was taking a pop at Taryn again. Then he heard his mate's voice.

"No need to take it out on me that you're so wrinkled you have to screw your hat on."

And just like that, he was smiling.

"Do you see what I have to put up with? She's always talking to me like this," said Greta, outraged—presumably talking to Don, Nick, and Derren.

"You know, I hear that bathing nightly in the blood of virgins is scientifically proven to reduce the effects of old age. Maybe you should try it."

Entering the kitchen, Trey went straight to where Taryn was perched on the counter and insinuated himself between her swinging legs. He took her mouth in a searing kiss that he hoped told her everything he didn't know how to say. Near her, surrounded by her scent, he could breathe better. It was odd how this tiny little female could anchor him the way she did. She really was the only thing keeping him rational right now, and he wondered if she knew it, felt the weight of that responsibility. Maybe she did, and maybe she felt how close he was to the edge, because she gave him what he hadn't even known he needed until then. She wrapped all her limbs around him and just held him to her.

CHAPTER SIXTEEN

———◆———

T rey was smiling as he made his way to the kitchen four mornings later. Waking up to the feel of his mate's plush lips around his cock could do that to a guy. Entering the room, he found a sight that made him halt. Gritting his teeth, he tore his eyes away and glanced at the people around him. Every member of his pack was there, though none of them had acknowledged his entrance. Each was occupied either with eating, staring into a coffee mug, or toying with a cell phone…as if there wasn't a small pile of gifts in the center of the table.

The pack knew better than to mark his birthday in any way, shape, or form—Trey wasn't the celebratory type and he didn't like being fussed over. It wasn't that he didn't understand why other people would want to mark their own special occasions, it was just that Trey didn't like that whole center-of-attention thing. His pack knew that. There was only one member who would ignore that and force fun on him.

He zoomed in on his little mate, who was sitting on the counter as usual, dipping mini cookies in her coffee. Slowly he approached her, but she didn't look up until he snatched the mug from her hand.

"Hey!" whined Taryn, not even slightly surprised by Trey's reaction.

"What's all that about?" He gestured with his thumb at the table behind him.

"What?" she asked innocently. "Oh, you mean the gifts."

"Oh, I mean the gifts."

"Well, it's like this: it's your birthday, people get gifts on their birthdays, and we're all nice, kind people who wanted to buy you something."

Trey copied her innocent shrug. "It's like that, huh?"

"Yes, and you're very welcome." If she hadn't been sure that it would have been taking things too far for Trey, they would all have sung "Happy Birthday" as he walked in.

"If people told you that my birthday was today, then they'll have also told you that I don't like to celebrate it. So why exactly have you ignored that?"

"Let me ask you something. If it had been my birthday, would you have ignored it?"

"If you had wanted me to, then, yes, I would've," he lied.

"I hope you're not going to make a habit of talking out of your ass, because liars go to hell." Gripping him by the shirt, she pulled him to stand between her legs. "Come on, Trey, it's only a few gifts and then a fun day out."

"No."

She followed after him as he stalked out of the room. Once in the tunnel, she leaped onto his back. "Can't you see I took pity on you? There're no banners or balloons and nobody sang anything." His response was a Ryan-like grunt. "Wouldn't you like to see what I bought for you? Aren't you just a little curious?"

He was, but he couldn't let her know that. She'd pounce on that weakness and use it against him.

"How about we make a deal," she proposed as they neared his office, which she knew he had every intention of locking himself in.

"No deals, Taryn."

"That's a shame," she said as she slid down his back, exhaling a heavy sigh. "It means I went to Victoria's Secret for nothing." She watched in satisfaction as he stopped still with his hand on the doorknob.

"Victoria's Secret?" he repeated without turning.

"Yeah, but never mind." She went to return to the kitchen, but then he spoke.

"Out of curiosity..."

She twirled to see that he was still facing the office door. "Well, I bought this kinky little baby-doll, all black lace like the one I tried on that time when I was tormenting you."

He cleared his throat. "Black lace?"

"Yeah." She took a few steps toward the kitchen, knowing what was coming next.

"What was this deal you had in mind?" he called after her as he finally turned. He was well aware that she had played him, but only an idiot would miss out on this.

She faced him and shrugged. "I was just going to propose that if you try to enjoy yourself and celebrate your birthday with us, then later—for one whole hour—I'll let you do whatever you want to me. I'll be kind of like your sex toy."

His cock jerked and quickly began to harden. "Anything I want?"

The look in his eyes told her that she was going to regret this, but Taryn was determined to make him learn to enjoy himself a little, and she wasn't above using sexual bribes to do it. "Anything you want."

He approached her slowly, his eyes narrowed. "You sure you can live up to your half of the bargain, Taryn? You can't make a guy a promise like that and expect him to go easy."

"You've never gone easy."

"I'm serious, Taryn, don't make this deal unless you can stick to it."

"I think I can handle whatever you've got in mind, Flintstone."

"Well, we'll find out soon, won't we?"

Smiling triumphantly, she took his hand. "Don't forget you've got to live up to your part of the deal first."

Reluctantly Trey allowed her to lead him back into the kitchen and over to the table. She nodded at the gifts, but he didn't select one. He felt a contrary mix of stupidity for what he was about to do, curiosity at what the gifts actually were, and horniness about the devilish deal he had just made. Rolling her eyes, Taryn picked up one of the small, gift-wrapped boxes and handed it to him. He stared at it for a full minute before making a tear in the wrapping, but then he stopped. Oddly enough, it wasn't because he still felt dumb, but because the anticipation was getting to him and he worried that he might actually enjoy the next few minutes. Like a big kid.

Black lace baby-doll, black lace baby-doll, he chanted to himself. And then he tore off the wrapping.

To his total surprise, he got some weird kind of rush. Before he knew it, he'd torn the paper from each and every one—and even felt a tiny bit disappointed to find that there were no more. He hadn't even minded opening the cards. It was kind of fun reading all the jokes in them. The gifts were actually pretty decent—especially the beer. Oh, and the sex toys for him to use on Taryn were definitely welcome. Although she hadn't seemed particularly happy with Dominic for buying those.

Trey had been surprised that not only had she bought him a designer shirt and a new cell phone, but she had also gotten him a voucher for a Ferrari Driving Experience.

"With an experienced instructor, you can drive a Ferrari on a range of circuits at all kinds of ridiculous speeds that will have me panicking for you," she explained.

It freaked Trey out that this female knew him better than he knew himself. He wouldn't have thought that such an experience would have appealed to him, but as he held the voucher in his hands, he felt a buzz of excitement. Leaning down, he nipped her bottom lip. It wasn't what anyone would call a proper thank-you, but her self-satisfied smile indicated that she knew he was happy with the gifts.

"Now that wasn't so bad, was it," she said, poking his chest.

"I don't know why you insisted on all this," griped Greta. "If he doesn't want to celebrate his birthday, he shouldn't have to." Seeing that Taryn was staring at her, she growled, "What, hussy?"

Taryn shook her head as if to clear it. "Sorry, I was just imagining you wearing a shock collar while I held the remote."

"Oh, there she goes again, giving me attitude."

"Not giving it, returning it."

Knowing this could go on for a while if he didn't distract them, Trey pulled Taryn against him. He whispered into her ear, "Now for a preview of the black lace baby-doll…"

She shook her head, whispering, "Oh no, not till later. Fun time first."

Fun, Trey thought a few hours later as he gazed up in disbelief. It was true he didn't know much about it, but he was pretty sure now that his and Taryn's ideas of fun were going to be very different. "I'm not going on that thing."

Taryn gaped as she heard the nervousness in his tone. "Trey, you've got to be kidding me. It's a roller coaster."

"It's a death trap, that's what it is." And how she could say *roller coaster* in the same tone that someone might use for the word *kitten* was beyond Trey's understanding.

"I think we might have finally found something that can shake our Alpha up," said Dante.

Trey scowled, running his gaze along his smirking enforcers. "I'm not scared of going on it, I'm just not convinced it's safe."

Marcus nodded, fighting fruitlessly to keep a straight face. "Sure."

"There's no way I'm letting you go on that thing either," Trey told Taryn.

She snorted. "Just when I thought you might have realized you can't control me, you try it again." She took his wrist and led him a little farther through the fairground entrance. "Don't worry, Flintstone, that big, bad ride's for later. We'll prep you first."

"Prep me?"

"We'll take you on some other stuff first. Once all that adrenaline's pumping through your system, you'll be gearing to get on that ride."

He snorted. "No amount of adrenaline will have me feeling suicidal."

In truth, he wasn't keen on going on any of the rides. He hadn't even wanted to come, but she had insisted he would love it and she had been so excited that it was kind of contagious. Others from the pack had easily been infected and before long Trey found himself being pulled into the backseat of his Toyota to sit with his mate as she led him to his death, it seemed.

Trey curled his arm around her and kept her close as they walked through the crowds, past tents, stalls, and sideshows. The tantalizing smells of cotton candy, popcorn, fries, hot dogs, burgers, onions, and doughnuts drifted through the air, making him suddenly feel hungry.

Everywhere brightly colored lights were blazing, flashing, and sparkling crazily. Screams, laughter, and a discordant mix of music came from every direction, irritating his wolf. There was really only one word to describe the place: eccentric. Fairgrounds were eccentric.

"You'll like this."

Trey followed Taryn's gaze, but couldn't see the ride itself due to the crowds. He arched a brow at the large, colorful sign above it. "What the hell are bumper cars?"

"You can't figure that out by yourself?"

He smiled at how his tiny little mate was able to push past the throngs of people like she was as big as...well, as he was. Then she was pointing to a roofed, metal, rectangular track on which several small electric cars surrounded by rubber bumpers and topped with large poles were dashing around and hurtling into each other. "You're supposed to crash into the others...on purpose?"

Although his tone said he didn't see the logic in the ride, Taryn could feel that he was intrigued. It was kind of cute seeing her serious, intense mate like this. Usually he was so sure of himself and completely confident, no matter his surroundings. A fairground, however, wasn't a place where anyone could easily maintain a serious air. People were helplessly drawn into the fun, even if it was just to laugh at other people making idiots out of themselves. She had known that Trey would be a little out of his element here, because this wasn't the kind of atmosphere he was used to. "You're a boy. Boys like to crash things. You'll like it."

"Taryn—"

She held a hand up to halt his argument. "See—your total lack of enthusiasm just proves you need to learn to let go a little. You would have learned to during adolescence if you hadn't spent most of that time running a pack. Time to make up for that. Don't you realize that you missed a crucial part of your development as a person?"

He frowned. "I turned out all right."

"Erections don't equal personal growth, Trey."

Ryan's laugh didn't wash down well with Trey, especially since he was generally a grunter.

Not wanting to admit that it did look kind of fun, Trey simply shrugged and gave a long-suffering sigh as he allowed her to drag him with her to join the line. Bouncing like little kids, Dante and his enforcers followed behind them, deciding whom they were going to pair with on the ride.

Trey shouldn't have been surprised when Taryn took a separate car and shot him one of her "come get me" smiles. Oh, he chased after her, all right, but then the sneaky little wildcat spun around and rammed right into the front of his car, laughing. And Trey found himself laughing along with her. The guys repeatedly came at him and Taryn as a group, and it amazed him how even while in a car that was no smaller in size than the others, she still found a way to wriggle out whenever she was surrounded.

"You *liked* it," said Taryn smugly when the ride ended and she made her way to him.

He jiggled his head and locked his arm around her. "It was all right."

Taryn chuckled and play-punched his chest. "Let's see what else we can find that's all right."

Trey groaned and huffed, but inside he was actually a little eager to try something else. Of course his little mate had sensed that and pounced on it, dragging him on rides such as the Hurricane, the Pirate Ship, the Log Flume, the Ghost Train, the Ferris wheel, the Orbiter, the Gravitron, and the Waltzer. Okay, the term *dragging him* was a little misleading. All she really had to do was point in the general direction of the ride, and he was there. She had been right—the adrenaline rush had him prepared to ride just about anything...except for the death trap.

What Trey wasn't able to understand was how he had become addicted to trying to win prizes at the side stalls, when it was obvious they were set up to make it practically impossible to win. Most of the prizes were crap too, so logic should tell him not to waste his money or time, but he'd been drawn to them like pigs to shit.

It hadn't been just him. The guys had also tried their luck repeatedly at ones like Coconut Shy, Hoopla, Cork Shooting, Tin Can Alley, Donkey Derby, and Ball in the Basket. Taryn had ended up with two bags full of cuddly toys in various sizes and colors, and a large, soft tiger that was almost as big as she was. As

Marcus had found that highly amusing—or been the only one dumb enough to *show* that he found it highly amusing—Taryn had elected him as the one who would carry it.

"Whoa, Bucking Bronco," announced Dominic.

All with hot dogs in hand, they followed Dominic as he dashed over to a large tent. Inside were two mechanical rodeo bulls covered in piebald blankets that had pieces of black leather for saddles stitched onto them.

"Come on, Taryn—you and me." Dominic smirked cockily. "Don't get me wrong, I already know I can hang on longest, I just want to watch you ride that thing."

Trey slapped the dirty pervert over the head.

"Hey!"

"Only be serious if you're happy to be beat by a girl," warned Taryn. She and Shaya would play that for hours when they were kids. Both of them still held records that beat anyone else in Lance's pack.

Dominic grinned impishly. "I like it when the person I'm up against actually thinks they'll win. It's more fun that way."

Sighing, Taryn handed her hot dog to Trey for safekeeping. "If you're so eager to humiliate yourself, I don't see why I shouldn't help you out with that."

"Oh, yeah, this will be a sight to see," Marcus drawled, laughing wickedly. Trick nodded his agreement, laughing along with him.

Knowing exactly what Marcus meant by that, Trey slapped both him and Trick over the head.

"What was that for?" complained Trick. "I didn't say anything."

"You didn't have to." Trey's heart was in his throat the entire time he watched her being spun about and bounced and bucked, but he still laughed and cheered her on. And still got as horny as all hell watching the way her body moved in sync with the bull as she maintained her balance, giving him a lot of dirty ideas to add to the many he already had.

Eventually, a cursing Dominic fell to the soft mat, scowling and laughing at the same time. He didn't even bother to get up, just remained flat on his back. "I only fell because I got distracted by your breasts. Could you tell them to stop looking at my eyes?"

"Idiot," she chuckled as she offered him her hand to pull him up.

"I've got a better idea. I'll stay here and you can sit on my face while I eat my way to your heart."

She groaned. "These dirty lines are getting worse. It's good for you that you're pretty." He laughed.

"You were awesome on that thing," Dante told her as she passed. Ryan grunted his agreement.

"You can ride me like that anytime," Trey whispered into her ear when she was back at his side.

She laughed and gave him a mysterious smile, gladly letting him enfold her with his arms. "How's the birthday boy?"

He smirked, cupping her ass. "Hard as a rock imagining what I'm going to do to you later."

Watching as his smirk turned mischievous, she narrowed her eyes. "And what would that be?"

"You'll find out tonight. You know what being my sex toy means, don't you? It means you can't fight me. For that entire hour, you have to do exactly as I say."

Yes, she knew that. She also knew it would absolutely kill her. "It's my gift to you. See, birthdays can be fun."

His smirk widened. "Oh, it'll be fun, baby, I can promise you that." He already knew exactly what he was going to do to her and just how much she would be tempted to fight him. Hell, the evening couldn't come soon enough.

Not liking that he was trying to make her nervous, she decided the teasing should go both ways. "Oh my God, oh my God," she rasped into his ear. Pulling back, she smiled. "Sorry, I was just practicing." He pinched her ass.

"So what's next?" asked Ryan before taking a swig of his cola.

Tao smiled. "We have to go in the fun house."

So they did, and Trey could admit it was kind of fun. Then they strolled through the house of mirrors, which he thought was the craziest and possibly also the dumbest thing ever. But he was too hyped up to give a shit that he had just wasted minutes out of his life looking at contortions of his own reflection—something he could do at home just by getting drunk.

Engrossed in the act of sharing cotton candy with Taryn— the worst sharer *ever*—and occasionally licking some from her lips, Trey hadn't realized they were so close to the death trap until Dante spoke.

"Well, Trey, you up for this or what?"

Peering up, up, up and taking in all the steep drops, sharp curves, and stomach-churning loops, Trey shook his head *hell no*. It looked even more hazardous and rickety up close. Not to mention the creaky "I'm going to snap any moment" noises coming from it. "I'll just stay here and hold the tiger and the bags."

"Oh, come on," implored Marcus.

"Yeah," said Taryn, "Come on."

Trey gave her a pointed look. "*You're* not going on it either."

"You'll love it, I promise."

He snorted. "No, I won't, because I'll be dead."

She pressed herself against him and instantly his arms went around her. "Don't worry. I'll protect you."

"I'm not scared."

"Liars go to hell, remember."

"Baby, look at that thing. It looks like there's only one screw holding the damn thing together."

She tugged on his T-shirt as if that would somehow help her get through to him. "It's *supposed* to look like that—dangerous, exciting, thrilling."

"If almost dying gives you a thrill, I'll beat you bloody and rush you to the hospital."

Frustrated, Taryn slapped his chest. "Buck up, Trey. It's just a ride. People go on it every day. People have been riding it tonight for hours."

"Maybe if we were at Disney World, then, yeah, I'd feel confident that it was all put together right."

"Big Thunder Mountain Railroad has crashed something like three times, you know," interjected Trick, earning a scowl from Trey.

She tugged on Trey's upper arm. "Come on, voice of doom and gloom, let's go. You'll love it, I swear."

No, he wouldn't love it at all, and Trey was resolved that he wasn't going on that thing. Until she tugged his head down to hers and whined, "Please?" She even pouted her bottom lip. The transformation reminded him of when Puss In Boots from the *Shrek* movies went from trained killer to helpless kitten. And, just for good measure, she ground against his cock, which was still semihard from having watched her on the rodeo bull. "You're dangerous."

Wearing a self-satisfied smile, she kissed him smack on the lips. "I knew you'd do me proud."

"Oh, I'll do you all right. As soon as we get home." After a twenty-minute wait—which gave him plenty of time to debate his decision and work himself up even more—he was taking a seat beside Taryn and reluctantly tugging down the padded bars to fit securely against his shoulders before connecting the thin little strap from between his legs to the bars. He pulled, testing the fit. And found that there was a nice, big, life-threatening gap. "This is loose."

Taryn rolled her eyes. "It's supposed to be or you'd suffocate. Look, mine's the same." When his eyes widened, she realized that was probably the worst thing she could have said. "It'll be fine." The attendant gave the bars a pull and, satisfied, continued on to check the others. "See, fine."

"You can't be serious."

"If you'll just relax, you'll enjoy it. Really, you don't need to be—"

"I'm not scared," he snapped.

"Trey, I understand that macho man law means you absolutely *have* to deny it, but—"

"Taryn, you—"

Abruptly the ride came to life. She smiled reassuringly while patting his hand. "Just relax."

Relax? If there wasn't so much damn noise, Trey would have informed her that she was dead either way. If the ride didn't kill her, he would, just because she wanted to ride the damn thing when her tiny body could easily slip out. Okay, maybe it couldn't *easily* slip out, but stranger things had happened. Like the fact that he was even on this ride at all.

Trey glanced at Taryn to find that, like the rest of the pack, who were all paired up in the rows in front of them, she had her hands in the air as they slowly chugged up the steep hill. She was even glancing down at the view below and then admiring the scenery beyond it, as if she was just on a bus or something. Trey didn't do either. When he wasn't checking on Taryn, he was keeping his gaze focused straight ahead.

"Did you ever see *Final Destination 3*?" Taryn asked, wearing a teasing smile.

Trey didn't find it funny. "You're a bitch."

"You say that like it's a bad thing."

"It is, and I'll be spanking your ass for it later."

"Promise?"

Growling, he focused his gaze on the seats ahead of him. He wasn't sure whether it was a good thing or a bad thing when they finally reached the peak. The silence that suddenly hung over them as they paused there didn't help his nerves at all. And then they were falling. No, they were plummeting toward the ground and the cool air was rushing up, stealing his breath. At the last moment, they sharply swerved, and then they were caught up in a series of twists, turns, loops, and bumps, and they were being jerked, shoved, squashed, and jostled. Then, just as quickly as it had begun, it was over.

Taryn laughed and clapped along with the others and then turned to Trey. He was, well, white. At least he wasn't green. He looked at her then, and although his scowl was there, his eyes were alight with the same lightheartedness she had seen whenever they played in the forest. "See, I told you that you'd love it."

"I'm still going to spank your ass."

CHAPTER SEVENTEEN

———◆———

T he little witch was stalling. Trey smiled to himself. Fifteen
minutes ago she had told him to get naked on the bed and
wait for her, and then she had disappeared into the bathroom.
Well, he was naked, and he was waiting, and he was so hard it
hurt—he had been since the moment she told him she had a
kinky piece of lingerie from Victoria's Secret. The only time his
cock had given him a brief reprieve was when he went on that
damn death trap. Now it was time for her to live up to her end of
the bargain, and he had a feeling his mate was regretting having
made it in the first place.

He could feel that she was nervous. She should be—he had
plenty in mind for her tonight. Now he would introduce her to
his ideas of fun. Or he would if she would just come out of the
damn bathroom. "Ready yet, baby?"

"Almost," she replied from behind the door.

Smiling, he asked, "You're not thinking of backing out of our
deal, are you?"

"Of course not," she snapped.

"Then get your ass in here." After a good thirty seconds, the
lock clicked open and she stepped into the room. His jaw hit the

floor. "Holy shit." Her gorgeous breasts were spilling out of satin cups that were held in place by spaghetti straps. The baby-doll had a loose-fitting skirt that fell to her upper thigh, barely hiding the matching black, lacy thong. Even better, the skirt split down the center, flashing him a strip of the velvety skin of her stomach. His wolf growled, wanting Trey to place her on her hands and knees and then fuck her until neither of them could move.

He sat up and moved to the edge of the bed. His voice was taut with lust. "Come here." When she hesitated, he arched a brow and said sternly, "You're my toy for the next hour, remember. You have to do as I say."

Damn caveman bastard. Anticipation, excitement, curiosity, and nervousness raged through Taryn as she went to stand between his legs. For a long moment, he didn't touch her, just caressed her entire body from head to toe with his gaze. The hunger in his eyes sent a bolt of heat through her. As if she wasn't hot enough just looking at him sitting there in his birthday suit! God, the man had one hell of a body. He was all muscle and power with a raw sexuality emitting from him that captivated her wolf. Oh, yeah, it was a body that promised gratification—something he had already delivered plenty of times.

"Mine. All mine." His expression dared her to deny it, but she didn't. "Hands behind your back." To his surprise, she immediately obeyed. He wondered just how long the good behavior would last. "Very good. Keep them there." He slid his hands through the split in the skirt and shaped her waist, enjoying the feel of her soft skin beneath his fingers. Snaking his hands farther around, he dipped them to cup her ass while licking along the swell of her breasts. He loved her ass—it was firm and pert and fit just right in his hands, much like the breasts he was staring at. "I think I'd like better access to these." He slipped his hands into the satin cups and scooped out her breasts. Perfect.

A moan slipped out of Taryn as he curled his tongue around one of her nipples. He sucked, bit, licked, and grazed it with his teeth before moving on to the other. Goose bumps broke out over her skin when he pulled back and blew on both wet buds until they tightened painfully. Needing his mouth on them again to take away the ache, she swayed forward slightly and arched into him. The piece of shit spanked her ass instead.

"Spread your legs a little for me. Good girl." Without any preamble, he slipped a finger inside her and groaned when her muscles gripped it tight and moisture greeted it. He slowly thrust his finger in and out of her, watching her face the entire time and the range of responses that played across it—pleasure, need, frustration, restlessness. "Do you like that?" He frowned at her nod. "Give me the words, baby."

"Yes, I like it."

"Good girl." Rewardingly, he drew a nipple into his mouth while circling her clit with the thumb of the hand that was finger-fucking her. Then he inserted another finger and gave her more of those lazy thrusts that never failed to drive her crazy—and that was the whole idea. He needed that nervous tension gone from her body, needed her mindless and so driven by the need to come that she wouldn't balk at those desires she pretended she didn't have. So he continued with the leisurely thrusts, occasionally curving to find her sweet spot, but then slowing almost to a halt whenever she came close to climaxing.

Motherfucking son of a goddamn cocksucking bitch! For the eighth time now he had refused to let her come. Taryn considered breaking his nose…but that would mean she would need to take the time to heal him and it would only prolong things. As he well knew, she wasn't much into soft, slow, and savoring every minute. Right now all she wanted was her mate to fuck her senseless. Was that really too much to ask? She was shaking with want and frustration, and the word *please* was actually on the edge of her tongue. Hell if she would say it though.

She gasped as he latched on to her nipple again, sucking hard and sending a zing of bliss to her clit. She didn't realize she'd moved her hands and threaded them through his hair until he pulled back and gave her a warning look. Growling her annoyance, she clasped her hands behind her. She almost sobbed when, for the ninth time, he brought her to the edge but didn't allow her to topple over. It was official—he was evil.

"Would you like to know what's going to happen next, baby?"

Taryn's eyes widened as he slipped his hand behind his back and brought out a thin piece of rope.

Just as he'd expected, she froze. He gave her a particularly hard thrust with his fingers and pressed his thumb down on her clit, wrenching a moan from her. "Oh yes, baby, I'm going to tie those hands behind your back while you suck me off."

The devious bastard. He'd purposely set out to get her into a desperate, mindless state where she wouldn't care about anything other than him letting her come—and it had worked! The submissive act wasn't making her bristle. She was going to kill him, really, she was. Tomorrow. After he'd made her come half a dozen times. Then she'd kill him.

"You'd like that, wouldn't you, baby? You might not like that you want it, but you do."

The dominant side of her was saying a resounding *no*, but that voice was buried below her overwhelming need to come. She'd be lying if she said she wasn't a little curious.

"Regardless of our deal, I won't force you. I'll never force you to do anything you don't want. But I know you're strong enough to do this. I wouldn't even suggest it if I didn't think you were." Again he curved his fingers to target her sweet spot, making his thrusts cajoling. "What do you think, baby? Shall we try?"

Swallowing hard, she eventually nodded.

He bit her lip. "You're nodding again. Give me the words."

"Yes, I'll try."

"That's my good girl."

Taryn gasped as the fingers of his free hand abruptly tunneled into her hair and his tongue drove into her mouth, stroking her own. As always, his kiss took her over and he greedily drank her into himself. All she could do was kiss him back and cling to him—the only solid thing in her world just then.

Finally he pulled back. "Turn around." Slowly, she did. "That's it." Gently he gathered her hands together and tied the rope around her wrists in a knot that was secure but not anything that would feel threatening to her. "All done, baby." Once she was again facing him, he said, "On your knees, Taryn. I want my cock in your mouth. I want you to suck me off while your hands are tied behind your back."

This was *not* revving her engines, Taryn told herself. Not one little bit. Obediently—hell, this obedience thing should be really pissing her off—she went to her knees and ran her tongue along the length of his cock from base to tip. She smiled at the sound of his groan. Holding his gaze, she licked the drop of pre-come from the slit.

He tapped her cheek lightly with his cock. "Open up." He groaned when she finally took him into her mouth. "Oh, yeah, that's it. You know how I like it." The sight of her down there, with her lips wrapped around him and her breasts spilling out of her baby-doll, had him close to coming already. He wasn't going to last long; his climax was approaching fast.

Roughly he speared his fingers into her hair and began to guide her movements, urging her to suck faster. He tugged on her hair to the point of pain, knowing she liked it, *feeling* she liked it. "I'm going to come, Taryn. Get ready. I want you to swallow it all." Both he and his wolf had wanted to mark his female, his mate, in this primitive way for months, had been craving it. A loud, guttural groan escaped him as his orgasm hit and jets of come shot down her throat. It felt so good he was surprised he didn't pass out, especially since he'd been waiting to come all damn day. He pulled her to her feet and gently skimmed his thumb along her jawline. "Very good. Now I think you deserve a reward. What do you think?"

If the reward involved coming, Taryn was game. Surprising her, he gently turned her and untied the knot binding her wrists. Hell, he'd taken it easy on her...which didn't seem like Trey. When he swerved her to face him again, he massaged her wrists gently—nothing sexual about it. Again, this did not seem like Trey. His mouth landed on hers, dominating her lips, as he slowly raised her arms above her head. She gasped as he again fastened the rope around her wrists, joining her hands as though in prayer. The sneaky fucker. Oh this, *this* seemed like Trey. His dark, hooded gaze ensnared her as he spoke again, his voice ringing with dominance and power in the way that never failed to make her shiver. Her wolf loved it.

"I want you to go and lie back on the bed with your legs spread and your arms above your head. Can you do that for me?"

Did bears shit in the woods? Instantly Taryn clambered onto the bed and did as he asked.

"Gorgeous." He gently breezed the tip of his finger through her slick folds. "So wet for me." He loomed over her. "Did you like sucking my cock, baby? Did you get off on it?" When she only nodded, he arched a brow. "I can't hear you."

"Yes."

Without missing a beat, Trey dropped to his knees and buried his face between her legs. Taryn bucked in surprise, groaning. He tormented her with his tongue, alternating between nibbling on her clit, swiping his tongue through her folds, and circling her entrance with that tongue—never delving inside. Instead of providing her with some measure of relief, he was only succeeding in working her into a frenzy. "I need to come."

Trey gave her a careless shrug. "I'm not done yet, baby. You'll just have to wait."

She kicked out at her asshole of a mate. "Don't be a jerk, Trey!"

He pinned her with a look. "Are you going to keep still, or do I have to come all over you and leave you like this?"

She cursed a blue streak at him but he simply chuckled, sending vibrations through her clit, which he was teasingly flicking with the flat of his tongue. Then he was nibbling, licking, and stabbing her with that talented tongue, and she was moaning, whimpering, and crying out, unable to keep quiet. "I really, *really* need to come."

"Good, because I'm ready to let you." Instantly he drove two fingers inside her and fucked her hard with them as he suckled on her clit—that was all it took. Her thighs squeezed his head as she came, screaming. He continued to deliver teasing licks to her clit, helping her ride out her orgasm, until finally she slumped onto the mattress. He held her gaze as he sucked his fingers clean, groaning.

The sex-crazed look on her face almost had Trey coming again. "I think my little bitch is ready to take my cock now." Trey knelt on the bed and pulled her legs up straight against his chest. Holding her eyes, he rammed his cock inside her and began roughly pounding into her, knowing that was what she craved. "Tight, wet, hot, and all mine. Aren't you, baby? You were made for me. The reason you exist is to take my cock inside you. Isn't that right?"

Taryn nodded, once again suppressing her reflex to challenge him. She could feel an orgasm ready to tear through her and the last thing she wanted was for him to stop. God, it was going to be a monster-big one. Then, abruptly, he slowed his pace and made his thrusts shallow. Urgh! She'd done everything he told her to do! She hadn't once complained! She hadn't spat any profanities at him—well, not aloud anyway. Yet here he was *being a fucking prick.* "Trey—"

"You didn't answer me, baby. You know I don't like it when you just nod. I'll ask again. The reason you exist is to take my cock inside you, *isn't that right?*"

She could absolutely kill him right now! How dare he treat her like, like, like…well, a toy. Dammit, why had she made that deal? "Yes! Now fuck me!"

Then he was hammering into her again and she was almost sobbing with the pleasure and pain of it, clasping at the bedsheet so hard she wouldn't be surprised if she tore it. Not that she could bring herself to care about that or anything other than the fevered pounding that he was subjecting her to.

"Shall I fuck you harder? Huh?" He gave her a painfully hard thrust. "Like that?" She nodded. "I can't hear you, Taryn."

Defiantly, she didn't answer. He stopped just as she was about to come. *Motherfucker.*

Trey wasn't surprised when her upper body sprang up and she snapped those teeth at him. He tutted. "Now, that wasn't very nice. Do you want to get fucked hard, yes or no?"

What she wanted was to bite his cock off and beat him over the head with it. Tomorrow, she'd do that tomorrow. "Yes," she growled.

"Then lie back, don't move, and take it." At that Trey began pounding into her at a frenzied pace that had her back arching and more husky cries escaping her throat. God, he loved being inside her, loved seeing that spark of defiance in her eyes, and he loved feeling her come apart around him. Using one arm to pin both her legs against his chest, he abruptly drove one finger into her ass. She cried out and bucked.

"I need to come!"

She wasn't the only one. Trey began drumming two fingers on her clit. Her muscles tightened around him again and he groaned. "Let me feel you come all over my cock." Seconds later she exploded around him, screaming. Feeling her pleasure as well as his own had him coming so hard he saw spots. "*Fuck.*" Trey collapsed beside her. Breathing in her scent and kissing her neck softly, he asked, "You okay, baby?"

"Mmm." That was all she could manage as she lay there, panting, lacking the strength even to keep her eyes open.

"Don't think you can go to sleep. I'm not done with this body yet." He lapped at his mark. "You know what's coming next, don't you?" The words rumbled out of Trey as anticipation rushed through him. "I'm going to fuck this sweet ass."

"Hell, no. I don't want to know what a stuffed turkey feels like." Or what it would feel like if it was alive while it was being stuffed. Her wolf didn't quite agree. Tramp.

"Now, now, Taryn, you said I could do whatever I want to you tonight. And I want my cock in your ass." She could pretend she didn't want this all she liked, but he could *feel* that she was intrigued, and he knew that she liked it whenever he finger-fucked her ass.

"You can stay away from my ass." She gasped in outrage as Trey flipped her over, pulled her ass in the air and spanked both cheeks hard. "Hey!"

"Be still."

"You'll slice me in half!"

"I'm your mate, Taryn. Your body was made to take mine—anywhere I want."

"I let you tie me up, isn't that enough?"

Draping himself over her, Trey spoke into her ear, "This is what's going to happen, Taryn. I'm going to finger-fuck your ass to get you ready for me. And you'll like it, whether you want to or not, you'll like it. You won't be able to help it. Then I'm going to sink my cock into your ass and you'll love it, baby, and you'll want more. And I'll give you more. I'll give it to you hard and fast the way you'll want it. And you'll come screaming, I can promise you that."

Using his and her come combined, Trey lubricated her ass with one finger, thrusting it in and out of her in a rhythm he found kind of hypnotic. When he added another finger, she jolted. "Shh, baby, I won't hurt you. You know I'd never hurt you." At those words she relaxed a little. He continued readying her with two fingers, and soon she was groaning and writhing, trying to counter his thrusts. "That's it. You like that?" She only nodded, but he didn't call her on it this time. Hell, he was too fascinated with the sight of his fingers moving in and out of her ass to care. When he added a third finger, and she groaned in pleasure rather than pain, he knew she was ready.

Thank God. "Baby, I can't wait any longer." He slowly withdrew his fingers and then pressed his cock into her ass. "Shh, relax, let me in." Releasing a long breath, she let the stiffness leave her body. He gave her back a soothing rub. "Good girl. Now push out as I push in." Ignoring the urge to ram himself inside her, he fed her an inch of his cock at a time, careful not to hurt her. "Oh, baby, you have no idea how hot it is watching my cock disappear in your ass. Good, Taryn. Take more." Finally he was fully sheathed. "Fuck, that feels incredible."

He was right, it did—which surprised the hell out of Taryn, who had never felt so full in her life. Sure, it hurt, but it was a good hurt. The bite of pain only intensified the pleasure. He'd been right—her body accommodated him, was made to accommodate him wherever he wanted to take her. If only he would move...

"Ready, baby?" Taking her moan as a yes, he slowly withdrew until only the head of his cock was inside, and then he slowly sank back in. A whimper escaped her. "Feel good?" She only nodded, but again he let it slide. Once Trey had given her a few more slow thrusts, she began to squirm restlessly. "You want more? You want it harder?" She nodded. "Taryn?"

She turned her head and met his gaze. "Yes, I want it harder."

"Good girl."

Trey gave her what she wanted, rearing back and then plunging back inside. His thrusts were hard but not hard enough to make her come. He knotted a hand into her hair and yanked her head back. "Tell me who you belong to, baby. Tell me."

"You," she rasped.

"That's right, you're all mine. *My* little bitch. *My* good girl. *My* mate." And then he was plunging hard, deep, and fast into her ass, knowing she wanted it, knowing she loved it. Loved it so much she was rearing back to meet his thrusts. "Scream my name for me when you come. That's right." The combination of *feeling* how violent her orgasm was and hearing her scream his name quickly triggered his own orgasm. "Son of a bitch!"

My thoughts exactly, thought Taryn.

CHAPTER EIGHTEEN

W*ell, shit.* Taryn plunked herself on the bathroom stool as utter shock overcame her entire being. Her breaths started coming in short, shallow pants and a slight tremor ran through her body. A cocktail of emotions swished through her, around her, over her, and she couldn't make any sense of them. A part of her wanted Trey, wanted his arms around her comforting her, but she knew that if she tried to stand, her legs wouldn't support her. She also knew that there was a very good chance that comfort wasn't what she would get.

It was her full bladder that had woken her early and made her slip out of Trey's secure hold. As she stumbled her way into the bathroom, still half-asleep, she found herself frowning as she became aware that something wasn't quite right. Nothing that set off any alarm bells, nothing that was making her wolf agitated or apprehensive. On the contrary, her wolf was extremely content, though maybe a little more on the alert than usual. Still, something was different and it was pissing her off enough that Taryn began to snap out of her drowsy state. And then she understood: her scent. It had changed again. For a second she'd wondered if it was something to do with the bonding, but an age-old instinct surfaced and told her exactly why it was different. Pregnant. She was pregnant.

Just how the hell had that happened? Okay, sure, she knew *how*, but she had been taking her pills on time; she hadn't missed a single one. The contraceptive pills designed for shifters were a lot stronger than those used by humans, and they were 99.9 percent foolproof. She realized that wasn't a guarantee, but no one expects to be in the 0.1 percent, do they?

No wonder her wolf was so content. Now that the fog had cleared, Taryn found that she herself was...happy. She had always wanted pups of her own, though she'd never dared hope too strongly that it would ever happen. How could she not be happy to know that growing inside her was a little person who was half her and half the person she loved? Now Trey, on the other hand...there was no telling how he would react.

In a few months he had gone from wanting jack shit in terms of relationships to being partially bonded—that was a lot for someone like him. He might not feel ready yet. Hell, given Trey's nature, there was a chance he hadn't pictured ever having any kids. Not that Taryn would have agreed to never have any, but she would have agreed to give him time. It would hurt to find out he didn't want this baby, but that could very well be the case and she knew she had to prepare herself for that—mostly so that she could refrain from clawing his eyes out. It was amazing just how protective she already was of this unborn life.

She wasn't sure how long she had sat there, planning what she would say and panicking as the right words wouldn't come, when she heard Trey call out her name. Shit. "I'll be out in a sec." Apparently, that wasn't good enough because she heard him rising from the bed and unsteadily making his way to the bathroom.

"Taryn, what's wrong?"

Great, so he had sensed her panic. "Nothing. I'm fine." The door swung open and, frowning at her, he stepped inside. He halted abruptly as his frown deepened and his nostrils flared. A few seconds later his eyes widened and his mouth dropped open. There was no mistaking the smell of a pregnant wolf. She gave him a cautious, wobbly smile. "Hi."

Although Trey had never had a way with words, he had never found himself knocked enough to be speechless. Until now. When he sensed her anxiety, he'd thought that maybe she'd had a nightmare or was worrying herself stupid about the challenge taking place tomorrow—what else was going to wake her up in a panic at dumb o'clock in the morning? The distinctive change to her scent had hit him immediately as he entered the room, but not harder than his understanding of what that meant.

The sight of his little mate huddled on the stool, as if bracing herself for a fierce impact, made something in his chest tighten. His reaction—she was bracing herself for his reaction. Her emotions were all over the place, but her primary emotion was happiness. She was happy. Scared and shocked, but happy. And she feared he wouldn't feel the same.

His wolf bucked at the reins, wanting to be near her, to protect her, to hold her. Wanting the same and knowing he needed to say something, Trey went to her and squatted in front of the stool. "You're pregnant." Oh, hell, he was getting worse with words if all he could do was state the obvious.

"Yeah. Pregnant. I've been taking my pills, but..." She let the sentence trail off, shrugging.

"I—I have no idea what to say, baby."

She smiled a little at his apologetic expression. "I don't need you to say anything. I just need to know if you're okay with this. I can't sense anything from you."

"That's probably because I'm numb." Her small smile fell and Trey wanted to kick himself. "No, I don't mean..." He sighed. "Baby, I don't know what I mean." This, here and now, showed just how much of an unfeeling bastard he was. He was supposed to be over the fucking moon, wasn't he? Wasn't this supposed to be one of the top moments of his life? Here was his mate telling him she was pregnant. Pregnant. His mate was pregnant. She was having a baby. *His* baby. His son or his daughter…and then the surreal quality of the situation cleared and it actually sank in that, shit, Taryn was pregnant with his baby.

Slowly he raised his hand and placed it on her stomach. A fierce sense of protectiveness surged through him, stealing his breath. Her half smile returned, but it was forced and shaky. Even as she had a fragile look about her, there was pure steel there. She was ready to kick his ass if he said anything negative. He leaned forward and closed his mouth over hers, kissing her greedily, and suddenly became aware that, hey, he was happy about this. No, more than happy. He was…kind of excited. He rested his forehead against hers as he spoke. "If someone had told me a few months back that I'd soon be mated with a baby on the way, I'd have laughed my fucking head off. You changed everything, Taryn."

She knew he didn't mean it in a bad way. Still, she couldn't resist teasing him. "Me? This is all me, is it?"

"All you. You've made me want things I never would have expected to want. Things I didn't think were in the cards for me." He massaged her stomach gently. "Like him."

She arched a brow. "Him? It could be a her."

"I'm not going to be very good at the dad thing. You know that, right?"

Taryn pinned him with a look as she cradled his face in her hands. "You will be. I know you will be."

"Baby, I don't know anything about being a dad—mine was an asshole."

"Exactly. Just do everything your dad didn't do."

There was actually logic in that, he thought. He could work with logic. His gaze was drawn again to her flat stomach. So slender. She was so slender and so damn small. He didn't see how she could carry a baby inside that body and not snap in half with the strain.

Sensing his fear that she might be hurt, Taryn kissed him softly. "I'll be fine."

"Nothing can happen to you, Taryn," he insisted.

"Nothing will. I'll be fine. We'll be fine."

He scrutinized her face as he asked in a low voice, "How does it feel? To know you hold my sanity in your hands?" If he lost her, if she left his life, his mind would go right along with her.

She smiled, brushing her nose against his. "Trey, whatever makes you think that you're sane now?"

He chuckled, shaking his head. He nipped her bottom lip, then sucked it into his mouth, liking the way her eyes flared with lust. She was so responsive—it was enough to drive him crazy. He kissed her softly, denying her his tongue just to tease her. "You better be okay, baby, or I swear I'll blister your ass with the palm of my hand."

"What about the pack? How do you think they'll all feel about the pregnancy?"

"There's only one way to find out."

When they stepped hand in hand into the kitchen half an hour later, they were greeted with the usual brief nods and smiles. Then everyone's nostrils flared, the chatter stopped, and all eyes zoomed in on Taryn.

She knew the pregnancy was an extremely significant thing. For some reason no one had yet been able to explain, wolf shifters couldn't produce their own offspring unless either their Alpha pair or their Beta pair had done so. Nature had really funny ways, in her opinion. Now that Taryn was pregnant, it meant that it was possible for Grace and Rhett or Lydia and Cam to begin their own families, which probably had a lot to do with why all four of them looked absolutely ecstatic.

Dante was the first to react. He jumped to his feet and strolled over to slap Trey on the back. "Congratulations." He quickly kissed her cheek and artfully dodged Trey's subsequent clout. "With his gene pool, he'll be a powerful Alpha." Suddenly they were surrounded by most of the pack, and Lydia and Grace were squealing excitedly.

Tao raised his hand. "I claim bodyguard duty!"

Ryan grunted. "Damn little shit, *I* was going to do that."

"I'm going to be an uncle," said Dominic excitedly. "If it's a boy, I'll teach him all he needs to know about reeling in women."

Trick snorted. "You mean you'll teach him those dirty lines you're always subjecting us to." He gave Taryn a quick hug and said, "Congratulations, honey."

"Speaking of dirty chat-up lines," Dominic drawled as he turned to Taryn, wearing that all-too-familiar wicked grin. When she shook her head, warning him to keep it to himself, he sighed. "I can't help it. I love your hair, your eyes, and your smile. Hell, I love every bone in your body. Want to add one more?" As usual, Trey hit him.

"Don't worry about Dom, Taryn." Marcus patted her stomach gently. "I'll teach the little guy in there the art of flirting so that he never has to use those lines."

"I'll teach him how to throw a ball," declared Dante. "And how to drive."

"That's nice and all," said Ryan, "but you know I'm going to be his favorite uncle, right?"

"Um, *hello*," said Taryn. "The baby could be a her, you know." They all gave her sympathetic looks, as if they pitied her for even thinking something they perceived to be dumb. She might have scowled at them if, to Taryn's astonishment, the old crone hadn't suddenly approached, wearing a genuine smile. Just like that, Trey, Dante, and the enforcers formed a wall in front of her. Oh, dear God, was she going to have to put up with this overprotectiveness for the entire five months of the pregnancy? It certainly looked like it. At least shifter pregnancies didn't last nine months like human ones did. Those poor women.

"I'm not going to hurt her."

Nobody moved to let Greta pass.

"She and I might not always see eye-to-eye, but that's my great-grandchild in there."

Their expressions said that wasn't relevant.

Sighing, Taryn hopped up onto the counter behind her. Immediately, Trey spun to face her. "Be careful jumping around like that."

Taryn double-blinked. "Oh my God, you've got to be kidding me. Chill, Flintstone. Grace, I need one of your magical coffees."

"No, no coffee," said Grace. "Caffeine's not good for you during pregnancy." As Grace then rambled on about all the other things Taryn wouldn't be able to drink or eat, she felt her mood plummet.

"You look tired, baby. Want me to take you back to bed?"

She looked at him in sheer disbelief. "No, I don't. None of you get to treat me like an invalid—let's just clear that up right now."

"It's great to have some good news for a change," said Brock with a smile. "It's been a long time since I've been around any pups." He turned to Kirk. "Well, son, aren't you going to congratulate our Alphas?"

Kirk said nothing. He just sat next to an equally mute Hope, looking kind of...defeated.

"She's pregnant?" hissed Selma. "Oh. Great. Not only are we stuck with her, but we've got Warner blood polluting our pack!"

"Selma," growled Trey, more protective of Taryn than ever before.

"Twelve weeks you said she'd be here! Twelve weeks! Then you try telling us she's your true mate! I've waited for you to see the truth, waited for you to see that you're wrong and she's just fooling you so she can be Alpha fe—"

"You know, Selma," began Taryn, interrupting her mid-rant, "you're behaving like a drug-crazed terrier trying to catch and chew off its own tail. Seriously, pursuing your *mated* Alpha is insane and suicidal. It really is time to get off the Selma Gets

Whatever She Wants plane and accept the facts. *I* am Trey's mate, *I* am Alpha female here, and *you* don't have a prayer of changing that. We've got enough things to worry about, so stop with your tantrum or I'll have to do what I like to call making my point in a way that no one can misinterpret. Others might refer to it as breaking your fucking nose."

"That wouldn't be so bad," said Grace, sounding hopeful.

Selma refused to drop the matter. "Trey, how can you not see her for what she really is? Everything was fine here until she came along."

Reminding himself that hitting females wasn't a good thing, Trey released his frustration with a long exhale. "If you're so unhappy, feel free to leave. In fact, you're more than welcome to leave with Darryl tomorrow after the challenge. If there's anything left of him. I can't guarantee there will be."

"M-maybe I will l-leave," she replied, seeming to be truly shocked that Trey would choose Taryn over her. "Maybe Hope and I w-will start our own p-pack."

"I never said anything about Hope. If she wants to leave, she can, but it won't be because you bullied her into it."

Predictably, Selma stormed out of the room, wearing the scowl from hell. For once, Hope didn't follow her, making her loyalties clear. Kirk also remained where he was.

Taryn spent the next few hours being fussed over by almost the entire pack. At first she was feeling pretty damn claustrophobic and fought the urge to bash everybody's skulls in with the cast-iron frying pan. But when she was nicely placed on the reclining end of the humongous sofa with a mug of hot milk and a pack of cookies while Marcus massaged her shoulders and Dominic rubbed her feet, she was thinking it was good to be a pregnant Alpha.

Then Trey had to go and mess it up. "I want you to stay here while I go to meet Lance about the challenge." They had notified her father yesterday via the pack web about the challenge and arranged a meeting for this morning at Mo's Diner.

She sat up straight in the recliner. "Oh, hell no!"

"Baby, don't fight me on this. You know it's a good idea for you to remain home, where you'll be protected."

"Alpha pairs deal with issues together. They go to meetings together."

"It's different now. You need to be careful, you're having our baby." God, it was weird saying that, but not in a bad way, which made it even weirder.

"Oh, *puhlease*, you'd have said the same damn thing if I wasn't pregnant. You don't get to use our baby as an excuse to keep me cooped up here. We both know that's exactly what you're doing."

He tilted his head, conceding that. "Okay. So I would have said the same thing no matter what. It's only because I want you safe. I don't like you being near your father, even if he does seem to have a newfound respect for you." She just stared at him, completely unmoved. "Taryn, you've got no idea just how protective and possessive my wolf is feeling right now. He's not going to cope well with you being around strangers, and he's really not going to like you being around a wolf who has repeatedly hurt you."

"So now your wolf is getting the blame?"

"Taryn," he groaned. "Your father isn't going to be the only Alpha male there. He's also bringing along ten very powerful Alphas from his collection of alliances. Ten wolves I don't know or trust. Then there'll also be whatever enforcers or bodyguards they each decide to bring along. That's a lot of strange wolves. Is it really so unreasonable to ask you to stay here, where you'll be away from them? Is it really so unreasonable to want you to stay away from any possible danger?" She didn't answer, just continued to stare at him blankly. "Taryn, are you even listening to me?"

"I pretended to, so let that be enough."

"He has a point though, Taryn," said Tao.

She raised an eyebrow at the traitor. "If I want your opinion, I'll kick it out of you, okay?"

When Tao went to speak again, Dante put a hand on his shoulder and shook his head. "You should know by now that when she's smiling like that, it's not a good sign, and best to leave her alone."

Suddenly Grace appeared and placed a glass in her hand. "Here, drink this. You need plenty of nutrients and lots of folic acid in your diet, so—"

Taryn grimaced. "What the hell is that?"

"Fruit juice."

"Really? Strange. Because it looks like vomit."

"Grace, will you tell her it's best to stay behind?" said Trey. "It's not a good idea for her to be going to stressful meetings while she's pregnant."

Taryn poked him in the chest. "Oh no, Flintstone, you don't get to drag Grace into this. I *am* going to this meeting."

"Don't make me lock you in our room." He was expecting an outburst. What he got was a smile. Dante was right; it only meant bad things when she smiled like that.

"Try it if you feel you must. But just remember this: I know where you sleep, I know where the cheese grater is, and I know it'll cause you a hell of a lot of pain if it makes contact with your cock. Don't think I won't do it. I know I can heal you afterward, so my conscience won't interfere." Her smile widened when he emitted a low growl.

He was still growling twenty minutes later when they left Bedrock for Mo's Diner. Taryn probably shouldn't have found it so amusing, but she did—much like a smiling Dante, who seemed to find humor in every dispute his Alphas had. Trey, in overprotective mode, had wanted to bring all six enforcers, so they took his gold, nine-seater Chevrolet Tahoe.

When his mood hadn't improved fifteen minutes later, she finally snapped. "Will you stop with the growling! If you really *must* brood, then do it quietly."

"This isn't brooding, baby, this is me so unbelievably pissed I'm considering just taking my chances with the cheese grater and having Dante drive you back home."

"Dante knows better than that."

The Beta winced. "Yeah, I'd kind of like to keep my foreskin."

Trey sighed at her. "Pain in my ass."

"Pain in your cock if you try sending me home."

And so the growling continued.

Finally, they arrived at the diner and, much like last time, Trey received many wary looks. To her surprise, so did Taryn. Clearly the Brodie incident was still fresh in everybody's minds. She picked up Lance's scent almost immediately. Sitting at a long table, surrounded by ten of his powerful allies, he looked exactly like the big man he wanted to look. Scattered around the diner were enforcers and bodyguards, ready to protect their Alphas at the slightest hint of danger. Trey subtly directed his own enforcers, other than Tao, who came to the table with him, Taryn, and Dante, to do the same.

All the Alphas stood, and all looked pretty insulted that Trey was keeping his Beta and Head Enforcer so close—it was considered a sign that he distrusted them. But then their eyes went to Taryn, and she guessed that they had scented her condition and, thus, the reason for Trey's cautiousness. She was proven right when her father spoke.

"Trey, Taryn. Congratulations." Strangely enough, he sounded like he meant it. All the Alphas followed suit, congratulating them both and inviting them to sit opposite Lance.

"Thanks," said Taryn while Trey gave them a nod. Dante and Tao stood directly behind their seats, alert and wearing "don't dare try anything" expressions. She hid a smile at the apprehension wafting from the wolves at the table. These might be very powerful Alphas, but they were still intimidated by Trey.

Lance introduced each of the Alpha wolves, though it wasn't necessary. Trey knew who each and every one of them was, just as he knew that each and every one of them had had problems with his father's pack in the past. Much like Lance, Rick Coleman had been good at making enemies. It was little wonder then that they were there, prepared to listen and possibly be present for the battle.

"Could you tell us exactly what the trouble is that you have with the Bjorn Pack?" asked Lance.

Massaging Taryn's nape the entire time, Trey explained about his banishment, his father's death, and his uncle's challenge. "My hope was that Darryl would back down at some point before the twelve weeks were up. Instead, as encouragement for me to give him what he wants, he ordered an attack on Taryn—"

"An *attack* on you?" If Taryn hadn't known better, she might have thought Lance actually cared.

"—which very much backfired, leaving her unharmed."

"It was most likely a trap," said one of the Alphas—a very muscular, redheaded guy with an accent Taryn couldn't place. She didn't bother to hide her smug "told you so" smile from Trey, petty though it was.

"Yes Quinn, and that was the only thing that kept me from reacting." Trey easily remembered the large male who had once dueled with Rick Coleman and probably would have won if Darryl hadn't distracted Quinn at a critical point in the fight. Hopefully, he was interested in getting a little payback.

"This happened while you were pregnant?" asked another of the Alphas.

"If it had, he'd be dead right now and we wouldn't be having this conversation," Taryn replied.

Damn right, thought Trey. "The challenge takes place tomorrow. My uncle won't keep this as a battle between two Alphas—he's too much of a coward for that. He has many alliances, so I'm expecting a large number of wolves to appear with him. Nick Axton, the Alpha of the Ryland Pack, has already offered us his support."

"Ryland Pack," repeated Lance. He looked at Taryn. "Your uncle Don mated into that pack, right?"

She nodded and smiled. "He sends his love." Lance rolled his eyes.

A roundish, grim-looking wolf looked at Trey curiously. "Nick's a powerful Alpha, but his pack isn't much larger than yours."

"Exactly," said Trey. "That's why I'm low on numbers, and that's why I'm here."

"If you win tomorrow, what do you intend to do with who is left of the Bjorn Pack and with their territory?" asked Quinn.

"Let me make it clear that *when* I win tomorrow, I don't intend to make any wolves outcasts or distribute the territory among others. I know a lot about being out there with no protection or territory, and I have no wish to place others in the same situation. Whoever is left of the pack will be permitted to keep their territory and choose a new Alpha, providing they swear their allegiance to me. They'll be expected to do the same for any packs who back me, but that is the most I can offer in terms of reward for anyone's backing. So, in other words, if that and a chance to settle some scores with Darryl isn't enough for any of you, it's important you say so now."

"So, all in all, we have the support of only one other pack?" asked Cam later that day over dinner, sounding both panicky and beaten.

"Two," corrected Dante. "Nick Axton also gave us his support, remember."

Taryn watched from her position on the counter as the expressions of those at the table all melted into despair. Seeing that she had—gasp—paused in eating her meal, Trey and Grace, who stood on either side of her, scowled at her until she jammed a chunk of steak in her mouth.

Kirk gave Trey an accusatory look. "You said that mating with Taryn would give us the alliances we need to get through this challenge."

"And *you* said Darryl would never follow it through," Dominic pointed out.

"Didn't I say it would all be for nothing?"

Taryn didn't even see Trey move. One moment he was at her side, the next moment he was clamping his hand around Kirk's throat and snatching him from his seat.

"All for nothing, huh?" Trey growled. "That's my mate you're talking about. My mate, who is pregnant with my child. My mate, who is also your Alpha female."

"Trey, I know he crossed a line, but he can't breathe." Brock tried appealing to Trey with a look, but it was useless.

"There's only so far you can push someone, Kirk, and you've pushed me too hard, too far, too many times. One more shove from you will be all it takes for me lose it." The fear wafting from his cousin satisfied both Trey and his wolf enough that they released him. Kirk flopped back into his seat, coughing and trying to gasp in air. Trey returned to Taryn's side and she kissed him lightly, easing his tension slightly.

"What time are Lance and Nick coming with their enforcers?" asked Lydia.

"They've agreed to arrive here at noon. I've no idea what time Darryl will appear, but I don't think it will be any earlier than then."

"We might not have only Lance and Nick," said Rhett. "You've had a lot of messages over the pack web, Trey. It seems that word's gotten around about the challenge. Apparently, Darryl has earned himself a number of enemies over the years, and they're all offering to be present tomorrow to stand at your side."

"Standing at his side as in actively getting involved in the battle, or as in literally just standing there like lemons?" asked Grace.

"They'll be present and act as backup if things go to shit," Taryn explained. "But unless Trey looks like he's losing, they won't get involved."

"They're more or less just people who want to watch like nosy bastards so they can go and tell everyone about how they were there," said Trick. Ryan grunted his agreement.

An unexpected yawn escaped Taryn, and she allowed her head to drop onto Trey's shoulder as she closed her eyes.

"Tired, baby? Come on, let's get you to bed. You need sleep."

"I'm not tired. I'm just checking my eyelids for holes. It could take awhile."

He chuckled and scooped her up, cradling her against his chest. "Bed."

"You'll get tired more easily over the first month of your pregnancy," Grace told her. "It's totally normal."

Having said their good nights, Trey carried her to their bedroom, liking that she didn't fight him and allowed him to carry her. Once inside he carefully laid her on the bed and peeled away her jeans before removing her long-sleeved T-shirt. "What's with the glum look on your face, baby?"

"You're kidding, right? Take your pick. There's the fact that you'll be in a battle tomorrow. There's the horrible knowledge that we have a traitor in our pack. Oh, and there's the little matter of me being hidden away tomorrow instead of being part of the battle."

He sighed and draped himself over her, kissing her neck softly, wanting to relax her. "Baby, you can't be upset with me for asking you to stay clear of a battle."

"I'm not. There's no way I'd endanger our baby like that. I just worry something will happen to you. Any of you. It's worse knowing I'm a healer and I *can* help, but won't be there to help."

"I can understand how you're feeling. I'd be going apeshit crazy now if I knew you were going to be near any danger and didn't even have me with you. But I need you to stay here, inside. Nothing can happen to you or the baby, Taryn, it just can't. I'd never get through it."

"Nothing can happen to you either, so make damn sure you come back to me." She fused her mouth to his, kissing him hard. He tangled a hand in her hair and tugged, reminding her who the more dominant was, and then he took over the kiss. His tongue plundered her mouth just as she wanted his cock to plunder her body, but for some reason he was holding himself back. He was so tense it was like he was bracing himself for some kind of impact. She arched against him and felt the very hard proof of his arousal. His entire body stiffened and he looked like he wanted to jump off the bed. "What's the matter?"

His eyes danced to her stomach and then back to her face. "I don't want to hurt you."

She groaned. "Is that why you're holding back? Trey, you won't hurt me or the baby by being inside me." He didn't look convinced. She sighed dramatically. "I suppose I could just get my old vibrator out or—"

He pinned her with his gaze. "Nothing goes inside you except my cock, remember."

"Yes, and I remember agreeing to that…but it was pending the applicable terms."

"Applicable terms?"

"In situations where you're denying me said cock, I get to dig out my vibrator and take care of the matter myself." His face molded into a menacing scowl. Or at least he thought she'd find it menacing. Instead, she laughed. And cupped the erection pressing insistently against the denim of his jeans. "I want it. It's mine."

"Yes, it's yours," he allowed, "pending the applicable terms. In situations where you're threatening to cheat on me with a fake cock, you don't get any."

Tricky little bastard. "It really is a good thing I love you and your cock, Trey, or I'd have to snap it off for that." An expression of shock replaced his scowl. She placed a finger to his lips. "Don't say it back. I don't want you to say what I know you don't mean. Maybe one day you can mean it, but we both know that's not today. I just want you to know."

This was why she deserved a better mate—he was so damn wrong for her it wasn't even funny. Still, she was staying exactly where she was. "You're all there is for me, Taryn. I'm broken, baby. You know that. Before you…it was like those bits of me were just scattered all over the place. I've never felt whole. Not until you. You hold those pieces together. It's not an exaggeration when I say you hold my sanity in your hands. Without you, I'd fall apart." If that made any sense to her, he'd be surprised.

She stroked his bottom lip with the pad of her thumb. "Thank you for that. Now do me, already."

He sighed dramatically. "I'm mated to a nympho."

"Ass."

CHAPTER NINETEEN

⬦

The ringing of Trey's cell phone had everyone in the kitchen stiffening, particularly Taryn, who was sitting on the counter with her legs wrapped around his waist. Without releasing her gaze, he dug it out of his pocket and answered. "Hello."

"They're here," Ryan informed him.

Trey wasn't surprised that they had arrived at ten o'clock. The only reason he had told the pack last night that he was expecting Darryl around noon was because Trey didn't want the informant telling Darryl he'd be ready for the bastard. "How many?"

"Dominic says there's something like one hundred and seventy out there, but it's likely that some of them are just there to stand at his side."

"What about the three packs that offered to come and stand at our side? Are they here?"

"Arrived an hour ago, just before Lance and Nick. Everyone's waiting just inside the gate." They had arranged for their allies to arrive early, suspecting Darryl would make an attack in the morning, believing he would be catching Trey unaware.

"Okay. Don't let Darryl and his crew through the gate until I get there."

"Sure."

Trey ended the call and handed his cell over to Taryn. "I'll lose it in the battle if I take it with me out there."

She tightened her legs around him, wishing she could just hold him there and ask the others to face Darryl. Yes, that was selfish and unfair, but she couldn't help wanting that and she wasn't going to apologize for it. This was her mate, the other half of her soul, the father of her child. If she had the right to be selfish about anything, it was him.

"I have to go, baby," he told her softly.

She nodded sadly. "I know. Be careful. You have to come back to me."

"There'll be a lot of blood on my hands by the end of this battle. You know that, right?"

She pressed her forehead to his. "Do you honestly think I'd judge you for protecting your family, your pack, your territory? Darryl obviously wants to die. Assist him."

Damn, this woman got to him. Never had she judged him—not for being who he was, not for what he could and couldn't feel, and not for anything he'd done or was capable of doing. He kissed her hard and deep, urging her into him, taking strength from her in a way that he had never been able to do with another person. Breaking the kiss, he buried his face in the crook of her neck and took her scent deep inside him, let it flow over him and center both him and his wolf. He hated to leave her, especially right now. Every primal instinct he had told him to stay at her side and be her constant protector, but there was no choice. He couldn't tell the other males of his pack to face the danger alone—that wasn't who he was and it wasn't what an Alpha did.

"I need you to promise me something," he said as he locked his gaze with hers. "I need you to promise me that no matter what you feel over our link, no matter what you think is happening, you stay here. You don't try to reach me; you don't take a chance out there just so you can heal me. You stay here with

Grace, Lydia, Greta, Hope, Brock, and Selma. You focus on keeping yourself safe and our baby safe. Promise me." He wasn't surprised when she gave him a look that could kill. A lesser man would have cowered.

"That's not fair," she said through her teeth. "Of course I don't want anything to happen to the baby, but by asking me to make this promise, you're asking me to choose between you two, and I can't do that."

He cupped her face with his hands as he insisted, "Yes, you can and you will. I'm not asking you to choose, I'm asking you to keep yourself and the baby safe."

She blinked back tears. Her wolf whined inside her head. "If you died I wouldn't survive it anyway."

"Yes, you would. You're so goddamn strong, you could get through anything." It made him proud to have her. For the first time, he was actually glad that the mating bond was only partially developed, as it meant that she had a better chance of surviving if the bond was broken. Not that he planned on dying today, but there was always a possibility. "I have to go."

Reluctantly she uncurled her limbs from around him. "I love you, even though you're being an unfair prick."

He chuckled, but the sound didn't hide the anger he felt with himself for not being able to give her those words.

Knowing what was going through his head, she gave him a cautioning look. "I don't need words, I just need you to come back."

"I plan on it." Having kissed her one last time, he turned to see Grace and Lydia both crying as they had private moments with their own mates, while Kirk and Brock hugged each other tightly. Although Cam, Rhett, and Kirk weren't enforcers and only ever worked as security guards for the gate, Trey couldn't afford to leave them behind. He needed all the wolves he could get, especially since Brock was staying behind—they wanted the females to have at least one male with them.

Dante had expressed concern about taking Kirk along with them, since he was one of their suspects, but somehow Trey just couldn't see him being the informant. They would find out soon enough—if it was Kirk, he would join Darryl when they reached the gate.

As Dante, Tao, Marcus, and Trick were saying their good-byes to Taryn, Greta came and hugged Trey tightly. "Take care, son. Rip the bastard apart."

"Always so bloodthirsty," he said with a smile.

"Don't worry, I'll make sure she's all right."

He narrowed his eyes at her, still smiling. "Since when do you care about Taryn's welfare?"

"Since I heard she was pregnant." At his skeptical look, she shrugged. "All right, I like her just a bit. She reminds me of me." She thumped him on the arm when he laughed. "She does. She's got spirit."

"Yep, she has plenty of that." He gave Taryn one last look—in it was a warning to do as he'd asked, a reminder that she was too important for him to lose, and a good-bye. He looked up at the others. "Everyone ready?"

Nodding, Dante, Tao, Marcus, Trick, Rhett, Cam, and Kirk followed Trey as he left the room. No one said a word as they exited the caves and descended the many steps of the mountain. As they entered the woods, Trey gestured for Dante to come close.

"You don't need to ask me to make sure she's okay if anything happens to you," said Dante quietly. "But we will win this, Trey."

"But if we don't, if you feel me die through the pack link, you leave the battle and you go to the caves—you take her where Darryl can't reach her."

Dante swallowed hard. "You have my word on that, although I don't know if she'd survive the bond being broken."

"She would. Taryn could survive anything. Besides, it's only partially developed. And another thing: I'd be lying if I said I hope she mates with someone else so she's not alone—I'm too much of a bastard to be that noble—but if she does you make sure that kid knows who its dad was." Satisfied by Dante's nod, Trey said no more as they progressed through the forest. His wolf was pacing inside him, all worked up by the adrenaline circulating through Trey's system. He hadn't wanted to leave Taryn's side, but he did understand that there was a nearby threat and that this threat needed to be eradicated.

It was odd to think that only a few months ago, the most important things to Trey had been his pack, his territory, and protecting both. He never would have thought anything could be more important than that, never would have expected that anyone could be as important to him. Now he had other things to fight for—his mate, his unborn child, their future. The woman had turned his life upside fucking down, turned him inside fucking out, and yet he wouldn't have it any other way.

It amazed him that he'd thought he was content before she came into his life. In reality he hadn't known the meaning of the word. With Taryn he was content. She anchored him and made him happy in a way that nothing and no one had ever done before. He didn't want to lose that, *refused* to lose that. Dante was right; they would win this, because no other ending was acceptable.

Finally the forest thinned and they stepped out into the clearing, bringing them within twenty feet of the main gate. Although Ryan had told him just how many wolves Darryl had brought along, Trey was still rocked by the intimidating sight it made. If he had been normal enough to respond appropriately to fear, he might have been tempted to stop the battle before it started. Not to save himself, but the others who might get hurt. He'd soon find out if it was a good thing or a bad thing that he wasn't normal.

Gathered on the fringe of the woods were Nick and a number of males from his pack, including his bodyguard, Derren. Not far from them was Lance, with several from his pack, including his bodyguard, Zack, and two of his enforcers, Perry and Oscar. They all gave him brief, respectful nods before resuming scowling at Darryl and his followers.

The wolf shifters—there were approximately fifty—who had come to stand at Trey's side and serve as backup were all grouped together near the security shack. They didn't look so eager to be there. Trey guessed it was because they hadn't expected him to be so outnumbered, placing them in a position where they would need to act as backup. He wouldn't be surprised if they instead slipped away during the fight.

He stalked toward the closed gate with Dante and Tao flanking him, blanking his expression the way he had done as a child whenever his father and uncle decided to torment him for their own entertainment—being stoic had always agitated the hell out of both of them. Trey stopped as he came to stand directly opposite Darryl. His wolf growled inside his head, affronted by this male's scent and reaching for the surface with his eagerness to get to him.

Looking as smug as all shit, Darryl grinned at him. "Time's up. You really should have just given in to me at the beginning, Trey. I'll tell you what, since you're my nephew and all, I'll give you one last chance to yield to me."

Trey couldn't help that his mouth twitched into a smile, especially since Dante and Tao were chuckling. "Yield? My mate's right; you do live in La La Land."

"You can't honestly mean to accept my challenge."

"And why's that?"

"Look around you." He gestured to his numerous supporters. "I think it's safe to say that you're outnumbered."

"If that bothers you so much, let's keep this as a one-to-one battle. Let's take care of this Alpha to Alpha."

Darryl's fear didn't show on his face, but it could be heard in his voice. "I don't think so, Trey—we both know your enforcers would attack me after I'd killed you. They have no honor."

Dante and Tao growled at the insult and gave Darryl looks that promised he'd pay for that. But Darryl was *Trey's*.

"You can't win this, nephew. You never had any chance of winning it. Not even mating with the daughter of an influential wolf could help you out with this. I'm looking forward to becoming better acquainted with her, even if she is latent."

A growl trickled from Trey's mouth. His wolf wanted to sink his jaws into this male's throat and feel his blood gush into his mouth. "I'm pissed enough with you as it is, *Uncle*. If I were you, I'd be very careful about pushing me even further."

Darryl laughed, but there was a nervous tremor to it. "One last chance. Give in to my requests, and we can avoid this battle."

As Trey backed away from the gate with Dante and Tao, his uncle smiled—obviously believing Trey was backing down. Snort. Like that would ever happen. "Ryan, open the gate." The smile immediately fell from Darryl's face and was replaced by a dark scowl.

As the gate creaked open slowly, more wolves stepped out of the trees—some from behind Trey, some from his left side, and some from his right, until there were approximately one hundred and fifty wolves standing with him. It didn't make the numbers strictly even, but it was pretty damn close. He noticed Quinn was grinning like a kid in a toy store. The other nine Alphas that Trey had met at the diner only yesterday looked just as eager and bloodthirsty.

Darryl's eyes widened and he swallowed hard. His face was a question mark.

Trey cocked his head. "You didn't really think I'd reveal to the entire pack just how many wolves were joining me, when I knew you had an informant who could tell you, did you?" Darryl's eyes widened even more, though Trey wouldn't have thought it was possible until then. "Oh, yes, I know all about that." Finally, the gate was fully open. "Know this: It doesn't matter how many wolves you have protecting you, Darryl. I *will* get to you and I *will* kill you."

Red in the face, Darryl howled. Taking that as a signal to attack, his supporters instantly shifted into their wolf forms and began galloping through the gate. Trey's own allies followed his lead as he ran and leaped, rapidly shifting midway through the leap into his wolf form, and clamped his jaws closed around one of his enemies' throats.

"It's started," Taryn told Greta, Brock, and Hope. Grace and Lydia, who were on either side of her, already knew through their links with their own mates. Echoes of Trey's anger and rage reached her through their bond, along with his determination and focus. Even though she knew just how strong and powerful he was, she was so damn scared for him and so damn pissed off that she couldn't be there. Of course she knew it was best that she wasn't, but the idea that he could be hurt and she wouldn't be there to heal him was haunting her, mocking her healing gift.

Lydia, who was fidgeting crazily with worry, rubbed a hand over her face. "God, this is nerve-racking."

Grace's smile was weak. "They're going to be fine." Shakily, she added, "They have to be."

At Taryn's wince, everyone looked at her. "Trey's gone feral."

"In this instance, it's a good thing," said Greta.

Grace grabbed the glass beside Taryn that was filled with another weird concoction of hers. "Here, drink the rest of this."

Taryn shook her head and placed a hand to her stomach. "I couldn't eat or drink a single thing right now. I feel too nauseous."

"So do I," mumbled Lydia.

"It's the nerves," Greta told them. "Where's Selma?"

"In her room," replied Hope. "She's refusing to come out and she won't let me in. She says I've betrayed her because I've chosen to give my loyalty to Trey and Taryn. To be honest, I always thought Selma would do that too, after a little while. I've never seen her so worked up before."

"Maybe you should go see her," suggested Brock with an understanding smile. "Selma acts tough, but she must be worried. No one should be alone right now." Hope nodded and left the room.

"How long do you think it will go on for?" Grace asked Taryn.

It was Brock who answered. "Could be twenty minutes, could be forty-five minutes. It depends whether Darryl's winning. If he's not, some of his allies might leave. It's unnerving to think that some of them might have already gotten past our own wolves and are on their way to the caves."

Lydia made a low whining sound. "Don't say things like that."

"We have to be prepared for it happening. There are only forty of us out there. Darryl will have brought at least a hundred, if not more."

Of course Taryn knew there were more than just forty on their side, and she might have said as much—after all, if the informant *was* sitting in this very room with her, there wasn't anything they could tell Darryl that he didn't already know at this point—but then her vision blurred a little, startling her.

"Taryn, you okay?"

Triple-blinking to clear away the haze, she looked to Grace. "Yeah, fine. Just feel kind of woozy. You don't think it's Trey, do you? You don't think he's hurt and—"

"Calm down, use your link."

Taking a deep breath, she felt for Trey and found him immediately. His ass had gone totally feral. Despite a few twinges of pain, he wasn't seriously hurt. She exhaled a sigh of relief. "He's fine."

"The pregnancy will have you feeling a little off balance at first. Don't worry."

Brock gestured to the half-empty glass. "Grace is right, you should drink some more of that…whatever it is. You need the nutrients."

Taryn shook her head, grimacing. "No, I don't feel good."

Lydia flinched and moaned. "Some asshole just chomped on Cam's hind leg. He's okay, though, thank God. Ryan helped get the other wolf off of him."

Grace gave her a sympathetic smile. "Rhett's received some pretty decent scratches and bites, but he's not tiring or in any real pain. God, I hate this shit."

"I need to walk around. Not outside," Lydia quickly assured them, shifting from foot to foot in restless, nervous movements. "Just through the tunnels. Standing still is killing me."

"I'll go with you. Coming, Taryn?"

"Thanks, Grace, but I feel too woozy. I need to sit."

"I can stay with you if you want."

"She's fine, she's got me and Brock," said Greta, waving Grace and Lydia out of the room. She turned back to Taryn, frowning. "Don't worry so much about him." It was chastising rather than comforting. "God knows he's been through enough battles and he's always come back, alive and well."

"That's not going to stop me from worrying." Nothing would stop her from worrying, short of Trey standing before her.

"Darryl's nothing but a little fart anyway. That's why he's brought so many with him—he knows he'd never win a one-to-one challenge with Trey."

"Why do you think he wants the packs united so badly?"

Greta huffed. "Darryl's problem is that although he was born an alpha, he was a weak one—too weak to be a pack Alpha. His little brother, Rick—Trey's father—on the other hand, was very strong. He was also a horrible bastard. Darryl spent his life walking in Rick's shadow, overlooked. But that didn't stop him from lodging himself so far up Rick's ass that he ended up being made Beta. Then Trey was born and even as a little boy you could tell he was a powerful alpha. Both Rick and Darryl saw him as a threat and treated him very badly."

Taryn couldn't help that her upper lip curled in anger. "Yeah, I heard a little about that."

"When Trey almost killed his father, Rick ordered Darryl to beat Trey, punish him. But Darryl wouldn't—he knew he couldn't. That was why talk of banishing him started. My guess is no one in the pack forgot Darryl's fear of a fourteen-year-old boy and so he's not being respected or obeyed as Alpha."

"Makes sense. If he had been, half of his pack wouldn't have turned up here to check on my welfare."

Greta nodded. "Unless he shows his pack that he *can* over-power Trey and fix the divide in the pack, he'll be challenged soon enough and lose his position."

Greta said more, but Taryn couldn't make any sense of the words, as her hearing suddenly went weird, like she was under-water or something. Seconds later it returned to normal, but then her vision went blurry again.

"Taryn. Taryn, you all right?"

She wasn't sure who asked and she didn't care as the sudden urge to vomit had her ready to dash for the nearest bathroom. But she didn't make it. She hadn't even gotten halfway out of the room when she doubled over with pain and projectile vomited all over the kitchen floor. Then again. And again. And again. Then she flopped onto her side, panting, moaning, and sweating. Worse, she was beyond woozy and close to passing out. She felt Brock pick her up.

"Go get Grace," he told Greta. "I'll take her to lie down in her room."

She retched again, but this time nothing came out. She doubted there was anything left in her stomach, especially since she'd hardly eaten anything that morning. The feeling she had now wasn't all that different from when she had hit her head. It was a little like she was weightless, like a dream state was creep-ing up on her. Her vision alternated from fuzzy around the edges to totally blurred. Her head seemed so unbelievably heavy and she felt sort of detached from her body. This could *not* be good for the baby. Fear shot through her as she wondered if this somehow meant she was losing the baby.

Shit, that sun was bright.

Wait, what? It occurred to her then that, hey, she was outside. And she should not be. "Where are we going?" she slurred. Her body jolted crazily and she realized they were descending the steps of the mountain face.

"Sorry, Taryn, but this is just the way it has to be."

His voice was sharp, clipped, cold. This was not the Brock she knew. "It's you. You're the informant."

He peered down at her, clearly surprised. "So you knew. Doesn't matter now. All that matters is getting you to Darryl quickly."

"What did you do to me?" she moaned as a spasm racked her stomach.

"It's just a drug to make you sleep. I slipped it in that weird juice. I've no idea how you can drink that stuff Grace makes."

Another retch. Still no vomit.

"I'm not sure why it's making you sick." Not that he sounded concerned.

"Why, Brock? Why help Darryl?"

"I couldn't care less about him. Trey, however…Now that's a different matter." The degree of anger and loathing in his voice was unsettling.

"If you were unhappy here, you could've left."

"No, I couldn't have. Not without Kirk, and he'll never leave. I know you don't think much of my son, but he's a good man. He is. A lot of people look down on him because his mom was human and he's not as strong an alpha as the others—a little like they did with Darryl. But he has good principles, has honor, he's a loyal wolf. That's why he wanted to leave with Trey when he was banished."

"You could have stayed behind."

He shook his head. "No. And not just because of Kirk, no. I couldn't have let her go alone."

"Who? Greta?"

He looked at her like she was insane. "Louisa."

The name tickled her memory. "Trey's mom?"

"You must've heard how I found my true mate, but she was already in love with another man. Oh, yes, Trey's mom. By the time I met Louisa, she and Rick had imprinted on one another. I didn't tell anyone, because I knew Rick would have exiled me to keep me away from her. I hated seeing them together, *hated* it, but I couldn't bring myself to leave her life. So I became good friends with her and let that be enough. I know she felt the pull between us. She never even came close to acting on it though. Louisa was a loyal woman. Then Trey was banished and, for once, she stood up to that bastard Rick and she left him. There was my chance. My chance to have her as I should have. And I would have…but Trey killed her."

"She turned rogue," she reminded him.

"If I'd been there when she slipped into that state, I could've pulled her back from it. I could've." No, he couldn't have—a wolf gone rogue was beyond all help. "But he executed her. Snapped her neck like it was a twig. I wanted to kill him, but just like Rick and Darryl, I knew I couldn't take him."

Her head swam again, but she fought the pull of sleep. "Why stay?"

"So one day I could make sure he knew the pain that I went through. The pain of losing a mate."

Oh, fuck. It suddenly hit her just how dangerous her situation was. She'd thought that maybe Darryl wanted to use her as collateral—a kind of "give me what I want, Trey, and your mate goes free" scenario. But this…*well, hell.*

"It made the whole thing even better when I realized you were true mates. You should thank Darryl, really. If it wasn't for him telling me to hold off, I would have killed you at some point.

The car and the raven—that was just for fun, just something to keep me going."

What a weird, sick bastard. "That day on the stairs?"

"I'd made an arrangement with Darryl. His goons were waiting not far out of pack territory. The plan was for me to hand you over to them so they could give you a beating as a warning. And, well, that plan went to shit. As did the one for you to be attacked while you were in town with Lydia. Unfortunately for you, your luck has run out, little one. It's really nothing personal, Taryn. I like you. You're strong, you have a good heart, but this is the way it has to be."

"You think Louisa would want this? Trey's her son. Darryl will kill him."

"Very true. Greta was right—all Darryl wants is for everyone to see him overpower Trey. He knows he can't do it. Trey's too strong. But there's one thing that will weaken him—the death of his mate. At the very moment your bond is severed, he'll lose all strength. It won't last more than a minute, but it will be long enough for Darryl to have this chance and end this once and for all. So you see, Darryl gets what he wants, and I get what I want."

Hoping he might have a conscience she could appeal to, she asked, "You're happy to hand over a pregnant female to be murdered?"

Nothing. Not an ounce of guilt or regret to be seen in his expression. "It's just the way it has to be," he said for the third time.

"You could take me back," she slurred, desperate now. "I promise you won't be punished. Don't punish this baby for something Trey did." Not that she blamed Trey at all, but if it made the psycho release her, she'd say whatever he wanted to hear.

He chuckled, but it was humorless. "Honey, Trey will tear me apart and you know it. Even if you could guarantee me that protection, my answer would be no. You have a mate, Taryn. Let me ask you, if someone killed him, took him from you, could you ever forgive them? Ever forget it? I've waited too long for this. He took my mate from me, and now I'm going to take his from him."

He might have said more, she wasn't sure, because at that moment she lost the strength to stay conscious any longer, and the blackness swamped her.

The gray wolf was just finishing a kill when the awareness struck him and penetrated the fog in his mind. *Mate.* She was close. She shouldn't be close. The same instinct that told him she was nearby was also able to guide him to where she was. Quickly he galloped through the trees, intent on reaching her. He skidded to a halt when he saw her. She smelled like him and like sickness and drugs and anxiety. Mixed in with all that was the scent of the male who held her—uncle.

The gray wolf threw back his head and howled, garnering the attention of every wolf around him. No other male should touch her. No one was allowed to hurt her. She was his. She belonged to him. The life in her womb belonged to him. They were both his to protect, to care for, to shelter. The only thing stopping the wolf from acting on his raging anger and going for the uncle's throat was that Darryl's claws were pressed threateningly against her stomach—the gray wolf understood the threat, understood cause and effect. Although the man's words made no sense, he also understood what he wanted. He wanted Trey. So the wolf drew back, though he remained closer to the surface than ever before.

Trey rose to his feet, panting and raging. The sight of Taryn, pale and flaccid, held with her back against Darryl's chest, had his blood boiling and something in his chest tightening. She was unconscious, had clearly been drugged. Seeing Darryl's claws placed threateningly against the place where his baby was growing made it even more difficult for Trey to remain where he was. Every cell in his body urged him to pounce on Darryl. "Release her." The words were barely distinguishable.

Darryl gave him a callous smile. "That's not going to happen, my dear nephew. How strange it is to see something finally pull emotions from you. Rick would be devastated to miss this. Not as devastated as you'll be when you watch her die, but still."

A part of Trey's brain registered that all had gone quiet and that his pack was gathering close. Another part of his brain noted that many of Darryl's supporters had been slain and that Trey's side was winning the battle, but his only care was for the limp woman in Darryl's arms. "Release. Her." The bastard didn't. "If you want me, I'm right here. I won't even fight you."

Darryl laughed. "It's tempting. After all, the only thing I really want is for the others to see me take you down. But, well, I'm afraid I don't believe you would truly allow that. Plus, letting her live would break my bargain with our cousin, Brock." That very male then stepped out of the trees on Darryl's left. His expression was cold, cruel.

"Dad?" Kirk choked out. "Dad, what're you doing?"

"He has to know what it's like, son."

"What're you talking about?"

"He has to know how it felt for me when he killed Louisa. What it was like to lose her."

The truth hit Trey like a slap. "She was your mate?"

"And you took her from me."

Kirk shook his head, his eyes dancing from Brock to Taryn. "Dad, tell me you didn't hand her over to Darryl."

"Like I said, *he has to know what it's like.*"

"How could you do this?"

"He doesn't deserve your loyalty, son, he never has. Darryl has agreed to make you one of his enforcers when this is over."

Pale, wide-eyed, and clearly devastated, Kirk shook his head again and stumbled backward. "I—I can't believe you've done this."

"Son—"

"No," snapped Kirk. "I'm no longer your son."

Trey honestly couldn't believe what he was hearing. Although he'd never been able to work out what kind of motivation one of his pack could have had to betray him, he never would have expected this. Any of this. It didn't matter what the motivation was though—it never had. The result would always have been the same. "You're dead," he told Brock.

"No, Trey, that would be your mate," said Darryl with a smile. "Oh, and your unborn child."

His mate, his child. He had thought that if any of them would die today, it would be him. He had comforted himself with the knowledge that at least Taryn and his child would live. Dante would have ensured that. But now Trey saw that he didn't have the luxury of knowing that they would survive his death, because Darryl intended to kill them first. He wanted Trey to watch them die, to feel his bond with Taryn die, to see the life drain out of the only person he had ever loved. A jolt went through him at the realization. He loved her.

Of course he fucking loved her!

And not just because she was his mate, but because of the person she was. Her inner strength, her spirit, her sensuality, her big heart, her loyalty, her tenaciousness, her bravery, hell, even her damn sarcastic streak—it all came together to make a package that called to him and made it impossible for him to feel anything *but* love for her. The realization didn't even scare him, as it would have once. So now that the thread of fear had been removed from the knot of emotions inside him, the rest of the knot unraveled and fell away. And those mental walls went right along with them.

Abruptly there was a bang in his chest and a strange sensation in his head, as though his brain had hiccupped or something. Then he could feel Taryn's heartbeat as if it was his own, feel her inside of him like she was burrowed under his skin. But she was, wasn't she? Because she was the other half of his soul. He understood immediately what had happened. Their bond had snapped fully into being. He *felt* as her pulse rate improved and she struggled to a conscious state. He realized then that his strength was bolstering hers through their bond.

He also realized that Darryl was still talking, totally unaware of what was happening. Funny, that—how such a significant, life-changing occurrence could happen, yet go unnoticed by every person around them. It was a very good thing in this case.

"—and I bet you've never felt so helpless before in your entire life, have you, Trey?"

No, he hadn't. And Darryl was going to die for that. Die for daring to touch her at all. Trey's heart practically jumped when he watched Taryn's eyes flutter open. A few seconds later they widened and—quick as fucking lightning—she had one of the hands that were pinned behind her back positioned at Darryl's crotch with her claws placed threateningly around his balls. Obviously having felt the prick of claws on his naked skin, Darryl froze instantly. Trey shot him a falsely sympathetic look. Clearly his uncle had forgotten that latent alpha shifters actually could partially shift, lengthening their claws and canines.

"Let go of me, fucker, or I'll dig my claws into your crown jewels and rip them off—I don't give a shit."

Taryn meant every word.

The threat to the life of her unborn child had rage pumping through her body, a rage that was beyond normal—her insides burned, her heart was working overtime, her skin felt too tight for her body, her fangs had lengthened, and her entire being itched to hurt him. The primitive urge to protect had adrenaline coursing through her, preparing for anything, preparing her to *do* anything.

Dimly she recognized that her bond with Trey was cemented, that he was alive and relatively unharmed, but the red-hot fury blasting through her was so overwhelming that it left no room for her to feel anything else right now. The only thought she had in her head was that if she and her unborn child were about to leave this world, then this asshole's balls were going with them.

Her wolf smelled his fear, loved it. She wanted this threat to herself and her pup dead. Wanted it with such desperation that she was warring with Taryn for control, pushing and struggling and twisting for freedom, much like someone trapped under a frozen lake. The force with which she beat at Taryn's skin was actually painful. So painful that it was weakening Taryn. Not physically though. Physically, she was still strong and steady. But mentally, she was weakening...Kind of like she was fading. Her wolf relentlessly continued her assault, wanting her stupid human half to step aside and let *her* deal with this. Then Taryn weakened that little bit more as a particularly hard shove fractured that layer of iced water. That was all it took—her wolf smashed her way out.

Utter shock rushed over Trey as the scene played out before him. Darryl's hold on Taryn broke as, with a speed that only an extremely experienced shifter should have been able to achieve, she shifted into a creamy-white wolf. She was absolutely beautiful. As a female, her muzzle and forehead were narrower and her neck was thinner than those of males. Her limbs had smoother fur, giving her a more graceful look. All that gorgeous fur looked so unbelievably soft that he couldn't wait to comb his fingers through it, just as he often did with Taryn's hair.

To his surprise, the she-wolf didn't take a moment to marvel at finally being free. No, she was only interested in Darryl—who was apparently too stupefied to move. She was on him in a blink, leaping up and snapping her teeth into his nose as she knocked him down. Damn, she was just like Taryn—went straight for the nose. No longer paralyzed by shock, Darryl began to take his wolf form.

Snapping back into action—Trey shouldn't be surprised that the crazy bitch was challenging a male wolf—he shifted shape and gave his wolf control again.

The gray wolf rushed at the black wolf that had now flipped over and was growling at his mate. Protectiveness surged through him, serving as an energy boost. She was not to be touched or harmed or threatened. He had to protect her—her and his unborn pup. He barreled into the black wolf, wrenching a yelp from him and sending him sprawling across the forest floor, away from the she-wolf.

The black wolf righted himself quickly, his chest heaving, and faced the other. The gray wolf could sense that his opponent was less dominant and less powerful. That wouldn't bring him any mercy from the gray wolf though—not when he had threatened his mate, not when his scent triggered memories of cruelty and pain being inflicted on a young Trey.

Hackles raised, ears upright, and lips curled back, they circled each other—never moving their eyes from the other. Many other wolves observed, but none of them moved, nor did any battle between themselves. All stood still and quiet, as all understood that the outcome of this battle now rested on which of the two Alpha males won the challenge.

Suddenly the gray wolf rushed at his challenger and knocked him onto his side. Growling, he bit down hard on the black wolf's shoulder, drawing first blood. In retaliation the black wolf swiped his claws at the other, aiming for his muzzle. The gray wolf was able to dodge the move and then clamped his jaws around the offending leg.

The black wolf yelped—the sound satisfying his attacker and psyching the observing wolves. He raised his head just enough to bite down hard on the gray wolf's ear. The surprise of it made the gray wolf jerk away while releasing a loud, high-pitched bark. Taking advantage of that, the other quickly stood and swiped his paw at the gray wolf. His claw managed to slash his shoulder, and the scent of the gray wolf's blood flavored the air and had the challenger growling with satisfaction.

Growling with rage, the gray wolf leaped at the other wolf. He wrapped his forepaws around his challenger's neck and, calling on every ounce of his strength, wrestled him to the ground. Just as the gray wolf wanted, the other was now flat on his back in a vulnerable position that exposed his belly. The black wolf didn't offer his submission, but continued to growl and snap his teeth, knowing that any offers of submission would be ignored.

In one fluid move, the gray wolf straddled his challenger, using his forepaws to pin down his shoulders as his back paws slashed open the black wolf's belly. The yelps of pain and the overwhelming scents of fear, blood, and defeat that wafted from his challenger didn't placate the gray wolf or give him any sense of satisfaction. Only one thing would give him that.

He clamped his jaws around the black wolf's throat, biting down hard into fur and flesh. Blood gushed into his mouth, warm and tasting of victory. It tasted better than the blood of the sandy wolf who had once coveted his mate, and it even tasted better than the blood of the male who had sired him. With a loud growl, the gray wolf twisted his head sharply, ripping out his challenger's throat. Only then did satisfaction fill him.

The creamy-white she-wolf approved of the act. Her mate—strong, dominant, powerful—had defeated the challenger, had eliminated the threat to them and their pack. Slowly she walked to him, pleased at finally being free and being able to have fur-to-fur contact with her mate, as she had hungered to do from the second she picked up his scent. She had known he was her mate from the beginning, had always been annoyed with her human side for not recognizing this, for not recognizing the importance of this male to her life and her soul. Apparently sensing her approach, he turned. The dominant, confident Alpha held his tail up high and his ears erect as he covered the short distance between them.

She kept her ears down and fur flat as she licked and nipped at his muzzle in greeting. He pushed at her nose and rubbed his cheek against hers, returning her greeting—a greeting that had been long awaited but not possible until now. Then they were licking each other's faces and placing their noses behind the other's ears to inhale each other's scent.

A number of wolves suddenly approached, trooping together around their Alpha pair, seeking contact. *Pack*, the she-wolf knew. They joined her in licking their Alpha's injuries, giving him the respect and thanks he was due for protecting them. A gray-black wolf with a white undercoat—*Beta*—threw back his head and released a loud, long howl. The melodic sound rang throughout the forest and mountains, and was answered far and wide as other wolves—both shifters and full-bloods—joined the pack in celebrating their victory.

CHAPTER TWENTY

Three weeks later

"It's not funny," Taryn said as she returned to Caleb's side. "Of course it's not funny."

She scowled at Caleb. He might have been more convincing if he wasn't grinning. Come on, surely it was unreasonable to need to pee so often—eight times in one hour was just ridiculous! She wouldn't mind so much if she was actually downing several mugs of coffee a day, like she usually would, but now that she was pregnant, coffee wasn't allowed. How humans went through this for a whole nine months she'd never know. Hell, elephants were pregnant for, like, a year and a half. Seriously, what was up with that?

Nervous and fidgety, she straightened the silky, slim-fitting, knee-length dress for the hundredth time. She wasn't a fan of dresses and only ever wore them when she was attending a special occasion, such as a mating ceremony. As this was her own mating ceremony, she couldn't exactly wear jeans and a T-shirt. She had wanted to have the ceremony before her belly got too big with the pregnancy—she had no desire to waddle down the aisle like a penguin.

Greta had been outraged to hear that Taryn was wearing white, as apparently she was too much of a hussy for that. Although the woman had softened slightly to Taryn, it was only *very* slightly, and she still took utter joy in insulting Taryn and being difficult. But then, Taryn took utter joy in returning Greta's insults with some of her own, so that worked out okay.

Taryn would have had the ceremony sooner, but she felt that it was better for everyone to have time to recover from the battle, emotionally and physically. Because she was pregnant, no one had let her heal them—which was both unreasonable and dramatic, since it didn't make any difference at all to her gift. Although there was still a lingering sadness about how they had been betrayed by one of their own, everyone was by now simply relieved and happy to have won the challenge.

Kirk, on the other hand, had been devastated and ashamed. No matter how often they had assured him that he wasn't responsible for his father's actions, Kirk hadn't been able to even make eye contact with either Trey or Taryn. A few days after Brock's public execution—as was traditional for traitors—and the ceremony that had been held to honor the few who had died in the battle, Kirk had decided to join with those remaining from Darryl's pack. Dante's older brother, Josh, had been elected as their new Alpha and had agreed to accept Selma as well as Kirk. Well, good luck to him with that.

There had been talk about some of Josh's pack now joining Taryn and Trey's, but so far nothing had been officially decided. It would be just her luck that she had gotten rid of Selma, only to end up with a group of females that were far worse. The universe did seem to enjoy playing jokes on her.

"Ready?" asked Caleb.

Taryn released a long, calming breath. "Ready. Thank you for doing this." Although Lance was—surprise, surprise—attending the ceremony, she hadn't wanted him to do the giving-away thing. In her opinion he'd more or less given her away a long time ago. Caleb, on the other hand, had been a good friend to her since childhood and had been there for her over the years whenever she needed someone. It seemed more appropriate for him to do it. Plus, it had put to rest all the arguments between Dante, Don, and the enforcers as they fought over who should give her away.

"You don't have to thank me."

"I know you didn't want me to mate with Trey."

Caleb sighed and jiggled his head. "Of course I wish your mate wasn't mentally unstable, but I've seen him with you. I've seen how much he cares for you. That's good enough for me."

"You don't still feel like I'm betraying Joey, even though he was never my true mate?"

"No, I don't. I never thought you were betraying him, just that you were wrong about Trey. Now I see that it was me who was wrong, and I'm happy for you. How can I not be happy for my best friend?"

Touched, Taryn went to hug him, but he shook his head fiercely. "If your mate smells my scent all over you, he'll kill me."

Rolling her eyes, she took the hand he offered her and allowed him to escort her out of the caves, down the mountain steps, and through the trees that led to the lake. As it was the place where she and Trey spent most of their quality time together, it seemed rather fitting that the ceremony take place there.

Caleb halted as the forest began to thin out, and then howled. A harmony of howls responded, giving Taryn goose bumps. Caleb held his arm out and, taking another deep breath, she looped her arm through his as they walked through the last of the trees until they entered the clearing near the lake. The entire pack was there, plus Shaya, Lance, Perry, Oscar, Derren, and Don and his mate. They had all formed a huge circle, and Taryn knew that Trey and Nick would be in the center. Any Alpha could perform a mating ceremony, and Nick had kindly offered to do it for them.

When they reached the slight opening between Shaya and Grace, Taryn entered the circle, leaving Caleb to fill the space. A smile surfaced on her face the second she looked at Trey. He was wearing...hell, she didn't know what he was wearing. She couldn't move her gaze from his—the intense mix of heat, possessiveness, and adoration in his eyes made her inhale sharply. She didn't remember moving her legs, but seconds later she was standing before him, hearing Nick's words and answering when required to, but all her focus was taken up by her mate.

Trey's entire body clenched at the sight of Taryn. She looked so beautiful in that figure-hugging dress that he planned to tear from her body as soon as possible. Another one of those chest pangs struck him, but now he knew what they meant. Now he knew that he didn't just care for her, he loved her. He hadn't been able to work up the courage to tell her, to say the words.

He knew what she'd meant now when she'd told him that love was giving someone the power to destroy you and hoping that they didn't. She had that power. She could break him, end him. It scared him, and he knew that the moment he gave her those words and admitted that she had that power, he would be utterly defenseless. Maybe other people didn't fear that, but it had always been important to Trey never to be vulnerable to another person. So he was shitting his pants.

As the other wolves repeated the ritual words and appealed to the power of the full moon to bless the mating, Taryn soaked up the lust that was pouring from Trey and feeding her own. When the ceremonial words were almost at an end, her anticipation levels rocketed. Feeling hypersensitive, she ran her hands along her dress—something she was pretty sure was going to be utterly destroyed in the next five minutes.

Finally Nick said the final words, and this was the part when she should demurely step forward and kiss her mate before allowing him once again to bite her for all to witness. Instead, she let a wicked smile curve her lips…and then she dashed toward the woods, shifting as she ran.

Fuck. Instantly, Trey removed his shirt and pants, intending to shift into his wolf form. The last thing he would have expected was for Taryn to want to complete their mating with a chase and have him mount her for all to see—she was still new to that aspect of being a wolf. A part of his brain noted that many of the guests were laughing in surprise and also removing their clothes, clearly intending to follow. All he gave a shit about was tracking Taryn.

The gray wolf didn't need to use his mate's scent to find her; their bond told him which direction she had taken. He was nearing a clearing when a ball of white fur suddenly barreled into him. His mate had managed to ambush him. The she-wolf stuck her rear in the air in a pounce position, inviting him to play. The gray wolf was happy to do that.

They ran together, keeping their bodies close and enjoying the contact. Then, finally, he mounted her, aware that other wolves were watching—some were also mounting their mates, others were simply observers. The gray wolf had no care, however, for what the others were doing. He was only interested in taking pleasure from his mate, releasing his semen inside her.

"Hussy, did you help with making all this?" Greta asked from her seat at the long table on which the feast was spread out under the huge outdoor gazebo. "A lot of the food has got a real funny aftertaste."

"That weird taste is just from the shit you're always talking," replied Taryn, who was sitting on Trey's lap directly opposite the old dragon. Once they all had shifted back into their human forms, they had thrown some clothes on and practically dived at the food.

Greta gasped. "I hope your language will improve when the baby's born. I don't want my great-grandchild going around cursing like that or being sarcastic."

Taryn sighed dreamily. "I really wish I'd known you when you were alive. I bet you weren't so sour, prudish, and senile back then."

"Trey, you can't let her talk to me like that! This rudeness is uncalled for."

"He's not going to help you," sang Taryn. "He likes sex too much to interfere."

"There she goes again with that language. You shouldn't talk like that in front of your elders, and you especially shouldn't mention it in the presence of your own father and uncle."

Lance *did* look as though the talk of sex was making him a little uncomfortable, but—petty though it might be—Taryn was fine with that. She cocked her head at Greta. "So let me get this right: I can't mention sex, but Dominic can deliver line after sleazy line, and that's okay?"

Dominic pouted. "Aw, come on, Taryn, smile. It's the second-best thing you can do with your lips."

Taryn flapped her arms. "I give up."

Trey threw the last of his cake at him, growling. Dominic, of course, just laughed.

"It was a very nice ceremony," declared Don, obviously hoping to change the subject.

"It was," agreed Taryn. "Thanks again, Nick, for performing it for us."

"No problem. I was happy to do it." For, like, the millionth time, his gaze wandered to Shaya, who, for like the millionth time, met his gaze and blushed. Caleb had also noticed and had been teasing her all night long about it, which was why she'd bitch-slapped him at one point. Not many people were capable of making Shaya blush—she was just so flirtatious and bubbly—so it would be interesting to see if anything happened between her and Nick.

"I still can't believe that *you* had a mating ceremony," Tao said to Trey. "There isn't a romantic bone in your body."

"Oh, and you're a regular Romeo, are you, Tao?" Taryn's question was rhetorical.

"Hey, I admit it—the likelihood of me ever having one is slimmer than slim."

"Same here," said Trick. Ryan grunted, agreeing with him.

Trey tsked. "You say that now, but it'll be different when you meet your mate. They have a way of always getting what they want." He gave Taryn a mock scowl. She smiled brightly.

Dante snorted. "Look, I'm not saying I wouldn't have a ceremony. You know me, I love parties, and if there's an excuse to throw one, I'll do it. But if you're insinuating that *anyone* could have me wrapped around their little finger, you're damn wrong."

Marcus turned to Dominic. "With all your lines, *they'll* be wrapped around *your* little finger," he said sarcastically. "There's no way a woman could possibly resist your charm."

Dominic smiled. "Or my dick. Don't worry, I won't get it out. I don't want you all to get intimidated. And in the interest of health and safety, I think it's better that he's not unleashed."

Taryn gaped when Greta laughed. *Laughed!* "Excuse me a sec," Taryn said, standing up. "I need to pee *again*." Seeing that Marcus and Trick were trying to hide laughs, she smacked them both over the head as she passed the table.

"Hey, wait, I'll come with you," called Shaya. "So how are you feeling?" she asked as they walked, gesturing to Taryn's belly.

"Fine, just irritated by the constant need to pee. How are you?"

"I'm good. Speaking of pee, I swear I almost peed in my pants earlier. Isn't Dominic hilarious! I haven't laughed that hard in a long time."

"Yes, he is. And very cute. So is Nick."

"Don't start trying to play matchmaker."

"Would I do that?" Taryn asked with mock innocence. Shaya snorted. After a quick journey to her en-suite bathroom to answer the call of nature, they both descended the steps of the mountain. To Taryn's complete surprise, Lance was waiting for her at the bottom.

"I'll just go back to the party and wait there," announced Shaya, her expression confused.

Taryn faced her father and raised a brow questioningly.

For a few seconds, he just looked at her. Then, having cleared his throat, he finally spoke. "I'm not going to make excuses for any of my behavior toward you, but I will tell you that a big part of it was that you looked so much like your mom that it made recovering from her death that much harder. I know that's not an excuse, and like I said, I'm not going to make any. Why are you looking at me like that?"

Her frown deepened. "It's just that you sound, well, normal. I'm not sure whether that means we need to increase your medication or mine."

He rolled his eyes. "Anyway, as I was saying, a decent father would have been there for you after your mom's death. Maybe another father wouldn't have shoved you aside on discovering that you were latent, or maybe he would've done exactly as I did. But I lied when I said that your mom would have turned her back on you. She never would have done that."

"I know. You'd also be lying if you said that we'd still be having this conversation if I hadn't managed to overcome my latency."

"Maybe. It's not something that anyone has ever done before, as far as we're aware. Your strength has made me see you in a different light, I suppose."

"I know you didn't do it for me, but I'm thankful that you helped with the battle—if we hadn't had the numbers we needed, many of us could be dead right now, including Trey and our child."

"You're right. I didn't do it for you. But still...I'm glad none of you are dead. And I'm glad you have found your true mate. I know from what I had with your mom that it's something that can't be equaled."

"Everything okay, baby?" Trey asked as he stepped out of the trees.

She'd known he was approaching and had sensed his concern for her through their bond. Clearly he'd felt the awkwardness she was feeling as she spoke with Lance. "Yes, fine."

He held his hand out to her, looking at Lance speculatively. "Come on, let's head back to the party."

"Perry, Oscar, and I are leaving now. They're waiting for me by the car."

Taryn pouted. "So soon? But I haven't had a chance to poison your beer yet."

Rolling his eyes and sighing, Lance gave both her and Trey a nod before disappearing through the trees.

She took Trey's hand and let him lead her back to the party. Just like the time they went to a mating ceremony at Nick's territory, Taryn and Trey didn't bother dancing with the others. They saw little point in embarrassing themselves in front of their guests by revealing just how little rhythm they had. As Taryn wasn't allowed to drink any alcohol, Trey was sweet enough to refrain from having any himself to be supportive. Who would have thought the psycho highlander could be so thoughtful?

Feeling Taryn's head lean on his shoulder, Trey smiled. "Tired?" Naturally she denied it and sat upright again. Every day she was usually wiped out by the time she'd finished dinner, and went for a nap. Today had been especially tiring for her, and she obviously needed sleep. He stood and lifted her from her seat, curling her legs around him. "Come on, you need to lie down for a little while."

"No, I don't. Stop fussing, I just wanted to lean on you and have some contact with my mate. God forgive me."

If she hadn't yawned, he might have believed her. "Shut up," he said gently when she went to object.

"How many times do you have to be told, hussy? Listen to your body—if it tells you that you need to sleep, then sleep."

Taryn smiled. "Thanks for reminding me how important it is that I take care of myself, Greta. I'm not sure what I'd do if you weren't around. Although it's fun thinking about it."

Before the argument could become heated, Trey carried her out of the clearing, inside the caves, and then into their bedroom. Placing her carefully on the bed, he lay beside her and pulled her flush against his body. She found her own little groove and fit there like the last piece of a jigsaw, making him whole. She made him whole both inside and out, and he couldn't understand how he'd functioned before she came into his life.

"Trey? You know the baby might be latent, don't you?"

Hearing how small her voice was, he kissed her reassuringly. "Yes, I know that, but it won't matter to me if the baby is latent. Obviously I'd like it if that wasn't the case, but I'm not going to turn my back on him if it is."

She snorted. "It could be a *her*, you know." Although she also had the feeling it was a he.

Trey smiled. "You do know that the whole shifter community is terrified of you now, don't you? What you did is unheard of—no latent has ever shifted before."

"I don't think it would have happened if my wolf hadn't been so frantic because the baby was in danger."

"Your wolf is gorgeous, slender, and graceful. My wolf loves running with her, especially since he hadn't thought he ever would."

"Yeah, he likes to mount her a lot too," she grumbled, not that her wolf minded so much. "He's just as horny as you are."

"I'm not the nympho in this mating."

"I'm not the one who has a thing for fucking people in the ass."

He groaned. "Just remembering that makes me hard. I will be doing that again soon."

"I don't think so, Flintstone."

"You loved it, and you know you did." He tensed when she ground herself against his erection. "You need to sleep."

"No, I need you inside me."

"Taryn."

"Trey."

"You need sleep." But even as he said that, he wasn't stopping her from reaching down and unbuttoning his fly. He cursed and closed his eyes as she began working her soft hand up and down his length. She kept her pace slow, no doubt just to tease him the way he always teased her, but each wicked stroke still pulled him under her spell. Groaning in defeat, he lifted her leg and curled it over his hip. He rocked his erection against her clit and groaned again. "You drive me fucking crazy, do you know that?" It came out sounding like a complaint.

Burying his face in the crook of her neck, he inhaled her scent, letting it settle into his lungs and tease him. She smelled of exotic fruits, of him, of pregnancy, and of home. He took her mouth with a slow sensuality, seducing her lips and tongue. A crushing sense of ownership assailed him, driving him to possess her and overwhelm his senses with her. "I need your taste in my mouth." He peeled her T-shirt from her body and removed her bra before rolling her onto her back.

Taryn moaned as he played her body like the master he was—molding her breasts with his hands, sucking and biting her nipples until she was writhing beneath him, and then he was journeying down her body but pausing now and then to nip and suck at little patches of skin. He knew exactly what she liked and he gave it to her, but what increased the raw ache in her body more than any of that was the mix of possessiveness and adoration blazing from his eyes.

Once Trey had finally removed her jeans and thong, he took a minute just to look at her lying there, his to take and possess. At some point in the past few months, he had licked, kissed, or bitten every inch of her body. He knew it better than even she did. Every curve, every indent, every slope, and every hollow was etched into his brain. He had every mark committed to memory, whether it was a birthmark, freckle, scar, or the brands he'd left on her body—he could find every one of them with his eyes closed.

A gasp flew out of Taryn as he cocked her hips and suckled hard on her clit. There were no teasing licks this time, no making her wait. He swirled his tongue around her clit, flicked it repeatedly, and then sank his tongue inside her. Holding her still, he unrelentingly fucked her with that clever tongue. His soft growls heightened the pleasure until she just couldn't take any more. "Trey, stop." He didn't. She threaded her fingers through his hair and tugged. He snarled in the back of his throat and that just made the whole thing worse. "Please."

He froze at that one word. He doubted any other word would have reached him—he'd been too absorbed by her taste, hadn't been able to get enough of it. She'd begged him. She'd actually begged him. He peered up at her face, expecting to see shock in her eyes or for her to give him a smart-ass comment that assured him she was teasing him. Instead, her expression was totally open, totally exposed; everything she felt was right there in her lust-dazed eyes for him to see. It rocked him like nothing else could have. He knelt between her legs and gripped her hips, positioning his cock at her entrance. "Say it again." He half expected her to tell him to fuck off, but she didn't.

"Please."

There went his self-control. He slammed himself home, groaning as her muscles clamped around his cock, and then he took her hard and rough. Hearing her beg, knowing that she'd completely surrendered to him, had him well and truly lost. She'd broken down that last wall, had let him in, was accepting that every part of her belonged to him. It wasn't a one-way street; this female totally owned him, would have even if she hadn't been his true mate.

Feeling the telling tingle in his spine, he draped himself over her. "You know what I want, baby." She raised her head and bit down hard on his shoulder, sucking and licking. "Fuck. Scream my name for me, Taryn. Do it, I need it."

As he clamped his teeth over his claiming mark, Taryn's back arched with the explosion of pure bliss that ripped through her body. His name escaped her mouth in a scream so loud it hurt her ears. She heard him growl-groan her own name as his own release hit and his cock pulsed deep inside her. Panting and quivering with aftershocks, they stayed there like that, with him draped over her and his face buried in the crook of her neck. Thankfully the big lug had been careful not to place all his weight on her, because she wouldn't have had the energy to shove him off.

"I love you, baby."

His words had her eyes snapping open. If she hadn't been able to feel it was the truth through their bond, she might not have believed him so easily. Curling all her limbs around him, she whispered into his ear, "And I love you." The shudder that ran through him told her just how much that affected him.

"I'm sorry I didn't realize what I felt before," he said softly into her ear. "I'm sorry I kept my walls up with you."

"It's okay."

He pulled back to look at her face. "No, it's not. You're my mate and I didn't let you in."

"Of course you didn't, Trey. You didn't know how to let someone in. I don't blame you for that. Hell, I had my own defenses up for long enough."

"Yeah, but you didn't have walls up so high that you didn't even see how much you cared for your own mate." A wicked smile took over his face. "But now that all our defenses are down...it makes me wonder just how often I can get you to beg for me."

"Sorry, that was just a one-off."

"Oh no. You let me behind those walls of yours, gave yourself completely to me, and I'm not giving you back. You're *all* mine."

"That works both ways, Flintstone," she snapped. "You belong to me too."

He smirked, enjoying the possessiveness in her tone. "Only ever you, baby."

"Great. Prove it. Do me again."

Unbelievable. "For the tenth time, you need sleep."

"I'm supposed to listen to what my pregnant body tells me, remember. It's telling me it wants to play Hiding Pedro."

He released a long-suffering sigh. "See—you're a total nympho."

"Do you want your mate to be happy or not?"

CHARACTERS:

THE PHOENIX PACK:
Trey Coleman Alpha
Taryn Warner Alpha
Dante Beta
Tao Head Enforcer
Dominic Enforcer
Marcus Enforcer
Patrick "Trick" Enforcer
Ryan Enforcer
Greta Trey's grandmother
Grace Mated to Rhett
Rhett Mated to Grace
Lydia Mated to Cam
Cam Mated to Lydia
Kirk Brock's son
Selma Subordinate
Brock Kirk's father
Hope Subordinate
Louisa Trey's mother, deceased

NOTABLE CHARACTERS FROM THE ONYX PACK:

Lance Warner Alpha, father of Taryn
Cecilia Warner Mother of Taryn, deceased
Shaya Critchley Friend of Taryn
Caleb Friend of Taryn
Perry Enforcer
Oscar Enforcer
Joseph "Joey" Winters Died when only nine, believed to be Taryn's mate
Brodie
Nicole
Ashley
Richie

NOTABLE CHARACTERS FROM THE BJORN PACK:

Rick Coleman Previous Alpha, father of Trey, deceased
Darryl Coleman New Alpha, uncle of Trey
Josh Brother of Dante
Summer Died as a baby, believed to be Trey's mate
Viv Mother of Summer
Martin

NOTABLE CHARACTERS FROM THE RYLAND PACK:

Nick Axton Alpha
Don Uncle of Taryn
Derren Nick's bodyguard
Glory

OTHER CHARACTERS:

Roscoe Weston Alpha wolf shifter who attempts to claim Taryn
Dean Milton Mediator
Quinn Alpha wolf shifter, ally of Lance Warner
Roger Owner of shifter club The Pulse

ACKNOWLEDGMENTS

The biggest thank-you has to go to my husband for sharing the housework—okay, doing the majority of the housework—and for helping me with the kids so that I can immerse myself in my stories.

A big thanks to my beta reader, Andrea Ashby, for the long hours she put in and for being the best second opinion a person could have. Andrea, seriously, you're talented enough to write your own book; go for it.

A special thanks to all the people at Montlake Romance, but especially to Eleni Caminis for all her input, advice, patience, and guidance.

Lastly, a huge thank you to all the people who have taken the time to read my book. I hope you enjoyed it!

About the Author

Author Suzanne Wright, a native of England, can't remember a time when she wasn't creating characters and telling their tales. Even as a child, she loved writing poems, plays, and stories; as an adult, Wright has published two romance novels, *Here Be Sexist Vampires* and *From Rags*. An avid reader of fantasy books, she particularly enjoys the works of Christine Feehan, Nalini Singh, and Stephen King. Wright, who lives in Liverpool with her husband and two children, freely admits that she hates housecleaning and can't cook, but she knows some great jokes and always shares chocolate. *Feral Sins* is the first book in Wright's Phoenix Pack series.